Commonwealth

Commonwealth is the story of two broken families and the paths their lives take over the course of forty years, through love and marriage, death and divorce, and a dark secret from childhood that lies underneath it all.

HARPER PERENNIAL OLIVE EDITIONS

This book is part of a special series from Harper Perennial called Olive Editions—exclusive small-format editions of some of our bestselling and celebrated titles, featuring beautiful and unique hand-drawn cover illustrations. All Olive Editions are available for a limited time only.

"*Commonwealth* feels both contemporary and instantly classic; it's a beautiful, empathetic novel that manages to be surprising but somehow comfortable as well. With each new book, Ann Patchett just keeps upping her game."

—Jill, Powell's, Portland, Oregon

"I have loved all of Ann Patchett's novels, but *Commonwealth* is one of her best! A dysfunctional group of people, all in some way related, try to love one another while moving through life that sometimes isn't what we want or thought it would be. I read this in one sitting on Amtrak from NYC and just fell in love."

—Annie, Bank Square Books, Mystic, Connecticut

"It is a tricky feat to create an ensemble cast exploring complicated family dynamics in which the reader genuinely connects with each of the flawed, realistic humans within the story, but Ann Patchett does this beautifully in *Commonwealth*."

—Jessica, Bookbug, Kalamazoo, Michigan

"I savored this book. Ann Patchett's writing is masterful. The story is full of poignancy, humor, and insight into human nature as well as the nature of families. It's also completely, soul-satisfyingly unpredictable."
    —Patty, Oblong Books and Music, Rhinebeck, New York

"A snapshot of the class system in American families. . . . Funny, sad collage of heartbreak and betrayal. Also a love story to the idea of family."
            —Frayda, Mrs. Dalloway's, Berkeley, California

"Ann Patchett is simply a magician with the nuances of words and the subtleties of emotion. *Commonwealth* follows the stories of six children over several decades as they trudge between two broken but interconnected families. And she does it with amazing ease and intimacy."
            —Bill, Book Passage, Corte Madera, California

"Beautifully written with skillfully wrought characters; this is one of Patchett's best."
—Sharon, Boswell Book Company, Milwaukee, Wisconsin

"A wonderful, insightful saga of the interconnection of two families. The descriptive and often unexpected twists and turns pulled me into their lives fully. I loved every minute of reading!"
    —Alexa, An Unlikely Story, Plainville, Massachusetts

ALSO BY ANN PATCHETT

Commonwealth

A Novel

Ann Patchett

This is a work of fiction. Names, characters, places, and incidents are products of the author's imagination or are used fictitiously and are not to be construed as real. Any resemblance to actual events, locales, organizations, or persons, living or dead, is entirely coincidental.

FIRST HARPER PERENNIAL EDITION PUBLISHED 2017.

FIRST HARPER PERENNIAL OLIVE EDITION PUBLISHED 2020.

ISBN 978-0-06-303762-5 (Olive edition)

20 21 22 23 24   LSC   10 9 8 7 6 5 4 3 2 1

To Mike Glasscock

Commonwealth

1

The christening party took a turn when Albert Cousins arrived with gin. Fix was smiling when he opened the door and he kept smiling as he struggled to make the connection: it was Albert Cousins from the district attorney's office standing on the cement slab of his front porch. He'd opened the door twenty times in the last half hour—to neighbors and friends and people from church and Beverly's sister and all his brothers and their parents and practically an entire precinct worth of cops—but Cousins was the only surprise. Fix had asked his wife two weeks ago why she thought they had to invite every single person they knew in the world to a christening party and she'd asked him if he wanted to look over the guest list and tell her who to cut. He hadn't looked at the list, but if she were standing at the door now he would have pointed straight ahead and said, *Him*. Not that he disliked Albert Cousins, he didn't know him other than to put his name together with his face, but not knowing him was the reason not to invite him. Fix had the thought that maybe Cousins had come to his house to talk to him about a case: nothing like that had ever happened before but what else was the explanation? Guests were milling around in the front yard, and whether they were coming late or leaving early or just taking refuge outside because the house was packed beyond what any fire marshal would allow, Fix couldn't say. What he was sure of was that Cousins was there uninvited, alone with a bottle in a bag.

"Fix," Albert Cousins said. The tall deputy DA in a suit and tie put out his hand.

"Al," Fix said. (Did people call him Al?) "Glad you made it." He gave his hand two hard pumps and let it go.

"I'm cutting it close," Cousins said, looking at the crowd inside as if there might not be room for him. The party was clearly past its midpoint—most of the small, triangular sandwiches were gone, half the cookies. The tablecloth beneath the punch bowl was pink and damp.

Fix stepped aside to let him in. "You're here now," he said.

"Wouldn't have missed it." Though of course he had missed it. He hadn't been at the christening.

Dick Spencer was the only one from the DA's office Fix had invited. Dick had been a cop himself, had gone to law school at night, pulled himself up without ever making any of the other guys feel like he was better for it. It didn't matter if Dick was driving a black-and-white or standing in front of the judge, there was no doubt where he came from. Cousins on the other hand was a lawyer like all the others—DAs, PDs, the hired guns—friendly enough when they needed something but unlikely to invite an officer along for a drink, and if they did it was only because they thought the cop was holding out on them. DAs were the guys who smoked your cigarettes because they were trying to quit. The cops, who filled up the living room and dining room and spilled out into the backyard beneath the clothesline and the two orange trees, they weren't trying to quit. They drank iced tea mixed with lemonade and smoked like stevedores.

Albert Cousins handed over the bag and Fix looked inside. It was a bottle of gin, a big one. Other people brought prayer cards or mother-of-pearl rosary beads or a pocket-sized Bible covered in white kid with gilt-edged pages. Five of the guys, or their five wives, had kicked in together and bought a blue enameled cross on a chain, a tiny pearl at the center, very pretty, something for the future.

"This makes a boy and a girl?"

"Two girls."

Cousins shrugged. "What can you do?"

"Not a thing," Fix said and closed the door. Beverly had told him to leave it open so they could get some air, which went to show how much she knew about man's inhumanity to man. It didn't matter how many people were in the house. You didn't leave the goddamn door open.

Beverly leaned out of the kitchen. There were easily thirty people standing between them—the entire Meloy clan, all the DeMatteos, a handful of altar boys plowing through what was left of the cookies—but there was no missing Beverly. That yellow dress.

"Fix?" she said, raising her voice over the din.

It was Cousins who turned his head first, and Cousins gave her a nod.

By reflex Fix stood straighter, but he let the moment pass. "Make yourself at home," he said to the deputy district attorney and pointed out a cluster of detectives by the sliding glass door, their jackets still on. "You know plenty of people here." Maybe that was true and maybe it wasn't. Cousins sure as hell didn't know the host. Fix turned to cut his way through the crowd and the crowd parted for him, touching his shoulder and shaking his hand, saying congratulations. He tried not to step on any of the kids, his four-year-old daughter Caroline among them, who were playing some sort of game on the dining room floor, crouching and crawling like tigers between the feet of adults.

The kitchen was packed with wives, all of them laughing and talking too loud, none of them being helpful except for Lois from next door who was pulling bowls out of the refrigerator. Beverly's best friend, Wallis, was using the side of the bright chrome toaster to reapply her lipstick. Wallis was too thin and too tan and when she straightened up she was wearing too much lipstick. Beverly's mother was sitting at the breakfast table with the baby in her lap. They had changed her from her lacy christening gown into a starched white dress with yellow flowers embroidered around the neck, as if she were a bride who'd slipped into her going-away dress at the end of the reception. The women in the kitchen took turns making a fuss over the baby, acting like it was their job to keep her entertained until the Magi arrived. But the baby wasn't entertained. Her blue eyes were glazed over. She was staring into the middle distance, tired of everything. All this rush to make sandwiches and take in presents for a girl who was not yet a year old.

"Look how pretty she is," his mother-in-law said to no one, running the back of one finger across the baby's rounded cheek.

"Ice," Beverly said to her husband. "We're out of ice."

"That was your sister's assignment," Fix said.

"Then she failed. Can you ask one of the guys to go get some? It's too hot to have a party without ice." She had tied an apron behind her neck but not around her waist. She was trying not to wrinkle her dress. Strands of yellow hair had come loose from her French twist and were falling into her eyes.

"If she didn't bring the ice, then she might at least come in here and make some sandwiches." Fix was looking right at Wallis when he said this but Wallis capped her lipstick and ignored him. He had meant it to be helpful because clearly Beverly had her hands full. To look at her anyone would think that Beverly was the sort of person who would have her parties catered, someone who would sit on the couch while other people passed the trays.

"Bonnie's so happy to see all those cops in one room. She can't be expected to think about sandwiches," Beverly said, and then she stopped the assembling of cream cheese and cucumbers for a minute and looked down at his hand. "What's in the bag?"

Fix held up the gin, and his wife, surprised, delivered the first smile she'd given him all day, maybe all week.

"Whoever you send to the store," Wallis said, displaying a sudden interest in the conversation, "tell them to get tonic."

Fix said he would buy the ice himself. There was a market up the street and he wasn't opposed to slipping out for a minute. The relative quiet of the neighborhood, the order of the bungalows with their tight green lawns, the slender shadows the palm trees cast, and the smell of the orange blossoms all combined with the cigarette he was smoking to have a settling effect on him. His brother Tom came along and they walked together in companionable silence. Tom and Betty had three kids now, all girls, and lived in Escondido, where he worked for the fire department. Fix was starting to see that this was the way life worked once you got older and the kids came; there wasn't as much time as you thought there was going to be. The brothers hadn't seen each other since they'd all met up at their parents' house and gone to Mass on Christmas Eve, and before that it was probably when they'd driven down to Escondido for Erin's christening. A red Sunbeam convertible went by and Tom said, "That one." Fix nodded, sorry he hadn't seen it first. Now he had to wait for something he wanted to come along. At the market they bought four bags of ice and four bottles of tonic. The kid at the register asked them if they needed any limes and Fix shook his head. It was Los Angeles in June. You couldn't give a lime away.

Fix hadn't checked his watch when they'd left for the market but he was a good judge of time. Most cops were. They'd been gone twenty minutes, twenty-five tops. It wasn't long enough for everything to change, but when they came back the front door was standing open and there was no one left in the yard. Tom didn't notice the difference, but then a fireman wouldn't. If the place didn't smell like smoke then there wasn't a problem. There were still plenty of people in the house but it was quieter now. Fix had turned on the radio before the party started and for the first time he could hear a few notes of music. The kids weren't crawling in the dining room anymore and no one seemed to notice they were gone. All attention focused on the open kitchen door, which was where the two Keating brothers were heading with the ice. Fix's partner, Lomer, was waiting for them and Lomer tipped his head in the direction of the crowd. "You got here just in time," he said.

As tight as it had been in the kitchen before they'd left, there were three times as many people crammed in there now, most of them men. Beverly's mother was nowhere in sight and neither was the baby. Beverly was standing at the sink, a butcher's knife in her hand. She was slicing oranges from an enormous pile that was sliding across the counter while the two lawyers from the L.A. County District Attorney's Office, Dick Spencer and Albert Cousins—suit jackets off, ties off, and shirtsleeves rolled up high above the elbow—were twisting the halves of oranges on two metal juicers. Their foreheads were flushed and damp with sweat, their opened collars just beginning to darken, they worked as if the safety of their city relied on the making of orange juice.

Beverly's sister Bonnie, ready now to be helpful, plucked Dick Spencer's glasses from his face and wiped them with a dish towel, even though Dick had a capable wife somewhere in the crush. That was when Dick, his eyes relieved of the scrim of sweat, saw Fix and Tom and called out for the ice.

"Ice!" Bonnie cried, because it was true, it was hot as hell and ice sounded better than anything. She dropped her towel to lift the two bags from Tom, placing them in the sink atop the neat orange cups of empty rinds. Then she took the bags from Fix. Ice was her responsibility.

Beverly stopped slicing. "Perfect timing," she said and dug a paper cup into the open plastic bag, knocking out three modest cubes as if she knew to pace herself. She poured a short drink—half gin, half orange juice, from the full pitcher. She made another and another and another as the cups were passed through the kitchen and out the door and into the waiting hands of the guests.

"I got the tonic," Fix said, looking at the one bag still in his hands. He wasn't objecting to anything other than the feeling that he and his brother had somehow been left behind in the time it had taken them to walk to the market and back.

"Orange juice is better," Albert Cousins said, stopping just long enough to down the drink Bonnie had made for him. Bonnie, so recently enamored of cops, had shifted her allegiance to the two DAs.

"For vodka," Fix said. Screwdrivers. Everyone knew that.

But Cousins tilted his head towards the disbeliever, and there was Beverly, handing her husband a drink. For all the world it looked like she and Cousins had a code worked out between them. Fix held the cup in his hand and stared at the uninvited guest. He had his three brothers in the house, an untold number of able-bodied men from the Los Angeles Police Department, and a priest who organized a Saturday boxing program for troubled boys, all of whom would back him up in the removal of a single deputy district attorney.

"Cheers," Beverly said in a low voice, not as a toast but a directive, and Fix, still thinking there was a complaint to be made, turned up his paper cup.

Father Joe Mike sat on the ground with his back against the back of the Keating house, staking out a sliver of shade. He rested his cup of juice and gin on the knee of his standard-issue black pants. Priest pants. The drink was either his fourth or his third, he didn't remember and he didn't care because the drinks were very small. He was making an effort to write a sermon in his head for the following Sunday. He wanted to tell the congregation, the few who were not presently in the Keatings' backyard, how the miracle of loaves and fishes had been enacted here today, but he couldn't find a way to wring enough booze out of the narrative. He didn't believe that *he* had witnessed a miracle, no one thought that, but he had seen a perfect explanation of how the miracle might have been engineered in the time of Christ. It was a large bottle of gin Albert Cousins had brought to the party, yes, but it was in no way large enough to fill all the cups, and in certain cases to fill them many times over, for the more than one hundred guests, some of whom were dancing not four feet in front of him. And while the recently stripped Valencia trees in the backyard had been heavy with fruit, they never would have been able to come up with enough juice to sate the entire party. Conventional wisdom says that orange juice doesn't go with gin, and anyway, who was expecting a drink at a christening party? Had the Keatings just put the gin in their liquor cabinet no one would have thought less of them. But Fix Keating had given the bottle to his wife, and his wife, worn down by the stress of throwing a good party, was going to have a drink, and if she was going to have a drink then by God everyone at the party was welcome to join her. In many ways this was Beverly Keating's miracle. Albert Cousins, the man who brought the gin, was also the one who suggested the mixer. Albert Cousins had been sitting beside him not two minutes before, telling Father Joe Mike that he was from Virginia and even after three years in Los Angeles he was still shocked by the abundance of citrus fruit hanging from trees. Bert—he told the priest to call him Bert—had grown up with frozen concentrate mixed into pitchers of water which, although he hadn't known it at the time, had nothing to do with orange juice. Now his children drank fresh-squeezed juice as thoughtlessly as he had drunk milk as a boy. They squeezed it from the fruit they had picked off the trees in their own backyard. He could see a new set of muscles hardening in the right forearm of his wife, Teresa, from the constant twisting of oranges on the juicer while their children held up their cups and waited for more. Orange juice was all they wanted, Bert told him. They had it every morning with their cereal, and Teresa froze it into Tupperware popsicle molds and gave the popsicles to the children for their afternoon snacks, and in the evening he and Teresa drank it over ice with vodka or bourbon or gin. This was what no one seemed to understand—it didn't matter what you put into it, what mattered was the juice itself. "People from California forget that, because they've been spoiled," Bert said.

"It's true," Father Joe Mike admitted, because he'd grown up in Oceanside and couldn't quite believe the extent to which this guy was going on about orange juice.

The priest, whose mind was wandering like the Jews in the desert, tried to focus again on his sermon: Beverly Keating went to the liquor cabinet, which she had not restocked for the christening party, and what she found there was a third of a bottle of gin, a nearly full bottle of vodka, and a bottle of tequila that Fix's brother John had brought back from Mexico last September which they had never opened because neither one of them knew exactly what to do with tequila. She carried the bottles to the kitchen, at which point the neighbors who lived on either side of their house and the neighbors across the street and three of the people who lived near Incarnation offered to go home and see what they had in their own cabinets, and when those neighbors returned it wasn't just with bottles but oranges. Bill and Susie came back with a pillowcase full of fruit they'd run home to pick, saying they could go back and get three pillowcases more: what they gave to the party hadn't made a dent. Other guests followed suit, running home, raiding their fruit trees and the high boozy shelves of their pantries. They poured their bounty into the Keatings' kitchen until the kitchen table looked like a bar back and the kitchen counter looked like a fruit truck.

Wasn't that the true miracle? Not that Christ had rolled out a buffet table from His holy sleeve and invited everyone to join Him for fishes and loaves, but that the people who had brought their lunches in goatskin sacks, maybe a little more than they needed for their family but certainly not enough to feed the masses, were moved to fearless generosity by the example of their teacher and His disciples. So had the people at this christening party been moved by the generosity of Beverly Keating, or they were moved by the sight of her in that yellow dress, her pale hair twisted up and pinned to show the smooth back of her neck, the neck that disappeared into the back of the yellow dress. Father Joe Mike took a sip of his drink. And when it was done the people collected twelve baskets of scraps. He looked around at all the cups on the tables and chairs, on the ground, many of which had a sip or two left in the bottom. Were they to gather up all the leftovers, how much would they have? Father Joe Mike felt small for not having offered to go back to the rectory to see what was there. He had been thinking about how it would look for a priest to show his congregants just how much gin he had squirreled away, instead of taking the opportunity to participate in the fellowship of a community.

There was a gentle tapping against the toe of his shoe. Father Joe Mike looked up from his knee, where he had been meditating on the contents of his cup, and saw Bonnie Keating. No, that wasn't right. Her sister was married to Fix Keating, which made her Bonnie-Something-Else. Bonnie-of-Beverly's-Maiden-Name.

"Hey, Father," she said, a cup just like his held loosely between finger and thumb.

"Bonnie," he said, trying to make his voice sound like he wasn't sitting on the ground drinking gin. Though he wasn't sure that this was still gin. It may have been tequila.

"I was wondering if you'd dance with me."

Bonnie X was wearing a dress with blue daisies on it that was short enough to make a priest wonder where he was supposed to rest his gaze, though when she'd gotten dressed this morning she probably hadn't taken into account that there would be men sitting on the ground while she remained standing. He wanted to say something avuncular about not dancing because he was out of practice, but he wasn't old enough to be her uncle, or her father for that matter, which is what she'd called him. Instead he answered her simply. "Not a great idea."

And speaking of not great ideas, Bonnie X then dropped down to sit on her heels, thinking, no doubt, that she and the priest would then be closer to eye level and could have a more private conversation, and not thinking about where this would bring the hem of her dress. Her underwear was also blue. It matched the daisies.

"See, the thing is, everybody's married," she said, her voice not modulated to reflect her content. "And while I don't mind dancing with a guy who's married because I don't think dancing means anything, all of them brought their wives."

"And their wives think it means something." He was careful now to lock his eyes on her eyes.

"They do," she said sadly, and pushed a chunk of straight auburn hair behind one ear.

It was at that moment that Father Joe Mike had a sort of revelation: Bonnie X should leave Los Angeles, or at the very least she should move to the Valley, to a place where no one knew her older sister, because when not juxtaposed to that sister, Bonnie was a perfectly attractive girl. Put the two of them together and Bonnie was a Shetland pony standing next to a racehorse, but he realized now that without knowing Beverly the word "pony" never would have come to mind. Over Bonnie's shoulder he could see that Beverly Keating was dancing in the driveway with a police officer who was not her husband, and that the police officer was looking like a very lucky man.

"Come on," Bonnie said, her voice somewhere between pleading and whining. "I think we're the only two people here who aren't married."

"If what you're looking for is availability, I don't fit the bill."

"I just want to *dance*," she said, and put her free hand on his knee, the one that wasn't already occupied by a cup.

Because Father Joe Mike had just been chastising himself about placing the propriety of appearances over true kindness, he felt himself waver. Would he have given two seconds' thought to appearances if it had been his hostess asking for a dance? If Beverly Keating were crouching in front of him now instead of her sister, her wide-set blue eyes this close to his own, her dress slipping up so that the color of her underwear was made known to him—he stopped, giving his head an imperceptible shake. Not a good thought. He tried to take himself back to the loaves and the fishes, and when that proved impossible he held up his index finger. "One," he said.

Bonnie X smiled at him with such radiant gratitude that Father Joe Mike wondered if he had ever made another living soul happy before this moment. They put down their cups and endeavored to pull one another up, though it was tricky. Before they were fully standing they were in each other's arms. From that point it wasn't very far to Bonnie clasping her hands behind Joe Mike's neck and hanging there like the stole he wore to hear confessions. He rested an awkward hand on either side of her waist, the narrow place where her ribs curved down to meet his thumbs. If anyone at the party was looking at them he was not aware of it. In fact, he was overcome by the sensation of invisibility, hidden from the world by the mysterious cloud of lavender that rose up from the hair of Beverly Keating's sister.

In truth, Bonnie had already managed one dance before enlisting Father Joe Mike, though in the end it wound up being not even half a dance. She had pulled the hardworking Dick Spencer away from the oranges for a minute, telling him he should take a break, that union rules applied to men who juiced oranges. Dick Spencer wore thick horn-rimmed glasses that made him look smart, lots smarter than Fix's partner Lomer, who refused to give her the time of day despite the fact that she had twice leaned up against him, laughing. (Dick Spencer *was* smart. He was also so myopic that the couple of times his glasses had gotten knocked off while wrestling with a suspect he had been as good as blind. The thought of fighting a man who may well have a gun or a knife he couldn't see was enough to make him sign up for night school, then law school, then ace the bar exam.) Bonnie took Spencer's sticky hand and led him out to the back patio. Right away they were making a wide circle, bumping into other people. With her arms around his back she could feel how thin he was under his shirt, thin in a nice way, a thin that could wrap around a girl twice. The other deputy DA, Cousins, was better-looking, sort of gorgeous really, but he was stuck on himself, she could tell. Dick Spencer was a sweetheart in her arms.

That was about as far as her thoughts had progressed when she'd felt a strong hand gripping her upper arm. She'd been trying very hard to concentrate on Dick Spencer's eyes behind his glasses and the effort was making her dizzy, or something was making her dizzy. She was holding on to him tight. She hadn't seen the woman approaching. If she'd seen her, Bonnie might have had time to dodge, or at least come up with something clever to say. The woman was talking loud and fast, and Bonnie was careful to lean away from her. Just like that Dick Spencer and his wife were leaving the party.

"Going?" Fix said as they sailed past him in the living room.

"Keep an eye on your family," Mary Spencer said.

Fix was on the couch, his older girl Caroline stretched out across his lap, sound asleep. He mistakenly thought Mary was complimenting him on watching his daughter. Maybe he had been half asleep himself. He patted Caroline lightly on the small of her back and she didn't move.

"Give Cousins a hand," Dick said over his shoulder, and then they were gone without his jacket or tie, without a good-bye to Beverly.

Albert Cousins hadn't been invited to the party. He'd passed Dick Spencer in the hallway of the courthouse on Friday talking to a cop, some cop Cousins didn't know but who maybe looked familiar the way cops do. "See you Sunday," the cop had said, and when he walked away, Cousins asked Spencer, "What's Sunday?" Dick Spencer explained that Fix Keating had a new kid, and that there was going to be a christening party.

"First kid?" Cousins had asked, watching Keating retreat down the hall in his blues.

"Second."

"They do all that for second kids?"

"Catholics," Spencer said and shrugged. "They can't get enough of it."

While Cousins hadn't been looking for a party to crash, it wasn't an entirely innocent question either. He hated Sundays, and since Sundays were thought to be a family day, invitations were hard to come by. Weekdays he was out the door just as his children were waking up. He would give their heads a scratch, leave a few instructions for his wife, and be gone. By the time he got home at night they were asleep, or going to sleep. Pressed against their pillows, he found his children endearing, necessary, and that was how he thought of them from Monday morning all the way to Saturday at dawn. But on Saturday mornings they refused to keep sleeping. Cal and Holly would throw themselves onto his chest before the light of day had fully penetrated the vinyl roll-down shades, already fighting over something that had happened in the three minutes they'd been awake. The baby would start pulling herself over the bars of her crib as soon as she'd heard her siblings up—it was her new trick—and what she lacked in speed she made up for in tenacity. She would throw herself onto the floor if Teresa didn't run to catch her in time, but Teresa was up already and vomiting. She closed the door to the bathroom in the hall and ran the tap, trying to be quiet about it, but the steady sound of retching filled the bedroom. Cousins threw off his two older children, their weightless selves landing in a tangle on the bedspread folded at the foot of the bed. They lunged at him again, shrieking with laughter, but he couldn't play with them and he didn't want to play with them and didn't want to get up and get the baby, but he had to.

And so the day went from there, Teresa saying she needed to be able to go to the grocery store by herself, or that the people who lived on the corner were having a cookout and they hadn't gone to the last cookout. Every minute a child was howling, first one at a time, then in duet, with the third one waiting, then the third one joining in, then two settling down so as to repeat the cycle. The baby fell straight into the sliding glass door in the den and cut open her forehead before breakfast. Teresa was on the floor, butterflying tiny Band-Aids, asking Bert if he thought she needed stitches. The sight of blood always made Bert uncomfortable and so he looked away, saying no, no stitches. Holly was crying because the baby was crying. Holly said that her head hurt. Cal was no-where in evidence—though screaming, be it that of his sisters or his parents, usually brought him running back. Cal liked trouble. Teresa looked up at her husband, her fingers daubed in the baby's blood, and asked him where Cal had gone.

All week long Cousins waded through the pimps and the wife-beaters, the petty thieves. He offered up his best self to biased judges and sleeping juries. He told himself that when the weekend came he would turn away from all the crime in Los Angeles, turn towards his pajama-clad children and newly pregnant wife, but he only made it to noon on Satur-days before telling Teresa that there was work at the office he had to finish before the first hearing on Monday. The funny thing was he really did go to work. The couple of times he'd tried slipping off to Manhattan Beach to eat a hot dog and flirt with the girls in their bikini tops and tiny cutoff shorts, he'd gotten a sunburn which Teresa was quick to comment on. So he would go to the office and sit among the men he sat among all week long. They would nod seriously to one another and accomplish more in three or four hours on a Sat-urday afternoon than they did on any other day.

But by Sunday he couldn't do it again, not the children or the wife or the job, and so he pulled up the memory of a christening party he hadn't been invited to. Teresa looked at him, her face bright for a minute. Thirty-one years old and still she had freckles over the bridge of her nose and spread-

ing over her cheeks. She often said that she wished they took
their kids to church, even if he didn't believe in church or God
or any of it. She thought it would be a good thing for them
to do as a family, and this party might be the place to start.
They could all go together.

"No," he said. "It's a work thing."

She blinked. "A christening party?"

"The guy's a cop." He hoped she wouldn't ask the cop's
name because at that particular moment he couldn't remember it. "Sort of a deal maker, you know? The entire office is
going. I just need to pay respects."

She'd asked him if the baby was a boy or a girl, and if
he had a present. The question was followed by a crash in
the kitchen and a great clattering of metal mixing bowls. He
hadn't thought about a present. He went to the liquor cabinet
and picked up a full bottle of gin. It was a big bottle, more than
he would have wanted to give, but once he saw the seal was still
intact the matter was decided.

That was how he came to be in Fix Keating's kitchen making orange juice, Dick Spencer having abandoned his post for
the consolation prize of the blonde's unimpressive sister. He
would wait it out, showing himself to be reliable in hopes of
scoring the blonde herself. He would juice every orange in
Los Angeles County if that's what it took. In this city where
beauty had been invented she was possibly the most beautiful woman he had ever spoken to, certainly the most beautiful woman he had ever stood next to in a kitchen. Her beauty
was the point, yes, but it was also more than that: there had
been a little jolt between their fingers whenever she passed
him another orange. He felt it every time, an electric spark

as real as the orange itself. He knew that making a move on a married woman was a bad idea, especially when you were in the woman's house and her husband was also in the house and her husband was a cop and the party was a celebration of the birth of the cop's second child. Cousins knew all of this but as the drinks stacked up he told himself there were larger forces at work. The priest who he'd been talking to earlier out on the back patio wasn't as drunk as he was and the priest had definitely said there was something out of the ordinary going on. Saying something was out of the ordinary was as good as saying all bets were off. Cousins reached for his cup with his left hand and stopped to roll his right wrist in a circle the way he'd seen Teresa do before. He was cramping up.

Fix Keating was standing in the doorway, watching him like he knew exactly what he had in mind. "Dick said I was on duty," Fix said. The cop wasn't such a big guy but it was clear that his spring was wound tight, that he spent every day looking for a fight to throw himself into. All the Irish cops were like that.

"You're the host," Cousins said. "You don't need to be stuck back here making juice."

"You're the guest," Fix said, picking up a knife. "You should be out there enjoying yourself."

But Cousins had never been a man for a crowd. If this had been a party Teresa had dragged him to he wouldn't have lasted twenty minutes. "I know what I'm good at," he said, and took the top off the juicer, stopping to rinse the buildup of pulp from the deep metal grooves of the top half before pouring the contents of the juice dish into a green plastic pitcher. For a while they worked next to one another not saying anything. Cousins was half lost in a daydream about the other man's wife. She was leaning over him, her hand on his face, his hand going straight up her thigh, when Fix said, "So I think I've got this figured out."

Cousins stopped. "What?"

Fix was slicing oranges and Cousins saw how he pulled the knife towards himself instead of pushing it away. "It was auto theft."

"What was auto theft?"

"That's where I know you from. I've been trying to put it together ever since you showed up. I want to say it was two years ago. I can't remember the guy's name but all he stole were red El Caminos."

The details of a particular auto theft were something Cousins wouldn't remember unless it had happened in the last month, and if he was very busy his memory might go out only as far as a week. Auto theft was the butter and the bread. If people didn't steal cars in Los Angeles then cops and deputy district attorneys would be playing honeymoon bridge at their desks all day, waiting for news of a murder. Auto thefts ran together—those cars flipped exactly as they were found, those run through a chop shop—one theft as unmemorable as the next but for a guy who stole only red El Caminos.

"D'Agostino," Cousins said, and then he repeated the name because he had no idea where that particular gift of memory had come from. That's just the kind of day this was, no explanation.

Fix shook his head in appreciation. "I could have sat here all day and not come up with that. I remember him though.

He thought it showed some kind of class to limit himself to just that one car."

For a moment Cousins felt nearly clairvoyant, as if the case file were open in front of him. "The public defender claimed an improper search. The cars were all in some kind of warehouse." He stopped turning the orange back and forth and closed his eyes in an attempt to concentrate. It was gone. "I can't remember."

"Anaheim."

"I never would have gotten that."

"Well, there you go," Fix said. "That was yours."

But now everything was gone and Cousins couldn't even remember the outcome. Forget the defendant and the crime and sure as hell forget the cops, but he knew verdicts as clearly as any boxer knew who had knocked him down and who he had laid out cold. "He went up," Cousins said, deciding to take the bet on himself, believing that any crook stupid enough to steal nothing but red El Caminos had gone up.

Fix nodded, trying not to smile and smiling anyway. Of course he went up. In a certain stretch of the imagination they had done this thing together.

"So you were the detective," Cousins said. He could see him now, that same brown suit all detectives wore to court, like there was only one and they shared it.

"Arresting," he said. "I'm up for detective now."

"You've got a death card?" Cousins said it to impress him without having any sense of why he would want to impress him. He might be a grade-one deputy DA but he knew how cops kept score. Fix, however, took the question at face value.

He dried his hands and pulled his wallet out of his back pocket, fingering past a few bills.

"Fourteen to go." He handed his list to Cousins, who dried his hands before taking it.

There were many more than fourteen names on the folded piece of paper, probably closer to thirty, with "Francis Xavier Keating" printed at the bottom, but half the names had a single line drawn through them, meaning Fix Keating was moving up. "Jesus," Cousins said. "This many of them are dead?"

"Not dead." Fix took back the list to check the names beneath the straight black lines. He held it up to the kitchen light. "Well, a couple of them. The rest were either promoted already or they moved away, dropped out. It doesn't make any difference—they're off."

Two older women in their best church dresses and no hats leaned against one another in the frame of the open kitchen door. When Fix looked over they gave him a wave in unison.

"Bar still open?" the smaller one said. She meant to sound serious but the line was so clever she hiccupped and then her friend began to laugh as well.

"My mother," Fix said to Cousins, pointing to the one who had spoken, then he pointed to the other, a faded blonde with a cheerful, open face. "My mother-in-law. This is Al Cousins."

Cousins dried his hand a second time and extended it to one and then the other. "Bert," he said. "What're you ladies drinking?"

"Whatever you've got left," the mother-in-law said. You could see just a trace of the daughter there, the way she held her shoulders back, the length of her neck. It was a crime what time did to women.

Cousins picked up a bottle of bourbon, the bottle closest to his hand, and mixed two drinks. "It's a good party," he said. "Everybody out there still having a good time?"

"I thought they were waiting too long," Fix's mother said, accepting her drink.

"You're morbid," the mother-in-law said to her with affection.

"I'm not morbid," the mother corrected. "I'm careful. You have to be careful."

"Waiting for what?" Cousins asked, handing over the second drink.

"The baptism," Fix said. "She was worried the baby was going to die before we got her baptized."

"Your baby was sick?" he asked Fix. Cousins had been raised Episcopalian, but he had let go of that. To the best of his knowledge, dead Episcopal babies were passed into heaven regardless.

"She's fine," Fix said. "Perfect."

Fix's mother shrugged. "You don't know that. You don't know what's going on inside a baby. I had you and your brothers baptized in under a month. I was on top of it. This child," she said, turning her attention to Cousins, "is nearly a year old. She couldn't even fit into the family christening gown."

"Well, there's the problem," Fix said.

His mother shrugged. She drank down her entire drink and then waggled the empty paper cup as if there had been some mistake. They'd run out of ice, and the ice had been the only thing to slow the drinkers down. Cousins took the cup from her and filled it again.

"Someone's got the baby," Fix said to his mother, not a question, just a confirmation of fact.

"The what?" she asked.

"The baby."

She thought for a minute, her eyes half closed, and nodded her head, but it was the other one who spoke, the mother-in-law. "Someone," she said without authority.

"Why is it," Fix's mother said, not interested in the question of the baby, "that men will stand in a kitchen all day mixing drinks and juicing oranges for those drinks but won't so much as set a foot over the threshold to make food?" She stared pointedly at her son.

"No idea," Fix said.

His mother then looked back at Cousins but he only shook his head. Dissatisfied, the two women turned as one and tipped back out into the party, cups in hand.

"She has a point," Cousins said. He never would have stood back here making sandwiches, though he felt he could use a sandwich, that he wanted one, and so he poured himself another drink.

Fix returned to the business of the knife and the orange. He was a careful man, and took his time. Even drunk he wasn't going to cut off his finger. "You have kids?" he asked.

Cousins nodded. "Three and a third."

Fix whistled. "You stay busy."

Cousins wondered if he meant *You stay busy running after kids,* or, *You stay busy fucking your wife.* Either way. He put another empty orange rind in the sink that overflowed with empty orange rinds. He rolled his wrist.

"Take a break," Fix said.

"I did."

"Then take another one. We've got juice in reserve, and if those two are any indication of where things are going most of the people here won't be able to find the kitchen much longer."

"Where's Dick?"

"He's gone, ran out of here with his wife."

I bet he did, Cousins thought, a vision of his own wife flashing before him, the shrieking bedlam of his household. "What time is it, anyway?"

Fix looked at his watch, a Girard-Perregaux, a much nicer watch than a cop might be wearing. It was three forty-five, easily two hours later than either man would have guessed in his wildest estimation of time.

"Jesus, I should get going," Cousins said. He was fairly certain he'd told Teresa he would be home no later than noon.

Fix nodded. "Every person in this house who isn't my wife or my daughters should get going. Just do me a favor first—go find the baby. Find out who has her. If I go out there now everybody's going to want to start talking and it'll be midnight before I find her. Take a quick walk around, would you do that? Make sure some drunk didn't leave her in a chair."

"How will I know it's your baby?" Cousins asked. Now that he thought about it, he hadn't seen a baby at the party, and surely with all these Micks there were bound to be plenty of them.

"She's the new one," Fix said, his voice gone suddenly sharp, like Cousins was an idiot, like this was the reason some guys had to be lawyers rather than cops. "She's the one in the fancy dress. It's her party."

The crowd shifted around Cousins, opening to him, closing around him, pushing him through. In the dining room every platter was stripped, not a cracker or a carrot stick remained. The conversation and music and drunken laughter melted into a single indecipherable block of sound from which the occasional clear word or sentence escaped—*Turns out he's had her in the trunk the entire time he's talking.* Somewhere down a distant hallway he couldn't see, a woman was laughing so hard she gasped for breath, calling, *Stop! Stop!* He saw children, plenty of children, several of whom were pulling cups straight from the unwitting fingers of adults and downing the contents. He didn't see any babies. The room was over-warm and the detectives had their jackets off now, showing the service revolvers clipped to their belts or holstered under their arms. Cousins wondered how he had failed to notice earlier that half the party was armed. He went through the open glass doors to the patio and looked up into the late-afternoon sunlight that flooded the suburb of Downey, where there was not a cloud and never had been a cloud and never would be a cloud. He saw his friend the priest standing still as stone, holding the little sister in his arms, as if they'd been dancing for so long they had fallen asleep standing up. Men sat in patio chairs talking to other men, many of them with women in their laps. The women, all the ones he saw, had taken off their shoes at some point and ruined their stockings. None of them was holding a baby, and there was no baby in the driveway. Cousins stepped inside the garage and flipped on the light. A ladder hung on two hooks and clean cans of paint were lined up on a shelf according to size. There was a shovel, a rake, coils of extension cord, a bench of tools, a place for everything and everything in its place. In the center of the clean cement floor was a clean navy-blue Peugeot. Fix Keating had fewer children and a nicer watch and a foreign car and a much-better-looking wife. The guy hadn't even made detective. If anyone had bothered to ask him at that moment, Cousins would have said it seemed suspicious.

About the time he started really looking at the car, which seemed somehow sexy just by virtue of its being French, he remembered the baby was missing. He thought of his own baby, Jeanette, who had just learned to walk. Her forehead was bruised from where she had careened into the glass yesterday, the Band-Aids were still in place, and he panicked to think he was supposed to be watching her. Little Jeanette, he had no idea where he'd left her! Teresa should have known he wasn't any good at keeping up with the baby. She shouldn't have trusted him with this. But when he came out of the garage to try and find her, his heart punching at his ribs as if it wanted to go ahead of him, he saw all the people at Fix Keating's party. The proper order of the day was returned to him and he stood for another moment holding on to the door, feeling both ridiculous and relieved. He hadn't lost anything.

When he looked back up at the sky he saw the light was changing. He would tell Fix he needed to go home, he had his own kids to worry about. He went inside to find a bathroom and found two closets first. In the bathroom, he stopped to splash some water on his face before coming out again. On the other side of the hallway there was yet another door. It wasn't a big house but it seemed to be made entirely of doors. He opened the door in front of him and found the light inside was dim. The shades were down. It was a room for little girls—a pink rug, a pink wallpaper border featuring fat rabbits. There was a room not unlike this in his own house that Holly shared with Jeanette. In the corner he saw three small girls sleeping on a twin bed, their legs crossed over one another's legs, their fingers twisted in one another's hair. Somehow the only thing he failed to notice was Beverly Keating standing at the changing table with the baby. Beverly looked at him, a smile of recognition coming over her face.

"I know you," she said.

She had startled him, or her beauty startled him again. "I'm sorry," he said. He put his hand on the door.

"You're not going to wake them up." She tilted her head towards the girls. "I think they're drunk. I carried them in here one at a time and they never woke up."

He went over and looked at the girls, the biggest one no more than five. He couldn't help but like the look of children when they were sleeping. "Is one of them yours?" he asked. They all three looked vaguely similar. None of them looked like Beverly Keating.

"Pink dress," she said, her attention on the diaper in her hand. "The other two are her cousins." She smiled at him. "Aren't you supposed to be fixing drinks?"

"Spencer left," he said, though that didn't answer the question. He couldn't remember the last time he'd been nervous, not in the face of criminals or juries, certainly not in the face of women holding diapers. He started again. "Your husband asked me to find the baby."

Finished with her work, Beverly rearranged the baby's dress and lifted her up from the table. "Well, here she is," she said. She touched her nose to the baby's nose and the baby smiled and yawned. "Somebody's been awake a long time." Beverly turned towards the crib.

"Let me take her out to Fix for a minute," he said. "Before you put her down."

Beverly Keating tilted her head slightly to one side and gave him a funny look. "Why does Fix need her?"

It was everything, the pale pink of her mouth in the darkened pink room, the door that was closed now though he didn't remember closing it, the smell of her perfume which had somehow managed to float gently above the familiar stench of the diaper pail. Had Fix asked him to bring the baby back or just to find her? It didn't make any difference. He told her he didn't know, and then he stepped towards her, her yellow dress its own source of light. He held out his arms and she stepped into them, holding out the baby.

"Take her then," she said. "Do you have children?" But by then she was very close and she lifted up her face. He put one arm under the baby, which meant he was putting his arm beneath her breasts. It wasn't a year ago she'd had this baby and while he didn't know what she'd looked like before it was hard to imagine she had ever looked any better than this. Teresa never pulled herself together. She said it wasn't possible, one coming right after the next. Wouldn't he like to introduce the two of them, just to show his wife what could be done if you cared to try. Scratch that. He had no interest in Teresa meeting Beverly Keating. He put his other arm around her back, pressed his fingers into the straight line of her zipper. It was the magic of gin and orange juice. The baby balanced between the two of them and he kissed her. That was the way this day was turning out. He closed his eyes and kissed her until the spark he had felt in his fingers when he touched her hand in the kitchen ran the entire shivering length of his spine. She put her other hand against the small of his back while the tip of her tongue crossed between his parted teeth. There was an almost imperceptible shift between them. He felt it, but she stepped back. He was holding the baby. The baby cried for a second, a single red-faced wail, and then issued a small hiccup and pressed into Cousins's chest.

"We're going to smother her," she said, and laughed. She looked down at the baby's pretty face. "Sorry about that."

The small weight of the Keating girl was familiar in his arms. Beverly took a soft cloth from the changing table and wiped over his mouth. "Lipstick," she said, then she leaned over and kissed him again.

"You are—" he started, but too many things came into his head to say just one.

"Drunk," she said, and smiled. "I'm drunk is all. Go take the baby to Fix. Tell him I'll be there in just a minute to get her." She pointed her finger at him. "And don't tell him anything else, mister." She laughed again.

He realized then what he had known from the first minute he saw her, from when she leaned out the kitchen door and called for her husband. This was the start of his life.

"Go," she said.

She let him keep the baby. She went to the other side of the room and started to arrange the sleeping girls into more comfortable positions. He stood at the closed bedroom door for one more minute to watch her.

"What?" she said. She wasn't being flirtatious.

"Some party," he said.

"Tell me about it."

In one sense only had Fix been right to send him out to find the baby: nobody knew him at this party and it had been easy for him to move through the crowd. It was something Cousins hadn't realized until now when everyone turned their head in his direction. A woman as trim and tan as a stick stepped right in front of him.

"There she is!" she cried, and leaned in to kiss the yellow curls that feathered the baby's head, leaving a wine stain of lipstick. "Oh," she said, disappointed in herself. She used her thumb to try to wipe it up and the baby tightened her features as if she might cry. "I shouldn't have done that." She looked at Cousins and smiled at him. "You won't tell Fix it was me, will you?"

It was an easy promise to make. He'd never seen the tan woman before.

"There's our girl," a man said, smiling at the baby as he patted Cousins on the back. Who did they think he was? No one asked him. Dick Spencer was the only person who knew him at all and he was long gone. As he cut a slow path to the kitchen he was stopped and encircled over and over again. *Oh, the baby,* they said in soft voices. *Hey there, pretty girl.* The compliments and kind words surrounded him. She was a very good-looking baby, he could see it now that they were in the light. This one looked more like the mother, the fair skin, the wide-set eyes, everybody said so. *Just like Beverly.* He jostled her up in the crook of his arm. Her eyes would open and then close again, blue beacons checking to see if she was still in his arms. She was as comfortable with him as any of his own children were. He knew how to hold a baby.

"She sure likes you," a man wearing a gun in a shoulder harness said.

In the kitchen a group of women sat smoking. They tapped their ashes in their cups, signaling they were done. There was nothing left to do but wait for their husbands to tell them it was time to go home. "Hey there, baby," one of them said, and they all looked up at Cousins.

"Where's Fix?" he asked.

One of them shrugged. "I don't know," she said. "Do you have to go now? I'll take her." She held out her hands.

But Cousins wasn't about to turn her over to strangers. "I'll find him," he said, and backed away.

Cousins felt like he had been walking in a circle around Fix Keating's house for the last hour, first looking for the baby and then looking for Fix. He found him on the back patio talking to the priest. The priest's girl was nowhere in sight. There were fewer people outside now, fewer people everywhere. The angle of the light coming through the orange trees had lowered considerably. He saw a single orange high above his head, an orange that had somehow been overlooked in the frenzy to make juice, and he raised up on his toes, the baby balanced in one arm, and picked it.

"Jesus," Fix said, looking up. "Where have you been?"

"Looking for you," Cousins said.

"I've been right here."

Cousins nearly made a crack about Fix not bothering to try and find him but then he thought better of it. "You're not where I left you."

Fix stood up and took the baby from him without gratitude or ceremony. She issued a small sound of discontent at the transfer, then settled against her father's chest and went to sleep. Cousins's arm was weightless now and he didn't like it. He didn't like it one bit. Fix looked at the stain on the top of her head. "Did somebody drop her?"

"It's lipstick."

"Well," said the priest, pushing out of his chair. "That's it for me. We've got a spaghetti supper back at the church in half an hour. Everyone's welcome."

They said their goodnights, and as Father Joe Mike walked away he grew a tail of parishioners who followed him down the driveway, Saint Patrick marching through Downey. They waved their hands at Fix and called goodnight. It wasn't night, but neither was it fully day. The party had gone on entirely too long.

Cousins waited another minute, hoping that Beverly would come back for the baby like she'd said, but she didn't come, and it was hours past time for him to go. "I don't know her name," he said.

"Frances."

"Really?" He looked again at the pretty girl. "You named her for yourself?"

Fix nodded. "Francis got me into a lot of fights when I was a kid. There was no one in the neighborhood who forgot to tell me I had a girl's name, so I figured, why not name a girl Frances?"

"What if she'd been a boy?" Cousins asked.

"I would have named him Francis," Fix said, yet again making Cousins feel he had asked a stupid question.

"When the first one was a girl we named her after Kennedy's daughter. I thought, that's fine, I'll wait, but now—" Fix stopped, looking down at his daughter. There had been a miscarriage between the two girls, fairly late. They were lucky to get this second one, that's what the doctor had said, though there was no point in telling that to the deputy district attorney. "It works out this way."

"It's a good name," Cousins said, but what he thought was, *Lucky you didn't wait.*

"What about you?" Fix said. "You've got a little Albert at home?"

"My son's name is Calvin. We call him Cal. And the girls, no. No Albertas."

"But you've got one coming up."

"In December," he said. Cousins remembered how it was before Cal was born, how he and Teresa would lie in bed at night saying names to one another in the dark. One name would remind her of a kid who got picked on in grade school, a kid who wore stained shirts and bit his thumbs. Some other name would remind him of a boy he never liked, a bully, but when they got to Cal both of them were happy. It was something like that when they were thinking up names for Holly, too. Maybe they'd spent less time on it, maybe they didn't talk about it in bed, her head up on his shoulder, his hand on her stomach, but they'd picked it out together. She wasn't named for anybody, just for herself, because her parents thought it was a beautiful name. And Jeanette? He didn't even remember talking about a name for Jeanette. He'd been late getting to the hospital just that one time and if memory served he'd gone into the room and Teresa said, *This is Jeanette.* She would have been Daphne if anyone had asked him about it. They should talk about what they were going to name this new one. It would give them something to talk about.

"Name this one Albert," Fix said.

"If it's a boy."

"It'll be a boy. You're due."

Cousins looked at Frances asleep in her father's arms. It wouldn't be the worst thing if they had another girl, but if it was a boy then maybe they would call him Albert. "You think?"

"Absolutely," Fix said.

He never did talk about it with Teresa but he was there in the waiting room when the baby was born and he filled out the birth certificate—Albert John Cousins—after himself. Teresa had never much liked her husband's name but when would there have been an opportunity to bring that up? As soon as they were home from the hospital she started calling the baby Albie, Al-*bee*. Cousins told her not to but he wasn't ever around. What was he going to do, stop her? The other kids liked it. They called the baby Albie, too.

2

"So you're telling me that you named Albie?" Franny said.

"I didn't name Albie," her father said, the two of them following the nurse down a long, bright hall. "If I'd named Albie I wouldn't have given him such a stupid name. You could trace a lot of that kid's problems back to his name."

Franny thought of her stepbrother. "There was probably more to it than that."

"Did you know I got him out of Juvenile once? Fourteen years old and he tried to set his school on fire."

"I remember," Franny said.

"Your mother called and asked me to get him out." He tapped his chest. "She said it would be a favor to her, like I was so interested in doing her favors. When you think about all the cops Bert knew in L.A. you have to wonder why they were bothering me."

"You helped Albie," she said. "He was a kid and you helped him. There's nothing wrong with that."

"He didn't even know how to set a decent fire. I drove him over to see your uncle Tom at the fire station once I got him out. Tom was back in L.A. then. I said to Bert's kid, 'You want to burn up a school full of children then these are the guys who can teach you how to do it.' You know what he said to me?"

"I do," Franny said, not pointing out that there had been no children in the school when Albie had set it on fire, and that he'd done a pretty good job. Say what you will for Albie, he knew how to set things on fire.

"He said he wasn't interested anymore." Fix stopped, which made Franny stop, and then the nurse stopped too to wait for them. "People don't still call him that, do they?" Fix asked.

"Albie? I don't know. That's what I've always called him."

"I'm trying not to listen to this," Jenny said. The nurse's name was Jenny. She was wearing a name tag but that didn't matter, they knew her.

"You can listen to anything you want," Fix said. "But we should be telling better stories."

"How are you feeling today, Mr. Keating?" Jenny asked. Fix had come to the UCLA Medical Center for chemotherapy so the question wasn't entirely social. If you didn't feel well they sent you home and the entire process was pushed even further out into the unknowable future.

"Feeling fine," he said, his arm hooked through Franny's. "Feeling like light on the water."

Jenny laughed and the three of them stopped in a large, open room off the hall where two women wearing head wraps sat with digital thermometers in their mouths. One of them gave the newcomers a tired nod while the other stared ahead. All around them the nurses came and went in their candy-colored scrubs. Fix sat down and Jenny gave him a thermometer and wrapped a blood-pressure cuff around his arm. Franny took the empty chair next to her father.

"Just to get back to the original point for a minute, you and Bert talked about what he should name his son before Albie was born?" Franny had heard the story about the fire and the phone call that came after it a hundred times but somehow the one about Albie's name had never come up before.

Fix took the thermometer out. "It wasn't like we talked about it later."

"Hey!" Jenny said, pointing, and Fix put the thermometer back in his mouth.

Franny shook her head. "It's just hard to believe."

Fix turned his eyes up to Jenny, who unwrapped the cuff. "What's hard to believe?" she said for him.

"All of it." Franny opened her hands. "You and Bert making drinks together, you and Bert speaking, you knowing Bert before Mom did."

"Ninety-eight on the nose," Jenny said, and ejected the plastic thermometer sleeve into the trash. Then she pulled a length of bright-pink tourniquet out of her pocket and tied it around Fix's upper arm.

"Of course I knew Bert," he said, as if he were being denied the credit he was due. "How do you think your mother met him?"

"I don't know." It wasn't a question she'd ever thought to ask. There was no time in her memory before Bert. "I guess I thought Wallis introduced them. You hated Wallis so much."

Jenny was kneading the inside of Fix's elbow with her fingertips, searching for a vein that might still be open for business.

"I've known junkies who shot between their toes," Fix said with something approaching nostalgia.

"One more reason you don't want a junkie for a nurse." She tapped another minute on the papery skin and then smiled, holding the vein in place with one finger. "Okay, mister, here we go. A little stick."

Fix didn't flinch. Somehow she had managed to slip the needle straight in. "Oh, Jenny," he said, looking into the part of her hair as she bent over him. "I wish it could always be you."

"Did you really hate Wallis so much?" Jenny asked. She plugged in a rubber-topped vial and watched it fill up with blood, then she filled another.

"I did."

"Poor Wallis." She slipped out the needle and taped a cotton ball in place. "Just hop up on the scale and then I'll be done with you."

Fix got on the scale and watched as she tapped the metal weight back with one fingernail. Tap-tap down, another pound, another, until the scale balanced at 133. "You're drinking your Boost?"

When they were finished with what were called the preliminaries, they went farther down the same hall, past the nurses' station, where doctors stood reading reports on computer screens or their phones. They went into the large, sunny room where the patients lay tilted back in recliners, tethered to trickling streams of chemicals. Someone had turned the volume off on all the televisions, which meant they were freed from commercials but left with the discordant beeping of monitors. Jenny led Franny and Fix to two chairs in the corner. It was a gift, considering how busy the chemo room was. Everyone with the energy for preference preferred the corner chairs.

"I hope you have a good day once this is over," Jenny said. Jenny didn't administer chemo. It was only her job to get the chart ready for the nurse who would take over his case from there.

Fix thanked her and then settled in, using both hands to push himself into the recliner. When his head tilted back and his feet levered up he gave the small sigh of a cop in his chair at the end of a long day on the beat. He closed his eyes. For five full minutes he stayed so still that Franny thought he'd gone to sleep before the line was even started. She wished she'd thought to bring a magazine with her from the waiting room and was just starting to look around the treatment room, because sometimes magazines got left in there, when her father went back to his story.

"Wallis was a bad influence," he said, eyes still closed. "She was always sitting in our kitchen going on about liberation and free love. What you have to remember about your mother is that she didn't have her own character. She turned into whoever she was sitting next to. When she was sitting next to Miss Free Love then free love sounded like a great idea."

"It was the sixties," Franny said, glad he was awake. "You can't pin the whole thing on Wallis."

"I'll pin anything I want on Wallis."

It probably wasn't a bad idea. Wallis had died ten years before of colon cancer, and for all her talk of free love and liberation, she had stuck it out with Larry, who she had married when she was a junior in college. Larry saw her out of her life as patiently as he had seen her through it—giving her bed baths, counting her pills, changing her colostomy bag. Larry and Wallis had moved to Oregon after Larry sold his optometry practice. They grew blueberries and paid an extraordinary amount of attention to their dogs because their children and grandchildren so rarely had the time to visit. Wallis and Beverly had been maintaining their friendship from opposite sides of the country since they were twenty-nine years old, since Beverly left for Virginia to marry Bert Cousins, so Wallis's late-life move hadn't affected them at all. Los Angeles, Oregon, what difference did it make when you lived in Virginia? If anything, they were closer after the move because Wallis had no one but Larry and the dogs to talk to. Beverly and Wallis had e-mail and free long distance now. They talked for hours. They sent birthday presents to one another, funny cards. When Beverly married her third husband, Jack Dine, Wallis flew from Oregon to Arlington to be the matron of honor, as she had been the maid of honor at Beverly's wedding to Fix, but not in Beverly's wedding to Bert, which had been conducted privately and without friends at Bert's parents' house outside Charlottesville. Later, when Wallis got sick, Beverly flew to Oregon and they sat up in the bed together and read Jane Kenyon's poetry aloud. They talked about the things in life that had mystified them—mostly their children and their husbands. Wallis hadn't liked Fix Keating any more than he liked her, and she never minded that he assigned to her full responsibility for things that could not possibly have been her fault. If she could shoulder the burden of his blame while she was alive, it was hard to imagine she'd be bothered by it now.

"Are you cold?" Franny asked her father. "I can get you a blanket."

Fix shook his head. "I don't get cold now. I get cold later. They'll bring me a blanket when I need one."

Franny looked around the room for the nurse without letting her eyes linger on any of the patients—the woman asleep with her mouth open, hairless as a newborn mouse, the teenaged boy tapping on his iPad, the woman whose six-year-old sat quietly in the chair next to hers and colored in a book. How had chemo gone for Wallis? Did Larry drop her off or did he sit with her? Did their sons come up from L.A.? She would have to remember to ask her mother.

"They're slow getting started today," Franny said, not that it mattered. The soup and the bread that Fix wouldn't eat were ready at the house. Marjorie would be waiting for them. They would watch *Jeopardy!* Franny would sleep in the guest room upstairs.

"Never be in a rush to have someone poison you. That's my motto. I can sit here all day."

"When did you get to be so patient?"

"The patient patient," he said, pleased with himself. "So do you and Albie keep in touch?"

Franny shrugged. "I hear from him." Franny had talked about Albie too much in her life, and now, as if she could make up for it, she made a point of not talking about him at all.

"And what about old Bert? How's he doing?"

"He seems okay."

"Do you talk to him very often?" Fix asked, the soul of innocence.

"Not nearly as often as I talk to you."

"It isn't a contest."

"No, it's not."

"And he's married now?"

Franny shook her head. "Single."

"But there was a third one."

"Didn't work out."

"Wasn't there a fiancée though? Somebody after the third one?" Fix knew full well that Bert had had a third divorce but he never tired of hearing about it.

"There was for a while."

"And the fiancée didn't work out either?"

Franny shook her head.

"Well, that's a shame," Fix said, sounding as if he meant it, and maybe he did, but he had asked her the same questions a month before and he would ask her again a month from now, pretending that he was old and sick and didn't remember their last conversation. Fix *was* old and sick, but he remembered everything. Keep examining the witness—that's what he had told her over the phone when she was a kid and her ID bracelet had gone missing from her locker. She had called him from Virginia at five o'clock, the minute the rates went down, two o'clock California time. She called him at work. She had never called him at work before but she had his business card. He was a detective by then, and he was her father, so she figured he'd know how to find the bracelet.

"Ask around," her father had told her. "Find out who was

changing classes and where they were going. You don't need to make a big deal about it, don't let anyone think you're accusing them, but you talk to every kid who walked down that hall and then talk to them again because either there's something they're keeping from you or there's something they haven't remembered yet themselves. You have to be willing to put in the time if you're serious about finding it."

Patsy was his nurse today, a child-sized Vietnamese woman who swam in her XXS lavender scrubs. She waved at him from across the crowded room as if it were a party and she had finally caught his eye. "You're here!" she said.

"I'm here," he said.

She came to him, her black hair braided and the braid caught up in a doubled loop like a rope to be used in the case of true emergency. "You're looking good, Mr. Keating," she said.

"The three stages of life: youth, middle age, and 'You're looking good, Mr. Keating.'"

"It all depends on where I see you. I see you at the beach lying on a towel in your swim trunks, I don't think you look so good. But here"—Patsy dropped her voice and looked around the room. She leaned in close. "Here you look good."

Fix unbuttoned the top buttons on his shirt and pulled it back, offering her the port in his chest. "Did you meet my daughter Franny?"

"I know Franny," Patsy said, and gave Franny the smallest raise of the eyebrow, universal shorthand for *The old man is forgetting*. She pushed a large syringe of saline to clear the port. "Tell me your full name."

"Francis Xavier Keating."

"Date of birth."

"April 20, 1931."

"That's the winning ticket," she said, and pulled three clear plastic pouches from the pockets of her scrub top. "Oxaliplatin, 5FU, and this little one is just an antiemetic."

"Good," Fix said, nodding. "Plug 'em in."

From outside the seventh-story window the bright Los Angeles morning came slanting in across the linoleum floor. Patsy skated off to the nurses' station to input the details of treatment while Fix stared up at the silent advertisement playing on the television that hung from the ceiling. A woman walking through a rainstorm was drenched and dripping, lightning shooting down around her. Then a handsome stranger handed her his umbrella and as soon as he did the rain stopped. The street was now some British gardener's idea of the afterlife, all sunshine and roses. The woman's hair was dry and billowing, and her dress trailed behind her like butterfly wings. The words "Ask Your Doctor" parked across the top of the screen, as if the advertisers had anticipated everyone turning off the sound. Franny wondered if the drug was for depression, an overactive bladder, thinning hair.

"You know who I always think about when I'm here?" Fix asked Franny.

"Bert."

He made a face. "If I ask you a question about Bert or his pyromaniac son, that's called making conversation, being polite. I don't think about them."

"Dad," Franny said. "Who've you been thinking about lately?"

"*Lomer*," he said. "You didn't know Lomer, did you?"

"I didn't," she said, but she knew that story too, or some version of the story. Her mother had told her a long time ago.

Fix shook his head. "No, you wouldn't remember Lomer. You were sitting in his lap the last time he came over. He was carrying you around everywhere with him. He didn't even put you down when he ate his dinner. It was just a couple months after your christening party, I remember now. You were a pretty baby, Franny, and you were sweet. Everyone made such a fuss over you and it drove your sister crazy. Before you came along, Lomer paid all his attention to Caroline, which was how she liked it. I remember Lomer saying to her, 'Caroline, come up here, there's plenty of room,' but she wasn't having it. She couldn't stand to see the two of you together."

"Well, there you go," Franny said. To the best of Franny's memory, the only lap Caroline had ever wanted to sit in was their father's, even after they had moved to the other side of the country.

Fix nodded. "Kids loved Lomer, all of them. He was always letting them get in the car, turn on the siren, play with the handcuffs. Can you imagine the lawsuits people would file if someone did that now, handcuffing a little kid to the rearview mirror for fun? They had to stand up on the front seat, they loved it. Lomer gave cops a good name. I remember when he left our house that night after dinner, your mother and I talked about how sad it was the guy didn't have any kids of his own. We thought he was so old and he was what then, twenty-eight, twenty-nine?"

"Was he married?"

Fix shook his head. "He didn't have a girlfriend, at least not when he died. He got his nose broken in the Navy and his nose was a mess but he was still a good-looking guy. Everybody used to say he looked like Steve McQueen, which was an overstatement because of the nose. Your mother was always wanting to set him up with Bonnie and I said no because I thought Bonnie was an idiot. Too bad I got my way on that one. It would have saved the world a priest."

"Maybe he was gay," Franny said.

Fix turned his head, a shadow of such bewilderment crossing over him that it was clear he thought there had been a misunderstanding. "Joe Mike wasn't gay."

"I meant Lomer."

And with that Fix closed his eyes again and kept them closed. "I don't know why you have to do that."

"There wouldn't have been anything wrong with it," Franny said, but she was already sorry. Once upon a time in the city of Los Angeles there was a smart heterosexual cop who loved kids and looked like Steve McQueen and didn't have a girlfriend; whether she thought such a thing was possible didn't matter. Gay or straight, Lomer was just shy of fifty years dead. The chemo bag had just gone up and they had another hour and a half to sit in this room and either talk or not talk. "I'm sorry," she said, and when he didn't answer her she gave his arm a small poke. "I said I was sorry. Tell me about Lomer."

Fix waited for a minute, deciding whether to nurse the grudge or let it go. Truth be told, Franny irritated him, the way she looked like Beverly but without Beverly's sense of knowing what to do with her looks—her hair in a ponytail, the drawstring pants, not so much as ChapStick on her face. He knew people here, sometimes his doctor came by during treatment. She could have made an effort.

And she didn't know the first thing about Lomer either. Sitting in his lap when she was a year old was as close as Franny ever got to a man of Lomer's caliber. That old guy she'd been so crazy about when she was young, the one who'd robbed her blind, and even her husband, who may be nice enough but had clearly married her because he needed a babysitter for his children—Franny had no taste in men. Fix had hoped that someday his girls would meet a man like Lomer but no luck there. The picture in his mind—his partner at the dinner table holding Franny, Beverly in the kitchen dressed like she was going out to dinner instead of making dinner—that was enough to make the decision to keep his eyes closed, but then he felt a single, electric jolt run through his esophagus, as if the poison coursing through him had suddenly washed against the side of the tumor, and Fix remembered again what he was constantly forgetting: this was going to kill him.

"Dad?" Franny said, and touched her hand very lightly to his sternum in exactly that place.

Fix shook his head. "Get me another pillow."

When she brought the pillow and arranged it behind his back, he started. Franny had come all the way from Chicago to see him. She'd left her husband and the boys for this.

"What you need to know about Lomer is that he was a funny son of a bitch," Fix said. "There was nothing better than going on a stakeout with him." He found his own voice to be small and cleared his throat to start again. "I looked forward to sitting in some piece-of-crap car until four o'clock in the morning in South Central because Lomer was there telling jokes. I'd laugh until I was sick, until finally I had to tell him to cut it out or we were going to blow the whole night's work."

Franny's father looked brittle and small. The cancer was in his liver now.

There were spots in his pelvis and one in his spine,
while Lomer was handsome and still twenty-nine.

That's what Lomer would have to say about it.

"So tell me a joke," Franny said.

Fix smiled at the ceiling, at Lomer sitting beside him in the car. He lay like that for several minutes, the silvered droplets of chemo sliding down the plastic tubing and into the hole in his chest, then he shook his head. "I don't know them anymore."

Which wasn't true exactly. He remembered one.

"So this woman is home when a cop knocks on the door," Lomer said. For the first second Fix didn't know he was starting in on a joke. That was the thing about Lomer, you never knew. "The cop has a dog with him, something like a beagle, maybe a little bigger than a beagle, and the dog looks guilty as hell. The beagle tries to look up at the woman and he can't do it, he can't meet her eye, so he's looking down at the grass like maybe he's dropped a quarter in there somewhere."

A joke. Fix was driving and the windows were down. The radio was squawking directives in numeric code and Fix dialed back the volume until the words and the numbers were nothing more than a slight crackling of static. Lomer and Fix weren't headed anywhere in particular. They were on patrol. They were looking.

"The cop," Lomer said, "he's trying. This is tough duty. 'Ma'am,' he says, 'is this your dog?' And she tells him it is. 'Well, I'm sorry to inform you there's been an accident. Your husband's been killed.' So you know what happens, she's shocked, she's crying, all of it. The dog still won't look at her. 'But ma'am,' the cop says, and he does not want to say this, 'there's something else I have to tell you.' He's just going to rip off the Band-Aid. 'Your husband's body, when we found him at the site, he was naked.' And the wife repeats the word, *'Naked?'* And the cop nods, then he clears his throat. 'There's something else, ma'am. There was a woman in the car with him, and the woman didn't make it either.' The wife makes some sort of sound, a little gasp, or maybe she says, *Ooh.* And then the cop finishes it off. He doesn't have any choice. 'Your dog here was in the car with them. It looks like he was the only survivor.' And the dog just stares at his front paws like he really wishes they'd all been killed together."

Fix turned the car down Alvarado. It was August 2, 1964, and even though it was nearly nine o'clock at night it still wasn't fully dark. Los Angeles smelled like lemons and asphalt and the muted exhaust of a million cars. There were kids on the sidewalk shoving each other and running away, one big game, but the night crawlers were coming out too: the gang-bangers, the working girls, the junkies with their insatiable needs, and together they created a market of exchange.

For everyone there was something to sell or buy or steal. The night was just getting warmed up. The night was still very young.

"So do you make these things up?" Fix asked. "Have you been riding around for the last three hours making this up in your head or do you read jokes in joke magazines and save them for the right time?"

"This isn't a joke," Lomer said, taking off his sunglasses now that the sun was nearly finished. "I'm telling you what happened."

"To you," Fix said.

"To someone I know. The cousin of someone I know."

"Fuck you. Seriously."

"Just be quiet and listen for a change. So the cop offers his condolences and hands the woman the leash and he's out of there. The dog has to go inside. The whole time the dog is looking over his shoulder at the cop, who's getting in his car. When the woman closes the door she starts in on the dog right away. 'He was *naked?* He was in the car and he was *naked?*'" Lomer's voice wasn't that of a grieving widow but a furious wife. "And the dog looks back at the door, just desperate to be anyplace else in the world, you know?" Lomer looked out the passenger window of the car for a minute, at a kid with a basketball parked under one arm walking home from the courts, at a guy standing on the corner, drunk or high, his head thrown back and his mouth open, waiting for rain. When he looked back at Fix he was the beagle, the saddest, guiltiest beagle in the history of beagles, and the beagle that was Lomer nodded his head.

"And the woman?" Lomer said in the wife's voice. "She was naked too?"

And just that quickly he was a beagle again, just barely able to look up at Fix. He nodded.

"Well, what were they *doing?*"

This question was almost too much for Lomer as the beagle, so painful was the moment to recall, but he touched his thumb to the fingers of one hand to make a circle, and then took the index finger of his other hand and jabbed it through. Fix flipped on his turn indicator and pulled the black-and-white to the curb. He was no longer watching the street.

"'They were having *sex?*' the wife asks."

Lomer nodded sadly.

"In the *car?*"

The beagle closed his eyes and very slowly nodded again.

"Where?"

Lomer lifted his chin just a quarter inch to indicate the backseat. A sadder beagle was never born.

"And what were *you* doing?"

Fix was laughing before the punch line came, as Lomer put his hands on an imaginary steering wheel and looked nervously, nervously but with real interest, into the rearview mirror in order to see the backseat of the car, where Lomer the beagle watched his master screw another woman.

"Where do you get these things?" Fix asked and for a second touched his forehead to the steering wheel. Lomer never told him but he could remember the feeling of laughing so hard he couldn't breathe. Then from underneath the laughing and the sound of the cars rushing past and the high Latin music that was coming from someplace neither of them could see, a series of numbers separated them from the steady barrage of numbers the radio spat out—their numbers. Lomer and Fix both heard them with the volume nearly off, and they were glad, though there was no need to say this. The night had been too quiet so far and the quiet had given them an itch. They never believed there was nothing going on in Los Angeles, only that it hadn't come to them yet. Now the lights were on and the siren was screaming out its loop. Lomer gave directions and Fix raced the car down the suddenly empty middle lane of the wide street. Pedestrians held to the curb, all eyes on the black-and-white. The two officers felt that kick inside which never failed to ignite them. The call was for a domestic disturbance, which could mean a screaming match that was annoying the neighbors or a husband beating his wife with a belt or some kids standing on the roof popping off rats in the palm trees with a BB gun. It wasn't armed robbery and it wasn't a murder. Most of the time the people were just embarrassed and whoever called the cops got all the blame. Though sometimes not.

They took Alvarado to Olympic and slid down into the warren of side streets. Night was full on them and Fix killed the siren but left on the lights so that house by house the curtains parted an inch or two and the occupants peered out, wondering who was in trouble and wondering who was thoughtless enough to bring the cops down on their quiet neighborhood where everyone had at least one thing to hide. The house they were going to was dark. When the residents of the house know you're coming for them, the residents of the house trouble themselves to get up and turn off the lights. Standard operating procedure.

"Looks like we're too late," Lomer said. "They've already gone to bed."

"Let's wake them up," Fix said.

Were they ever afraid? Fix would wonder about this later. In the years that followed there was not a single thing Fix Keating didn't know about fear, even though he would eventually learn to set his face in such a way so as not to show it. But in the years he spent with Lomer, he walked through every door certain he would walk back out again.

It was a small box of a house with a small, square yard. It was like every other house on the street except for a cascading hedge of bougainvillea covered over in flowers the burning pink of antihistamine tablets. "How did this even *get* here?" Lomer said, running his hand across the leaves. Fix knocked on the door, first with his knuckles and then with his flashlight. In the flashing blue light from the car he could see he was making small dings in the wood. He called out, "Police!" but whoever was inside knew that already.

"I'll check around back," Lomer said and walked off whistling through the narrow side yard, shining his flashlight in the windows while Fix waited. There were no stars above Los Angeles, or they were there but the city threw out too much light to see them. Fix had his eye on the slim quarter moon when he saw a bright light coming through the dark house. Lomer switched on the porch light and opened the front door. "The back was open," he said.

"The back door was open," Fix said.

"What?" Franny asked. She put down her magazine and pulled the blanket up to his shoulders. He'd been right about the blanket. Patsy had brought him one.

"I was asleep."

"It's the Benadryl. It keeps you from itching later on."

He was trying to put it all together—this room, this day, his daughter, Los Angeles, the house just off Olympic. "The back door was open and the front door was locked. You would've stopped to think about that, wouldn't you?"

"Dad, tell me what house we're talking about? Your house now? The Santa Monica house?"

Fix shook his head. "The house we went to the night Lomer was shot."

"I thought he got shot at a service station," she said. That's what her mother had told them, and if it was forty years ago, more than that, she still remembered it. Her mother had been fighting with Caroline. Whenever Caroline stayed out past curfew or said something really horrible to Bert or gave Franny enough of a slap to make her nose bleed, she took the opportunity to remind their mother that had Beverly been a decent wife and stayed with their father then none of this would have happened. If Beverly had stayed married to Fix then Caroline would have been a model citizen; her good behavior had been entirely within their mother's grasp and she'd blown it by choosing to run off with Bert Cousins, so no one should be blaming Caroline for how her life was turning out. It was old news. By the point at which they'd come to this particular fight they'd been living in Virginia for longer than either girl had lived in Los Angeles, but the story of her alternative existence was Caroline's trump card and she brought it out for every occasion. Franny remembered the time the three of them were in the car coming home from school, she and Caroline both in the plaid uniform skirts and white perma-press blouses of Sacred Heart. She couldn't remember what Caroline had done that had started the fight, or why this fight seemed more serious than the others. But something that was said had made their mother tell them about Lomer.

"That's right," her father said to her. "He was shot at the Gulf station on Olympic."

Franny leaned over in her chair and put her hand on her father's forehead. His hair, which had been gray for as long as she could remember, had grown back a luminous white brush after the last round of chemo. Everyone talked about her father's hair. She swept it back with her palm. "I really want to know what you're talking about," she said, her voice low even though no one was listening. No one in that room was thinking about them at all.

Fix, who had never been big on sharing, suddenly wanted to explain it to her. He wanted Franny to understand. "The house was so small we knew it wasn't going to take any time to find them. There were three doors off the hall—two bedrooms, one bathroom. These places were all put together the same way. They were in the first bedroom. It was a father, a mother, four kids. They were on the bed together in the dark. We flicked on the overhead lights and there they were, all sitting up straight, even the littlest one. It was the father who'd been beaten. That's not one you see a lot. Usually it's the woman who's taken the hit but this guy looked like someone had just scraped him up off the freeway, his lip had sliced open on his teeth, one of his eyes was already shut, his nose was everywhere. I can see his face as clear as I see you. It's crazy how much of that house and those people I remember—their feet were bare, and all of them had their feet up on the bed. We started asking them questions and we got nothing, no response at all. The father was looking at me with his one eye and I was wondering how he was even upright. There was blood on his neck that was coming out of both of his ears. I would have thought the beating had popped his eardrums if it weren't for the fact that no one on that bed seemed like they heard us. Lomer radioed in for an ambulance and backup. I kept talking to them and finally the oldest girl, maybe she was ten, tells me they don't speak English. The mother and father don't speak English but the kids do. There were three girls and a boy. The boy was maybe seven or eight. I said, 'The person who did this, where did he go?' And then they all turned mute again, the girl was staring straight ahead just like her parents until the little one, who was five or something like that, not so much bigger than Caroline was then, looked at the closet plain as day. She didn't turn her head but she was very clear. The guy was in the closet. The older girl grabbed her wrist and squeezed the hell out of it but Lomer and I turned around and Lomer opened the closet door, and there he was, smashed into the clothes. It was a small closet, the kind people used to have, and everything they've got in the world was in there, including this guy. He understood the situation. He wasn't going to make it past us. He had blood on his shirt and his hand was cracked up from beating the poor son of a bitch on the bed. I don't think he spoke any more English than the one he'd come over to bust up. He'd stuck his gun in the pocket of a dress in the closet. Maybe he figured nobody would find it and he could come back and pick it up later. Right about that time the backup came in and then the ambulance. There were no Miranda rights back then, no calling in a guy who spoke Spanish. The family on the bed, they're all shaking now and the kids were crying, like it was fine when he was in the closet and they didn't have to look at him but now that he's standing in the bedroom again they were all stirred up. His name was Mercado. We found that out later. He had a regular job beating Mexicans who'd borrowed money to be smuggled into the country and hadn't made enough yet to pay off the debt. Nobody who had any money or any way to get their hands on money screwed these guys over. They beat people in front of their families, in front of their neighbors. That was the wake-up call, and if the money still didn't come a week or two later they'd swing by and shoot you in the head. Everybody knew it."

"You're awake!" Patsy said, making Franny jump. Patsy took down the smallest bag, the antiemetic, which was already empty. The others still had a way to go. "Did you get some rest?"

"I got some rest," Fix said, but he looked exhausted, whether from the chemo or the story or both. Franny wondered if Patsy didn't see it but then maybe he didn't look so different from anyone else in the room.

Patsy yawned at the mention of sleep, covered her mouth with a small gloved hand. "One day I'm just gonna stretch out in one of those chairs. I'm gonna pull the blanket up over my head and go to sleep. People do that, you know, the light bothers their eyes. Who'll know that it's me under a blanket?"

"I wouldn't tell," Fix said and shut his eyes.

"Are you thirsty?" Patsy patted the blanket on top of his knee. "I could get you some water, or there's soda if you want it. Do you want a Coke?"

Franny was just about to tell her they were fine but Fix nodded. "Water. Water would be good."

Patsy looked at her. "You?"

Franny shook her head.

Patsy went off to get his water and Fix waited, opening his eyes so that he could watch her go.

"So then what happened?" Franny said. This was the deal of taking her father to chemo when none of the doctors spoke in terms of a cure: this was the time she had, these were all the stories she was going to get. It was why she and Caroline took turns flying out to Los Angeles, because they'd never been with him for very long. It was to give Marjorie a break because it was Marjorie who did all the work, but more than anything it was to have a chance at the stories he was going to take with him. She would call Caroline tonight after their father had gone to sleep and tell her about Lomer.

"The house filled up with people—cops, the ambulance guys working. Lomer found an envelope in the trash and he drew some mice on the back for the littlest girl. It was clear she was in serious trouble with her parents and Lomer felt bad for her. The father went to the hospital in the ambulance, the mother and the kids, my God, we probably left them in the house for somebody else to finish off, I don't even know. It must have been two years before I thought about them again. We took the guy Mercado back to the station and booked him. When we were done it was nearly one in the morning and all we wanted was coffee. The coffee at the station was unfit. That was Lomer's word—*'unfit.'* I used to find myself thinking that if they'd troubled themselves to get decent coffee then Lomer would have had a cup at the station, but those are the kind of thoughts that make you crazy. We went to a gas station over on Olympic. Not close but close enough. The guy who owned the place spent real money on his coffee and he taught all the kids who worked for him the importance of dumping it out and making a fresh pot. People would drive an extra couple of blocks to buy their gas from a guy who had good coffee. It wasn't like it is today where there's nobody to fill up your tank but you can get a goddamn cappuccino. A coffee pot in a gas station, especially if the coffee was good, that was full-on innovation. The guy made the coffee and the cops came around and sat in the parking lot drinking the coffee, and then more people would come because they felt safer because of the cops. It was a little ecosystem based on coffee, so that's where we went. I was driving. The guy who drives drives all night, and the guy who isn't driving gets the coffee, so Lomer went in. I have to think he didn't see what was going on. He was eight, ten feet in the door before he was shot. And I didn't see what was going on because I was writing in the log. I heard the shot and I looked up and Lomer was gone. What I saw was the kid behind the cash register raising up his hands, palms out, and then this guy Mercado turned around and shot him too."

"Wait," Franny said. "Mercado? The guy from the house?"

Fix nodded. "That's what I saw. The gas station was just like all gas stations were back then—like a fish tank with a bright light on top—so I got a very clear look: Latino, twenty-five, five seven, white shirt, blue pants, some blood on the shirt. I'd been looking at this guy for the past two hours. He'd been sitting at my desk. I knew him, he knew me. He looked out the window and saw me there. He fired one more shot but he must have been rattled because the bullet didn't even hit the car. All it did was punch out the glass in the front of the station. Mercado ran out the door and went around the back. I heard a car but I didn't see it. I went in the station and Lomer was on the floor." Fix stopped there, thought for a minute. "Well," he said finally.

"What?"

Fix shook his head. "He was dead."

"What about the other guy, the service-station guy?"

"He made it maybe an hour, long enough to get him into surgery. He died in surgery. He was a high school kid, summer job. All he had to do was make the coffee and keep the gas station open."

Patsy came back with two Styrofoam cups of water, each with a bent-neck straw. "You never think you want any until you see it. That's the way it goes around here."

Franny thanked her and took the cups. Patsy was right, she wanted the water.

"But that's crazy," Franny said to her father, though she remembered that this was part of the story her mother had told them in the car, that her father had gone crazy after his partner was shot, that he hadn't been able to identify the man who killed Lomer. "How did Mercado get out of the police station? How did he know where you were?"

"It was a quirk of the brain, or at least that's how they explained it to me later. Too much had happened and somehow

I mixed up the slides, exchanged one suspect for another. But to this day I'll tell you: I saw what I saw. This was my partner dead. I didn't know how it happened but the guy was standing under a light maybe fifteen feet in front of me. We looked straight at one another, just like you're looking at me. When the cops came to the scene I described him to the letter. Hell, I gave them his name. But Jorge Mercado was in a holding cell in Rampart. He'd been there all night."

"And the guy who killed Lomer?" Franny said.

"Turns out I never saw him."

"So they never found the person who did it?"

Fix bent down the neck of the straw and drank. It was hard for him to drink because of the strictures in his esophagus. The water went down in quarter teaspoons. "No," he said finally, "they found him. They put it together."

"But you identified another man."

"I identified another man to the police. I didn't identify another man to a jury. They found someone who'd seen a car driving crazy near the gas station. They made it a point to find the driver and then they made it a point to find the gun he'd thrown out the window of the car. You shoot a kid in a gas station and the police department will make a sincere effort to find you. You shoot a cop in a gas station, that's a different story."

"But they didn't have a witness," Franny said.

"I was the witness."

"But you just said you didn't see the guy."

Fix held up a single finger between them. "To this day I haven't seen him. Even when I was sitting across from him in court. It never straightened out. The psychiatrist said when I saw the guy I'd remember him, and when I didn't remember him the psychiatrist said it might come back over time, that I might just wake up one day and it would all be there." He shrugged. "That didn't happen."

"So how were you a witness?"

"They told me who the guy was and I said yes, that's him." Fix gave his daughter a tired smile. "Don't worry about it. He was the right guy. What you've got to remember is that he saw me too. He looked out of the fish tank just before he tried to shoot me. He knew who I was. He killed Lomer and he killed the kid and he knew I was the guy who saw him do it." Fix shook his head. "I wish I could remember that kid's name. At the funeral home his mother told me he was a serious swimmer. 'Very promising' is what she said. Half the things in this life I wish I could remember and the other half I wish I could forget."

Beverly had stayed for another two years after Lomer died, even though she'd already made a promise to Bert that she was leaving. She stayed because Fix needed her. She'd pulled the car over to the side of the road on that day of the bad fight after school in Virginia and told Caroline and Franny to stop thinking she had just walked out on their father because she hadn't. She had stayed.

"I managed to get Lomer out of my head eventually," Fix said. "I carried him around for years, but one day, I don't know, I put him down. I didn't dream about him anymore. I didn't think what he'd want for lunch every time I got lunch, I didn't look at the guy riding next to me in the car and think about who he wasn't. I felt guilty about that but I have to tell you, it was a relief."

"But now you're thinking about him again?"

"Well, sure," Fix said, "all of this." He raised his hand to the plastic tubing that tied him down to life. He smiled. "He'll never have to do this. He'll never get old and sick. I'm sure he would have wanted to get old and sick if anyone had asked him. I'm sure that we both would have said yes, please, give me the cancer when I'm eighty. But now . . ." Fix shrugged. "I can see it both ways."

Franny shook her head. "You got the better deal."

"Wait and see," her father said. "You're young."

3

On the day before Bert and his soon-to-be second wife, Beverly, were to drive from California to Virginia, Bert came by the house in Torrance and suggested to his first wife, Teresa, that she should think about moving with them.

"Not *with* us, of course," Bert said. "You'd have to pack, sell the house. I know it would take some time, but when you think about it why shouldn't you come back to Virginia?"

Teresa had once thought her husband to be the handsomest man in the world, when in fact he looked like one of those gargoyles perched on a high corner of Notre Dame that's meant to scare the devil away. She didn't say this but it was clear by his change of tone that the thought was written on her face.

"Look," Bert said, "you never wanted to move to Los Angeles anyway. You only did it for me, and not, if I may remind you, without a great deal of bitching. Why would you want to stay here now? Take the kids back to your parents' place, get them started in school, and then when the time is right I can help you find a house."

Teresa stood in the kitchen they had so recently shared

and tightened the belt of her bathrobe. Cal was in second grade and Holly had started kindergarten, but Jeanette and Albie were still home. The children were hanging on Bert's legs, squealing like he was a ride at Disneyland, *Daddeee! Daddeee!* He patted their heads like drums. He patted them with a beat.

"Why do you want me in Virginia?" she asked. She knew why but she wanted to hear him say it.

"It would be better," he said, and shot his eyes down to those dear tousled heads, one beneath each hand.

"Better for the children if both of their parents lived near each other? Better for the children to not grow up without a father?"

"Christ, Teresa, you're *from* Virginia. It's not like I'm suggesting you move to Hawaii. Your entire family is there. You'd be *happier* there."

"I'm touched to hear you're thinking about my happiness."

Bert sighed. She was wasting his time. She'd never had any respect for his time. "Everyone else is moving forward except for you. You're the one who's determined to stay stuck."

Teresa poured herself a cup of coffee from the percolator. She offered one to Bert, who waved her away. "Are you asking Beverly's husband to come with you too? So he could see more of his girls? It would be better for them that way." Teresa had been told by a mutual friend that the reason Bert and the soon-to-be second Mrs. Cousins were moving back to Virginia was that Bert was afraid the new wife's first husband would try to have him killed, that he would find a way to make it look like an accident and so never be caught. The first husband was a cop. Cops, some of them anyway, were good at things like that.

It was a brief conversation which ended in Bert's being demonstrably irritated with her in the way he was always irritated with her, but that was all it took for Teresa Cousins to spend the rest of her life in Los Angeles.

Teresa had gotten a job in the secretarial pool at the Los Angeles County District Attorney's Office. She put the two little ones into day care and the two older ones into an after-school program. The lawyers in the DA's office had a small, collective sense of guilt about having covered for Bert during his long affair. They thought they owed Teresa a break now that he was gone and so they offered her the job. But it wasn't too long before they were talking to her about going to night school and becoming a paralegal. Teresa Cousins was exhausted, angry, and misused, but they had come to find out she was no dummy.

Bert Cousins had made very little money as a deputy district attorney, and so he had been obliged to pay only a modest alimony and child support. His parents' wealth was not his wealth and therefore did not figure into the settlement. He petitioned for custody of his children for the entire summer, from school's end to school's start, and his petition was granted. Teresa Cousins had fought hard to give him only two weeks, but Bert was a lawyer and his friends were lawyers who were friends with the judge, and his parents sent him enough money on the side to keep the case in court for all eternity if that was what the situation required.

When Teresa was told that she had lost summers, she made a point to curse and weep, but she wondered silently if she hadn't just been handed the divorce equivalent of a Caribbean vacation. She loved her children, there was no doubt about that, but she could see that one season out of four spent without having to deal with every sore throat and fistfight, the begging for ballet classes she couldn't afford and didn't have the time to drive to, the constant excuses made at work for being late and leaving early when she was just hanging on by a fingernail anyway, one season every year without her children, though she would never admit it, might be manageable. The thought of a Saturday morning without Albie jumping over her in the bed, back and forth and back and forth like he was skiing some imaginary slalom course, was not unappealing. The thought of him jumping over Bert's second wife, who no doubt slept in a cream silk negligee trimmed in black lace, a nightgown that had to be dry-cleaned, the thought of Albie actually jumping *on* her, well, that would be just fine.

For the first few years the children were too young to travel alone and so arrangements were made for their supervision. One year Beverly's mother flew them out, the next year it was Beverly's sister. Bonnie was anguished and apologetic in front of Teresa, never exactly able to meet her gaze. Bonnie had married a priest and was capable of experiencing guilt about all sorts of things over which she had no control. Another year it was Beverly's friend Wallis who played chaperone. Wallis had a loud voice and a big smile for all of them. She wore a bright-green cotton dress. Wallis liked children.

"Oh, kiddos," she'd said to the four little Cousinses.

"We're going to eat every peanut on the plane." Wallis acted like she just happened to be flying to Virginia herself that day, and wouldn't it be fun if she and the children could all sit together? Wallis had made it so easy that Teresa didn't even think to cry until she returned to the house alone.

It was one of Teresa's people who accompanied the children on the return flight: one year her mother, another year her favorite cousin. Bert would buy a ticket for anyone willing to brave six hours on a plane with his children.

But in 1971 it was decided that the children were old enough to go it alone, or that Cal at twelve and Holly at ten were old enough to wrangle Jeanette, who at eight needed absolutely nothing, and Albie, who at six needed everything in the world. At the airport, Teresa handed over the tickets Bert had sent and put her children on the plane to Virginia without suitcases, a bold maneuver she would never have attempted when Bonnie or Wallis was on duty. Let Bert hit the ground running, she thought. They needed everything: he could start with toothbrushes and pajamas and work his way up. She gave a letter to Holly to give to her father. All four of the children needed to have their teeth cleaned. Jeanette, she knew, had cavities. She sent copies of their immunization records, putting a check mark beside all the boosters that were due. She couldn't keep taking off work to run to doctor's appointments. The doctors were always late, and sometimes it was hours before she made it back to the office. The second Mrs. Bert Cousins didn't have a job. There would be plenty of time for her to take the children shopping, to take them to doctors. Holly fainted whenever she had a shot. Albie bit the nurse. Cal refused to get out of the car. She had wrestled with him but he had braced a foot against either side of the car door and wouldn't get out and so they missed his last booster. She wasn't sure if Jeanette had had her shots or not because she couldn't find Jeanette's immunization records. She made note of all of this in the letter. Beverly Cousins wanted her family? Have at it.

The children were seated across the aisle from one another, the boys on the left and the girls on the right, and each was given a set of junior airman wings, which only Cal refused to wear. They were glad to be on the plane, glad to be free of direct supervision for six hours. As much as they hated to leave their mother—they were unquestionably loyal to their mother—the four Cousins children thought of themselves as Virginians, even the youngest two, who had been born after the family's move west. All of the Cousins children hated California. They were sick of being shoved down the hallways of the Torrance Unified School District. They were sick of the bus that picked them up on the corner every morning, and sick of the bus driver who would not cut them a break, even thirty seconds, if they were made late by Albie's dawdling. They were sick of their mother, no matter how much they loved her, because she had on occasion cried when they returned to the house after missing the bus. Now she would be late for work. She went over it all again in the car as she drove them to school at terrifying speeds— she had to work, they couldn't live on what their father gave them, she couldn't afford to lose this job just because they weren't responsible enough to walk to the goddamn corner on time. They blocked her out by pinching Albie, whose screams filled the car like mustard gas. More than anything they were sick of Albie, who had spilled his Coke all over the place and was at this very moment kicking the seat in front of him on the plane. Everything that happened was his fault. But they were sick of Cal too. He got to wear the house key on a dirty string around his neck because their mother told him it was his job to get everybody home after school and make them a snack. Cal was sick of doing it, and on most days he locked his sisters and brother out for at least an hour so that he could watch the television shows that he wanted to watch and clear his head. There was a hose on the side of the house and shade beneath the carport. It wasn't like they were going to die. When their mother came home from work they met her at the door screaming about the tyranny of their situation. They lied about having done their homework, except for Holly, who always did her homework, sometimes sitting Indian-style under the carport with her books in her lap, because she lived for the positive reinforcement her teachers heaped on her. They were sick of Holly and the superiority of her good grades. Really, the only person they weren't sick of was Jeanette, and that was because they never thought about her. She had retreated into a silence that any parent would have asked a teacher or a pediatrician about had they noticed it, but no one noticed. Jeanette was sick of that.

They reclined their seats as far back as they could go. They asked for playing cards and ginger ale. They reveled in the sanctuary of an airplane which was for the time being neither in California nor Virginia, the only two places they had ever been in their lives.

Fix would take his week's vacation to be with Caroline and Franny when they went to California in the summer, whereas when Bert's children arrived in Virginia, Bert told Beverly his caseload at work had mysteriously doubled. Bert worked in estates and trusts law in Arlington, having decided the life of an assistant district attorney was too stressful. It was difficult to imagine how so many people needed new wills drawn up on the very day his children arrived. He sent her to the airport alone in the station wagon. He had thought that he was going to be able to pick them up himself but at the last possible minute a motion that no one was expecting had been filed, and not only could he not get to the airport, it really didn't look like he was going to make it home for dinner. Beverly had picked Bert's children up at the airport before, but in reality she had been going to pick up her mother or Bonnie or Wallis who had kindly agreed to come and visit her on a free ticket. It had been such a joy to see any one of them getting off the plane that she could very nearly overlook the children. She would lock arms with her mother or sister or dearest friend and together they would shepherd the lambs through baggage claim and out to the parking garage. It had been something to look forward to.

But now Beverly felt oddly paralyzed as she waited at the end of the jet bridge alone. When all the other passengers had disembarked, the stewardess brought the Cousins children out and she signed for them. Four little stair-steps, boy-girl-girl-boy, each one a glassy-eyed refugee. The girls gave her a disappointed hug at the gate while the boys hung back, walking behind her to baggage claim. Albie was singing some indecipherable song, possibly Cal was too, though she wasn't sure, they stayed so far away from her. The airport was noisy and crowded with happy families reunited. It was hard enough to hear herself think.

They waited at the baggage carousel and watched the bags rotate past. "How did the school year turn out? Did you make good grades?" Beverly launched the question to the group but the only one who looked at her was Holly. Holly made A's in every class except for reading and there she'd made an A-plus. Beverly asked if the weather had been good when they left Los Angeles, if they'd eaten on the plane, if it had been a good flight. Holly answered everything.

"The flight was delayed thirty minutes out of the gate because of traffic on the runway. We were twenty-sixth in line for takeoff," she said, her little chin lifted up, "but we had a good tailwind and the pilot was able to make up most of the time in the air." The part that divided her pigtails was wildly uneven, as if it had been made by a drunken finger rather than a comb.

The boys had wandered off in opposite directions. For a second she caught sight of Cal standing on the conveyor belt of a luggage carousel three carousels away, gliding by with the bags from Houston. No sooner had she seen him than he hopped off to avoid the charge of an oncoming skycap.

"Cal!" Beverly called out over the crowd. She couldn't yell at him, not publicly, not at a distance, and so she said, "Go get your brother!" But Cal looked back at her as if it were some weird coincidence that his name was Cal and this complete stranger had said something to someone who was also named Cal. He turned away. Jeanette stood just beside her, looking at the strap of her little shoulder bag, staring at it. Had anyone had this child tested?

Finally, every last bag from the nonstop TWA flight from Los Angeles to Dulles had slid onto the conveyor belt and been pulled away by the waiting travelers. There was nothing left to claim. The crowd dispersed and she caught sight of Albie trying to pry an ancient piece of chewing gum off the floor with what from a distance almost looked like a knife. She turned away.

"Okay," she said, calculating the time of day and the traffic back to Arlington. "I guess the bags didn't make the flight. That's not a problem. We'll just have to go to the office and fill out some paperwork. Did you keep the claim checks?" she said to Holly. Best to just direct everything to Holly, who seemed to have a natural desire to please. Holly was her only real chance.

"We don't have any claim checks," Holly said. She had very pale skin and dark straight hair, a face full of freckles. She had the kind of Pippi Longstocking looks adults found charming and other kids made fun of.

"But you had them at some point. Didn't your mother give you the claim checks?"

Holly started again. "We don't have any claim checks because we don't have any luggage."

"What do you mean you don't have any luggage?"

"I mean we don't have any." Holly didn't see how she could be any clearer than that.

"You mean you forgot it in Los Angeles? You lost it?" Beverly was distracted. She was looking for Cal and didn't see him. There were signs every ten feet warning people not to sit or stand on the carousels.

Holly's lip trembled slightly but her stepmother failed to notice. Holly had thought there was something fishy about taking a trip without bags, but her mother had assured her this was the way their father wanted it. He wanted them to have everything new—new clothes, new toys, new bags in which to carry home the loot. Maybe he'd just forgotten to tell Beverly. "We didn't bring any," she said quietly.

Beverly looked down at her. Goddamn Bert for saying she could manage this no problem. "What?"

It was terrible to have been made to say it once, unforgivable to be made to say it again. Tears welled up in Holly's eyes and started their run across the freckles. "We. Don't. Have. Any. Luggage." Now she would be in trouble with her father and she hadn't even seen her father yet. What was worse, her father would be mad at her mother again. Her father had been calling her mother irresponsible forever but she wasn't.

Beverly's eyes shot from one end of the baggage claim to the other. The passengers and the people who had met them were thinning out, two of her stepchildren were missing, the third stepchild was crying and the fourth was so consumed by the vinyl strap of her handbag it was hard not to assume she was handicapped. "Then why have we been standing at the baggage carousel for the last half hour?" Beverly didn't raise her voice. She wasn't mad yet. She'd be mad later when she had time to think about it but for now she simply didn't understand.

"I don't know!" Holly screamed, her eyes streaming. She pulled up the hem of her T-shirt and wiped it across her nose. "It's not my fault. You brought us down here. I never said we had luggage."

Jeanette unzipped the zipper on her little purse, dug around, and handed her sister a tissue.

Every year Beverly's second trip to the airport was worse because she always thought it was going to be better. She left her four stepchildren at home (first with her mother, then Bonnie, then Wallis, and now under Cal's supervision. They stayed home alone in Torrance after all, and Arlington was safer than Torrance) and drove back to Dulles to reclaim her girls. While Bert's children came east for the entire summer, Caroline and Franny traveled west for two short weeks: one with Fix and then one with her parents, just enough time to remind the girls how greatly they preferred California to Virginia. They shuffled off the plane looking like they were in an advanced state of dehydration from having cried for the entirety of their flight. Beverly dropped to her knees to hug them but they were nothing but ghosts. Caroline wanted to live with her father. She begged for it, she pleaded, and year after year she was denied. Caroline's hatred for her mother radiated through the cloth of her pink camp shirt as her mother pressed Caroline to her chest. Franny on the other hand simply stood there and tolerated the embrace. She didn't know how to hate her mother yet, but every time she left her father crying in the airport she came that much closer to figuring it out.

Beverly kissed their heads. She kissed Caroline again as

Caroline pulled away from her. "I'm so glad you're home," she said.

But Caroline and Franny were not glad they were home. They were not glad at all. It was in this battered state that the Keating girls returned to Arlington to be reunited with their stepsiblings.

Holly was certainly friendly. She hopped up and down and actually clapped her hands when the girls came through the door. She said she wanted to put on another dance recital in the living room this summer. But Holly was also wearing Caroline's red T-shirt with the tiny white ribbon rosette at the neck, which her mother had made Caroline put in the Goodwill bag before she left because it was both faded and too small. Holly was not the Goodwill.

Caroline had the bigger room with two sets of bunk beds, and Franny, being smaller, had the smaller room with twin beds. The two sisters were connected by neither love nor mutual affinity but by a very small bathroom that could be entered from the bedroom on either side. Two girls and one bathroom was a workable situation from the beginning of September through the end of May, but in June when Caroline and Franny returned from California they found Holly and Jeanette had made themselves at home in one set of bunk beds while Franny had lost her room completely to the boys. It was four girls in one room and the two boys in the other with a bathroom the size of a phone booth for the six of them to share.

Caroline and Franny lugged their luggage up the stairs. Luggage: that which is to be lugged. They passed the open door of the master bedroom where Cal was lying across their mother's bed, his dirty feet in dirty socks resting on the pillows, watching a tennis match at top volume. They were *never* allowed to go into the master bedroom or sit on the bed, even if they kept their feet on the floor, nor were they allowed to watch television without an express invitation. Cal didn't lift his eyes from the screen or give the smallest recognition of their arrival as they passed.

Holly was behind them, close enough to bump when they stopped walking. "I was thinking that all four of us could dance in white nightgowns. Would that be okay? We could start practicing this afternoon. I've got some ideas about the choreography if you want to see."

As for there being four girls in the dance recital, only three were in evidence. Jeanette was MIA. No one had noticed she was gone, but Franny's cat Buttercup was missing as well. Buttercup had not come to the door to greet Franny as surely she would have after two weeks away. Buttercup, the lifeline to normalcy, was gone. Beverly, drowning in the sea of child-life, had no clear memory of the last time she'd seen the cat, but Franny's sudden, paralyzing sobs prompted her to do a thorough search of the house. Beverly found Jeanette beneath a comforter on the floor in the back of the linen closet (how long had Jeanette been missing?). She was petting the sleeping cat.

"She can't have my cat!" Franny cried, and Beverly leaned down and took the cat from Jeanette, who hung on for only half a second and then let go. The entire time Albie followed Beverly around the house doing what the children referred to as "the stripper soundtrack":

Boom chicka-boom, *boom-boom* chicka-boom.

When their mother stopped walking the soundtrack stopped. If she took a single step it was accompanied by Albie saying only "boom" in a voice that was weirdly sexual for a six-year-old. She meant to ignore him but after a while he proved too much for her. When finally she snapped, screaming "Stop that!" he only looked at her. He had the most enormous brown eyes, and loose, loopy brown curls that made him look like a cartoon animal.

"I'm serious," she said, making an effort to steady her breathing. "You have to stop that." She tried to find within her own voice a sound that was reasonable, parental, but when she turned to walk away she heard the small, quiet chug, "*Boom* chicka-boom."

Beverly thought about killing him. She thought about killing a child. Her hands were shaking. She went to her room, wanting to close the door and lock it and go to sleep, but from the hallway she heard the thwack of a tennis ball, the roar of a crowd. She stuck her head around the doorframe. "Cal?" she said, trying not to cry. "I need my room now."

Cal didn't move, not a twitch. He kept his eyes on the screen. "It's not over," he said, as if she had never seen a tennis match before and didn't understand that when the ball was in motion it meant the game was still going on.

Bert didn't believe in television for children. At its most harmless he saw it as a waste of time, a bunch of noise. At its most harmful he wondered if it didn't stunt brain development. He thought Teresa had made a huge mistake letting the children watch so much TV. He had told her not to do it but she never listened to him when it came to parenting, when it came to anything. That's why he and Beverly had only one television in this house, and why it was in their bedroom, which wasn't open to children, or wasn't open to her children during the regular course of the year. Now Beverly wanted to unplug the television and cart it off to what the realtor had called "the family room," though no member of the family ever seemed to light there. She went down the hallway, Albie following at a safe distance, churning his music. Did his mother teach him that? Someone taught him. Six-year-olds didn't hang out in strip clubs, not even this one. Beverly went into the girls' room but Holly was there reading *Rebecca*.

"Beverly, have you ever read *Rebecca*?" Holly asked as soon as Beverly stepped into the room, her little face bright, bright, bright. "Mrs. Danvers is scaring me to death but I'm going to keep reading it. I don't care if I had the chance to live in Manderley. I wouldn't stay there if someone was being that creepy to me."

Beverly nodded slightly and backed out of the room. She thought about trying to lie down in the boys' room, the room that had once been Franny's, but it had a vaguely nutty smell reminiscent of socks and underwear and unwashed hair.

She went downstairs again and found Caroline banging around the kitchen in a rage, saying she was going to make brownies for her father and mail them to him so he'd have something to eat.

"Your father doesn't like nuts in his brownies," Beverly said. She didn't know why she said it. She was trying to be helpful.

"He does too!" Caroline said, turning on her mother so fast she spilled half a bag of flour on the counter. "Maybe he didn't when you knew him but you don't know him anymore. Now he likes nuts in everything."

Albie was in the dining room. She could hear him singing through the kitchen door. His single-pointed focus was astounding. Franny was in the living room, pulling the cat's front legs through the armholes of a doll's dress and crying so quietly that her mother was sure that every single thing she had ever done in her life up until that moment was a mistake.

There was no place to go, no place to get away from them, not even the linen closet because Jeanette hadn't come out of the linen closet since surrendering the cat. Beverly took the car keys and went outside. The minute she closed the door behind her she was underwater, the summer air hot and solid in her lungs. She thought about the back patio of the house in Downey, how she would sit outside in the afternoons, Caroline on her tricycle, Franny happy in her lap, the smell of the orange blossoms nearly overwhelming. Fix had had to sell the house in order to pay her half of what little equity they had and make the child support. Why had she made him sell the house? No one could sit outside in Virginia. She got five new mosquito bites just walking to the driveway and each one puffed up to the size of a quarter. Beverly was allergic to mosquito bites.

It was easily 105 degrees inside the car. She started the engine, turned on the air conditioner, turned off the radio. She lay across the scorching green vinyl of the bench seat so that no one looking out the front window of the house could see her. She thought about the fact that if she were in the garage rather than the carport she'd be killing herself now.

Because California public schools ran slightly longer than Virginia Catholic schools, Beverly and Bert had had five days alone in the house between her children's departure and his children's arrival. One night after dinner they made love on the dining room carpet. It wasn't comfortable. Beverly's weight had steadily dropped since their move to Virginia, and the bony protrusions of her vertebrae and clavicles were so clearly displayed she could have found work in an anatomy class. Every thrust pushed her back a quarter inch, dragging her skin against the wool blend. But even with the rug burns it made them feel daring and passionate. It hadn't been a mistake, Bert kept telling her as they lay on their backs afterwards, staring up at the ceiling. Beverly counted five places where the glass crystals on the chandelier were missing. She hadn't noticed it before.

"Everything that's happened in our lives up until now, everything we've done, it had to happen exactly the way it did so that we could be together." Bert took her hand and squeezed it.

"You really believe that?" Beverly asked.

"We're magic," Bert said.

Later that night he rubbed Neosporin down the length of her spine. She slept on her stomach. That was their summer vacation.

Here was the most remarkable thing about the Keating children and the Cousins children: they did not hate one another, nor did they possess one shred of tribal loyalty. The Cousinses did not prefer the company of Cousinses and the two Keatings could have done without each other entirely. The four girls were angry about being crowded together into a single room but they didn't blame each other. The boys, who were always angry about everything, didn't seem to care that they were in the company of so many girls. The six children held in common one overarching principle that cast their potential dislike for one another down to the bottom of the minor leagues: they disliked the parents. They hated them.

The only one who was troubled by this fact was Franny, because Franny had always loved her mother. During the regular part of the year they sometimes took naps together in the afternoons after school, spooning so close they fell asleep and dreamed the same dreams. Franny would sit on the closed toilet lid in the morning and watch her mother put on makeup, and she would sit on the toilet lid again at night and talk to her mother while her mother soaked in the bath. Franny was secure in the knowledge that she was not only her mother's favorite daughter, she was her mother's favorite person. Except in the summer, when her mother looked at her as if she were nothing more than the fourth of six children. When her mother was sick of Albie, she announced that all children had to go outside, and "all children" included Franny. Ice cream had to be eaten outside. Watermelon— outside. Since when had she not been trusted to eat watermelon at the kitchen table? It was insulting, and not just to her. Maybe Albie couldn't eat a dish of ice cream without dropping it on the floor but the rest of them were perfectly capable. They went outside all right. They went outside and slammed the door and took off down the street, loping across the hot pavement like a pack of feral dogs.

The four Cousins children didn't blame Beverly for their miserable summers. They blamed their father, and would have said so to his face had he ever been around. Cal and Holly gave no indication that they thought Beverly's behavior was inexcusable (and Jeanette never said anything anyway, and Albie, well, who knew about Albie), but Caroline and Franny were horrified. Their mother made everyone line up in the kitchen according to age and come to the stove with their plate instead of putting the food on the table in dishes as she did every other night of the year. In the summers they wandered out of the civilized world and into the early orphanage scenes of *Oliver Twist*.

It was a Thursday night in July when Bert called a family meeting in the living room and announced that in the morning they were going to Lake Anna. He told them he had taken the next day off from work and rented three rooms at the Pinecone Motel. On Sunday morning they would drive to Charlottesville to see his parents and then come home again. "It's a vacation," Bert said. "All arranged."

The children blinked, vaguely stirred to think of a day that wasn't going to be like all the other days, and Beverly blinked because Bert hadn't mentioned any of this to her. The children could see Beverly trying to catch Bert's eye but Bert's eye could not be caught. A motel, a lake, meals in restaurants, a visit to Bert's extremely unwelcoming parents who had horses and a pond and a fabulous black cook named Ernestine who had taught the girls how to make pies the summer before. If the children had been inclined to speak to the parents they might have said it sounded like fun, but they weren't inclined, so they didn't.

The next morning it was hot as a swamp. The birds stayed quiet in an effort to conserve their energy. Bert told the children to go and get in the car, though everyone knew it wasn't as simple as that. First there would have to be an ugly fight over who had to sit with Albie and they all stood around in the driveway waiting for it. The front seat, which was restricted to parents, was never an option, even though Caroline and Franny rode there with their mother all the time in the regular parts of the year. That left the backseat, the way-back, and the way-way-back of the wagon. In the end, the children were always arranged in pairs by gender or age, which meant that either Cal or Jeanette got stuck with Albie, occasionally Franny, never Caroline or Holly. Albie would sing an impassioned version of "Ninety-nine Bottles of Beer on the Wall" in which the numbers did not diminish sequentially—fifty-seven bottles, seventy-eight bottles, four, a hundred and four. He would talk about how he was going to be carsick and make convincing gagging noises that forced Bert to the shoulder of the interstate for no reason, although Jeanette inevitably threw up, never having said anything about it. At every exit sign Albie would ask if that was the exit they were supposed to take.

"Are we there yet?" he would say, then burst out laughing at the pleasure of it all. No one wanted to sit with Albie.

Just as they were starting to shove one another around the driveway, Bert came out carrying a canvas bag the size of a shoe box. Bert was a very light packer. "Cal," he said. "You ride with your brother."

"I rode with him last time," Cal said. Whether or not this was true no one could say, and what constituted "last time" anyway? The last time in the car? The last time on a trip? They never took trips.

"So you'll ride with him this time too." Bert threw his bag in the back and swung the door shut.

Cal looked around. Albie was darting towards the girls, poking them lightly with his index finger and making them scream. All four of the girls blurred together in Cal's mind: his own sisters, his stepsisters, it was hard to single out one of them to take the fall. Then Cal looked at Beverly, her purple striped T-shirt, her long yellow hair curled and brushed into stylish order, her sunglasses big as a movie star's. "Make her," he said to his father.

Bert looked at his oldest child and then his wife. "Make her what?"

"Make her ride with him. Make her sit in the way-back."

Bert smacked Cal with his open hand. It made a sound but it was hardly a serious blow, it only glanced off the side of his head. Cal stumbled back to make it look worse than it was. He'd taken harder hits at school, and this one was worth it just to see what little color Beverly had drain out of her face. Cal could tell that for a split second she hadn't known whose side Bert would be on, and she had seen herself riding all the way to Lake Anna in the backseat with Albie, and she had died. Bert said he was sick of all the horseshit. He told them to get in the car. And they did it, even Beverly, silently, and with grave bitterness.

On the road Bert kept the window down, his elbow pointing out towards the rolling hills, and said nothing.

Three hours later when they got to the Arrowhead Diner he had everyone line up and count off, Cal being one, Caroline being two, Holly being three.

"We're not the goddamn Trapp Family Singers," Cal said under his breath.

Franny looked up at him with a mixture of fear and disbelief. He had taken the name of God in vain. That was a big one. "You can't swear," she said. Bert could swear, even though it was a bad idea, but children could never swear. She was sure of that. Even in the summer she was a Sacred Heart girl.

Cal, both the oldest and the tallest of all the children, put his right hand on the top of her head, and, curling his fingers down towards her ears, squeezed. It wasn't as hard as he would have squeezed the head of one of his real sisters, but still, he maintained control.

Caroline, being the oldest of the girls, got to decide who would share beds at the Pinecone, and at dinner made the pronouncement that she would sleep with Holly. That meant Franny got Jeanette. Franny liked Jeanette. She liked Holly too as far as that was concerned, she just didn't want to sleep with Caroline, who was not above trying to smother her with a pillow in the middle of the night. The boys got their own room, and each his own bed. At seven o'clock that night the parents began to fidget and yawn, and then announced that they were exhausted, it was bedtime, and there would be fun in the morning.

But what the children got in the morning was a note slipped under the door of the girls' room. *Have breakfast in the coffee shop. You can charge it. We're sleeping late. Do not knock*. It was their mother's handwriting but the note was not signed *Love* or even *Mommy*. It wasn't signed at all. One more document in the ever-growing mountain of evidence that they were on their own.

Every door in the long row of bright-blue doors at the Pinecone was closed and the drapes over every window were pulled together. The cars parked in front of the rooms were wet with dew, or maybe it had rained during the night. The girls stood outside and knocked on Cal's door, the one to the right of theirs. Cal opened the door a crack. He kept the chain on and looked out at her with a single eye. "We're going to breakfast," Holly said. "Come or don't come."

Cal closed the door, took off the chain, and opened it again. Behind him they saw Albie sitting on his double bed watching cartoons, his feet rhythmically kicking the end of the mattress. Whenever any of the girls thought to complain that there were four of them in a room sharing two beds, they thought of Cal, sharing a room with Albie. Cal shared a room with Albie at home so maybe he was used to it but probably not.

"Let's go," Cal said.

Cal was built on his father's model. He was a tan boy with tan hair, and in the summer both the boy and his hair took on an undertone of gold. Cal had blue eyes, his father's eyes, while the other three had dark eyes like their mother. Albie may have looked a little bit like freckled Holly but Holly's good sense and Albie's lack of it scrubbed out any physical resemblance between them. All four of the children were thin but Jeanette was too thin to look like any of them. She was never described by her pretty face or by her hair, which was glossy and the color of dark honey. Jeanette was referenced only by her elbows and knees, which did, in fact, resemble doorknobs. When the six of them were together they looked more like a day camp than a family, random children dropped off on the same curb. There was very little evidence of their relation, even among those who were related by blood.

"They'll sleep until noon," Holly said, meaning the parents. In the diner she pushed her eggs around in circles with her fork.

"And when they do finally get up they'll just tell us they have to take a nap," Caroline said. It was true. The parents napped like febrile toddlers. All the children nodded their heads. Cal was next to the window in the booth and he turned away from the rest of them to stare at the road. Albie was pounding the bottom of a ketchup bottle with the flat of his palm until finally the ketchup poured out onto his pancakes.

"Jesus," Cal said and snatched the bottle away. "Can't you sit here without doing something disgusting?"

"Look," Albie said, and held up the pancake, dripping ketchup, in front of his face.

Jeanette pinned her toast to her plate with two fingers and removed the crusts with a knife.

"I'm not just going to sit here all day waiting for them," Caroline said.

"What else can we do?" Franny asked, because there wasn't anything to do. See if the motel had any board games maybe? A deck of cards? It was still so early, just now seven o'clock, and the sun came through the window of the diner like an invitation delivered to their table on a silver tray. It would have been a good day to swim.

"We came here to go to the lake so we should go to the lake," Caroline said, reading her sister's mind, or half of it. She was wearing her swimsuit under her clothes. They all were. Caroline was a lot angrier than the rest of them. It was there in her voice all the time. Then again, it could have been that Cal was the angriest and his anger just manifested itself in different ways.

Jeanette lifted her eyes from her toast. "Let's go," she said. It was the first thing she had said since they left Arlington the day before and so that settled it. Why should they wait for the parents to wake up? When they did go out with the parents, the children were divided into two groups—the big kids: Cal, Caroline, and Holly; and the little kids—Jeanette, Franny, and Albie. The big kids were allowed to wander off, swim in deep water without life jackets, hike out past anyone's view, and decide what they wanted for lunch. The little kids might as well have been tied to a tree and made to eat from a single dish. The little kids were never to be trusted. With no further discussion, the six of them decided it would be better to see this as an opportunity.

At the cash register they added a six-pack of Coke and twelve candy bars to their breakfast tab, enough to see them through to lunch if necessary.

"How far is it to the lake?" Holly asked the waitress who was ringing them up.

"Maybe two miles, a little less. You just get back on Route 98."

"What if you walk?"

The waitress studied the children for a minute. So many of them looked to be exactly the same size. Franny and Jeanette were thirty-eight days apart in age. "Where're your parents?"

"Getting dressed," Caroline said in the voice of a bored child. "They want us all to walk together. They said it was going to be an adventure. We're supposed to get directions."

The other children beamed at her for lying so deftly. The waitress took a paper placemat off the stack and turned it over. "There's a shortcut if you walk." On one end of the placemat she drew a rectangle to represent the motel (which she labeled "P") and on the other end a circle for the lake ("L"). The broken line she drew to connect the two was their ticket out.

In the parking lot, Cal tried all the doors to the locked station wagon. Franny asked him what he needed out of the car and he said, "Something. Mind your own business." He cupped his hands around his eyes and peered in the window, trying to see whatever it was he wanted.

"I can break in," Caroline said. "If it's something you really need."

"Liar," Cal said, not bothering to look at her.

"I can," she said and then she pointed at Jeanette. "Go get me a coat hanger out of the closet."

It was true. Their father had shown them how that very summer. Their uncle Joe Mike had locked his keys in Aunt Bonnie's car when they were all at their grandparents' house that last weekend, and their father had unlocked the door with a coat hanger to save Joe Mike the twelve dollars it would have cost to call a locksmith. After that Fix had both girls practice because they were interested. He said it was a good thing to know.

"The mistake people make is that they think they're supposed to pull up on something and you're not, you push down," he'd told them.

Caroline set about untwisting the wire hanger. That was the hardest part.

"You're wasting time," Cal said.

"Whose time?" Holly said. "If you're in such a hurry then go." She was curious, and it was plain to all of them that Cal was curious too.

Albie walked in wide circles around the car, swinging his hips from side to side and doing the boom-boom thing.

"Pipe down," Cal said to him. "If you wake Dad up he'll take your head off." That was when the rest of them remembered whose room the car was parked in front of and made a point to be quiet.

Caroline picked back the rubber seal at the bottom of the window with her pointer finger and stuck the coat hanger in while the other children pressed close to watch. Caroline was a little worried that locks might be different from one car to another. The station wagon was an Oldsmobile and Aunt Bonnie's car was something else, a Dodge maybe. The tip of her tongue pushed up at the corner of her mouth while she guided the coat hanger blindly towards what her father called the sweet spot about ten inches down from the button lock. Then she felt it, the wire against the mechanism of the lock. She didn't try to hook it though the temptation was there. It was just a little bump and she pushed straight down the way she'd been taught.

The lock popped up.

It was a victory for all the girls that they remembered not to scream. Caroline pulled the coat hanger out and opened the door like it was some sort of natural act. Even Albie put his arms around her waist. "You broke the car!" he said, his loud whisper making him sound like a movie gangster.

"That's right," she said and gave him the hanger as the morning's souvenir. Albie immediately went to the car next to theirs and began jamming the hanger down against the window. Oh, what Caroline wouldn't have given to call her father from the motel phone! She wanted him to know what a good job she'd done.

Cal took the coat hanger from his brother and studied it in light of this new potential. "You can teach me how to do this?" he said, either to Caroline or the coat hanger.

"Only police officers are allowed to do it," Franny said. "And their children. Otherwise you're a criminal."

"I'd be a criminal," Cal said. He slid into the front seat of the station wagon, opened the glove compartment. He took out a gun and a fifth of gin, the seal still on.

No one was surprised that there was a gun in the car, even though Cal was the only one who'd known it was there, and he only knew about it because he'd been nosing around in the glove compartment a few days before while Beverly was in the grocery store and he'd found it, proving yet again that sometimes a person just has to look. What surprised all of them though, Cal included, was that Bert had left it in the car. It made them think he must have another gun in his motel room. Bert liked a gun in his briefcase, in the nightstand, in the drawer of his office desk. He liked to talk about the criminals he had put away, and how a person never knew, and how he had to protect his family, and how he wasn't going to let the other guy make the first move, but really it was just that Bert liked guns.

The mesmerizing item was the gin. The parents might enjoy a drink every now and then but it wasn't like they had to take it with them. They had never seen gin in the car before. That was something special.

"You know you can't take it," Holly said, looking back to the door of the parents' room. She was talking about both the gun and the gin.

"Just in case something happens," Cal said. He put the gun in the brown paper sack along with the candy bars and Cokes. Jeanette had taken her Coke and two candy bars out of the bag already and put them in her purse. She took the bottle from her brother and started working on the seal, teasing it loose so gently that it finally gave itself up to her little fingernails in a single, replaceable piece. She put the seal in her coin purse and gave the bottle back to her brother. Then they set out for the lake, Caroline carrying the map.

It was hotter than they expected it to be, though no hotter than it had been the day before or the day before that. The sky was already turning white, clamping a pervasive dullness onto the landscape. Holly scratched at her arms and complained about the mosquitoes. Like her stepmother, she was particularly sensitive to mosquitoes. The grass in the field across from the motel, the field that the waitress had told them to cut through, came up to their waists and was as high as Albie's chest, but being right up in it they could see the tiny flecks of yellow flowers blooming on the stalks. "Can you see the lake?" Albie asked. He had ketchup smeared across the blue-and-yellow-striped shirt that Beverly had bought for him. His hands were sticky.

"Stop," Cal said, and put up his hand flat to the sky. They stopped like soldiers, all at once. "Turn around," he said, and they turned around.

"What's that building right there?" Cal was talking to his brother, pointing just across the street.

"The Pinecone," Albie said.

"How far did she say it was from the Pinecone to the lake?"

In the quiet they could hear the cars whizzing past. Deep in the grass the crickets rubbed their wings together, the birds called out overhead. "Two miles, maybe a little less," Franny said. She knew it wasn't her question to answer but she couldn't stop herself. There was something about standing there that was making her uneasy, the dry weeds pricking at her shins. There was no path through the field.

Cal pointed at his brother. It was funny the way he could be so much like his father while being nothing like him at all. "Albie?"

"Two miles," Albie said. He started chopping at the grass with his open hand, and then began swinging his arm back and forth like a scythe.

"So now you know we're not there and you know I can't see the lake." Cal started walking again and the rest of them pushed ahead. The field was bigger than it had looked from a distance, and after a while they couldn't see the Pinecone anymore and they couldn't see anything else either, just the grass and the washed-out sky. Several members of the party wondered if they were still going in the right direction.

"Are we there now?" Albie said.

"Shut up," Holly said. A grasshopper the size of a baby's fist jumped up from the dry grass and attached itself to her shirt and she screamed. Franny and Jeanette moved to the left of the pack, and when they ducked down they were pretty sure no one could see them. They were very close, almost nose to nose, and Jeanette smiled at her before they popped back up again.

"*Now* are we there?" Albie hopped forward, both feet together, but his progress was thwarted by the density of the grass. He looked back at his brother. "*Now* are we there?"

Cal stopped again. "I can send you back." He looked behind them. There was still the beaten-down vestige of the trail they had made in the grass.

"Where are we?" Albie asked.

"Virginia," Cal said, his voice as tired as an adult's. "Shut up."

"I want to carry the gun," Albie said.

"People in hell want ice water," Caroline said. It was an expression of her father's.

"Cal's got a gun," Albie sang, his voice surprisingly loud in the open landscape. "*Cal's got a gun!*"

They stopped again. Cal moved the brown bag higher up under his arm. Two swallows came from nowhere and shot past them. Albie wouldn't stop singing. Jeanette pulled the can of Coke out of her purse.

"It's too early to drink it," Holly said. She was in her first year of Girl Scouts and she had read the chapter about survival tactics in the handbook. "You have to make it last."

Jeanette cracked the can open anyway. Watching her

drink, they all decided they were thirsty. There would be more Cokes once they got to the lake.

"Cal's got a gun," Albie called, though with less interest.

Holly looked up at the sky. It was a complete blank. There wasn't a single cloud to offer them protection. "I wish I had a Tic Tac," she said.

Cal thought for a minute and then nodded his head. He reached into his back pocket and pulled out a tiny plastic bag about the size of three postage stamps where he kept the Benadryl tablets his mother made him carry for his allergy. They all sat down, pushing back the grass, and Caroline opened up the brown bag. She was very formal about the way she picked up the gun and set it beside her, and then she handed out the Cokes. Cal came behind her and gave everyone two garish pink pills. "I shouldn't give you any," he said to Albie. "You're annoying the hell out of me today."

But Albie kept his palm up in silent demand until finally Cal sighed and gave him his two.

"This is what I needed," Holly said, having brought the pills up to her mouth and then brought them down again, pressed beneath her thumb. She took the bottle of gin out of the bag and swigged it like Coke, but it surprised her. For a second she almost spit it out but she managed to keep her lips pressed together. She handed the bottle to her sister and then stretched out on her back. "Now I won't mind walking to the lake," Holly said.

Jeanette took a hit of the gin and coughed, then she leaned over and gave her pills to Albie. "You can have mine."

He looked at the two extra pills in his palm. Now he had four. They were so pink in the bright light, in a background of so much colorless grass. "Why?" he said, maybe suspicious and maybe not.

Jeanette shrugged. "Tic Tacs give me a stomachache." This was possible. Everything gave Jeanette a stomachache. That's why she was so thin.

Franny watched Caroline, how she pushed the pills into her palm with her thumb and threw back her head as if to swallow them with a big slug of Coke. Caroline was always convincing. Franny could see she didn't really drink the gin either. Her mouth wasn't open when she tilted the bottle back. But when the bottle came to her, Franny decided she would compromise—swallow the gin and palm the pills. The gin could not have surprised her more. She followed the burning sensation as it went down her throat and through her chest and stomach. It was as hot and bright as the sun, settling between her legs—a beautiful sensation, as if the burning had brought about a sort of physical clarity. She took a second mouthful before handing the bottle to Albie. Albie drank the most of all.

The children didn't mind waiting. Waiting was all part of it. It was hot outside and the Coke was still cold. It was nice just to lie there for a while and stare up into the emptiness of the sky, to not have to listen to Albie go on and on about nothing. When they finally got up Cal put his empty Coke can next to Albie's leg.

"That's littering," Franny said.

"We'll pick them up later," he said. "We'll have to come back for him."

So they all left their cans beside Albie, who was sleeping the sleep of four Benadryls and a big slug of gin in the hot morning sun. Cal took back the other pills from Holly and his stepsisters and put them in the baggie and put the baggie back in his pocket. The candy bars were starting to melt and the gun was hot from being out in the sun and they put them all together back in the bag and headed for the lake.

When they got there, the five of them swam out farther than they would ever have been allowed to had the parents been with them. Franny and Jeanette went to look for caves and were taught to fish by two men they met standing off by themselves in a grove of trees on the shore. Cal stole a package of Ho-Ho's from the bait shop and had no need to use the gun in the paper bag because no one saw him do it. Caroline and Holly climbed to the top of a high rock and leapt into the lake below again and again and again until they were too tired to climb anymore, too tired to swim. All of them were sunburned but they lay in the grass to dry because none of them had thought to bring a towel, but the drying-off bored them and so they decided to head back.

Their timing turned out to be perfect. Albie was awake but he was just sitting there in the field, quiet and confused amid the Coke cans, trying hard not to cry. He didn't ask them where they had been or where he was, he just got up and followed in the line behind them as they passed. He was sunburned as well. It was just past two o'clock in the afternoon. The most amazing thing of all was that minutes after they came back to the Pinecone and stretched across the beds in the girls' room in their damp swimsuits to watch television, the parents knocked on their door, bashful and apologetic. They couldn't believe how long they'd slept. They had no idea how tired they must have been. They would take everyone to the movies and out for pizza in order to make it up to them. The parents seemed not to notice the swimsuits, the sunburns, the mosquito bites. The Cousins children and the Keating children smiled up with beatific forgiveness. They had done everything they had ever wanted to do, they had had the most wonderful day, and no one even knew they were gone.

It was like that for the rest of the summer. It was like that every summer the six of them were together. Not that the days were always fun, most of them weren't, but they did things, real things, and they never got caught.

4

The music didn't change. The tape churned out the same two-hour loop again and again. The management figured that either the customer would have paid up and left or be too drunk to notice before the songs began to repeat. A person would have to stay in the bar, sober and attentive, for more than two hours before realizing that George Benson was singing "This Masquerade" for a second time. That meant the only people who could be troubled by the repetition were the people who worked in the bar, and the standard of sobriety and attention knocked several of them out of the running. During the course of an eight-hour shift an employee could expect to hear the tape four times in its entirety, four and a half for whoever was closing. Franny spoke to Fred about it at the end of her first month. Fred, the better of the two night managers, oversaw the bar and the larger, busier, and less profitable hotel restaurant. He told her it didn't matter.

"It does matter," Franny said. "It's driving me batshit." She was wearing a slim black dress, sleeveless and short, over a fitted white blouse. She was wearing black high-heeled shoes. With her straight blond hair in a single loose braid, she looked like the music-video version of the Catholic school-girl she'd once been. Before she took the job she wasn't sure if she'd be able to bear the indignity of the uniform, but it turned out the uniform didn't actually bother her. It was the music. It was Sinatra singing "It Was a Very Good Year" that made her feel like she might step into the revolving door at the front of the lobby, a tray of cocktails balanced on her open hand, and swing out into the dark winter night.

Fred gave her a nod. He was not paternalistic or dismissive, though he looked like somebody's father and gave her an answer that was in no way helpful. "Trust me. I've been here almost five years. You get used to it."

"But I don't want to be here in five years. I don't want to get used to it." The smallest flash of discomfort registered in the night manager's eyes. Franny tried again. "Couldn't you just get a couple different tapes? It could be the same people. I'm not complaining about the kind of music. I mean, different music would be appreciated but that's not my problem. The repetition is my problem. Those people sang other songs."

"We have more tapes somewhere," Fred said, glancing around the tiny windowless office, "but no one ever changes them."

"I could change them."

He pushed up from his cluttered desk and gave her shoulder a small, conciliatory squeeze. Everyone in this place was a toucher: the waitresses kissed at the end of their shifts, the managers rested their hands on your shoulders, a busboy, not correctly tipped, could deliver a forceful hip check when squeezing past you at the dishwash station. And the customers, Jesus, the customers liked to touch. Two years in law school and not a single person had put a finger on her, but that was law school, where everyone who had made it through the first two weeks understood the concept of liability. Standing this close, she could catch just the smallest trace of vodka in the air around Fred and was surprised that she could still register the smell of alcohol. "Just wait," he said, his voice full of reassurance. "It goes away."

Franny trudged down the narrow hallway from the office to the kitchen where the cooks played bootlegged cassettes of NWA on a boom box coated in grease, the volume so low it barely whispered above the clanging of pots, *fuck da police*. The men mouthed the words and bobbed their heads, all within the low limits of the management's tolerance.

"Little House," Jerrell called out to her from the line. "Be sweet and get me some lemonade." He reached across the searing cooktop and through the pickup window to hand her his jumbo Styrofoam 7-Eleven cup with lid and straw.

"Sure," Franny said. She took the cup. The cooks, every one of them a large black man, were reliant on the waitresses, every one of them a small white woman, to bring drinks back from the bar to keep them from dying in the Sahara of the fry station.

"I count on you," Jerrell said, and pointed at her with a raw steak before dropping the meat on the incandescent surface in front of him.

But Franny never forgot the lemonade, nor how many extra packets of sugar he liked, nor the bar pretzels needed to make up for the body's lost salt, flushed away in the rivers of sweat that dropped onto the cooktop with an explosive sizzle and vanished. She knew what every man in the kitchen wanted in his cup. Franny was a professional. She remembered orders for tables of ten, who got the Ketel One, who got the Absolut. She could soothe a single businessman without letting him monopolize her time. Stepping out into the frozen slap of Chicago in the small hours of the morning, it was not lost on her how much better it would have been to be a bad cocktail waitress and a good law student. She had dropped out of law school in the middle (though closer to the beginning) of the first semester of her third year. She had racked up an enormous debt predicated on the salary of the partnership she would never obtain. For someone who had no skills and no idea what she wanted to do with her life other than read, cocktail waitressing was the most money she could make while keeping her clothes on. Those were her only two criteria at this point: not to be a lawyer and to keep her clothes on. She had tried regular waitressing, wearing black sneakers and hoisting trays of food, but there wasn't enough money in it to cover the minimum payments in her coupon book. In the dark, velvety plush of the Palmer House bar, men regularly, inexplicably, left two twenties sitting on top of an eighteen-dollar check.

She filled up the Styrofoam cup with crushed ice and lemonade and, seeing that Heinrich the bartender was listening to a customer outline the seven sorrows of the world, laced the frozen slush with Cointreau. Cointreau was the bottle at the very end of the bar near the soda station and was therefore the easiest to snatch, plus she thought it made a certain sense with lemonade. She would have paid for the shot but employees were not allowed to buy alcohol during their shift, and they were especially not allowed to buy alcohol for the men who operated the knives and heated surfaces. Jerrell had told her he'd give her ten bucks any time she could get something extra in the cup, but she wouldn't take his money. This, too, made her a sort of mythical creature among the members of the kitchen staff, because while the other waitresses would take drink orders from the cooks, they often forgot to fill them, and when they did remember, they never turned down a tip.

Franny ran tort law in her head in an effort to block out the music, covering the thing she hated with the thing she despised. The elements of assault: the act was intended to cause apprehension of harmful or offensive contact; and the act indeed caused apprehension in the victim that harmful or offensive contact would occur. The night was winding down. The high tide of gin and tonics had receded into the quiet ebb of after-dinner drinks: snifters of brandy and small, syrupy glasses of Frangelico purchased by customers who realized they weren't quite drunk enough to go up to their rooms. It was Franny's night to close, and for the moment she'd been left alone to oversee the room: two tables of two and one lone soul at the bar. Both of the other cocktail waitresses clocked out, one to pick up her sleeping child from her ex-husband's couch, the other to have drinks with a Palmer House waiter in some less-expensive bar. They had both kissed Franny before they left, and then they kissed each other. She guessed that Heinrich had gone to smoke in the hallway outside the kitchen, which gave Franny the chance to slip around to the other side of the bar and step out of her shoes. She flexed her toes back before grinding them down against the damp honeycomb of the black rubber bar mat, then she ate three maraschino cherries from the garnish bins along with an orange slice because they were best when chewed up together. That was what she was doing when she saw Leon Posen, her mouth full of chemically altered fruit. She should only have had a glimpse of him but when he looked up she had neither the opportunity nor the will to turn away.

"Hello," he said. Leon Posen, sitting two seats away from her. He was wearing a dark-gray suit and a white shirt with only the top button of his collar undone. He may well have had a tie folded in his pocket. Had he reached out his hand and she reached out her hand their fingers very easily could have touched. As a rule Franny didn't pay attention to the people at the bar. They were people who had chosen not to take a table and therefore were not her responsibility. She had no idea how long he'd been sitting there. Ten minutes? An hour?

"Hello," she said.

"You're shorter than you were," he said.

"Am I?"

"You've taken off your shoes."

Franny looked down at the sore red curve bitten into the top of either foot, clearly visible through her stockings. It was an impression that stayed for hours after she was home. "Yes."

He nodded. His hair was iron gray, sheeplike. Effort must have gone into combing it down. "It's a nice effect but I'd think it would destroy your feet after a while."

"You get used to it," Franny said, and thought of Fred, and how he had told her she'd get used to it. She made herself listen now as a way of orienting herself in the world, in the bar where she stood across from Leon Posen. Lou Rawls was singing "Nobody But Me," which was funny because that was the one song in the rotation she never got tired of, the perfect union of nouns and verbs. *I've got no chauffeur to chauffeur me. I've got no servant to serve my tea.*

Leon Posen nodded, his fingertips resting on a drained glass of ice. Franny was shaping the story in her head even as he was sitting in front of her. She was thinking of how she would pull out her copies of *First City* and *Septimus Porter* as soon as she got home. She would go back over the parts she had underlined in college and read them again. Then she would wake Kumar up and tell him she had talked to Leon Posen in the bar, and how he had asked her about her shoes. Kumar, who was a genius when it came to not being interested in anything, would want to hear every detail, and when she was finished he would tell her to start again. Even as it was happening, she knew that the story of meeting Leon Posen at the Palmer House was one she was going to tell for a long time. *If I hadn't gone to law school in Chicago and then dropped out, I wouldn't even have been working in the bar.* She would tell that to her father and to Bert.

But Leon Posen hadn't finished. He was still in front of her, waiting for her attention while she imagined him. "Why get used to it?"

"What?" She had lost her place in the conversation.

"The shoes." He looked like his pictures, the nose taking up all the real estate, and then the soft, hooded eyes. His face was a caricature of his face, a face that was meant to be sketched beside a book review in *The New Yorker*.

"Well, you have to, the shoes are part of the uniform, and

you wear the uniform because you make more money." And though she wouldn't mention it, the uniform was polyester, which you can laugh at all you want but it washed really well and didn't need to be ironed. Franny never had to figure out what she was supposed to wear to work, which had also been the great thing about Catholic school.

"You mean I'll tip you more for wearing uncomfortable shoes?"

"You will," she said, because she'd been there long enough to know how things work. "You do."

He looked at her sadly, or maybe that was just the way he looked, as if he felt the pain of every woman who had ever crammed her feet into heels. It was a beguiling effect. "Well, I haven't tipped you yet so if that's the reason you might as well put your shoes back on. We could see what happens."

"I'm not your waitress," she said, regretting it deeply. *Leon Posen, step away from the bar! Come and sit at one of the little tables with the flickering candles. Make yourself comfortable in the rounded, red leather chairs.*

"You could be if I ordered another drink." He held up his glass, rattled the lonesome ice. "What's your name?"

She told him her name.

"I never meet Frannys." He said it like her name was a favor to him. "Franny, I'd like another scotch."

It was her job to get him a drink if he was sitting at a table but not if he was sitting at the bar. They were not union workers at the Palmer House but the division of labor was ironclad. She knew her place. "What kind of scotch?"

He smiled at her again. Two smiles! "Dealer's choice," he said. "And remember, I may be that rare individual who tips off the percentage of the bill instead of your heel height so knock yourself out."

She had just worked her left foot back into the shoe when Heinrich, fresh from his cigarette and breath mint, rounded the edge of the bar and came towards them. He was raising two fingers to Leon Posen, a gesture that asked if he was ready for another without troubling himself to form the question into words, as if theirs was a relationship so sacred it had transcended language. Franny, stepping out of her left shoe as she rushed to cut him off, all but threw herself into the bartender, who in turn was forced to catch her. He looked down at her stocking feet. Heinrich was a man of Leon Posen's age, her father's age, which was to say somewhere in the dark woods past fifty. He came from a more decorous time. She had no business being behind the bar in the first place, she knew that. It was his country.

"I need a favor," she said. It was easy to be quiet. She was in his arms.

Heinrich turned to Leon Posen and raised his eyebrows slightly, formally, asking the question. Leon Posen nodded.

"Come with me," Heinrich said. He steered Franny down to the end of the long bar where the curaçao and the Vandermint sat on high glass shelves, waiting to be dusted.

"That's Leon *Po*sen," Franny said, keeping her voice low.

Heinrich nodded, though whether the nod meant *I know that* or *What's your point?* there was no way of telling. Franny had heard Heinrich speaking on the phone in German once, his voice more forceful in his native tongue. What language did he read in, or did he read at all? Was Leon Posen well translated in German?

"Just let me take care of him," Franny said. "I'm asking you."

Franny's skin was so translucent it acted more as a window than a shade. She was the only waitress who tipped the busboys out the full ten percent they were due, and she tipped the bartenders with equal consideration. Heinrich had always thought there was something German about her, the yellow hair, the clear blue ice of her eyes, but Americans were never Germans. Americans were mutts, all of them. "You're not a bartender," he told her.

"I can pour scotch in a glass."

"You have tables. I do not serve your tables because I find the customer interesting." He was wondering how much to ask for. Too much briefly crossed his mind. They wouldn't be the first ones to retire to the storeroom.

"For Christ's sake, Heinrich, I was an English major. I can recite the first three paragraphs of *Nevermore* from memory."

Heinrich had been an English major himself when he was a student in West Berlin, though for him it had been English literature with a concentration in nineteenth-century British. What a luxury it was to read Trollope, knowing that one wall away such a thing would be impossible. He wanted to say to her, *Where have these books gotten us?* but instead he reached behind her, between her shoulder blades, and ran his hand down the length of her cornsilk braid. He had always wanted to do that.

It didn't matter. At that moment she would have cut it off and given it to him as a souvenir. She went back to her place at the bar and took down a bottle of the Macallan, not the twenty-five-year but the twelve. She had no intention of sticking him. She put fresh ice in a fresh glass and covered it over with scotch. The silvered spouts stuck into the top of every bottle made pouring an absolute pleasure. It gave her accuracy, control. No one could convince her that this was the more difficult job.

Leon Posen glanced down to the end of the bar where Heinrich was unloading a rack of wine glasses, wiping out every one for good measure. "So what do you owe him?"

"I'm not sure yet." She put down the napkin, the glass.

"Always ask the price. That can be the lesson of our time together." He lifted his glass to her, *Thank you, dear Franny, and goodnight.* But Franny, who knew that this was the point at which the conversation ended and she was supposed to go and check on her tables, didn't go. It wasn't that she wanted to ask him about the books, or what he had been doing with himself since the publication of *Septimus Porter* twelve years ago. She had no intention of spoiling his night. It was that she could see her own life very clearly standing there in front of him, and her life was boring and hard. Going to law school had been a terrible error in judgment that she had made in hopes of pleasing other people, and because of that error in judgment she was in debt like some sort of Dickens character, like the kind of person who wound up on the Oprah show weeping, without a single skill to show for it, when into the bar of the Palmer House came Leon Posen. He was drinking the drink she had poured in his glass. The brightness of him, the brightness that she felt standing just on the other side of the bar, was more than she was willing to let go of. It was like throwing out breadcrumbs to the birds day after day and then suddenly having a passenger pigeon alight on the back of the park bench. It wasn't just that it was rare, it was *impossible*, and she wasn't going to make any abrupt movements that could startle him away.

"Do you live here?" she said. *What's it been like*, she asked the passenger pigeon, *the whole world thinking you're extinct?*

He looked behind his shoulder at the room, the great eyelids lifting. "At the Palmer House?"

"In Chicago."

A couple came in, unbundling a tangle of coats and scarves and hats, and sat at the bar two stools away. Why, she wanted to ask them, with all the empty stools to choose from, would they want to sit so close? She could smell the woman's perfume, dark and not unpleasantly musky, from where she stood. Then she realized they had meant to sit in front of her. She was the bartender.

"Los Angeles," Leon Posen said, after a great deal of internal wrestling. "Depending on how you look at it."

"Whiskey sour," the man said, heaping their winter wear on the stool beside them. The pile of woolens immediately began to slide off and he grabbed onto the sleeve of a coat and then tipped his head in the direction of the woman. "Daiquiri."

"Up," the woman said, pulling off her gloves.

Franny wasn't sure how to tell them that this wasn't her job, but Leon Posen knew how to say it. "She doesn't mix drinks," he told them. "She can pour scotch in the glass but if it's got two ingredients or more you're going to need someone else." He looked at Franny. "Is that fair?"

Franny nodded. She represented herself falsely just by standing there.

"I could make you a whiskey sour," he said to the man, then, looking at the woman, shook his head. "But not a daiquiri. I bet you there's a mix back there somewhere."

"I don't know," Franny said.

"You should ask the German." Leon Posen pointed the couple to Heinrich, who was still polishing glasses at the far end of the bar, ignoring with intent. "It would be a gift to him. He's had his feelings hurt."

"You know a lot about this place," the woman said. It was very late. Underneath her glove there was no ring.

"It isn't this place," Leon said. "It's bars." He asked Franny the name of the bartender, and Heinrich, with ears pitched to frequencies higher than a dog could imagine, heard the question and put his towel down.

"Whiskey sour," the man began again.

When they had placed their orders and Heinrich had made a tasteful showing of his skills with a cocktail shaker, the couple did indeed gather up their belongings and carry them off to a small table in the corner, a table that would have been Franny's except for some unspoken exchange in which it was decided that Heinrich would serve the drinks as well, taking both the table and the tip.

"I was born in Los Angeles," Franny said, once the couple were mercifully gone. She'd been waiting such a long time to say it she wasn't sure the point still had any conversational relevance.

"But you had the sense to get out."

"I like Los Angeles." In Los Angeles she was always a child. She swam the length of Marjorie's mother's pool, skimming its blue bottom in her two-piece bathing suit. The shadow of Caroline, half-asleep on her inflatable raft, was a rectangular cloud above her. Their father was just at the water's edge in a lounge chair reading *The Godfather*.

"You say that because we're in Chicago and it's February."

"If L.A.'s so awful why do you live there?"

"I have a wife in Los Angeles," he said. "That's something I'm working on."

"That's why people come to Chicago," Franny said, "To get away from wives." She was thinking of divorce law, thinking now there was a practice she'd never touch, before she remembered that she'd never touch any of them.

"You sound like a bartender."

She shook her head. "I'm a cocktail waitress. I can't mix a drink."

"You're the bartender to those of us who don't need their drinks mixed, and I'd like another scotch. You did a very good job getting that first one in the glass." He studied her then as if she had only now stepped in front of him. "You're taller again."

"You told me it might improve my tip."

He shook his head. "No, you told *me* it might improve your tip, and it won't. I don't actually care how tall you are. Take off your shoes and I'll buy you a drink."

When had Leon Posen finished his scotch? It was a remarkable trick. She hadn't seen a thing and she'd been watching. Maybe it had happened while the whiskey sour was being made. She had been distracted for a minute. Franny took the bottle from the counter behind her. "You can't buy me a drink. It's against the rules."

Leon leaned forward. "Verboten?" he asked quietly.

Franny nodded. The ice in the glass looked bright and undiminished so she didn't see the point in changing it. She didn't measure out the scotch either, she just poured it in on top of what had been there before. The silver spout made her overconfident and she poured the scotch from too great a height and spilled some on the bar beside the glass. She wiped up her mistake and set the glass on a fresh paper napkin. In truth, she wasn't a good bartender, even for drinks containing a single ingredient. "So why are you in Chicago?"

"Maybe you're an analyst." He took his cigarettes out of his jacket and shook one free from the pack.

"When I tell people I waited on Leon Posen they'll ask me what he was doing in Chicago."

"Leon Posen?" he asked.

This was a possibility she hadn't considered, but it wasn't as if she'd ever met him. She was working off jacket photographs, old ones at that. "You're not Leon Posen?"

"I am," he said. "But you're younger than my regular demographic. I didn't think you'd know."

"Did you think I was just an extraordinarily helpful cocktail waitress?"

He shrugged. "You could have been trying to pick me up."

Franny felt herself blush, something that didn't usually happen in the bar. He waved his hand as if to dismiss the observation. "Strike that. A ridiculous thought. You're a smart girl, you read books, and now you've poured a scotch for Leon Posen, but you should call me Leo."

Leo. Could she call Leon Posen Leo? "Leo," she said, trying it out.

"Franny," he said.

"It isn't just that you're Leon Posen," she said. "Leo Posen. I'm interested in people in general."

"You're interested in why I'm in Chicago?"

Somehow this wasn't going the way she had intended it. "All right, I'm not interested. I'm conversational."

He lifted his glass and took the smallest sip, dipping in his upper lip as if he were only tasting it to be polite. "Are you a journalist?"

She put her hand on her heart. "Cocktail waitress." Actually, Franny had been saying this to herself every day in front of the bathroom mirror, after she brushed her teeth, before she left for work, *I am a cocktail waitress*. Practice had made perfect. She took the heavy Zippo lighter out of her apron pocket and flipped open the lid with her thumb. He leaned forward and then back, shaking his head.

"No, you don't look at the cigarette, you look at me. When you light a cigarette you have to look the person in the eyes."

So Franny did this, even though it was nearly impossible. Leo Posen leaned towards the little flame in her hand and kept his eyes steady on her eyes. She felt a rocking in her chest.

"There," he said and blew the smoke aside. "That's how you get a better tip. It isn't the shoes."

"I'll remember that," she said, and shut down the flame.

"So I've come to Chicago to have a drink," he said. "I'm living in Iowa City for now. Have you ever been to Iowa City?"

"I thought you lived in Los Angeles."

He shook his head. "Don't be slippery. I asked you a question."

"I've never been to Iowa City."

He took another sip to see if his drink had improved now

that he had a cigarette, and obviously it had. "It's not the kind of place you go unless you have specific business there. If you grow corn or trade in pigs or write poetry then you go to Iowa City."

"That's why I haven't been."

He nodded. "The bars are full of students. It wouldn't be my choice to drink in a bar full of students, but that isn't the real problem." He stopped there. He was waiting for her. Leo Posen liked a straight man.

"What's the real problem?"

"It turns out the ice in the drinks contains a certain amount of herbicides—herbicides, pesticides, and what I think must be liquid fertilizer. You can taste it. It's not just the ice in the bars, of course, it's in all the water, all the water that doesn't come from France in bottles. I've heard it actually gets much worse in the spring when the snow starts to melt. There's a higher concentration. You can taste it on your toothbrush."

She nodded. "So you come to Chicago to have a drink because the ice in Iowa has agricultural chemicals in it."

"That and the students."

"You're teaching there?"

He took a casual pull off his cigarette. "One semester. It was a mistake I made. It sounded like a lot of money at the time but nothing's a lot of money when you weigh it out against the costs. Nobody sits you down and explains the situation with the water before you sign the contract."

"Wouldn't it be easier to make ice at home? Use the water from France. You can brush your teeth with it, too."

"In theory, yes, but there's no good way to implement it.

Either you have to carry your ice bucket with you to the bar or you have to drink at home by yourself, which I don't do."

"So come to Chicago and have a couple of drinks," Franny said, because she was glad he was there, she didn't care about his reason. "It's good to get away."

"Now you're seeing it," he said, slapping the bar with his open hand. "Cedar Rapids doesn't solve the problem."

"Des Moines doesn't solve the problem."

"You're shorter again."

"You told me to take my shoes off."

"Are you saying that I told you to take your shoes off and you did it?"

"I'd rather have them off."

He shook his head, though whether to marvel or despair she didn't know, then he crushed what was left of his cigarette into the small glass ashtray. "Did you ever want to be a writer?"

"No," she said, and she would have told him. "I only wanted to be a reader."

He patted the top of her hand, which she had left close by on the bar in case he needed it. "I appreciate that. I've come a long way so that I could have a drink and not be anywhere near another writer."

"Can I get you another drink?"

"You're a great girl, Franny."

The problem, and it was one she took seriously, was that Franny didn't know how long Leo Posen had been sitting at the bar before she saw him, how long Heinrich had been doing his job before she took his job away. Because while Leo Posen appeared to be perfectly sober, she would bet that he seemed that way regardless of how much he had drunk. Some men were like that. They went from sober to more or less dead without intermediate steps. "Are you staying here at the hotel?" she asked, her voice gone small.

He tilted his head ever so slightly and waited, his face full of benevolence.

Franny shook her head. "It's only because if you were to get in your car and run someone down on your way back to Iowa tonight I might have to go to jail."

"*You'd* go to jail? That hardly seems fair."

"Dram shop civil liability, state of Illinois." She held up her hand to demonstrate seriousness.

"'*Dram* shop'?"

"They should update the name."

"Are the other dispensers of dram aware of this?"

Only the ones who had dropped out of law school, she wanted to say, but nodded instead.

"Well, not to worry. I only have to get to the elevator."

Franny brought back the bottle of scotch. "What happens in the elevator is your own business." Just then the lights came down two settings. Heinrich always shut down the night too abruptly, turning the lights so low so fast that it felt like a straight fall into darkness. Every time it happened she had a split second of wondering if something small and important had ruptured inside her head.

"It's a sign," Leo Posen said, looking up at the ceiling. "Make it a double."

After bringing out a larger glass to hold twice the scotch, Franny stepped into her shoes and went to settle up with her two tables. She felt sheepish about asking them for money when she had abandoned them so long ago, but neither table seemed to hold it against her. One gave her a credit card and the two businessmen handed her a mysteriously large amount of cash and then pulled on their coats to leave. When she came back to the bar, Heinrich was putting plastic wrap over the stainless-steel garnish bins, tucking the maraschino cherries into the refrigerator for the night.

"Did they tip you for the shoes?" Leo Posen asked. The scotch was gone and now he was leaning into the bar. His eyes weren't focused on anything.

"They did."

"How much?"

Heinrich looked up from his work. He didn't mind that it was an inappropriate question. No one ever asked about tips and he wanted to know.

She hesitated. "Eighteen dollars."

"That tells us nothing unless we know the amount of the check. They could have been drinking a vintage montrachet, in which case they stiffed you."

"It wasn't montrachet," Heinrich said.

Franny sighed. There was no way to explain that she needed the money, that she was sleeping on Kumar's couch so that she could pay the next coupon in her loan booklet. "Twenty-two dollars."

A small, involuntary sound passed Heinrich's lips, the puff of air that comes after the punch but without the punch itself.

"I picked the wrong business," Leo Posen said.

Heinrich looked at him doubtfully. "That's not what they would have tipped you."

"What about the other table?" Leo said.

Franny held up her hand, enough.

"I never would have guessed it," he said to Heinrich. He reached into his pocket and pulled out a brown leather wallet thick with credit cards, photographs, cash, folded receipts. He dropped it on the bar, where it made a soft thud like a baseball falling into a glove. "Here," he said. "Take the whole thing. I can't do the math."

Franny rang up his check, folded the little piece of paper, and left it there in a clean highball glass. That's the way they did it at the Palmer House, just to remind you how you came to rack up such a magnificent bill in the first place. The passenger pigeon had stayed beside her on the bench all evening, but then what do you do? You can't stuff the thing in your purse and take it home with you, and you can't sleep in the park, waiting for it to go on its own. It was cold now, it was dark.

Leo Posen sighed and opened his wallet. "You aren't even going to help?" he asked.

Franny shook her head and started wiping down the bar. She did suspect that math was part of the problem, that the drunker people were the more they struggled with percentages and so decided to err on the side of extravagance. But then she also wondered if they tipped her more because they felt embarrassed for their drinking. Or they tipped her more in hopes she might run after them and suggest that for eighteen dollars she would like to have sex.

Leo Posen continued to sit, though he had stacked his money neatly over the top of his bill and his glass and napkin were gone. Every other customer in the bar of the Palmer

House Hotel was gone. Jesus, a busboy, had come over from the restaurant to make sure that everything was off the tables. He had his eye on Leo Posen's back. It was time to run the vacuum.

After Franny had clocked out and put on her coat, she came back to the bar. It was the long puffy coat her mother had bought for her when she got into law school, a sleeping bag with sleeves, her mother had called it, and it was true, many were the nights she threw it on top of the blankets on the couch before climbing in. She stood next to Leo Posen's chair. "I'm going now," she said, wishing for the first time since taking the job that the night were longer. "It's really been something."

He looked at her. "I'm going to need your help," he said in a level voice.

The pigeon fluttered off the back of the park bench and into her lap, pushing its head against the folds of her coat.

"I'll get Heinrich." Her voice was very quiet even though it was just the two of them there. This was why she shouldn't take Heinrich's customers, even the famous novelists, because in the end they would still be his responsibility. "He can take you to the elevator."

He turned his head slightly to the left, as if he had meant to shake it *no* and then lost his train of thought. "Don't get the German. I just need—" He waited, looking for the word.

"What do you need?"

"Guidance."

"We'll find someone bigger."

"I'm not asking you to carry me."

"It would be better."

"Is the elevator not on your way?"

Wasn't it a sort of honor to be asked? It would be the most interesting part of the story and the part she wouldn't tell—that Leo Posen was too drunk to walk himself out of the bar and so she had to help him. It wouldn't be the best decision Franny had ever made, but it wouldn't even be in the running with the worst. And he'd done so much for her already in the years before they met, those beautiful novels. She took his hand off the bar and pulled it around her shoulder. He gave himself over to her. "Stand up," she said.

Men can be surprisingly tall once they've been unfolded from the high bar chairs. Franny's shoulder, raised by the height of her heels, barely came to his armpit. He put more weight on her than she would have expected but she could hold him up. "Just stand here for one second and get your balance," she said.

"You're good at this."

She tried to rearrange his hand, which covered her left breast without intention. Where was Heinrich now? Mercifully smoking? He could use this against her, though with the German it was always hard to say what would offend him. Franny had her arm around Leo Posen's waist as she steered the course between the dark icebergs of her tables.

"Wait," he said. Franny stopped. He raised his chin. He looked like he was trying to remember something, or that he was going to ask for another drink. "That song," he said.

Franny listened. The tape was playing to the empty room. Gladys Knight and the Pips were singing. The gist of the story was that the relationship was over and neither party was willing to own up to it. The first thirty times she heard that song she'd loved it. Then she didn't anymore. "What about it?"

Leo lifted his hand from Franny's breast and pointed at the air. "That's the song that was playing when I came in. *I keep wondering what I'm going to do without you,*" he sang lightly.

The bar, Heinrich liked to say, was West Germany, and Franny understood its progressive, flexible approach to the workforce. But the lobby was under the control of the East, full of Soviet spies you never suspected. "Stay out of the lobby," Heinrich had told her when she'd first taken the job. "Once you're in the lobby, you're on your own. The bar can't save you."

Still, she had to figure they didn't know her any better than she knew them. Her cocktail uniform would have sold her out but it was hidden by her coat, and the shoes could have been the shoes of any foolish woman in the hotel. The Palmer House had a grand lobby with massive chintz sofas both overstuffed and piped; some were circular, with a tall middle section pointing up to the chandeliers like a fez. The oriental carpet could have covered a basketball court. The ceiling, which opened through the second floor, was a small-scale Sistine which traded Adam and God for the stars of Greek mythology: Aphrodite and random nymphs tucked between wandering clouds. It was the kind of lobby where tourists came and took pictures of one another standing in front of the towering floral arrangements. Peonies in February. Even at one o'clock in the morning there were people milling around aimlessly, and a line of young men and women in smart dark suits waited behind the marble counter to help them. At least the bar closed. The front desk staff stood there all night.

Franny and Leo had a moment to consider their reflection in the brass elevator doors after she pressed the arrow pointing up. "You don't look like you should be with me," he said, falling into the enchantment of the movie they made together. He was starting to sway a little so that he could watch them sway, left to right, right to left.

In a whispered voice she told him to hold still. The numbers lit up as the elevator came for them—five, four, three, two—and then the doors slid open. "There you go," she said, and tried to move him forward on his own. She was not hopeful.

He looked at her under his arm. "There I go where?"

"Into the elevator, like you said." But he hadn't taken an ounce of his weight off her, and she had to say the inability felt sincere. She didn't think he *could* actually walk into the elevator without her. Leo Posen said nothing. The doors started to close and, in a perilous demonstration of balance, she pushed them open again with one foot.

"Okay," she said, though she was talking to herself. "Okay, okay, okay." She pulled them both inside and the doors slid closed. "What floor are you on?"

"Okay what?"

"What floor are you staying on?"

"I have no idea." His words were heavy but distinct, each one a cannonball dropped into dust.

"Do you have a room at this hotel?"

"I'm sure I do," he said, though with a slight trace of defensiveness that planted a seed of doubt in her mind.

The doors started to open again and Franny pushed the Door Closed button, then the button for the twenty-third floor. There was a twenty-fourth floor but it was a penthouse. The twenty-fourth floor required its own elevator key. "Do you have the key in your pocket? Check your pocket."

"Do you not want to be seen with me?"

Franny leaned Leo Posen into the corner of the elevator and he balanced there nicely. She went through the pockets of his suit jacket, inside, outside, and then his pants pockets. These were the games she and Caroline had played with their father in the summers: how to question the suspect, how to pat him down, how to pop the lock on a car door. Fix saw everything as a learning experience for police procedure. In Leo Posen's pockets she found a folded handkerchief (pressed, no monogram), a pair of readers, a roll of wintergreen Life Savers (two missing), a baggage check for a flight to LAX, and his wallet. She proceeded to go through his wallet. The hotel's keys looked like credit cards now. Sometimes people put them in there.

"Hey," Leo said in a tone of small amusement that was just about to flicker out, "do you not want to be seen with me?"

The elevator made an unassuming ding to herald their arrival. The doors opened up to show them the enormous elevator bank of the twenty-third floor: it contained a long lozenge-shaped sofa with seating on all four sides, ten-foot mirror, and an old-fashioned house phone on a table. Franny punched five. "I don't want to be seen with you."

He lightly touched the pockets of his jacket to see if there was anything she had missed. "I'm a nuisance."

"You made a show of giving me a pile of money in the bar and now I'm going to your room. They fire the cocktail waitresses for that." Of course she could call the office of student legal aid at the University of Chicago, where third-year law students offered free legal advice that was worth exactly what you paid for it. She had friends there. They might move her to the top of the pro bono pile. She could explain that she had been fired for solicitation when in fact all she was doing was what any English major would have done: seeing that Leo Posen made it safely back to his room (though was that a convincing case? Wouldn't many English majors want to have sex with Leon Posen? Did she? Not at the moment, no. No she did not). It was, after all, in the university's best interest to see that she kept her job so that she could pay back her loan, but then she remembered that she didn't owe them money anymore. Her loan had already been sold twice and was now held by the Farmers' Trust of North Dakota. It was her loan that had been forced into prostitution. The fifth floor came and went: the doors opened onto an identical elevator bank and then the doors closed. They were headed back to twenty-three. Did anyone in the lobby monitor suspicious elevator activity? In his wallet: a Pennsylvania driver's license in the name of Leon Ariel Posen; American Express, MasterCard, Visa, Admirals Club, and a Pasadena Library card; several school pictures of a little red-haired girl who aged as Franny flipped ahead; folded receipts she didn't unfold; and a Palmer House Hotel key card. Bingo. Franny looked at it, the pleasant hunter green, the hotel's name printed in an overly ornate script, a magnetic stripe on the back that would unlock the door to one of the rooms in this hotel. "What's your room number?"

"Eight twelve."

The doors opened again. Hello, twenty-three. Franny pushed eight. "You said before you didn't know."

"Before I didn't know," he said, looking away. The ride wasn't agreeing with him. There was that little jostle with every stop and start, two fast inches up and then down again to remind the passenger of the cable from which the box hung. He may have come up with a number just so she would take them back onto solid ground. The doors opened again and he struggled forward as if trying to leave without her. She draped his arm around her shoulders again. It was hot inside her coat, which had been designed to sustain human life at twenty degrees below zero. A sheen of sweat brightened her face. Sweat ran down the backs of her legs and into her shoes.

"You wouldn't lose your job," he said. He kept his voice down and for this Franny was grateful. Not all drunks were capable of such restraint. "I'll tell them we're friends. That's what we are."

"I'm not sure they would appreciate our friendship," she said. The halls, like the elevator banks, were very wide. So much wasted space was an Old World luxury. She had never been upstairs before, and what she was feeling she imagined must be akin to breaking and entering. The halls were endless, seemingly without a vanishing point, and were lined with black-and-white photographs of famous people at the height of their beauty: Dorothy Dandridge, Frank Sinatra, Judy Garland. They went on and on. Franny kept her eyes on

them. Hello, Jerry Lewis. The carpet was dizzying, a mash-up
of peacock feathers in yellow and peach and pink and green.
It was hard to look down for very long, and she was sober.
It couldn't have been a good match for scotch. There was a
room-service table in the hall, a half-eaten Reuben sandwich,
scattered fries, a single rose in a bud vase, the bottle of wine
upended in its silver bucket . . . 806, 808, 810, 812. Home.
She shifted her hip into Leo Posen to balance his weight, then
dipped the key in the lock. A small red light flashed twice and
then disappeared.

"Fuck," she said quietly, and tried again. Red light.

"What if I came home with you?"

"That wouldn't work."

"I could sleep on the couch."

"*I* sleep on the couch," she said, except for the nights she
slept with Kumar, which weren't many because that was not
the nature of their relationship. He was a friend. She needed
a place to stay.

"Eighteen twelve," he said, straightening himself imperceptibly. "That's what it is."

She could take him back to that lovely lozenge-shaped
sofa; a place to relax if the wait for the elevator became
too strenuous. It was plenty big enough. She could leave
him there. She could go downstairs and call the front desk
from the house phone, explain that she had seen a man
sleeping on the eighth-floor sofa.

"Eighteen twelve."

Franny shook her head. "You're thinking of the overture,
or you're thinking of the war. You're not staying in room
1812."

He considered this, still looking at the locked door in front of them. "I could be thinking of the war," he said. "Could we stop for a while? I need a little rest."

"I do too," Franny said. She had clocked in for her shift at four-thirty. She wasn't going to the eighteenth floor. They might as well start on two and dip the key in every lock in the hotel.

"You seem nervous," he said, his voice coming up as if from sleep. "Have you been in trouble before?" He was getting more comfortable with the transference of his weight across her shoulders, and he wasn't doing as good a job picking up his feet, which made it feel like she was dragging him over an uneven path of rocks. Franny passed the elevator bank and kept going.

"I'm in trouble right now," she said. She would give him one more chance and then she would leave him. He wouldn't blame her. He wouldn't even remember her. Were they to fall in the hallway that would be it for both of them. He was ten inches taller, eighty pounds heavier. She would be pinned beneath him, broken ankle, broken wrist, until the kid who slid the bills beneath the doors at three a.m. came down the hall and found them there. She didn't have health insurance. When they got to room 821 she took the key out of her coat pocket and dipped it. It flashed red, red, then green. The lock clicked and she turned the handle. Eight twenty-one. She was thrilled that at the very least she understood the nature of mistakes.

Leo Posen hadn't thought to leave a light on. Franny walk-dragged him over to the bed and sat him down on the edge while she clicked on the lamp. A pretty room, padded headboard, heavy drapes, an imitation of a fine desk where a famous novelist might sit and write a novel. All in all too nice a room if its only purpose was to sleep off a drunk. There was an overnight bag on the overstuffed chair with a topcoat draped over the back. The good and merciful turn-down service had come before them and folded back the bedspread, exposing the white pillows, white sheets, the deep envelope of sleep so inviting that she wondered if she were to lie down on the far side of the king-sized mattress for an hour whether anyone would know the difference. It would make the case much harder for legal aid after she'd been fired for solicitation, finding her hair on the pillow. "Help me with your arm."

Leo Posen leaned forward and held his arm back, and with that adjustment she was able to work him out of his suit jacket. He was a man who had been helped out of a suit jacket before. He gave a long, tired sigh, as if the world's weight had finally caught up with him.

She laid the jacket on top of his coat and then leaned down for his shoes. Leo Posen had lovely lace-up shoes, polished and worn soft as gloves. She put them far enough away from the bed that he wouldn't trip on them in the night. Then she picked his feet up off the floor and put them in the bed with the rest of him, turning him around in the process. The pants, the belt, she didn't even consider them.

"Next time I'll know," he said, sinking into all that softness, cool sheets, warm blankets.

She put her hand on his shoulder just to call him back for a moment. "Sleep well," she said. She made her voice as soft as the pillows because now that this was over and he was safely in bed she could love him again. She covered him up.

"You can stay for a while, can't you?" There was no embarrassment there, only peace, only enough time left to ask for one more favor, which Franny thought was the deepest difference between women and men. His eyes were closed and by the end of the sentence he was asleep, and so she said nothing. She pulled the spread over him and turned off the lamp, then she sat down on the edge of the bed in the dark, on the far far side, and changed her shoes. She kept a pair of flats in her bag. The soles of her work shoes had only touched the carpet of the hotel and so they were as good as new. She would have them for years.

*   *   *

Had anyone asked Fix Keating and Bert Cousins what they agreed on, neither man would have been able to come up with much of a list. Still, without ever having discussed the matter (without ever having discussed any matter) they had both decided that Caroline and Franny should go to law school. The girls were very young when this idea first took hold, Caroline was in middle school and Franny still sleeping with dolls, but Fix and Bert had mapped out the future like generals in their separate camps. Neither Caroline nor Franny exhibited any interest in American history. They were not particularly given to rational thought. They showed no skills at debate, though their energy for screaming at one another was limitless. But then again it wasn't about what either man had seen in Caroline or Franny. It was about what each had seen in himself.

Bert held similar expectations for all the children in the family, even Jeanette, who he thought could at least do title searches if she ever made it through school. By expecting the same thing of everyone he saw himself as fair-minded and devoid of favoritism, and by coming up with a plan so many years before it would need to be implemented he figured he was bound to have at least some measure of success. The law, after all, was what Cousinses did. Bert's great-grandfather had been a lawyer for the Pennsylvania Railroad, and his grandfather had been a circuit court judge. Bert's father, William Cousins, called Bill, had practiced a gentleman's version of real estate law out of substantial offices in downtown Charlottesville, mostly drawing up contracts for friends who bought swaths of Virginia farmland, waited for the zoning to change, and then turned the land into strip malls. It was a good source of income from which Bill retired early, his wife having come into the Coca-Cola bottling rights for half of the commonwealth through the bequest of her childless uncle. Bill Cousins liked to stand in his living room and look out the front window, down the allée of noble sycamores that lined the drive, and think the world was beautiful and should never change.

Bert held a Jeffersonian belief that a basic understanding of the law was the foundation for any successful life, so even if one of the children wanted to be a nurse or teach school he expected they should secure law degrees first. His belief that a person without an understanding of the law could not actually be intelligent or interesting had been a problem in both of his marriages.

Fix's take on the law was more straightforward: he wanted his girls to be lawyers because lawyers made money. If Caroline and Franny made money themselves there would be a smaller chance that they would one day leave the guy they were married to for a guy who was rich. Fix was a great believer in history repeating itself, and he never tried to dress it up as anything else. If it happened once, it could damn well happen again.

The year that Caroline was thirteen and Franny was ten, Fix bought them each a Kaplan study guide to the LSAT. He wrapped them up in red foil paper and mailed them to Virginia for Christmas along with the regular presents that Marjorie had picked out: board games, a stuffed rabbit, a watercolor set, a sweater, two music boxes.

"It's a little crazy but it's not a bad idea," Bert said, picking up Franny's copy while she scratched around in the piles of crumpled wrapping paper, searching for some overlooked present that might have gotten lost under the tree.

"Are you serious?" Beverly said. She was wearing a zip-up floor-length robe of dark-green velour, a homemade Christmas present from her own mother. On any other mother in the world it would have looked dumpy, but on their mother it was startlingly chic.

"If they read one chapter a month," Bert said, flipping through to the index, "that wouldn't be too much. They don't have to understand it. At this point it would just be a matter of familiarizing themselves with the vocabulary, but if they really stuck with the program they'd wind up with perfect scores someday." He had yet to articulate his own plans to raise up an entire firm of lawyers, but he saw Fix's initiative as a good place to start.

Caroline, in her red-flannel reindeer pajamas and fluffy socks, was torn between the desire to tell Bert to go fuck himself and remembering that the gift was from her father. She decided she would look at the book later when Bert wasn't around to take any pleasure in seeing her do it. Franny on the other hand was just now opening the hardback copy of *A Tree Grows in Brooklyn* from her grandmother. Even from the first sentence, from the look of the words on the page, she could tell that that was what she would be reading over Christmas vacation, not an LSAT prep book. But when their father called later that morning to wish them a merry Christmas and to tell them he missed them more than anything in the world and wished that they could all be together (which made the girls cry on their separate extension phones, Caroline in the kitchen, Franny sitting on the floor beside the bed in Bert and her mother's room), he also broke the news that he had gotten into law school. Starting in January, Fix Keating would be attending Southwestern College of Law at night. Going at night meant it would take four years instead of three, but that was okay, that was the way Dick Spencer had done it. He wished he'd started earlier, the way Dick had, but you can't spend your life regretting things.

"If I'd started when I was your age I'd be a senior partner by now," he said to the girls. *When I was a boy I took a turn, as an office boy in an attorney's firm* their father liked to sing in the morning. "You two have all the time in the world to study. If you start now and I start now then we could all study together when you come out next summer."

It was Christmas vacation and Franny didn't want to study, nor did she want to commit to studying in the summer. He had already told them he'd take them to Lake Tahoe that summer and rent a pontoon boat they could swim off of. She wasn't about to trade that in for all of them sitting around the kitchen table quizzing each other for what amounted to a giant spelling test.

But when Caroline hung up the phone she might as well have already filled out her application. She went to her room, the Kaplan guide under her arm, and closed the door. She was going to law school with her father.

Franny blew her nose and wiped her eyes and went back to the living room. Her mother was gathering the trampled paper scraps and dazzling end-bits of curled ribbon into a Hefty bag while Bert sat on the couch with a cup of coffee and gazed at the holiday tableau: Christmas tree, beautiful wife, fire in the fireplace, sweet stepdaughter.

"Daddy's going to law school," Franny said, making herself comfortable with her novel in the blue armchair. "That's why he wants us to study. He wants us to go to school with him."

Beverly stood up, her leaf bag overstuffed and feather-weight. "Fix is going to law school?"

Bert shook his head. "He's too old for that."

"He isn't," Franny said, glad to be able to explain. "He's going like Dick Spencer." Franny liked the Spencers, who took them all to lunch at Lawry's every summer when they were in Los Angeles.

The name rang its small bell in the back of Bert's mind. Dick Spencer from the DA's office who had once been a cop; in fact, Dick Spencer who had invited him to come along to the christening party at Fix's house. Franny's christening party.

"Where's he going?" Bert asked. He seemed to remember Spencer had gone to UCLA.

"Southwestern College of Law," Franny said, impressed with herself for having committed it to memory.

"Dear God," Bert said.

"Well," Beverly said, brushing a strand of yellow hair out of her eyes. "I say good for him."

"Sure," Bert said. "It's going to be tough though, trying to go to law school every night after work. I don't know when he'll have time to study."

Franny looked at him, her own yellow hair long and slightly stringy. She hadn't bothered to brush it this morning in her rush to get down to the presents. "Didn't you go to law school?"

"Sure I did," Bert said. "I went to the University of Virginia. But I didn't do it at night. I went the regular way."

"So that wasn't hard," Franny said. She felt proud of her father, who would be doing two things at once. The nuns had led her to believe that God gave preference to people who did things the hard way.

"It was hard enough," Bert said and took a sip of coffee.

Caroline came back downstairs and stalked through the living room on her way to the kitchen to get a snack, a second piece of Christmas coffee cake which she felt would aid in her studying.

"So your father's going to law school," Beverly said to her, smiling. "That's great."

Caroline stopped dead, as if her mother had shot her in the neck with a blowdart tipped in neurotoxins. The expression on her face blossomed into something between horror and rage. They could all see the mistake had been made and that there would be no undoing it. "You *told* them?" Caroline said, turning the full force of herself onto Franny.

"I didn't . . ." Franny's voice started small and then

trailed into nothing. She meant to say she didn't know she wasn't supposed to tell, or she didn't know it was a secret, but the words just dried up in her mouth.

"Did you think Dad *wanted* them to know? Did you wonder why he didn't just call and ask to talk to them?" Caroline took two fast steps to Franny and struck her sister's bony shoulder with an open hand, the blow knocking the younger girl sideways out of the chair. It hurt, both the arm that was hit and the arm that she fell on. Franny couldn't help but think that Caroline must have really been mad at her, madder than usual even. Caroline almost never hit her in front of people.

"Jesus, Caroline," Bert said, putting down his cup. "Stop it. Beverly, don't let her hit Franny like that."

Christmas is particularly hard. All four of them were thinking some variation of that same sentence. Beverly leaned imperceptibly away. Nobody liked to see Franny hurt, but the truth was that Beverly was afraid of her older daughter and she didn't step in unless there was blood.

"Don't tell me anything," Caroline said to Bert, spitting just the tiniest bit in her fury. "Tell your snitch." Franny was crying now. The red imprint of her sister's hand would be a purple bruise by the time she went to bed. Caroline turned around and pounded up the stairs, every step a blow. She would be forced to study without her piece of cake.

Once Fix started law school, his conversations with the girls revolved around torts. "Mrs. Palsgraf was in the East New York Long Island Rail Road Station standing next to a scale," he said conversationally, like he was telling them a story about his neighbor. He was only saying it to Caroline because Franny had put the phone down and gone back to reading *Kristin Lavransdatter.* During the "Law School Summers," as they would later be remembered, Caroline and Fix sat together at the kitchen table, Fix explaining the cases. He said it helped him, that if he could explain a case to the girls then he would have learned the law that was embedded in it. "People will tell you that law school is about learning to think, but it's not. It's about learning to memorize." He held up his hand and counted off on his fingers, "Negligence, wrongful death, invasion of privacy, libel, noncriminal trespass . . ." Caroline took notes. Franny read. Franny credited her father's time in law school for her reading *David Copperfield* and *Great Expectations,* all of Jane Austen, the Brontë sisters, and, eventually, *The World According to Garp.*

There had always been a particular bond between Caroline and Fix, only now that they had the ten exceptions to the Dead Man's Rule to discuss they were closer. Caroline and Fix agreed there was nothing as boring as property law, with five times the details and little intuitive reasoning to help them. There was nothing to do but plow through the cases with endless repetition and clever mnemonics. What's an offer? What's an acceptance? What's a contract? What creates a third-party beneficiary? Property law required vigilant attention.

"It's a good thing there're going to be two lawyers in the family," Fix said to Franny over dinner, meaning Caroline and himself. "Somebody's going to have to make the money to buy you all those books."

"They're free," Franny said. "I check them out of the library."

"Well, thank God for libraries," Caroline said.

Astonishing how much condescension could be packed into the words *Thank God for libraries*. Fix laughed, and then caught himself. Franny didn't think he meant to laugh.

Fix had favored Caroline even before he started law school. It was because she was older, because they'd had more time to get to know one another before the divorce. It was because Caroline's hatred for Bert burned like a clean white flame, and because she went out of her way to make their mother's life miserable and then report the whole thing back to her father. Fix would tell her to ease up, while at the same time enjoying the meticulous detail of her reportage. He would have liked to have had the chance to make Beverly's life miserable too. Caroline looked like Fix—the brown hair, the skin that tanned to gold the minute they hit the beach. Franny was too much like their mother, too delicate and fair and uncoordinated. Too pretty while at the same time never as pretty. When their father took the girls to the alley behind the grocery store at six o'clock in the morning with their racquets and fresh cans of tennis balls, Caroline would have as many as twenty-seven consecutive hits without missing. *Thwack, thwack, thwack*, into the blank wall that was the back of the A&P, her long arms intuitively graceful in their swing. Franny's personal best was three consecutive hits, and that had only happened once. But the real difference between Caroline and Franny was that Caroline cared. She cared about the law and tennis and her grades in classes she didn't even like. She cared what their father said about their mother, what he said about everything. Franny just wanted to go back to the car and read Agatha Christie. Most of the time they let her go.

After their father had finished the second day of the California State Bar Exam, he called the girls in Virginia to tell them how crazy people were. They came into the test lugging their own desk chairs, their lucky study lamps. One guy was so superstitious he came with a friend and together they dragged in the guy's desk. Crazy! The test was long and hard, like running all the way from MacArthur Park to the police academy in summer, but that's why you practice, so that when the time comes to perform you'll be ready. Fix had been ready, and the test was behind him now. He was done.

Franny told Bert. She went into his study and shut the door before she told him, and even then she kept her voice down. "Dad took the bar."

Franny and Bert got along, even when Bert and Beverly no longer got along, even though Caroline and Bert had never gotten along. Bert looked up from the stack of file folders in front of him. "Did he pass?"

"He just took the test," she said. "But I'm sure he passed." Four years of doing nothing but working and studying and going to school, sacrificing vacations and what money he had—he had passed. There was no other possible outcome.

Bert shook his head. "California's tough. A lot of people have to take the bar a couple of times before they pass."

"Did you take it a couple of times?"

Bert, who was quick to be brash with everyone else, was kinder to Franny. He looked at her there, her very straight shoulders, and gave his head a shake as if he were sorry about it, then he went back to his work.

Fix didn't pass the bar.

Marjorie was the one who called and told the girls. "Nobody passes the first time. I know plenty of lawyers and they all say forget it. Your dad is just going to have to take it again. The second time you know what you're up against. The second time it all makes sense."

"Will it be the same test the second time?" Caroline wanted to know. Caroline was crying and she was trying to be quiet about it, keeping her hand over the receiver.

"I don't think so," Marjorie said with hesitation. "I think the test is always different."

"So what did he do?" Franny said from the extension, knowing that it was up to her to carry the conversation now. "What happened when he found out?" Fix had asked Franny and Caroline to pray for him on the day of the test, and they had. They had asked the nuns at Sacred Heart to pray for him too, and still he hadn't passed.

"We went to my mom's and she made your dad a nice dinner."

"Oh, that's good," Franny said, because Marjorie had a mother who could make anybody feel better about anything.

"She made him a gin and tonic and fixed a meatloaf. She told him it was a shame that he didn't pass the test but at least he'd get to take it over. She said most of the tests you take in life you only get one shot at. I think that made him feel better."

For the second test Fix made index cards. He knew a guy who had done that the second time and that guy had passed. Fix showed the cards to the girls that summer. He kept them lined up in a shoebox, divided by topic. There were more than a thousand cards. Caroline quizzed him even when the car was going through the car wash, except she wasn't quizzing him. She was telling him the answers, holding the card flat against her chest. "The doctrine under which a person in possession of land owned by someone else may acquire a valid title to it, so long as certain common law requirements are met, and the adverse possessor—"

Franny stood at the long set of windows and followed the car as it passed down through the slapping cloths that dangled from the ceiling (continuous), through the soap suds (hostile), the rinse (open and notorious), the spray wax (actual). She let the car wash fill her, every part of her, but still it was not enough to bear away the four elements of adverse possession.

As brilliant as the index cards were they didn't work, even though the second time he took the test he brought his own desk lamp. Marjorie's mother made him dinner again and told him he was going to have to take the bar a third time, nothing to be ashamed of, plenty of people had, and so Fix sat for the test the third time, and when he didn't pass it then, he stopped. No one talked about law school anymore, except insofar as it applied to Caroline and Franny.

By the time Caroline took the LSAT her senior year at Loyola, her Kaplan guide was held together by duct tape, highlighted in three colors, and bristling with Post-it notes. Test takers are a superstitious breed, so while she was careful to read updated versions in her study groups, the copy she read in bed in her dorm room before going to sleep was the one her father had given her that Christmas in Virginia. Fix's and Bert's mutual theory that a consistent practice over so many years would result in a perfect score had not been correct. A perfect score on the LSAT is 180. Caroline Keating came in at 177. She didn't know where she had lost those three points but she never forgave herself for them.

*   *   *

Almost two weeks after Franny had so miraculously deduced that Leo Posen's room number was 821, and had gotten him to that room and gotten herself out of the hotel without anyone's being the wiser, she got a phone call at the bar. Ten minutes past six and every table was full, every barstool taken. People stacked up behind the people in the chairs, drinks in hand, laughing and talking too loudly while hoping that a seat would open up. One of the other waitresses, the girl named Kelly who had the ex-husband and the child, put her hand on the small of Franny's back and nearly touched her lipsticked lips to Franny's ear while whispering to her. Everything these people did was intimate, even the delivery of messages. "Phone call," she said, her voice slipping beneath the din.

Franny had never gotten a phone call at the bar. Kelly got them all the time, from her ex-husband and her babysitter and her mother, who sometimes watched the baby. The child was never able to make it through the entire shift without facing some unsolvable need. Franny did a quick scan in her mind of all the people who might be dead, then realized there was no guessing. The room was so loud—competing voices, the eternal clink of glasses, Luther Vandross on the goddamn tape which meant that Bing Crosby was coming next. Heinrich held the phone straight out to his side as if it were some nasty bit of carrion scraped up off the road, while continuing his conversation with a customer. He kept his chin down slightly, his shorthand for disapproval. He didn't need to say it. She put a hand over one ear as if that could actually block out the noise.

"It's Leo Posen," the voice said.

"Really?" she said. It's not what she would have said had she taken a moment to think about it. She had reread *First City* since escorting him to his bed and that had kept him very present in her mind. Franny doubted he would have remembered any aspect of that evening, and even if he had, it would never have occurred to her that she would hear from him again. Thinking that Leo Posen might call her required a level of self-aggrandizement that Franny Keating did not possess.

"I should have called sooner."

"Why?" she said.

"I put you in a bind. I never checked to see if you got in any trouble."

"Oh, no trouble," she said. She looked out over the bar and imagined they were his characters drinking there, Septimus Porter himself holding a highball glass, his girls making all the racket.

"I didn't hear you."

"I said it was *no trouble*. It's really noisy in here. It's happy hour." Heinrich was staring at her and she put her hand over the receiver. "Leon *Posen*," she said to him, but he only shook his head and turned away.

"Could you come to Iowa City on Friday?"

"Iowa?"

"There's a party I have to go to and I thought you might like it." He stopped for a minute and Franny strained to hear any noise from where he was calling but the bar was too loud.

She pressed the receiver even harder against her poor ear.

Finally he started to speak again. "Actually, that's not true. I don't think you'd like it, but I thought I might be able to stand it if you came. I'd get you a room at the hotel. It's not the Palmer House but it would be okay for the night."

"I don't have a car," Franny said.

"I'll send you a bus ticket! That's even better. You never know about the weather out here. I'd worry about you if you were driving. Would you mind taking the bus? I could send the ticket to you in care of the hotel. Franny of the Palmer House bar. What's your last name?"

From across the room she could see a man at one of her tables holding up a glass, tilting it side to side. It should never come to that, customers having to beg for a drink. "Keating. Listen, I have to run," she said, her eyes fixed on that one glass, how the ice caught the light above the heads of the crowd. "I'm going to lose my job again. I can take a bus."

Franny was on the schedule but there was never any problem getting someone to take a Friday. That's where the money was, and as soon as she had given the night away she felt the loss of it. Even if she wasn't paying for her ticket or her room, the trip was going to cost her.

"He wants to sleep with you," Kumar said when she told him about the phone call. He was still up when she came home from work, sitting at the kitchen table amid piles of books and Post-its. He seemed the slightest bit dejected, even though he had to expedite a review of an article that was a hundred pages long with over a hundred footnotes. He didn't have the energy to think about Franny, much less sleep with her.

Kumar was right, of course—why else would anyone im-
port a cocktail waitress from another state?—but somehow
that wasn't what it felt like. Leo Posen had waited two weeks
before he'd called her, which meant what? That he'd tried to
forget her and couldn't? That the cocktail waitresses in Iowa
weren't putting out? "Maybe he likes my mind," she said, and
laughed at her own cheerful stupidity. "My charming company."

He gave her a small, conciliatory shrug but said nothing.

She had woken Kumar up the night she met Leo Posen
and told him the story just like she knew she would. It
was nearly two o'clock in the morning when she'd climbed
into his bed in the dark room and shaken his shoulder.
"Guess who I met! You have to guess!" Kumar loved those
books. They had talked about them not long after they'd
met. He'd been looking at her bookshelves when she went
into the kitchen to make a pot of coffee and when she returned with the cups he was holding her copy of *Septimus
Porter*. He left the Updike on the shelves, the Bellow and
the Roth.

"You read Leon Posen?" he said, just to make sure they
hadn't been left behind by some old boyfriend.

Franny and Kumar had met not long after coming
to the University of Chicago. They sat beside each other
in torts and decided to study together. They had become
friends without realizing that soon there would be no time
for friendship. Now that Franny was broke and sleeping on
his couch, it was hard to say what was bothering him most
about her trip to Iowa, that a woman he would have liked
quite a bit had there been time was going to a party in an-

other state with another man, or that he wished he were going with her, or that he wished he were going instead of her.

Leo Posen was waiting for her in the bus station in Iowa City. He was wearing his black topcoat and gray felt hat, studying the bus schedule that was mounted under Plexiglas on the wall as if he might be thinking about going somewhere himself. When he saw Franny coming towards him he smiled a smile much larger and more grateful than any he had given her at the bar.

"I didn't think this would actually work," he said, showing her for just a second the sweet, awkward overlap of his lower teeth. He held out his hand to shake her hand. She would remember to tell this to Kumar because if the plan was to sleep with her, if that was his sole intention, he would have kissed her right off.

"It was an easy trip," she said.

"You don't understand," he said with great cheer. "I thought I was going to sit here freezing my ass off and watch every person get off the bus from Chicago and that none of those people would be you. I might even have come back to check the next bus from Chicago just to see if maybe I'd gotten the time wrong. After that I was going to feel like an idiot, tell myself how ridiculous it was to think I could send a bus ticket to a stranger and expect that she would get off the bus just because I wanted her to. I had it all planned out. In fact, I was so sure that you weren't coming I had thought about not even coming to the station just to show you."

"That would have been awful," Franny said, because she realized now she didn't have his phone number or his address.

He shook his head. "I was going to feel terrible and foolish and old for the rest of the day, and then I was going to call the department chair and tell him that given the circumstances I couldn't possibly come to his party."

"Well," Franny said, not quite understanding any of it, "I guess I ruined your plans."

"Oh, you did, you did! You shot the entire day." He rubbed his hands together to warm them up and then sank them deep into his pockets. It was a nicer bus station than she expected to see, the floors were swept and there was no one sleeping on the benches in the waiting area, but it was nearly as cold inside as it was outside, the deepest cold of the windswept midwestern prairie in late February. The one ticket agent in his window wore a hat and gloves along with his heavy coat.

"Do you want to go to your hotel first, freshen up? Take a rest?"

Franny shook her head. "Not particularly." It didn't make any sense that he should be so surprised: of course Franny Keating would visit Leo Posen. The question then, she supposed, was to what extent did he see himself as Leon Posen? If he saw himself as a famous novelist then he would have known she would be there, but if he saw himself as someone she had met in the bar, well, he was right. She never would have gotten on a bus for anyone she'd met in the bar, not for a single other circumstance that she could think of. She wouldn't have taken anyone else to his room either, in fact the thought of it gave her a chill that was in no way connected to the freezing bus station. Still, when she looked at him, she didn't feel that familiar sensation of having made a real mistake. She only saw Leo, and was glad to be in Iowa.

He took the canvas bag off her shoulder, the one she'd used to carry her schoolbooks in back in her school days. It had always been so heavy. Now there was just a nightgown and toothbrush, a change of clothes for tomorrow, the volume of Alice Munro stories she'd been reading on the bus.

"It doesn't seem like you're planning to stay," he said.

"Just the night."

"Well then, I should show you a little bit of Iowa before it gets any darker."

"I saw an awful lot of it on the bus coming in. It looks like Illinois, the parts that aren't Chicago." The ride had taken five and a half hours. In between the Munro stories, she'd watched all of those endless snowy fields poked through with a hundred thousand broken stalks of corn, and the long shadows those stubbled cornstalks threw across the snow in the late-afternoon light. She'd leaned her head against the window. Field after field after field, and not an inch of space wasted on something as decorative and meaningless as a tree.

"You've already figured it out then," he said, and pointed to the big double doors that led out to the parking lot. "I'll take you to dinner instead." Together they stepped into frozen air, a soft sweep of snow just beginning to cover the recently shoveled walks.

Old snow was layered over the ground, the parked cars that hadn't been disturbed, the tough little shrubs that would bear the snow's impossible weight until spring. She could feel her own brittleness as the frozen air did battle with her coat. It was no worse than Chicago, it might even have been two degrees warmer, and still it was like walking into a wall of broken glass. She pictured those early settlers in their covered wagons crossing the prairies in search of a better life. Why did they stop here? Were the horses lame? Was it springtime? Were they so hungry that they brought their wagons to a halt and said, *This is far enough*?

"Tell me again why this is better than Los Angeles?" Franny asked. She wished she could put her arm through his arm and lean into him. He was tall enough to block the wind.

"I'm not married to anyone in Iowa."

"Let's hope that's true for most of the states."

"That's what I like about you. You have a positive take." He put his hand flat on her back and steered her into an Italian restaurant which looked like it might have recently been a diner. "I'm overestimating," Leo said, looking at his watch. "There probably isn't time for dinner. There's probably only time for a drink. Can you manage with just a drink for now? There'll be plenty of food later on."

Franny was just glad to step out of the weather. The wind blew in the door behind them, making an arctic puff across the tables and causing the other diners to look up. The restaurant, unlike the bus station, had a zealous heater. "I'll manage fine." She started to zip herself out of her coat and unwrap her scarf, pull off her hat. She wore boots with rubber soles and rubber covering over the toes. They were lined with the pelts of cast-off teddy bears. There was no vanity in winter.

The bartender was a woman who could have been on either side of sixty, with a swept-up pile of blond curls nested on the top of her head and a black vest which nearly failed at its job of containing her bust. The name *Rae* was stitched across the left breast in looping cursive.

"There he is!" Rae said. "Ducking in before you have to go to work?"

"I thought I should," Leo said.

"I tried to get off," she said to Franny, her eyes bright inside their spiky cages of dried mascara, "but I couldn't do it. What are you going to have, darling?"

"The same," Franny said, tilting her head to Leo. "And maybe some breadsticks and a glass of water."

"That's good thinking," the woman said, taking a bottle of scotch from the shelf behind her. "That soaks it up. Are you going to introduce him?"

"Have you not met?" Franny asked, confused. It seemed the barmaid had mistaken her for someone else. She held out her hand to the man beside her. "Do you know Leo Posen?"

This pleased them both to no end, Leo and the bartender, and they both gave a nice big laugh that brightened up their end of the bar in this dismal little restaurant. "Rae," she said, and held her hand out to Leo, who took it in both of his hands for a shake, hail fellow well met.

"She makes me ice," he said.

"I keep it in a Ziploc bag." Rae reached into the freezer beneath the bar and pulled out the bag on which she had written *No Touch* with a heavy black marker. "He thinks that Iowa is trying to poison him with bad ice."

"He told me," Franny said, nodding.

"I told you that?" Leo asked, taking off his scarf and helping himself out of his coat. He was wearing a suit again, this one dark blue, and a regimental tie.

"Who am I supposed to introduce you to?"

"You introduce him to the audience at the reading to-night," Rae said, and used a highball glass to scoop up two servings of the ice. "Big-deal famous writers hardly mean anything in this town but I like to go when I've got a free night. I've been going for years. That way I get to see all my customers while they work. And you know what all of them tell me? They say, Rae, you should be the one writing books."

Leo nodded his head in sincere agreement. "You should."

Rae smiled at him and then turned her attention back to Franny. "Sometimes they have one of the kids in the program introduce the old men. Speaking of, I should get a look at your ID."

Franny rummaged around in her purse for her wallet and then handed her driver's license to the bartender, who took a pair of readers out of her pants pocket and actually looked at it, which was more than Franny ever did. Franny almost never carded anyone, and when she did, she figured that someone handing you identification was tantamount to being of age.

When Rae was satisfied she handed both the glasses and the license to Leo. "Look at this," she said. "Frances is almost twenty-five. Honest to God, I would have thought you were seventeen. That's the thing about getting older. Everybody else starts looking younger."

Leo took the glasses and looked for himself. "The Commonwealth of Virginia?" he said, and turned the license over, maybe wondering if she had chosen to donate her organs. "I thought you were from Los Angeles."

"I am, but I learned to drive in Virginia."

"So if she isn't your student and she doesn't know you're supposed to start reading in twenty minutes, who is she?" Her tone was still jolly but Rae was looking only at Leo now, and Leo continued to look at the driver's license.

"She's my bartender," he said in distraction, and then, remembering himself, he looked up at Rae and smiled. "My other bartender."

Franny didn't correct him. The woman behind the bar did not wish to hear another word from her. Rae poured Dewar's in two glasses and pushed them forward. "That's eight," she said. The breadsticks and water were not her problem. A crowd was starting to form at the warm end of the bar, farthest away from the door, and she went to attend to them.

Leo Posen put a ten-dollar bill on the bar. If he understood what had just happened with his friend who made him ice at home and brought it to work in a baggie, he gave no indication. He was paying attention to his drink. "I have to give a reading and then there's a party for me afterwards. It's one of the obligations. There aren't many of them and they're all written down in my contract. I don't have to go to any of the other parties."

"Were you going to tell me about the reading?"

Leo gave his head a small shake. "The way I was figuring it, I didn't think I'd have to. In the first place, I didn't really think you'd come from Chicago on a bus, and if you did come, then you'd be tired and want to rest in your hotel room. I'm always tired when I come to a new place. Travel makes me tired, newness makes me tired, and I never go anywhere on a bus, so I was thinking that if you came you'd need to go straight to bed. Clearly, you have more resources than I do."

"Even if you managed to ditch me at the hotel while you read and picked me up afterwards for the party, wouldn't you think that someone might say, 'Didn't you enjoy the reading?'" If she had never met him she would have come. Had she known that Leon Posen was giving a reading in Iowa City, she would have come by herself on the bus. Kumar would have shirked his responsibilities as editor of the law review, something he'd never done, for the chance to go with her. That was the thing Leo Posen didn't understand.

"Or they would say, 'My God, what an interminable reading.' And by the way, I wouldn't be ditching you. I would be sparing you. The impulse was polite."

Franny smiled and Leo Posen looked at his watch, then he stretched his neck in Rae's direction. She was laughing with her new customers at the other end of the bar, the broad beam of her back squarely towards them. "You're a professional. What's the best trick you know for getting your bartender back when you're in a rush?"

"Take them to your reading as your date," Franny said. "It works every time."

He tapped the face of his watch as if questioning the news. "It's just that it would be so helpful to have one more before we go."

Franny slid her glass over to him. The ice, so thoughtfully made, was just beginning to melt, softening the Dewar's with water bottled from an ancient spring in France. "I don't actually drink," she said. "This is a trick I figured out a long time ago. It makes people like me."

Leo looked at the glass, and then he looked at Franny. "My God," he said. "You're a magician."

5

An unfamiliar bicycle was parked in the hallway outside her apartment where people were not supposed to park their bikes but of course that did nothing to tip her off. Jeanette opened the door, the grocery bags cutting into her wrists, her coat and boots made heavy and hot by the four flights of stairs, and found her brother sitting on the couch with her son in his lap.

"Look! Look!" her husband said. In his excitement Fodé hugged her before thinking to free her from the plastic bags. Bintou, their babysitter, rushed to wrestle the bags from her other arm and then helped her out of her coat. They treated her like this, the two of them, like she was the queen of Williamsburg.

"Albie?" There was no question that this was her brother but it was the difference between seeing a boy and a man. Albie's hair, which had been a sweet mess of dark curls, was now a thick braid long enough to make Jeanette wonder if he'd cut it even once since she'd seen him last. And where had the cheekbones come from? There were rumors of the Mattaponi tribe slivered into the DNA on their mother's side. Maybe the

Mattaponi had risen again in the youngest Cousins child. He looked like he was playing the part. "My wild Indian," Teresa used to say when he would run through the house screaming. Now here he was, as thin and as quiet as a knife.

"Surprise," Albie said, the word a flat statement of fact: *I am surprised to be in your living room. You are surprised that I'm here.* Then he added the thing that had been the most surprising to him, "You have a baby." Dayo, the baby, was holding on to the rope of Albie's hair. He gave his mother an enormous smile, both to say he was glad she had come back to him and also he was very pleased with their exotic guest.

"Scarf," Bintou said, and unwound the damp wool from Jeanette's neck. She plucked the hat from her head and shook off the melted snow. It was February.

Jeanette turned to her husband. "This is my brother," she said, as if he were the one who had just walked through the door. It felt almost accidental seeing Albie in her living room, the way some other long-lost siblings might run into one another in an airport, at a funeral.

"I saw him on the street!" Fodé said. "He was walking a bicycle away from our building just as I was coming home from work."

Albie nodded to confirm the implausible story. "He came running after me. I thought he was some crazy guy."

"New York," Bintou said.

The good news washed over Fodé, poured from him, the thrill of it still so fresh. "Except I was calling your name, Albie! Albie! The crazy guys don't know your name."

Jeanette wanted nothing but to step into the hallway for

five minutes and pull her thoughts together. The room was too cramped: Albie and Dayo sat on the couch like guests while she and Fodé and Bintou remained standing. Had they just now come in the door or had they been waiting for her for a while? How much of their discussion had she missed?

"You were just walking down the street?" she said to Albie, *My street, of all the streets in all the world?*

"I was coming to see you," he said. "I rang the bell." He shrugged as if to say that was it, he'd tried.

"But he rang the wrong bell," Bintou said. "It didn't ring here."

Then Jeanette turned to her husband. None of this made sense. "So how did you know it was my brother?" There were no pictures of Albie in their apartment, and certainly Fodé had never met him. Jeanette tried to think of the last time she'd seen her brother. He was getting on a bus in Los Angeles. He was eighteen. Years and years and years.

Fodé laughed, even Bintou covered her mouth with her hand. "Look at yourself," he said.

She looked at her brother instead. He was an exaggeration of her: taller, thinner, darker. She wouldn't have said they were too much alike except when compared to the West Africans in the living room. Funny to think of someone in the apartment looking like her when Dayo looked like no one but his father and babysitter. When Bintou met her at the door at night, Dayo bound to her chest ingeniously with yards of bright-yellow cloth, Jeanette couldn't help but think, *Really? This is my son?*

"Do we look that much alike?" she asked her brother, but Albie didn't answer. He was trying to unlace the tiny fingers from his hair.

"I wanted to wait and see you so happy," Bintou said, squeezing Jeanette's arm. "Now I'll go. Family time." She leaned over the baby and kissed the top of his head repeatedly. "Tomorrow, little man." Then she added something else in Susu, a few swooping words of birdsong meant to connect him to Conakry and the motherland.

"I'll walk her," Fodé said. "Then you'll have time." He had to leave them. He could not possibly contain his good cheer another minute, his elation in the face of visiting family. He put on Jeanette's coat and hat and scarf because they were there, because Fodé had very little sense of what was his and what was hers. "Goodbye, goodbye!" he said, waving and then waving again, as if he would be walking Bintou back to Guinea. There was pageantry in the smallest of Fodé's departures.

"Explain this," Albie said once the door was closed, the two sets of footsteps receding down the stairs, the animated elegance of French drifting behind them. Fodé and Bintou spoke French when they were alone. "They're a couple?"

Jeanette hated to admit it but it was better once they'd gone, just having the extra space in the cramped room, the extra air. "Fodé's my husband."

"And he has two wives?"

"Bintou's our babysitter. They're both from Guinea, they both live in Brooklyn. It doesn't make them a couple."

"You believe that?"

Jeanette did believe that. "You don't need to look for ways

to make me crazy. Just seeing you is enough. Does Mom know where you are?"

He ignored her. "So this one's really yours." He held out his arms as far as his braid would allow and waggled Dayo back and forth while the baby laughed and pumped his legs up and down. "Can't you just imagine what those old Cousinses would have to say about this? They'd make you give him to Ernestine."

"Ernestine's dead," Jeanette said. It was the diabetes—first her foot, then she was blind. Her grandmother had tallied Ernestine's losses in her annual Christmas letter until finally the news came of the housekeeper's death. Jeanette hadn't thought about Ernestine much since then, and in the clear picture of Ernestine's face so suddenly returned she could see her own disloyalty. Ernestine had been the only person in her grandparents' house Jeanette had ever liked.

Albie sat with this information for a minute. "Anybody else?"

Other people had died, of course they had, but she couldn't think of any people who were Albie's people. She shook her head. The baby began to stuff her brother's braid in his mouth and so she took him, not sure that Albie would want the baby's saliva in his hair, not sure she wanted that hair in the baby's mouth. She offered Dayo her wrist and immediately he began to work it over with his sore gums, his few teeth cutting against her skin. He turned his eyes up to stare into her eyes as he sucked and chewed. There was something about the gnawing that settled her, brought her back to herself, to this room, this moment.

"If you were going to have an African baby, couldn't you

at least have named him something a little less African?"

Jeanette brushed her fingers along the plush density of her son's hair. "To tell you the truth I named him Calvin, but it turns out I could never bring myself to call him that. For a long time we just called him 'the baby.' Fodé was the one who started calling him Dayo."

Albie's spine straightened involuntarily, then he leaned down to look into the baby's eyes. "Cal?"

"Where have you been?" Jeanette said.

"California. It was time to go."

"California all this time?"

Albie gave a small smile at such an impossible thought, and in that smile she saw something of the brother she had known. "Not even close," he said. The sleeves of his black sweater were pushed up towards his elbows, showing off patterned bands of black tattoos that circled his wrists in wide bracelets. Everything was black: the tattoos, the sweater, the jeans, his work boots. Jeanette wondered if he had kohl around his eyes or if his lashes were just very dark.

"So do you live here now?" That wasn't the question, but then there was no single question.

"I don't know." He reached out and touched his finger to Dayo's chin, making the baby laugh again. "We'll see how it goes."

Then she saw the duffel bag in front of the couch, inches away from the toe of her winter boots. She had somehow overlooked it by looking so intently at him.

Albie shrugged as if none of it had been his idea. "Your husband said I could sleep on the couch until I find a place."

It would have to be the couch, unless it was the coffee ta-

ble or the single armchair where Fodé studied or their tiny
kitchen table. The baby slept with them in the bedroom in a
bassinet wedged in between the bed and the wall. If she had
to go to the bathroom in the middle of the night she worked
herself out of the blankets and crawled off the foot of the
bed. Jeanette sat down on the couch, and the baby, who was
just starting to crawl, stretched his arms away from her in
an effort to get to the floor. She put him down.

"It's not like I'll ever be here," Albie said.

It was the closest he could come to an apology and it startled her, because even though they didn't have the room or the
time or the money to keep him, even though she did not forgive
him for disappearing for the last eight years with only the occasional postcard to let them know he wasn't dead, the thought of
his going made her want to get up and lock the door. How many
nights must he have needed a place to go but never called her
or Holly or their mother? If he was with her now it meant that
something had changed. The baby had hold of the zipper on the
duffel and was trying to figure it out. "You'll be here," she said.

*   *   *

Albie and Jeanette were not from Virginia. They had both
been born in California and in that sense the two of them
had been a team, albeit a team neither one of them wanted
to be on. Jeanette had applied for her first passport when
she was twenty-six, after she had gotten pregnant, after she
and Fodé were married. He wanted to take her to Guinea to
meet his family. The question that made her stop as she filled
out the forms in the post office was *Place of Birth*. What she
wanted to write was *not Virginia*. *Not Virginia* was where she

was from. Cal had tortured Albie and Jeanette with the lesser state of their birth. "Take a good look around," Cal had said once when they were driving to Arlington from Dulles, the passing landscape a multidimensional shade of green never witnessed in Southern California. "They only let you in now because you're little. Dad got permission. Once you're older they'll stop you in the airport and put you back on the plane."

"Cal," their stepmother said. Just his name. She was driving and she didn't want to get into it but she flashed her big Jackie Onassis sunglasses in the rearview mirror to show him she meant business.

"They'll send you back too," he said to her, his face turned to the window. "Sooner or later."

After Cal died, there was never any mention of Jeanette and Holly and Albie going back to Virginia. Every now and then their father would fly out to Los Angeles and take them to SeaWorld and Knott's Berry Farm, take them to that restaurant in West Hollywood where girls swam in the giant fish tank along the wall while you ate your dinner, but the endless unsupervised summers of the commonwealth were over. Albie, of course, moved back later for a single, disastrous school year after the fire, and Holly went back for two nights as an adult in an attempt to measure just how much peace and forgiveness she had mastered through the dharma, but Jeanette wrote off both the state and its residents, including, but not limited to, her father, both sets of grandparents, her uncles and aunts, a handful of first cousins, her stepmother, and her two stepsisters. Goodbye to all that. She hunkered down with what she considered to be her real family: Teresa, Holly, and Albie—the three people who were with her in the house in Torrance when she brushed her teeth at night. It was a funny thing but until that point she hadn't fully understood the extent to which her father was *gone*, that he had left them years ago and would never come back unless it was to spend the day at an amusement park. Her mother slept alone in her room like Albie slept alone in his. Jeanette, thank God, had Holly. She would lie in her bed at night watching Holly breathe and make a promise to herself to hate Albie less. Even if he was simultaneously irritating and unknowable, he was also her brother, and she was down to just the one.

But those were lean years for emotional charity, and no matter how many nights Jeanette tightened down on her resolve to be kinder, kindness failed. Without her father, without Cal, the four remaining members of the Southern California Cousinses became more profoundly themselves, as if whatever social ability each had achieved in his or her life had been wiped away in the time it took a bee to sting a boy. The speed at which their mother ran from work to school to the grocery store to home had doubled. She was always arriving, always leaving, never there. She couldn't find her purse, her car keys. She couldn't make dinner. Holly found a box of cancelled checks in the desk drawer in the living room and practiced her mother's signature, *Teresa Cousins, Teresa Cousins, Teresa Cousins*, until she could do it with exactly the right amount of pressure, the pen angled perfectly against the paper. Holly's hard work at the art of forgery meant they could still go on field trips and turn their report cards back in. Holly, who believed in credit where credit was due, took her good work straight to her mother, and Teresa put Holly in charge of paying the bills without ever telling her if it was punishment or reward. Teresa's inabilities in household accounting were legendary, going back to the time when she and Bert were happily married. Before Holly took over the checkbook, third notices and disconnection warnings arrived in the mailbox and were promptly misplaced, so that once or twice a year the house snapped into darkness. The electricity wasn't such a loss if you didn't count the television, and candles flickering in the middle of the table while they ate cereal for dinner made them think of the very rich and the very much in love. But when the toilets stopped flushing and the showers went dry, well, that was intolerable. Everyone agreed the water bill had to be paid on time. Holly, who at almost fourteen was good at pretty much everything, was good at math. She started balancing the checkbook the way she'd been taught in home economics (a class that had also enabled her to do emergency mending and make inventive casserole suppers). When she was able to identify the disaster that was their financial state, she taped a rudimentary budget to the refrigerator every week just like her teacher Mrs. Shepherd had told the girls they would need to do later on in their married lives. The last line Holly wrote in red Magic Marker: *This is what we have to spend: $____*. Even Albie paid attention to that.

For her part, Jeanette dragged the kitchen stepladder out to the backyard and pulled the low-hanging oranges off the trees, then carried them back to the kitchen in a bucket to make juice with the old metal juicer. It was a lot of work but she did it because orange juice was the way it used to be in their family. At night their mother took the pitcher out of the refrigerator and made herself a screwdriver. She never asked which one of them had been so thoughtful as to make orange juice, and Jeanette, unlike her sister, couldn't bring herself to say. Their mother was still capable of responding to a situation—had she spilled the pitcher of juice she would have mopped it up—but she exhibited zero curiosity. She never wondered about anything except Cal.

For the most part she didn't talk about Cal, but there were little things that gave her away, like the fact that they used to get stacks of Tombstone frozen pizzas from the grocery store and now their mother visibly flinched if they so much as walked by them in the freezer aisle. Was it because Cal had eaten so many Tombstone pizzas with sausage and pepperoni, or was it really just the name she couldn't stand? Not discussed. Now they called for delivery and the pizzas came to the door.

But then one night when they were all eating pizza and watching television, their mother came right out and said what was always on her mind. "Tell me about Cal." They had been watching an old Jacques Cousteau program. It had nothing to do with anything.

"What about him?" Holly asked. They really didn't know what she meant. It had been more than six months since he'd died.

"What happened that day," Teresa said, and then added, in case they didn't understand what she was talking about, "At your grandparents' house."

Had no one ever told her? Hadn't their father explained things? It wasn't fair that everything fell to Holly but it did. Jeanette kept her eyes on her plate, and Albie, well, Albie didn't know the story either. That was when Holly was grateful to Caroline for having given her a script to follow.

Otherwise she wouldn't have known what to say. She told her mother the girls had left the house after Cal because Franny decided she wanted to go back and change into long pants because of the ticks, and how there were two ways you could go to the barn from the Cousinses' kitchen door, how Cal and the girls had taken different routes because they found him when they were coming back. Her mother knew the Cousins house, of course. She and Bert had been married on the front porch and danced in front of two hundred guests beneath a tent on the lawn. There was still a cream-colored leather album of wedding pictures in the hall closet. Their father was handsome. Their mother, freckled and pale, with her tiny waist and dark hair, had been like a bride in a fairy story, a child bride.

"Why would you wait for her to change her pants?" their mother asked. "Why wouldn't her sister have waited with her?"

"Caroline did wait," Holly said. "We all did. The girls stayed together." She told her they saw him lying in the grass, and how at first they thought he was playing a joke. The other girls ran back to the house but Franny stayed with Cal just in case.

"Just in case what?" Teresa didn't like the fact that it was Franny who stayed.

It was hard for Holly to say the words because they came from a time in her life when she still believed in the possibility of a different outcome. "In case he woke up," she said.

"I saw it," Albie said, still looking at the television screen. It was a commercial, a pretty woman spreading peanut butter onto a slice of bread.

"You didn't see anything," Holly said. Albie hadn't been with the girls and he hadn't been with Cal either. Albie had been asleep. On this point everyone was clear.

"I left before you got there. I saw everything that happened before you came."

"Albie," their mother said. Her voice was sympathetic because she thought she understood the way he felt. She too had been shut out of the story.

"You were asleep," Holly said.

Albie spun around and threw his fork at his sister, threw it like a javelin in hopes of piercing her chest but it bounced off her shoulder without incident. Albie was ten and his gestures tended to be sloppy. "He got shot and I'm the only one who saw it."

"Albie, stop that," their mother said. She pushed her hands through her hair. She was regretting having asked them, the children could see that.

"It's fine," Holly said, cool and dismissive in a way that made Albie's head burst into flames.

"It was Ned from the barn!" he screamed. "He shot Cal with dad's gun. The one from the car, the gun that Caroline got out of the car! I saw it and you didn't see it because I was the one who was there. They didn't even know I was there."

Jeanette and Holly were both crying then. Their mother was crying. Albie was screaming that he hated them, *hated them*, and that they were liars. That was how it ended.

On that worst of all August days in Virginia, Caroline had already decided to become a lawyer, and so she told the other girls—Holly and Franny and Jeanette—exactly what had happened even though they'd been right there. This was after they had run fast as horses to the house and Ernestine had called the ambulance, after they had taken Ernestine back to Cal. Ernestine, fifty pounds too heavy and in ill-fitting shoes, was running with the girls through the back field while Mrs. Cousins waited at the house to direct the ambulance. Somewhere in all of that Caroline had worked out the story in her head. When did she find time? While they were all still running? Once they were back in the house? Cal was in the ambulance speeding away with the lights spinning and the siren wailing for no reason (oh, but he would have loved it though), and the Cousinses were in their car following Cal's ambulance to the hospital. Ernestine was trying to find Albie who somehow, in all the confusion, was missing. Their father was running through the parking lot of his law office in Arlington to jump in his car and race to Charlottesville to see his son for the last time. No one knew where Beverly was. That was when Caroline rounded the three other girls into the upstairs hall bathroom of the Cousinses' house, pushed them in and locked the door behind them. Only Franny was crying, presumably because she had spent those extra fifteen minutes with Cal while the other girls had run to the house and then run back again. Franny alone understood that Cal was dead. Even the people from the ambulance wouldn't say the word *dead* when all they had to do was look at him. Caroline told her sister to shut up.

"Listen to me," Caroline said, as if they didn't always listen to Caroline. She was fourteen that summer. Her voice was sharp, rushed. Flecks of cut grass were stuck to her legs and tennis shoes. "We weren't with him, do you understand me? Cal went to the barn by himself. We came up later and we found him in the grass right where he was, and when we found him we ran straight back to the house to tell. That's all we know. When anyone asks us, that's what we say."

"Why do we have to lie?" Franny said. What was there to lie about when they weren't supposed to lie anyway? Weren't the facts of the day bad enough without compounding them? Caroline, with the full force of her frustration at both the circumstances and Franny's stupidity, slapped her sister hard across the face. Franny hadn't seen it coming, hadn't braced herself, and the blow spun her sideways and knocked her head into the door of the linen closet. The knot on her left temple began to inflate before their eyes. It would be one more thing to explain.

Caroline was irritated by the crack her sister's head had made against the door when she was working to keep them quiet. She turned back to Holly and Jeanette, the more reliable two. "We can be as upset as we want. They'll expect us to be upset. But we're upset because we found him, we're upset because it happened, that's all, not because we were there." At that moment she could have told them that their only way out was to grow tails and swing through the trees and they would have done it. Caroline was thinking of their culpability, and maybe, because she was Caroline, how it might affect her own college admission. She would be in high school in the fall.

"Tell me again what happened," Teresa said one evening to Jeanette. By this point it had been well over a year since Cal died. As a rule the people in her family didn't ask Jeanette anything. Holly was studying at a friend's house down the street, and Albie was riding his bike with the pack of boys he had recently assembled. Jeanette and her mother were for the moment alone together even though they were pretty much never alone. Her mother said it so casually, like it was just another thing she'd forgotten. *Where is my lipstick? Who was that on the phone?*

Jeanette could still see Caroline in the bathroom, hear the barking clarity of her directions. She could see how sweat had dampened Caroline's hair at the temples and soaked through the collar of her yellow T-shirt. But she couldn't see Cal anymore. In just a year his face had slipped away from her. "I wasn't there," Jeanette said.

"But you were there," her mother said, as if Jeanette had forgotten.

"If you want to find the person who did it, you have to ask the same questions over and over again," Franny had told Jeanette one summer when they were in Virginia. It was years ago, before Cal died. It was one of the police skills Franny was trying to teach her, along with breaking into cars and taking apart the phone receiver so that you could listen in on other people's calls without their knowing. "Sooner or later someone always slips up," Franny had said.

Jeanette wondered if her mother was trying to slip her up.

"He got tired of waiting for us," she said. "He was going to go see the horses and we were going to catch up."

"You caught up," her mother said.

Jeanette shrugged, an awful gesture given the circumstances, disrespectful. "It was too late." It was after Cal died that her mother finally lost her freckles, as if even they had abandoned her. Jeanette was looking at the bridge of her mother's nose, trying to stay focused, trying to remember what she had looked like before all this happened.

"So who gave the pills to Albie?" their mother asked.

"Cal," Jeanette said, surprised by how good it felt to tell the truth about something. "He always did that."

With all that had happened that day, no one cared that Albie was missing except Ernestine. After checking in the attic and the cellar, she said he must have gone with Beverly. No one knew where Beverly was. She'd taken one of their grandparents' cars and hadn't told anyone she was leaving. If she'd gone into town she must have taken Albie with her. If it had been any other day the very thought of Beverly taking Albie with her anywhere, *ANYWHERE*, would have cracked the girls up.

* * *

The Goddamn Boys on Bikes is what the neighbors in Torrance called them, and later it was what they called themselves. They heard the words yelled after them as they cut over lawns, flashed between cars to the high-pitched skid of slamming brakes, swooped across grocery-store parking lots in fast, tight circles for the pleasure of terrorizing the mothers with loaded carts. People simultaneously wanted to kill them, believed that they had almost killed them, and were afraid of being killed by them. Albie, a member of the Mattaponi tribe, Raul, Salvadoran born on this side to parents born on that side, and two black kids, the smaller, handsomer, sleepier-looking one called Lenny and the other, the tallest of the four, Edison. They had all started riding together when they were eleven and ten, when they were still just irritating boys whose mothers wanted them out of the house in the afternoon. They were dangerous right from the start, forcing the cars they cut in front of to swing hard into people's lawns. One car jumped the curb and went straight into a phone pole while the boys sailed on, whooping the way they imagined the Indians would. The summer they were mostly twelve a car door opened unexpectedly and sent Lenny straight up in the air. The other three slammed on their brakes in time to see their young friend tumble gymnastically across the backdrop of blue sky. It should have killed him, would have killed him had he landed anywhere near his head, but instead he reached out his right hand to catch himself and snapped his wrist so that the bone came through the skin. Albie crashed not two weeks later, a sudden downpour pulling up the oil embedded in the pavement and sending his bike spinning out from under him. Albie broke his shoulder and tore back one ear, which required thirty-seven stitches to reattach. Edison and Raul pedaled carefully around the bike paths in the park for the rest of the summer, scaring no one, not even themselves. Edison came to Albie's house to visit and stood beside the recliner in the darkened living room. Albie had to stay in the recliner pretty much all of the time because of his shoulder.

"Everybody has a bad summer sometimes," Edison said, and Albie, who knew this to be true, gave his friend a Tylenol with codeine while they watched cartoons.

By the time they had graduated from Jefferson Middle School, Albie and Lenny and Edison were fourteen and Raul was fifteen. They were tall but not as tall as they would be.

From a distance it was impossible to tell if the bicycles were ridden by boys or men. They went too fast, and since they were always trying to see which one could outdo the other, the pack of them shifted in furious rotation, like the lead men in a race.

The Goddamn Boys on Bikes stole less candy after middle school, concentrating instead on the cans of Reddi-wip they slipped into the kangaroo pockets of their sweatshirts when they went to Albertson's. Later they would ball up together on the floor of Albie's bedroom to take in the small, sweet kick of nitrous oxide, or huff airplane glue from paper lunch bags. Each of the four mothers despaired at the bad crowd her son had fallen in with and, with the exception of Teresa, each of the mothers believed the other boys were entirely to blame.

Then one hot day in the summer they were mostly fourteen, Raul's bike slipped its chain. They were miles from home, on a narrow service road that ran beside a field that stretched out wide behind an industrial park. The boys waited while Raul squatted beside his bike and worked on the chain. The field was unmown and given over to tall grasses and various weeds, all of which had died months before. That was Torrance. Albie lay on his back on the pavement, which was maybe two degrees away from being hotter than he could stand. It felt good on his shoulder. He wished he had sunglasses but none of them had sunglasses. He took a blue Bic lighter out of the giant buttoned pocket of his long shorts. He had a little pipe in there too, with a little wooden slide over the tiny mesh basket, but that was just for show. He was long out of pot and out of the money he had stolen from Holly's babysitting stash to buy more, so instead of getting high he raised his arm straight up and flicked his lighter at the sun.

"What?" Lenny asked. He had tried to sit on the pavement but it was too hot. He couldn't believe that Albie was lying on it.

"Fire communicates with fire," Albie said, thinking that sounded profound. Then he turned his head to the right, towards the field, and saw two brown moths dipping over the dry grass, and just like that he brought his arm straight down to the right, the Bic flame turned to high, and touched the fire to the grass.

This was a field made to be burned. The flame licked at Albie's wrist as he snatched his hand away and rolled twice across the pavement before jumping up and grabbing his bike. The fire made a whooshing sound and then an ecstatic crackling like stiff sheets of cellophane balled up by human hands.

"Fuck, man," Raul said, stumbling back. "What did you do?" They were pulling their bikes farther and farther away, swinging a leg over to get out of there but none of them turned to go. All four of the boys were frozen, mesmerized, the weirdest chill washing over their skin while they watched this miraculous growing animal devouring the earth in every direction, every direction where there was grass and not bothering them at all on the pavement. The fire came as high as their waists, their chests, gorgeous beyond anything they'd seen, the rippling orange sheets hanging in the air like a desert mirage, like something that was there and not there. Black smoke curled above the flames, announcing to the neighborhood this very private thing that Albie had made. *Fire! Fire!* they'd be calling in the industrial park, even though it was already starting to die out around the edges. The fire needed so much. The boys could see it looking for more grass, anything to keep itself alive. It would have happily burned them up if it meant going for another minute.

"We should get out of here," Edison said, though for all the world it sounded like, *Would you look at that?*

Forget the whip-its, the huffing, the pot. Forget the bikes even. From that first minute all they wanted was primordial fire. In the distance they heard sirens. Yesterday they would have ridden towards the noise, followed the bright-red trucks to the action like a bunch of little groupies after a band. Today they were the action, and they knew enough to get the hell out of there.

It was his grandfather Cousins who had first taught Albie and Cal how to make match guns one summer in Virginia. All the device required was an old-fashioned spring clothespin, a couple of rubber bands, a box of kitchen matches, and a scrap of sandpaper. The boys had been instructed to pay attention to the unspeakably boring old man, who had been instructed to impart some piece of family wisdom to the boys. A match gun was what he'd come up with. It meant something different in Virginia, of course, where at least for that one freakish summer of incessant rain the world had been rendered deep and lush and essentially fireproof. In Virginia people stored wood in the garage in the hopes that one day it would be dry enough to burn. Having made their guns, their grandfather adjusted a match into position and, *zing*, sent the missile sailing off the front porch in a pretty arc of flame.

"Never in the barn," their grandfather had said to them when he handed over his invention. "In fact, never by yourselves. Are you listening to me? If you're going to shoot matches, I have to be with you."

Cal was underwhelmed. Whenever he got the chance he took his father's handgun out of the glove compartment and stuck it in his tube sock under his jeans, tying the butt to his ankle with a tight bandanna. He was wearing it that day on the front porch while his grandfather fussed over the clothes-pin.

But Albie didn't have a gun and so the little flame thrower held his interest, enough that when he tried to reconstruct one from memory five years later in Torrance, he found he could. Spreading out his materials on the dining room table, he made a match gun for each member of his posse. After a single practice session in Edison's backyard, in which they burned up paper towels and Kleenex laid out on the grass at varying distances, they set fire to a mountain of empty card-board boxes banked behind the liquor store and two dead shrubs in front of an Exxon station. On the days they got up early enough, they shot matches into the newspapers that waited on the sidewalks and front steps of their neighbors' homes. When they were much better at it they shot those pa-pers while on bikes. They took a city bus all the way to the Sunset Strip and shot matches into the palm trees, standing back to wait for the rats to tumble down the slender trunks as the dried out fronds burst into flames overhead. They tried to shoot the rats but that never worked. Rats were fast and not particularly flammable.

All through the summer they set things on fire despite the drought and the winds, despite the roadside admonish-ments of Smokey Bear. Fuck Smokey. They weren't interested in anything as sloppy as a forest fire. They liked precision, the art of flame, the single burning newspaper, one abandoned lot. They lit matches through the first two months of their freshman year at Shery High. As shoplifters they had had a spotty record, but as arsonists they were remarkably adept at not getting caught, or they were until they set their school on fire.

Raul had art last period on Fridays, a peaceful moment at the end of his week in which he was free to draw meticulous dragons breathing fire into trees. Just before he left the classroom, in the second after the bell rang and everyone began to shove their notebooks frantically into their backpacks, he leaned over and flipped the catch on the window sideways, to the unlocked position. The art room was in the basement of the school and the windows were big and at ground level. No one was looking in his direction and so no one saw him do it. He did it only because he could. Miss Del Torre the art teacher would turn it back before she went home, or if she didn't think to do it, and Miss Del Torre was an idiot so who knew, the janitor would do it when he mopped up after school.

"I want to go see something," Raul said to the other boys on Saturday morning. Nothing else was going on and so they didn't even bother to ask him what it was he wanted to see, they just got on their bikes and followed him over to school. He led them behind a low hedge that blocked the window's view to the street and, looking into the art room, Raul pushed on the glass, barely tapped on it, and the window swung open. Albie, elated by the possibility of an interesting Saturday, dragged the four bikes behind the hedge, while Lenny, who was smallest, squeezed through first. Once he was inside and straightened up he smiled at them through the glass, and waved. He found another window at the other end of the room that opened wider, a portal to another world, and one by one the Goddamn Boys on Bikes slipped inside.

There was no explanation for how the school, which was the major source of misery in their lives, could have been transformed into the most compelling place on earth simply by virtue of its being Saturday. *What a difference a day makes*, Albie's mother used to sing back when she still did things like that. *Twenty-four little hours*. The halls were silent and wide without the hordes of furious children and bitter, defeated adults. Without the buzzing overhead lights the sunlight fell down the walls and across the linoleum tiles, collecting in watery pools around their feet. Edison wondered what it would be like to be old, as old as his father, and come back here then. He figured it would be like this, the building entirely his, because he didn't take into account that other children might be coming in the future. Raul stopped and looked at the winners of the art contest lined up on a cork board. Only two of the pictures were any good: a charcoal drawing of a girl in a sundress, and a small painting of two pears in a bowl. Both had only been awarded honorable mentions while a ridiculous collage of a skyscraper made out of tiny magazine pictures of skyscrapers had won. He wondered if Miss Del Torre, who, it couldn't be said too often, was an idiot, hadn't been able to see which of the students had actual talent because there were always too many people around.

They had lost Lenny at some point. None of them had noticed he was gone and then he came back again, walking towards them down the hall. "Guys," he said, waving his arm as if they might miss him. "Come here. You've got to see this."

The squeak of their tennis shoes echoed in the halls and the sound made Albie laugh, and then they all laughed as they passed the endless row of lockers, all of them closed, all of them exactly the same. "Look at this," Lenny said, and he turned into the boys' bathroom.

For a freshman in public high school in Torrance, and especially for Lenny, who was not as tall as the other boys and skinnier despite his efforts, no place was more terrifying than the bathroom. He used every means he could think of to stay out of there, though sometimes he suspected it was thinking about it so much that made him need to go. But this room, which as recently as yesterday had been as foul and dangerous as a junkie's den, a haze of boy sweat and shit and piss, the acrid stink of boy fear, this room was now perfectly clean. It smelled vaguely, even pleasantly, of Clorox, like a public swimming pool. In fact, the way it was all arranged—the mirrors and sinks on one side, the line of toilet stalls with their green metal doors on the other—had a sort of peaceful symmetry. There was a huge amount of space between the toilets and the sinks so that you wouldn't have to bump up against any other kid unless that kid was very specifically trying to bump you. For the first time the boys noticed three bands of tiles that went around the entire room, three bands of blue that served no purpose whatsoever except to be decorative. Raul went to a urinal and, tilting back his head with the flow, noticed sunlight. "When did they put windows in here?"

Because no one was around to stop them, they went in the girls' bathroom as well and found it to be exactly the same, except that the three stripes of tile that ringed the walls were in shades of pink, and instead of urinals there was a Tampax dispenser bolted by the sinks on which someone had scratched the words *EAT ME* into the white enamel. Someone else had tried, unsuccessfully, to sand it out. The room was disappointing somehow. Even Albie and Raul, who both had sisters, thought there would be more to it than that.

All the supply closets in the school were locked, as was the principal's office, which was too bad because they would have liked to rifle through the desk drawers. They talked about taking everything out of one classroom and switching it with another, or maybe just moving a few things around to make people wonder if they were losing their minds, but in the end they decided not to touch anything. It felt too good to be in school on Saturday, and if they wanted to come again they were better off leaving everything the way it was.

So it was senseless that Albie dropped his matches in the art room trash can just when they were getting ready to leave. He kept books of matches in his pocket all the time now, to practice opening them up and striking a match with one hand. Then he would give the matchbook a hard shake and put the fire out. Except this time when he lit the match he dropped the whole book in the trash can in the far corner of the room near the window where they had come in, much the same way Raul had flipped the lock open on the window. There wasn't any reason, no reason for lighting the match or dropping it. It wasn't to impress the other boys, who were themselves always dropping lit matches everywhere these days. There was no reason that it was in the art room, except that the art room was the room where they happened to be, and really no reason they were in the school on a Saturday in the first place. It was a big metal trash can that took the match, waist high, ten times the size of anything they had in the regular classrooms where all a kid would throw away was a pop quiz he got a lousy grade on. The trash can in the art room should have been empty, everything in the school was empty and clean, but down in the bottom of the green plastic trash liner there were still some crumpled-up pieces of news-print and a couple of oily rags that had been used to wipe down the paintbrushes after they had soaked in the turpentine, and so the trash can lit up like the very mouth of hell, shooting a flame that made Albie jump back as if on springs and made the other boys turn. The flame caught the nubby green polyester draperies that were double-lined to make the room dark for that point in the semester when Miss Del Torre made a slide-show presentation on the highlights of art history. The draperies were the age of their parents and burned faster than the dry grass in the field, the flames tearing straight up to the acoustical tiles in the ceiling and spreading over the boys' heads to the other side of the room where the paints and brushes and pastels and papers and jars of solvents waited like Molotov cocktails to ex-plode. The smoke was nothing like the smoke they loved out-side. This smoke was somewhere between ink and tar, oily and viscous and black. It came for them, sucking up the air while the clear orange flame sucked up the drapes. The whole room was coming for them now with the fire in every corner. They had entered the room through the window but when they checked the window they found it was no longer an available exit.

They had never set a fire inside before, had never seen one, and so they wrongly used the skills they had developed by set-ting fires outside: they stood perfectly still and watched, the theory being that they had made the fire and so the fire was bound to respect them. Then the school's fire alarm went off. They knew that bell, so loud it seemed to be going off inside their brains. They loved fire drills, everything dropped, the girls always so upset because they weren't allowed to take their purses with them, everyone lined up and rushed outside in an orderly manner. The bell brought them back to their senses. The bell saved them. They had practiced and practiced so that in this moment the boys did what they had been drilled to do: duck low, stay together, run for the door. A flame reached out and caught hold of Albie's Red Baron T-shirt, burning his back. In the hallway Edison pulled it off him and burned his hand. As they ran for the door, the sprinklers they had never noticed doused the long, empty hallway, dissolving the entries for the art contest. They pushed out the side door, ran into the sunlight, and fell on the grass by the parking lot, gasping and coughing, panting and singed, the smell of smoke ground into their skin. Albie thought for an instant of his brother. He wondered if dying had been anything like this for Cal. The four boys lay there in the grass, tears streaming over their blackened cheeks, so exhilarated by the force of their own lives they were unable to move. That was where they were when, a scant minute later, the firemen found them.

It had been a nearly impossible decision for Teresa to send Albie to Virginia to live with Beverly and Bert. Clearly he needed a father, but some other father, any other father, would have been preferable. Beverly and Bert had not killed Cal. Teresa knew this very quietly inside herself. They had been negligent in the details of supervision but as Albie's most recent catastrophe confirmed, so had she. Still, it felt better to blame them. It felt almost good, although good probably wasn't the word. She could call Bert up on the phone and ask him, "Does it feel good to blame me for Albie? Is 'good' the word?"

What Teresa knew for certain was that she couldn't keep her second son, and since there was no one else volunteering to take him, she didn't see what else she could do. In the end, Albie went to Arlington, and when he failed in the private school there he was sent to a boarding school in North Carolina, and then military school in Delaware. He was eighteen the summer he came back to Torrance, a junior in high school given the fact that the boarding school had held him back. Holly and Jeanette were both home from college and tried to take him to the beach, to parties with their friends he might remember, but Albie was lodged like an anvil on the couch, watching game shows and eating bowls of cornflakes covered over with a thick sludge of sugar. He kept his collective communication to twenty words a day. He counted them. He worked his way through the liquor cabinet from left to right, though the cabinet itself had no organizing principle. He never started in on any bottle until he'd finished the one preceding it.

Then one day he claimed to have gotten a call from Edison. His old friend had a job setting up bands in a club in San Francisco, and he said that all Albie had to do was carry the amplifiers off the buses and plug them in. Edison had an apartment with some other guys and Albie could throw a mattress on the floor. Albie seemed to be almost excited about this, as excited as Jeanette and Holly and their mother could remember him being about anything. Lifting things, plugging things in, sounded like a job he was qualified to do, so Teresa bought him a bus ticket to San Francisco and made him a stack of peanut butter sandwiches. Holly and Jeanette each gave him a hundred dollars out of their savings. He loaded his bike underneath the bus with his duffel bag, and Jeanette and her sister and their mother waited until he took his seat by the window so that he could see them wave good-bye. He was going away again. He would be someone else's impossible problem to solve. They were each privately giddy in their relief.

Fodé came into the bathroom that night while Albie was brushing his teeth, one tap and he let himself in, shutting the door behind him. The bathroom was a good place to talk, even if there really wasn't the space for two adult men to stand comfortably together. Albie was pressed up against the sink, and Fodé, wearing flannel pajama bottoms and a white T-shirt, moved around the stacked plastic milk crates full of folded towels and bath toys and Pampers. "My brother," he said, "listen to me, I want to tell you, you will stay here with us. A week, a year, the rest of your life, as long as you need to be here, we welcome you."

Albie had the toothbrush in his mouth, minty foam trailing from his lower lip, when his sister's husband put a hand around the back of his neck and touched their foreheads together. A tribal custom? A sign of earnestness? A pass? All he knew about his sister was what he dimly remembered from when they were teenagers, and about her crazy African husband he knew nothing at all. Forehead to forehead, Albie nodded. He still needed a place to sleep tonight.

Fodé smiled. "Good, good, good. Your sister needs her family. Calvin needs his uncle. And I could use a brother. I am very far away from home."

"Sure," Albie said.

"You can talk to me. That's what we do. You look around this house, your house, and you think things are busy." He shook his head. "I am very good at stopping. You say, 'Brother, stop, come and sit with me,' and here I am. You tell me what you need." Then Fodé stopped and looked at him again, his face so close it was difficult to focus. "Albie, what do you need?"

Albie thought about this. He leaned forward to spit his toothpaste into the sink. His head was about to split open. "Tylenol?"

At this small request Fodé beamed, his teeth, his glasses, his broad forehead, so many reflective surfaces for light. He reached across Albie and opened the medicine chest, pointing to the second shelf. "Tylenol," he said proudly. "Are you unwell?"

"Headache." His eyes did a quick inventory of what was available, which was pretty much the Tylenol and the pediatric Tylenol, eardrops, eyedrops, nosedrops.

Fodé filled the small yellow cup on the sink and handed it to him, the communal cup. "Soon you will sleep. That's what will help. You've had a long trip home."

Albie swallowed four pills and nodded, a nod which was also meant to cover thank you and goodnight. Fodé nodded solemnly in return and backed out of the bathroom, shutting the door behind him. Jeanette had told him where this friendliest of creatures had come from but damned if he could remember, Namibia, Nigeria, Ghana? Then it came to him.

It was Guinea.

Even with the additional incentive of Bintou, who, if she wasn't actually the second wife of his brother-in-law could probably be made while the baby was down for a nap, Albie could not sit in that apartment for the entire day. For one thing it was tropically hot. The radiator hissed and clanked like someone was beating it to death with a lead pipe down in the basement. Neither Bintou nor Dayo even flinched at the noise but it made Albie want to take off his skin. Small wonder Jeanette and Fodé left for work so early. A humidifier blew a steady mist through the tiny room, very possibly an attempt to re-create a sub-Saharan climate in this Brooklyn terrarium. "Good for the lungs," Bintou said, smiling when Albie got up to see if it could be turned off. The window that led to the fire escape was jammed and so he went down the four flights of stairs to smoke. The third time he went to smoke he carried his bike with him and rode away into the softly felted snow. By one o'clock he had a job as a bike messenger.

It was the work he found in every city, the only employment he felt that life had prepared him for. He couldn't even call himself an arsonist since he was now twenty-six and hadn't so much as set a fire in a fireplace since he was fourteen. When asked when he could start work he said now, and then went on to spend the day figuring out Manhattan. It wasn't a complicated place.

"I am so proud of you! And this means you will stay. Visitors don't get jobs on their first day in town. Houseguests don't get jobs. You are a resident now. One day here and you own the city."

Jeanette smiled at her brother, a small Jeanette smile, rolling her eyes slightly. *Africans*, she seemed to be saying. *What can you do?* She was still dressed in her own work clothes, a skirt and sweater. She had been in her second year of graduate school for biomedical engineering when she got pregnant. Jeanette, it turned out, was the smart one. She had explained to Albie the night before that instead of following her original plan to have an abortion, she and Fodé had decided to conduct a radical social experiment they called Having The Baby, and because of the outcome of that experiment, she had dropped out of school and now worked as a field service engineer for Philips. She did set-up, instruction, and service for MRI machines in hospitals stretching from Queens to the Bronx.

"I plug them in," she said flatly. "I show people the man-ual." She would have to continue to do so, she explained to Albie last night while making up his bed, despite the mind-less, soul-crushing nature of the work, at least until Fodé had finished his doctorate in public health at NYU and Dayo was of an age that it seemed bearable to send him to day care. *Dayo care*, they called it. "If I don't go back to school," she whispered while she tucked a sheet over the sofa cushions, "the radical social experiment will have failed because I'll have to kill myself."

Albie held the baby while Jeanette heated up the dinner Bintou had left for them. Fodé set the table and opened a bot-tle of wine, telling them the story of his day. "Americans love the idea of vaccinating Africans. What could be nicer than a photograph of dusty little Nigerian children lined up for inoculation on the front page of the *New York Times*? But for their own children the mothers of New York City find vaccinations passé. They say the vaccination is not sufficiently natural, that it could possibly cause something worse than it could prevent. I have spent the day trying to convince women with college educations to vaccinate their children and they argued with me. I must go to medical school. No one will listen to me if I am not a medical doctor."

"I'll listen to you," Jeanette said. "Don't go to medical school."

"One woman told me she did not believe in epidemiology." He covered his face with his hands. "It is appalling."

"Measles are no longer applicable in New York." Jeanette patted his shoulder. "We've transcended measles."

Jeanette washed the salad greens. Fodé wrapped the sliced bread in tinfoil and put it in the oven. They worked around one another in the tiny space, each one stepping out of the other's way.

"Tell me about *your* day instead," he said to her. "Let's think of something better."

"You want to think about MRI demonstrations in hospital basements?"

Fodé stopped for a moment, then smiled and shook his head. "No, no." He turned then to his brother-in-law, so pleased to have another opportunity. "What I meant to say is—Albie, please, tell us about your day."

Albie shifted the weight of his nephew in his arms. He spoke to the baby. "I was stopped by security guards in four buildings today. I showed my ID, was told I could go up, and then I was stopped by a second guard at the elevator who told me I couldn't go up."

Fodé nodded with appreciation. "This is most impressive for a white man."

"And I was almost hit by the M16 bus."

"Stop it," Jeanette said, putting a bowl of salad in the middle of the table. "No more about your day either."

"That leaves us with Dayo," Albie said.

Fodé took the baby from his arms. "Dayo. There is no one I would rather hear from. My son, tell us, was it a beautiful day to be alive?"

"Uncle," Dayo said, and held out his arms to go back.

Albie, who had lived close to the edge for so long, and at times had strayed past the edge, looked out the window to see the lights shining down from all those countless Brooklyn apartments. He wondered if this was what people were doing—were they making dinners with their family, holding babies, recounting days? Was this what life was like for them?

Albie's bicycle was an amalgamation of so many different replacement parts it could no longer rightfully be called a Schwinn. It was his job to deliver small packages and notarized insurance forms and promising manuscripts. Sometimes it was a contract and he was to wait for a signature before riding it back to where it had come from. Sometimes he was asked to sign as a witness. New York was the land of limitless deliveries. There was always someone who had something that needed to be someplace else, and so the day went on until he stopped it. He cut in front of buses and between taxis, startled drivers from Connecticut like the Goddamn Boy on a Bike he had once been. The tourists saw him bearing down on them and hung to the curb. When he arrived at his destination, he lifted his bike onto his shoulder like it was his younger brother and carried it with him into the elevator. While Albie was three inches taller than his father, he was only very tall and not extraordinarily tall. He was, however, extraordinarily thin, and the thinness gave him the illusion of additional height. Often the receptionists would blanch ever so slightly to see Albie approaching their desk with a manila envelope in his hand, the bicycle wearing a dent into his acromion. He was a living skeleton with his black tattoos and his thick black braid, like Death himself had come for them, ready to ride them out on his handlebars.

"You should consider upping your caloric intake," Jeanette said when he came limping back into the apartment in the evenings.

"Occupational hazard," he said. True and not true—he'd seen some fat messengers in his day.

Albie made money, and after a couple of months of thinking he would leave tomorrow or the next day, he started giving half of it to Jeanette for rent and coffee and wine and Dayo's education or her education. The other half he changed into hundreds and folded into the zipper compartment of his duffel. He had tried to give the money to Fodé first but Fodé wouldn't even look at it. The next day he waited for his sister at the subway station and gave it to her instead. Jeanette nodded and pushed the bills into her pocket.

"Don't you think we should go into therapy someday?" she said as they went past the yogurt shop, the shoe-repair place, the Korean markets with their buckets of daffodils out front. Maybe she thought he was giving her money for therapy. "Once we were on our feet psychologically we could patch Mom and Holly in on conference calls so they could be in therapy with us." Albie had told her he wasn't ready to call their mother yet, but Jeanette had called her. She called Teresa most days from work and told her everything.

"What about Dad?" Albie said. The street was crowded and he put his arm around her shoulder while they walked. He didn't know why. It wasn't anything he'd done before but it was nice. They had a similar gait.

"I bet Dad's been in therapy for years. I bet he's finished with therapy by now."

"Without ever conferencing us in?"

Jeanette shook her head. "It wouldn't have crossed his mind."

Albie had come to Brooklyn to get on his feet, and in certain respects he was on them now, except for the drinking, which he made possible by taking in limited amounts of alcohol with rigorous consistency, and the speedballs, which got him through the latter half of his days. Smoking didn't count. Bad habits were all a matter of perspective, and as long as the present was viewed through the lens of the past, anyone would say he was doing a spectacular job. He had saved enough money to find a place of his own but he never looked. Somehow, despite the nearly comical lack of space, Fodé and Jeanette made him feel like he should never go. Dayo wanted to hold on to his legs the minute he walked in the door, to stand with both of his feet on Albie's foot and wrap his arms around the muscled calf to hold himself up.

"Uncle" was his best word, perfectly enunciated. He could not say it enough. Albie liked the couch that was too short for him. He liked the days he would ride all the way home in the afternoon and tell Bintou she could take a few hours off while he took the baby to the park. He liked the feeling he didn't have a name for when he saw Fodé on the front steps waiting for him late at night with a beer. He would leave them eventually, but until he did he would bring home cold sesame noodles from Chinatown, he would fold up his blankets every morning and put them behind the couch, he would find reasons to stay out late several nights a week in order to ensure their privacy, and when he came home very late, he would turn his key in the lock so quietly that he would never wake them.

"Where were you last night?" Jeanette would ask, and Albie would think, *You missed me.*

At first Albie went to bars and to movies on his nights out but quickly saw that bars and movies in New York could eat a day's wages. He stayed at the library until the library closed, and then went to the Christian Science Reading Room until the Christian Science Reading Room closed, and then, depending on the quality of the book he was reading and the amount of speed still hopping him up, he went to the Laundromat that never closed and sat amid the dead moths and thumping dryers and the pervasive smell of dryer sheets. Because he had gotten to know the receptionists at the publishing houses where he delivered envelopes and asked them what they were reading, he always had books. There was no other place Albie delivered to or picked up from that ever gave him gifts, but the receptionists at publishing houses didn't mind giving a copy of a book to a bicycle messenger, even the bicycle messenger of death.

"Tell me what you think of that," one would say, and in return he would smile at her. Albie's smile was a dazzling thing, the wonders of his childhood orthodontia never what one would expect from the rest of the package. With that smile the receptionist felt that she had been given a gift in return.

One night after midnight in the early part of June, Albie was in a Laundromat in Williamsburg. The taxis still rushed by but they were quieter. The people on the street were quieter. Albie was reading the novel he had started the day before, and in reading it he'd lost track of time. It was considerably better than the usual fare of detective stories and thrillers he read, because the receptionist at Viking tended to give him better books. She didn't just give him what had come out that week either, though sometimes she gave him those too. She'd given him a copy of *David Copperfield* once and said she thought he'd like it, just like that, like he was the sort of person someone would look at and think of Dickens, and so he read it. It was a book he was supposed to read for school the year he was in Virginia. He had carried it around with him for a month, just like all the other kids in his class carried *David Copperfield* around, but he'd never cracked it. "If I'd known you when I lived in Virginia," he told the receptionist after he'd finished it, "I might have passed the class."

"You're from Virginia?" she asked. Maybe she was his mother's age, maybe a little younger, and she was smart, he could tell that. These conversations never lasted more than two or three minutes but he liked her. Albie had places to go and the telephone at her desk never stopped ringing. She picked it up and asked the person if she could put them on hold, which she did without waiting for an answer.

"Not from there," he said. "I just lived there for a while when I was a kid."

"Stay right here," she said. "One second." When she came back she gave him a paperback called *Commonwealth*. "It was a very big deal last year, won the National Book Award, sold through the roof. Do you know it?"

Albie shook his head. Last year he was still in San Francisco, the money from messengering then going to heroin. A meteor could have taken out the Eastern Seaboard and he wouldn't have known about it.

She turned the book over and tapped the tiny photograph of the man on the back. "It was the first book he'd written in fifteen years, maybe more than that. Everybody here had given up on him." The phone rang. All the hold lights were blinking now. It was time to go back to work. She handed him the book and waved goodbye. He gave his head a small bow, smiling at her before he left.

In retrospect he would say that he knew right from the beginning, maybe the middle of the first chapter, that there was something going on, though everything is clear in retrospect. The nearer truth was that the book had taken hold of him long before he saw himself in it. That was the part that seemed so crazy, how much he had loved the book before he knew what it was about.

It was about two sets of neighbors in Virginia. One couple has been in their house a long time, the other couple has

just moved in. They share a driveway. They get along well.
They can borrow things from one another, watch each other's kids. They sit on each other's decks at night and drink
and talk about politics. One of the husbands is a politician.
The children—there are six of them altogether—wander in
and out of each other's houses, the girls sleep in one another's beds. It was easy enough to see where things were going
except that it wasn't so much about the miserable affair. It
was about the inestimable burden of their lives: the work,
the houses, the friendships, the marriages, the children, as
if all the things they'd wanted and worked for had cemented
the impossibility of any sort of happiness. The children, who
seem only to be atmospheric and charming at first, are more
like a ball of snakes. The oldest and the youngest are boys
and there are four girls between them. Two girls in the politician's house, two girls and two boys for the doctor whom the
politician is in love with. An extra husband, an extra wife.
The youngest child, a son, is unbearable. Maybe that's the
real problem. He is emblematic of what can never be overcome. The lovers, with their marriages and houses and jobs,
employ any trick to find a moment away together, but what
they're really trying to get away from is the children, and that
youngest son in particular. The children, who are so often
stuck with the youngest one, give him Benadryl in order to
ditch him. The older son carries it in his pocket because he's
allergic to bee stings. They feed the little boy Benadryl and
stuff him in the laundry basket under a pile of sheets so they
can ride their bikes to the swimming pool in town unencumbered. Isn't that what everyone wants, just for a moment to
be unencumbered?

Albie put his thumb on the page and closed the book on top of it. The Laundromat was quite suddenly cold. There were two young punks, the boy with his hair spiked out with glue, the girl with two safety pins through her nose. They sat and smoked while their black laundry made circles in the washer. The girl gave Albie half a smile, thinking maybe he was one of them.

Did he know it was Benadryl? They called them Tic Tacs but did he know? He woke up under the bed, in a field, in the car, on the couch covered over in blankets. He woke up on the floor of the laundry room in Virginia, buried in sheets. He never knew why he woke up in places he didn't remember going to sleep in. "Because you're the baby," Holly said. "Babies need more sleep."

His hands were cold. He put the book back in his messenger bag and walked his bike out onto the street, hearing the *tick-tick* of his spokes, the little punks watching him, thinking he was leaving without his laundry. He knew the next part in the book, the part he hadn't read, how the older son called Patrick would die, how the younger son had been given all the pills so that when they were needed there would be nothing. He knew that wasn't even what the book was about.

Albie walked his bike down the street. Did he see himself in the Danish detective novels? In the postapocalyptic thrillers? Was there any chance the problem was that he put himself in the center of everything?

That wasn't the problem.

When he got back to the apartment it was almost two o'clock in the morning. He went into their bedroom and stood at the foot of the bed, Jeanette and Fodé and Dayo all sound asleep. Maybe their subconscious minds had accepted that he lived there now and so no longer heard the sound of his footsteps, or maybe they were so dead tired at the end of their day that anyone could be standing in their bedroom now and they'd sleep right through it. Even with the shades down there was light in the room. That was New York. Nothing was ever really dark. Dayo was in the bed with them, between them, sleeping on his back. Jeanette had her hand on his chest. It was almost unbearable to watch other people sleep. Had she told Fodé what had happened? She would have told him she had a brother who died but what did he know beyond that? Albie had told no one. Not the boys on the bikes or the messengers he had coffee with in the mornings or Elsa in San Francisco with whom he had shared a needle. He had never mentioned Cal. Albie covered his sister's foot with his hand, her foot and then a sheet, a blanket, a bedspread. He squeezed her foot and in her sleep she tried to pull away but he held on until she opened her eyes. No one wants to wake up to see a man in their bedroom. Jeanette made a noise that was small and choked, a sound of pure fear that broke her brother's heart. Her husband, her son, they slept right through it.

"It's me," Albie whispered. "Get up." He pointed to the bedroom door and then went out into the living room to wait for her.

6

Leo Posen had taken a house in Amagansett for the summer. There was no view of the ocean, a person would have to write an entirely different kind of book in order to afford an ocean view, but it was a beautiful house with wide halls and sunny rooms, a porch swing the size of a daybed, a kitchen with an enormous table that looked like it had been pegged together by Pilgrims to celebrate a later, more prosperous Thanksgiving. The house belonged to an actress who was shooting a movie in Poland for the summer, and summer was the only time she used it. The real estate broker had made it clear that this property was never rented, but the actress was a great admirer of Leo's. In fact, she was hoping for a part in the movie of *Commonwealth*. She wanted to play the doctor who was having the affair, and hoped that Leo, surrounded by her pretty things, her pictures, would think of her.

In the spirit of full disclosure, Leo told the broker there was no movie deal.

The broker was stopped by this. Even she, who knew next to nothing about the movie business, knew that the rights should have been snapped up before publication. For the briefest instant she wondered if the option for *Commonwealth* was something she herself could acquire. "Don't worry about that," the broker said. "When they do make the movie she's still going to want the part."

Leo had rented the house in hopes that he would spend the summer working on a new novel, the one his literary agent had sold to his publisher without so much as an outline while *Commonwealth* was ringing the slot machines. He had also rented the house in hopes of pleasing Franny. He'd told her she wouldn't have to do anything but lie on the big down sofa in the front room and read all day, or she could ride her bike to the beach and read. "Sand, waves, beach roses," he said, picking up a strand of her fascinating hair and letting it fall between his fingers. At night after dinner they would sit together on the porch and he would read her everything he'd written that day. "That doesn't sound like such a bad vacation."

But it was a bad vacation. The problem, they realized much too late, was the glorious house itself, which sat atop a hill to catch the afternoon breeze while a great hedge surrounded the property for privacy. The fruit trees scattered over the wide lawn had been late to bloom because of the long, hard winter, so that even now in early June the cherry trees were weighted with dark pink blossoms. The jumbled flower beds that spoke of glorious disarray were tended by a gardener who came on Wednesdays, the same day a Peruvian man with a skimmer net came to remove the cherry blossoms from the swimming pool. There were five bedrooms with variations on the sloping-ceiling-dormer-window theme: window seats, puffy comforters, hand-braided rugs over floors of quarter-sawn oak. Leo Posen had told the broker that he was looking for something considerably smaller but she dismissed the idea. "Smaller will still be more expensive because of the deal you're getting," she told him. "You cannot imagine what this house would cost you if you were renting at fair market value. If you don't want to use the extra rooms I suggest you close the doors."

That might have solved the problem were it not for the fact that nature abhors an empty bedroom in summer in Amagansett, especially when those rooms are owned by an actress and rented by a novelist. People wanted to visit. Eric, his editor, who should have been the one to hire a sentry to patrol the property line with a gun, was the first to call and say how nice it would be to get together outside of the city and talk over Leo's ideas for the new book. Eric could come out Thursday, beating the rush, but Marisol, his wife, had an opening she needed to go to that night. He supposed that Marisol would have to brave the Jitney on Friday.

Marisol? Leo stumbled for an instant but then agreed pleasantly to everything—yes, yes, a great time would be had by all. He hung up the phone and looked at the yellow legal pad in front of him, then he looked out the window. It was raining, and for a while he sat and admired the cherry trees, wondering if anyone had ever made a legal pad out of a cherry tree. Then he went downstairs to see if Franny thought they should drive into town for lunch.

"It's good that Eric's coming," Leo said to Franny. The rain was light and they sat outside under an awning at the café where they'd had lunch three days in a row. It was extremely pleasant. "I can ask him about finding you a job. You're a terrific editor, you know, better than he'll ever be, not that I'd mention that."

Franny shook her head. "Don't ask him."

The waitress came by and Leo touched the rim of his empty wineglass. It was after two o'clock, a very late lunch. "If I don't ask him he'll figure it out himself. I might just mention that you're looking for something. Or maybe I'll mention it to Marisol."

"Eric knows me," she said. "If he wants to hire me he knows where I am." Of course, Eric had probably noticed that Leo and Franny didn't live in New York, and in fact didn't live anywhere for more than four months at a time, which would make taking on a regular job difficult. Anyway, Franny wasn't sure she wanted to be an editor.

"Eric knows you from dinner parties. He hasn't gotten to spend any real time with you. That's why this is going to work out so well."

When Eric came on Thursday afternoon he said he'd rather stay in for dinner. He'd been out every night that week, and anyway it would be so much easier to talk at the house. Eric was in every sense a wiry man, a runner with a small frame who must have once been told that blue complemented his eyes. Franny had never seen Eric in anything other than blue. He looked up the staircase, touching the banister with affection.

Leo looked at Franny. "That would be all right, wouldn't it?"

She should have seen it right then but she didn't. She was thinking in terms of one dinner, one night. Franny went into the kitchen and called Jerrell at the Palmer House to ask him how to cook steaks. He would just be at the beginning of his shift now. He would be chopping parsley.

"Little House," he said. "Get the fuck back here. You know can't nobody else fill my cup."

She laughed. "I'm going to give up my summer to go get your lemonade at the bar? Be a friend and help me here."

Jerrell was standing in the manager's office and the manager was staring at him. The cooks never got calls. He told her to rub a little bit of Old Bay on the meat and let it sit. "I mean a *little* bit. That shit is not for steaks." Then he walked her through the basics of asparagus and baked potatoes. "You buy the salad and a cake. Somebody out there's got money. Don't you go doing everything yourself."

Franny went to the grocery store, the butcher's, the bakery. She went to the liquor store and picked out the wines, stocked up on scotch and gin. When she got back to the house she unloaded the car. Leo and Eric had begged off the trip to town, saying they were going to talk about the novel first, get business out of the way. She could hear them laughing out on the screened porch on the side of the house where Leo had decided it would be all right to smoke. Great, raucous laughter. Franny carried out two glasses of ice and a bottle of Macallan to be friendly. She was wearing her beach clothes: cut-off shorts and flip-flops, a plain white T-shirt. She was twenty-nine years old. They were playing house. She was playing hostess.

"Eric, will you look at this girl?" Leo said from his chair, putting his arm around her hips and pulling her towards him. "Is she a dream?"

"A dream," Eric said, and then asked Franny if he could have a tall glass of Pellegrino or Perrier with ice.

Franny nodded, glad that she'd thought to buy seltzer. She went back to the kitchen. They were talking about Chekhov, not the novel. Eric was wondering whether there was a market for a new translation, a series of ten volumes, all of it. She wondered which of the stories had struck them as funny.

As a feminist, Franny had to ask herself why it was she'd made dinner for Leo and Eric on Thursday night without ever expecting that they would offer to help her, but that when Marisol came out from the city the next day in her embroidered linen tunic and red linen scarf, and sat down on the screened-in porch and said what she could really use was a glass of white wine, a nice chablis if they had it, Franny felt a little ping, like someone had just shot her in the neck with a rubber band. She *had* asked Marisol what she could get for her, and Marisol, digging in her purse to find her own cigarettes, so thrilled to see that someone else was smoking, had answered. What was the problem with that?

"This place is gorgeous!" Marisol said, smiling as she took the glass from Franny's hand. "But then I've never known anyone as lucky as Leo."

For much the same reason as the night before, it was decided that they wouldn't go out for dinner that night either. Marisol gestured in the direction of the cherry trees. "Leave this place and go into town? Have dinner with all those people from the Jitney? Not on your life." Marisol managed an art gallery in SoHo. The thought of staying in the actress's house, listening to the actress's crickets, was enchanting.

Franny kept her face neutral but Leo was able to catch just a flicker of the problem. He clapped his hands in a single burst of good cheer. "We can do the exact same thing we did last night. Last night's dinner was perfect. We'll have it again. That shouldn't be any problem, do you think?" he said to Franny.

"Marisol doesn't eat meat," Eric said, using his nicest smile. Eric and Marisol were more or less Leo's age, in the general camp of just past sixty. They had a son who was completing his residency in dermatology at Johns Hopkins and a daughter who was home with a baby.

"Fish," Marisol said, holding up her hand in a Girl Scout pledge. "I'm really a vegetarian but I'll eat fish socially."

They looked at Franny, all innocence and expectation, the three of them nestled into the soft ivory cushions that covered the wicker chairs. She couldn't call Jerrell again. He'd just tell her she was a fucking idiot. For fish she'd have to call her mother. "Anything else?" Franny asked.

Eric nodded. "Something crunchy? Some nuts or little crackers, maybe a mix?"

"Bar snacks," Franny said, and went to the kitchen to find her keys.

This was not the way things went between Leo and Franny. Their relationship, which had been going on five years, was built on admiration and mutual disbelief. After all this time he could not believe that she was with him: not only was she young (not just younger but categorically *young*) and more beautiful than he had any right to deserve at this point, but she was the cable on which he had pulled himself hand over hand back into his work: she was the electricity, the spark. Franny Keating was *life*. For her part, Franny could say the name *Leon Posen*, like she was saying *Anton Chekhov*, and find him there in the bed beside her. It did not cease to be astonishing with time. And more than that, he had found her life meaningful when she could make no sense of it at all.

Which was not to say they were without problems: there was the future, always unknowable but, realistically speaking, doomed at some point by the thirty-two-year spread in their ages, and the past, because Leo was still technically married. His wife in Los Angeles was holding out for a cut of future royalties, a touchingly optimistic demand considering how long it had been since he'd published a book. Leo flatly refused to give up any piece of work he had not yet written. Then he had published a best seller that came with a sizable advance which had already earned out, prize money, and extensive foreign sales. As they entered into the new phase of royalty checks, his wife confirmed her belief to her lawyer that she had been right to dig in her heels.

Leo should have been rich at this point but he had to keep accepting prestigious visiting-author positions at various well-heeled institutions just to make ends meet, and these positions made it nearly impossible for him to work on his new book. Yes, there was a tremendous amount of money but it flowed from a single river and into countless tributaries. He already had one ex-wife, truly divorced and behind him, to whom he paid a significant alimony, as well as payments to the wife who should have been his second ex-wife. She cost him a fortune. His daughter from the first marriage always needed money because she needed so much more than money but money was the easiest way for her to express those needs, and then there were two sons from the second marriage who refused to speak to him at all—one a sophomore at Kenyon and the other a junior at Harvard-Westlake in Los Angeles. Their tuition, along with their every wish, was Leo's command.

Franny knew it was past time for her to figure out her life but Leo clung to her like a child to a blanket, and honestly, it was a wonderful thing to be needed by the person she most admired, to be told she was indispensable. It was infinitely preferable to applying to graduate schools when she didn't know what she wanted to study, and so she tended to go with him, showing up in pretty dresses to faculty dinners at Stanford or Yale. Sometimes she would go back and work at the Palmer House for a couple of months, living in the apartment they kept on North Lake Shore Drive. Leo made the payments on her loans so she was safe, but she missed making money of her own. Anyway, it was good to see her friends. The Palmer House would always take her in.

"This is madness," he would say to her over the phone, too many drinks past the point at which he should have been calling. "I'm here by myself so that you can be a waitress? Go to the airport, please, tonight, first thing in the morning, just get on a plane. I'll send you a ticket." It was something of a joke between them, him sending her a ticket, though in this case he wasn't joking.

"You're going to be fine." Franny made a point not to say anything that mattered in conversations like these. Tomorrow he wouldn't remember a word of it. "And this is good for me. I need to work every now and then."

"You *have* worked! You have consistently inspired me when the entire world failed at the job. I'll give you a salary. I'll write you a check. It's your fucking book, Franny. It's you."

Of course, when he was writing the book he said that wasn't the case. He said that what she had told him was nothing but the jumping-off point for his imagination. It wasn't her family. No one would see them there.

But there they were.

Other than the difference in their ages, and the fact he had an estranged wife, and had written a novel about her family which in its final form made her want to retch even though she had found it nothing less than thrilling when he was working on it, Franny and Leo were great. And it wasn't as if she begrudged him the novel, it was a brilliant novel, it was the brilliant work of Leon Posen which she had brought down on herself.

But as long as anyone was making a list, there was one other problem that deserved mention, even if Franny refused to acknowledge it as a problem: Franny didn't drink. Leo felt her abstinence as a judgment no matter how lightly she passed it off. He noticed it when they were with friends, and he noticed it when she went around to the driver's side of the car after lunch in town because he'd had three lousy glasses of pinot gris. He noticed it when he was alone, when she was on the other side of the country. What she had told him was that she had been in an accident a long time ago, that she had caused the accident because she'd been drinking, and so she stopped drinking. He brought this up again on several occasions but he always felt like he was talking to the part of her that had gone to law school. Franny, he believed, was missing out on a great opportunity by not going back to finish her education.

He would begin: "Did you kill anyone in this car accident?"

"I did not."

"Injure anyone? Run over a dog?"

"Nope."

"Were you hurt?"

She gave him a deep sigh and closed the book she was reading, *The Radetzky March* by Joseph Roth. He had recommended it to her. "Could you give me a pass on this?"

"Are you an alcoholic?"

Franny shrugged. "Not that I know of. Probably not."

"Then why won't you just have a drink, keep me company. You could have a drink in the house. I'm not going to ask you to drive the car."

She leaned over and kissed him then, as kissing was her best means of ending arguments. "Put your big brain to it," she said kindly. "You can think of something better to fight about."

Franny went into the kitchen and called her mother in Virginia. "Fish for dinner," she said, "four people, something I can't screw up."

"Can't you go out?" her mother asked.

"It's not looking that way. It turns out this house is the Hotel California. People walk in the door and they don't want to leave again. I'd probably feel the same way if I wasn't the one doing the cooking."

"You, cooking," her mother said.

"I know."

"Have you looked in her closet?"

Franny laughed out loud. Her mother could go right to the heart of the matter. "Etro bikinis, a fleet of little silk slip dresses, lots of long cashmere sweaters, featherweight, shoes like you have never seen shoes. She must be the size of an eyedropper. You can't believe how tiny everything is."

"What size are the shoes?"

"Sevens." Franny had tried to push her foot into a sandal, Cinderella's ungainly stepsister.

"If I came up I could help you cook," her mother said.

Franny smiled, sighed. Her mother had tiny feet. "No more company. Company's the problem right now."

"I'm not company. I'm your mother." She said it lightly.

For a minute Franny thought how nice it would be, her mother on the other end of the sofa reading books. For the most part Franny went home alone to Virginia, or her mother came to visit when Franny was in Chicago working at the bar. The few times Leo and her mother had been together they were cool and polite. Her mother was younger than Leo. She had read *Commonwealth*, and while she was glad she got to be a doctor, she would have been gladder still to have been left out altogether. Beverly didn't believe that Leo Posen had her daughter's best interest at heart. She had told him that once when she and Leo were drinking. Franny's mother was not what they needed to complete their summer vacation.

"Please," Franny said. "Just help me with the fish."

Her mother put the phone down so she could go and get her recipe for seafood chowder. "If you follow my instructions as you have never followed my instructions even once in your life you will be a tremendous success."

And oh, but her mother was right. They raved and praised. Eric and Marisol said they couldn't have had a better meal in Manhattan. Franny's mother had worked everything out, the salad with nectarines, which brand of cheese biscuits to buy, Franny was as impressed as her guests. But Leo again had failed to go to the grocery store with her, and none of them came into the kitchen to ask if they could chop the bell peppers, and when she came out to the porch to tell them dinner was ready, Eric, in the middle of another funny Chekhov story, had held up his hand so that she would know to wait until he was finished, but it took him nearly fifteen minutes to finish, and Franny could not help but think of the shrimp that were only supposed to simmer three minutes. By the end of the meal the guests were tremendously grateful, really, they couldn't have been nicer, and Eric made a show of rolling up the sleeves of his blue linen shirt before he picked up the plates and put them in the sink, but that was it.

Leo's agent, Astrid, called the house on Saturday morning. Her secretary had called Eric's office the day before on a matter having nothing to do with Leo and was told in the course of the conversation that Eric was at Leo's place in Amagansett. Astrid had a house in Sag Harbor. She came out every Thursday night in the summer and went back Monday mornings. Did they really think they weren't going to see her? Astrid said they were coming to Amagansett that afternoon. "They" included one of her authors, a young man of exceeding promise who was spending two weeks at her place while he nailed down a few last revisions.

"I'll give you the address," Leo said with some resignation.

"Don't be silly," she said. "Everyone knows the house."

"Astrid?" Eric's face arranged into an expression of mild despair. He was working the crossword puzzle from the Saturday paper. He hadn't shaved and didn't want to shave.

"She didn't ask," Leo said, though Leo liked Astrid. The very fact that Eric didn't like her was proof that she was doing her job.

"There goes lunch," Eric said.

Marisol came down the stairs in a red swimsuit and a wide-brimmed hat. "I'm going to the pool," she said.

"Astrid's coming," Eric said.

Marisol stopped and put on her sunglasses. "Well, she lives in Sag Harbor. It's not like she's going to stay over."

Franny drove to Bridgehampton and bought lunch at a ridiculously expensive gourmet shop that sold prepared foods, put the food in the car, and then, struck by the clear and sudden understanding that no one would be leaving, walked straight back in and bought dinner. Leo had given her his credit card. The total for the two meals came to an unspeakable fortune. By the time she got back to the house Astrid was there with a pale young writer named Jonas who had shiny black hair and yellow linen pants. He ate twice as much as the rest of them put together. Franny realized sadly there would be no leftovers for tomorrow's lunch.

"Why reprint Chekhov?" the young writer said to Eric, taking both the herbed chicken breast and the lemon-poached salmon to his plate. "Why not have the courage to publish some young Russian writers instead?"

"Maybe because I don't work at a publishing house in Russia." Eric poured himself a glass of wine and then topped off Marisol's glass. "Oh, and I don't speak Russian."

"Jonas speaks Russian," Astrid said, the proud mother.

"*Konechno*," Jonas said.

Astrid nodded. "He's very involved with the refuseniks."

"There *are* no refuseniks," Leo said. "They opened up the gate and let them out in the seventies."

"The refuseniks were my field of study," Jonas said. "And believe me, there are still plenty of oppressed Jews in Russia."

"So shouldn't I be publishing some young Russian writing about the refuseniks instead of an American who's studied them? Wouldn't that show more courage?"

"You don't publish me."

Eric smiled at so pleasing a thought. "Let's call it a draw, shall we? Chekhov is my field of study, the refuseniks are yours. We're both old news."

"Is that couscous?" Marisol asked Franny, pointing at the salad with the cucumbers and tomatoes.

"Israeli," Franny said, passing the dish. "It's just bigger."

Franny's premonition in the gourmet shop proved to be correct. Come dinner, Leo and the guests were still lounging on various sofas throughout the house. Jonas appeared to be working on a manuscript, or at least he had a stack of paper in his lap, a pencil between his teeth. It was odd to think he'd brought a manuscript to lunch. Eric came in from the pool and allowed that while the idea of more food had seemed impossible just two short hours ago, he thought he might be getting hungry again. At the very least he needed a drink.

Leo looked up and smiled. "Now there's a thought."

After a very long evening, in which Franny didn't have to cook but did need to heat and plate and serve, after the consumption of an extraordinary amount of wine and then the raiding of the actress's Calvados and Sauternes for after-dinner drinks ("Franny, make a note of what we're stealing," Leo said, rifling through the rack in the pantry. "I want to remember to replace it.") when everyone had wandered back out to the side porch to smoke, Franny was left with a dining room that looked like Bacchus had thrown a bash. She drew in her breath and began to stack plates.

The tall young novelist followed her to the kitchen. For a minute she thought he was interested in helping before realizing that he was in fact just interested. He was wearing glasses now, though she didn't remember him wearing them earlier when he was reading.

"My contract is with Knopf," he told her, picking up a wineglass and holding it in a dish towel. "*Entre nous*, I was hoping for FSG. Ever since I was in college I've wanted to be published by FSG, but"—he shrugged at Franny and leaned against the sink—"you know."

"They didn't want the book?" she asked.

Jonas looked hurt. "Money," he said. "Everyone knows FSG never has real money."

Franny was rinsing the plates when Leo came in. "There you are!" he called to the young novelist. His arms were wide open and he was holding a highball glass in one hand. "I've been wanting to show you a tree." He could bellow sometimes when he was drinking, and Franny wondered, with all the windows open, if the neighbors could hear him.

"A tree?" Jonas said. His glasses were lightly steamed from his proximity to the sink.

Leo put his arm around the young man's shoulder and led him away. "Come and see it. There's a beautiful night sky."

"Really, Leo?" Franny called after them. "A tree? That's the best you can come up with?"

Astrid didn't spend the night but somehow the young writer did. Jonas said he was prone to car sickness if he'd been drinking and certainly he'd been drinking. He looked around the house and declared the entire situation straight-up Fitzgerald, so much so that sleeping over would have to be part of it. Astrid, who would have stayed herself had an invitation been extended, volunteered to drive back for him tomorrow around lunch.

When the last of the actress's Danish china had been returned to the glass-fronted cabinets and the zinc counter-tops had been wiped down and the trash taken out, Franny stopped to survey her good work. The houseguests had pro-vided her with three days' hard labor, but it was a kind of labor she was used to. Not the cooking maybe, but the refill-ing of glasses and the emptying of ashtrays, the straightening and fetching, the quiet audience to conversation. Tomorrow was Sunday and on Sunday it would be over. Franny felt proud of herself: she'd been a good sport. Leo would be grate-ful for all the many kindnesses she'd shown his friends.

After a hungover breakfast in which everyone who re-quested eggs requested them cooked a different way, Leo an-nounced that he had to work. He put his legal pad and pens and scotch and two volumes of Chekhov (Eric had convinced him to write the introduction to the new edition, though, of course, not until his own novel was finished) in a canvas tote bag and walked across the lawn to the tiny one-room cottage at the back of the property. With its little desk and single bed and overstuffed chair, its ottoman and floor lamp, it was easy to imagine that the place had been built for exactly this purpose: not to write, because Leo was not writing, but to get away from the hordes of moths that had been drawn to the house's magnificent flame.

"It's good that he's working," Eric said to Franny. He was holding his coffee cup with both hands, looking wistfully in the direction where Leo had disappeared, the way a woman standing on the beach will look at the place on the horizon where the whaling vessel had disappeared. "We've got to encourage him, make sure he keeps at it. He can't lose his momentum again."

Franny didn't mention that there was no momentum because there was no book. She wondered what Leo had told him. "He will," she said vaguely, "once everything settles down and gets quiet." Could she ask him what Jitney he was planning to take back to the city? She looked at Eric, his gray hair long and curling, his glasses pushed to the top of his head. "Let me know about the Jitney," she said. "I'll drive you down. There can be a line on Sunday if you wait too long."

Marisol shook her head. "Friday was enough for me. I can't even imagine Sunday." She looked at her husband. "When are you going back?"

Eric tilted his head back and forth as if he were trying to calculate a tip. "Tuesday? Maybe Tuesday. I'll have to check and see."

Marisol nodded and pulled the style section out of the

paper. "Well, I get an extra day. I came out a day later than you did."

Jonas arrived in the kitchen wearing green swim trunks and a T-shirt. "Can I just have coffee for now?" he said, squinting against the morning light. "I'm going for a swim."

Franny had so much to say, but in that exact moment she was distracted by the writer's swim trunks, stunned by them. "Where did you get swim trunks?"

Jonas looked down at himself. "These? I don't remember. REI?" In the T-shirt, in the bright light, he looked no more than twenty.

"They're yours? You brought them here?"

They were all looking at her now.

"I brought them here," he said. He plucked at the fabric with two fingers. "Are they okay?"

"You brought extra clothes?"

He caught her line of questioning and came back at his hostess with an ill-prepared defense. "I get carsick. And I don't like to ride in cars at night. Astrid said it was a big house."

Franny had been at the market when they arrived. She hadn't seen him come in with a suitcase. She would need to wash the sheets in his bedroom unless he wasn't planning to leave. The phone started to ring and Jonas, in a gesture of independence, poured his own coffee and went out the back door.

"I want to talk to my father," the voice on the phone said.

"Ariel?"

There was no answer, because the answer would be that Leo had three children and two of them were boys and only the girl was speaking to him these days, so if a woman called asking for her father, then, yes, it was going to be Ariel.

"Hold on a minute," Franny said. "He's out in the back. I'll have to get him."

Eric gave her a look to inquire as to the nature of Ariel's call but Franny ignored him. She crossed through the wet grass, beneath the cherry trees and past the pool where Jonas was already lying shirtless on the diving board, the cup of coffee beside his head. When she got to the cabin door she didn't knock.

"Ariel's on the phone," she said.

Leo was stretched across the single bed with a volume of Chekhov in his hands. He looked up at Franny and smiled. "Would you tell her I'm working? Tell her I'll call her back."

"Not on your life," Franny said.

"I can't talk to her now."

"Well, neither can I, so I suggest you go down to the kitchen and hang up the phone."

She walked out of the cabin and to the back of the property. She knew where there was a break in the hedge and she took it: through the neighbor's yard, down their driveway, and out onto the street, her flip-flops slapping against her feet. She wished she had her bicycle, a hat, some money, and at the same time she wished for nothing in the world but to be alone. Franny couldn't help but believe that she had brought every discomfort she experienced down on herself. Had she done something with her life no one would be asking her to make them cappuccino, and had she done something with her life she would be perfectly happy to make them cappuccino, because it would not be her job. She would make the coffee because she was a gracious and helpful person. She could feel good about being kind without continually wondering if she were anything more than a nice-enough-looking waitress. She wished, as she approached thirty, that she had figured out how to be more than a muse, or, as her father had put it the last time she had seen him in Los Angeles, "Being a mistress isn't a job."

Her father hadn't read *Commonwealth* but her sister had.

"There's nothing particularly libelous about it," Caroline said to Franny. "He's covered his tracks."

"I'm grateful that you don't review for the *Times*."

"I'll put it another way: I didn't enjoy it but I'm not going to sue him."

"You're hardly even in the book."

Caroline laughed. "Maybe that's what irritated me about it. Anyway, if I was going to sue I'd make it a class-action case, get the whole family involved."

"Well," Franny said, "that would be one way to get us all together again."

It was funny how much Franny missed Caroline now. For as much as they'd hated each other growing up, a peculiar fondness had crept in somewhere along the way. Franny and Caroline knew all the same stories. Caroline practiced patent law in Silicon Valley. There was nothing harder than that. She was married to a software designer named Wharton. Wharton was his last name but no one ever called him anything else because his first name was Eugene. Franny believed that Wharton had softened her sister up. He made Caroline laugh. Franny had no memory of her sister ever laughing about anything when they were growing up, at least never in front of her. Caroline and Wharton had a baby named Nick.

Franny got to spend a lot of time with Caroline the semester Leo was teaching at Stanford. Caroline still badgered her about going back to law school, and Franny was able to believe that the badgering came from a place of affection.

"Believe me," Caroline said, "I know school is miserable. I even know that practicing law can be miserable. But sooner or later you have to do *something*. If you think you're going to find one thing that will be perfect for you, you're going to spend your eightieth birthday reading the want ads."

"You sound like you're trying to talk me into a bad marriage."

"But it doesn't have to be a bad marriage. Why can't you see that? Get a law degree and go fight housing discrimination, or go get a job for a publisher and write book contracts for authors."

Franny smiled and shook her head. "I'll figure it out," was what she had said to her sister.

But she hadn't figured it out, and now she was in Amagansett walking through town in order to avoid the man she loved and his friends. Franny looked in shop windows, and when she saw a newspaper on a bench she sat down and read the entire thing. The light was so soft, so honeyed, that she could almost forgive her houseguests for wanting to stay. She waited until she was sure it was too late for anyone to ask her to make them lunch. She passed the restaurant she and Leo liked, hoping that by some chance she would see him there. Finally she decided to go back. There was nothing else to do.

She had planned to sneak up to the bedroom undetected, but they saw her from the side porch and waved.

"Franny, what a day we've had without you!" Leo said, as if there had been nothing strange about her leaving or her return.

Astrid, back from Sag Harbor, nodded. "I had to bring the sandwiches for lunch. There's still some sorbet."

"And Eric and I went into town and bought things for dinner," Marisol said.

"Someone's still going to have to go back into town," Eric said. "We didn't get enough."

Franny looked at them up on the porch, everyone softened by the veil of the screen, by the light that was slanting in behind them, by the bank of yellow lilies that separated them from her. It was not unlike seeing tigers at the zoo.

"Hollinger called," Leo said. "He's driving in from the city with Ellen. They should be here in an hour or so."

"Hollinger?" Astrid said. "You didn't tell me that. How did he know where you were?" John Hollinger was not Astrid's client. His novel *The Seventh Story* had beaten out *Commonwealth* for the Pulitzer, and both men made a great show of how this fact had not affected their friendship, even though they hadn't exactly been friends in the first place.

Marisol gave a single, dismissive wave. "It won't be an hour. He's always late."

There was a time when Franny would have been overwhelmed by the thought of John Hollinger coming for dinner, but that time had passed. Now he and his wife represented nothing more than two extra place settings at the table. This brought them up to eight, assuming that Jonas and Astrid would never leave.

"What about you?" Eric said, glancing down at Franny as if finally remembering she'd been gone. "Nice day?"

Franny shaded her eyes with her hand and looked up at him, puzzled. "Sure," she said. That was all they needed to release her from the conversation.

There were six cardboard boxes on the long wooden table in the kitchen, a half a dozen ears of corn still in their green sleeves. She heard the sound of scratching, and then one of the boxes jerked abruptly forward.

Leo came into the kitchen and stood behind her. "I'm sorry about Hollinger," he said, kissing the side of her head. "He wasn't asking. He called to announce his impending arrival. We should have rented a motel room in the middle of Kansas for the summer."

"They would have found us."

"I spent the day hiding in the cabin so that everyone would think I was writing a novel. Where did you go?"

"What's in the boxes?" Franny said, though of course she knew exactly what was in the boxes.

"Marisol thought it would be fun to have lobster."

Franny turned and looked at him. "She said she was a vegetarian. Does she know how to cook them?"

"I don't think it's a science. You just drop them in water. Listen," he said, putting his hands on her shoulders and looking at her straight on in a way that made him appear very brave. "I have to tell you this and I'd rather not: Ariel is coming out for a couple of days."

Many things were possible but Franny and Ariel in the same house was not one of them. For Ariel's sake Franny stayed out of the entire neighborhood surrounding Gramercy Park when she went to New York. It was the single way they respected one another: they did not overlap. "She wouldn't come out when she knows I'm here," Franny said. "I answered the phone."

"I think she really just wants to see the house. I made the mistake of telling her about it months ago. I didn't think we were going to rent it then. She said she needs a vacation."

Franny was distracted by the scratching. The boxes, she could see now, were shuffling across the table in microscopic increments. The thought of each separate lobster in the dark was every bit as excruciating as the thought of Ariel Posen coming to Amagansett, either that or she was experiencing some sort of emotional transference. Leo followed her gaze to the table.

"I should have been a pair of ragged claws," he said, looking at the sad containers trying to get away. "Scuttling across the floors of silent seas."

"Leo, she hates me. That's been made clear."

Leo mustered the energy for a wan smile. "Well, maybe this is the summer she stops hating you and we all get along. It's got to happen sooner or later."

"When?" Franny asked. Not *When will she stop hating me?*—Franny knew the answer to that one—but *When is she coming?*

He sighed and pulled her to him, the wide, warm chest of literature. "She didn't know. Probably tomorrow, possibly Tuesday. She said if she got everything together she could come out tonight, but I don't think we need to worry about tonight."

"Is she bringing Button?" Button was Ariel's daughter, the four-year-old granddaughter of Leo Posen, the only grandchild.

Leo looked at her, surprised. "Of course she's bringing Button."

Of course. "Anyone else?"

Leo went to the refrigerator and found a bottle of pinot gris unfinished from lunch. He poured what was left in a glass sitting out on the sink. "Maybe a boyfriend. There's someone named Gerrit. I think he's Dutch. She said she didn't know what Gerrit's plans were yet. She might be on better behavior if she has someone to impress."

"Should I, after tea and cakes and ices, have the strength to force the moment to its crisis?" Franny asked the lobsters.

"And what's that supposed to mean?" Leo said.

Franny shook her head. "Nothing. It's the next line."

"It's not the next line," he said, and took his wine out to the porch.

Franny put a pair of scissors in her purse and carried the six boxes out to the car. Franny, who felt herself to be without talent, was very adept at carrying more things than anyone would have thought possible. She could feel the lobsters scrabble as their bodies slid heavily into the dark cardboard corners of the boxes.

"Need a hand?" Jonas said, speeding up his pace when he saw her. He was coming back from the pool, his chest and back unevenly scorched.

"I've got it," she said, setting the boxes down to open the car door.

"Are you going into town?"

"Back into town." She arranged her passengers on the floor of the backseat—three on either side.

"Let me just run inside and get my shirt," he said, his face bright with opportunity. "I need some things in town. I'll keep you company."

She started to tell him no, to explain, but instead she nodded. She waited until the kitchen door had closed behind him, waited another ten seconds, and then got in the car and drove away.

Franny and Leo didn't talk about marriage, except sometimes sentimentally in bed, his hands spreading wide across her back, and even then it was only to say how quickly they would have married had it not been for the future and the past. What they never spoke of was the prohibitive element in the present, which was Leo's daughter.

For the most part, Franny tried her best not to think about Ariel, whom she had met on several disastrous occasions early on in her relationship with Leo. Franny didn't aspire to like Leo's daughter, but she hoped to someday achieve a low level of distant compassion towards her. To that end she disciplined herself to think of her own father whenever Ariel came up, to imagine Fix showing up with someone younger than she was, poor dear Marjorie pushed to the side. Fix taking up with his favorite cocktail waitress, not just for the weekend but going on five years. Her father in love with this cocktail waitress who had no means of supporting herself but who would wait for him in motels when he went on stakeouts. When she could think of things that way, the lava of Ariel's rage against her was easier to bear. The simple truth was that Franny couldn't stand to be hated. Sacred Heart hadn't prepared her for it and college hadn't prepared her for it. Law school had been doing its best to toughen her up but then look how she'd done in law school.

Franny found a parking spot two blocks from the water and carried the six boxes down to the end of the pier, past the fishermen with their buckets and lines, past the tourists holding hands. She wanted the lobsters in deep water. Maybe they'd be stupid enough to crawl into someone else's pot tomorrow but she didn't want them walking straight up on the beach minutes after their exoneration. She set the six boxes out in a line and opened them up. Christmas at the pier. Christmas for crustaceans. They were a dappled black and green now, not the electric red they would have been after boiling. They were still frisky, energized by their proximity to salt water, waving their bound claws in impatience. They would never know what they had missed, though being lobsters, they would probably never know anything. She took the scissors and stuck them in the box, doing her best to cut off the wide rubber bands without nicking a claw or losing a finger. (The first band on each one was easy, the second a challenge.) When she finished, she tipped them one at a time out of their boxes and into the ocean, where they made a pleasing smack against the water and then sank from view.

By the time Franny had loaded down the car with all the necessary provisions and driven back to the house it was late in the afternoon. She caught a glimpse of Leo on the front porch talking to someone by the door (Nine for dinner? She had enough) while the rest of them were off who knows where. There was a sleek silver Audi pulled to the back, the Hollingers must have arrived by now. Franny thought how nice it would have been to have taken a shower before she saw them but that wasn't going to happen. She started carrying the boxes and bags into the kitchen. She'd made three trips when Leo came in with a tall young man with a long black braid.

"Franny," Leo said.

Franny put the heavy box she was holding down on the table, half liquor, half wine. There was a second case of wine still in the car. She kept her hands on top of the box to keep them steady. That first moment she saw him she knew exactly what it was she'd done, how serious and wrong it was to have given away what didn't belong to her. She had known it at the time, too, but she hadn't cared. It was the way Leo had listened to her, the way he had asked her so many questions and then told her to tell him everything again. There had been nothing in her life to equal the light of his attention.

"Christ," Albie said. "You look exactly the same."

He was taller and thinner than she could have ever imagined he would be. He wore a sleeveless T-shirt and some oversized pants covered in pockets. His arms were dark and muscled, his wrists tattooed. He was at once someone she knew as a brother and someone she had never met. "Not you," Franny said.

Hadn't she thought he'd show up sooner or later? She had expected him around every corner in those first months after the book came out, but time passed. Did she forget about him then? "How did you find us?"

"I found him," Albie said, motioning to Leo. "It turns out he's the easiest person in the world to find."

"That's good to know," Leo said.

"I wasn't thinking about you," Albie said to Franny. "But I guess it makes sense. Somebody had to have told him."

They had wanted to go to the barn and brush the horses. If they brushed the horses and mucked out a few of the stalls then usually Ned would let them take turns riding the mare for the afternoon. But Albie was driving them crazy. What was he doing that was so intolerable? Standing here in front of him now, Franny couldn't remember. Or maybe he wasn't doing anything wrong. Maybe it was just that someone had to watch him around the horses and none of them wanted to do it. He wasn't the monster they told him he was, in fact there wasn't anything so awful about him. It was only that he was a little kid.

"Albie has terrible breath," Franny announced. Then she turned to him. "Didn't you brush your teeth this morning?"

That was how the ball got rolling. Holly leaned in and sniffed the air in front of her brother's face. She rolled her eyes. "Tic Tac, please."

Caroline looked at Cal. "You might as well. You know he's never going to brush his teeth. I don't think he's brushed them since we got here."

Cal pulled the little plastic bag out of his pocket. He had four in there and so he gave him four.

"All of them?" Albie asked.

"You stink," Cal said. "If you don't you're going to scare the horses."

Jeanette left the room then. She didn't say where she was going but the rest of them said they had to wait for her.

"I want to go!" Albie said.

Franny shook her head. "Ernestine told us we had to stay together."

They waited until he fell asleep. It never took that long. Cal carried Albie down to the laundry room and left him under a pile of towels on the floor. It was Sunday and Ernestine was making a big supper. She never did laundry on Sunday.

And now twenty years later here was Albie in the actress's summer house, having read about that day he had largely slept through in a novel written by someone he'd never met. Franny shook her head. Her hands were cold. She had never been so cold before. "I'm sorry," she said. The words came without volume and so she said them again. "I know that isn't worth anything but I'm sorry. I made a terrible mistake."

"How did you make a mistake?" Leo said. He reached into the box and took out the bottle of Beefeater. "I'm going to have a drink. Would anyone else like a drink?"

"Did you think I was never going to see it?" Albie asked. "I mean, maybe that was a good guess. It took me long enough."

"I was trying to explain to him before you got here," Leo said, pouring some gin in a glass. "Writers get their inspirations from a lot of places. It's never any one thing."

Franny looked at Leo, willing him to pick up his glass and go back out to the porch to smoke with his guests. "Just give us a minute," she said to him. "This isn't about you."

"Of course it's about me," Leo said. "It's my book."

"I still don't understand this," Albie said, pointing at Franny and then at Leo. "How did he wind up with my life?"

"It isn't your life," Leo said. "That's what I'm trying to explain. It's my imagination."

Albie swung around like a whip, his hands coming up to Leo's shoulders, pushing him back. Leo, startled, dropped his glass on the floor, and for a moment the room was suffused with the clean smell of gin.

"You don't understand why I'm here, do you?" Albie said. "You have no idea how hard I'm trying not to kill you. I really might. And if you made me up then you'll understand just how little there is at stake for me here."

There was a clear case for stepping towards Leo then, for putting her hands on Leo's arm, but Franny turned to Albie instead. Albie was the one she had wronged. She and Leo had wronged him together.

"Listen to me, let's go and talk," she said to Albie. "Come outside and talk to me."

Leo stumbled back as if struck, his face flushed. Leo— shorter, heavier, more than twice Albie's age—would later swear there had been a blow. The highball glass rolled past his feet, miraculously unbroken. "I'm calling the police," he said. He could hear the unevenness in his own breathing.

"Nobody's calling the police," Franny said.

"What in the hell are you talking about?" Leo said.

Marisol came in the kitchen through the swinging door, Eric behind her. "Franny, where are my lobsters?" she said.

Franny couldn't think of what she was talking about at first or why she was even still in the house, but then she remembered. "Go," she said. She kept her eyes on Albie.

"Do you even know what lobsters cost?"

Eric touched his wife's shoulder. "Come back to the living room," he said. "They've got company."

"We're the company!" Marisol had put on a silk shift

dress of emerald green, a flat gold necklace. The Hollingers had come and she was dressed for dinner. Only Hollinger was a bigger name on the marquee than Posen, and some might disagree with that. Hollinger had been more consistent in his career, he'd had the bigger wins. Dinner, unassembled, was on the table in the boxes, in the shopping bags. "Jonas told me you put them in the car. Was something wrong with them?"

Albie turned to Franny. "Do you work for them?"

Franny took her hand off Albie's arm and put her hand in his hand instead. "We have to go."

"Who is this?" Marisol said. Marisol, who wasn't part of anything, who had never been invited.

"This is my brother," Franny said.

"He is *not* your goddamn brother," Leo said, his voice loud enough to go through the windows and out across the lawns.

Franny had made a mistake when she'd left the house that morning without taking her purse and she did not make the mistake again. "Stay here," she said to Leo. "Everything's going to be fine."

Albie picked up the bottle of gin.

"You're not leaving with him," Leo said.

"If I don't leave here with him I'm going to invite him to dinner. I'm going to put him upstairs in the guest room, okay?"

"I'll tell you what," Eric said. "Why don't we take some drinks out to our guests? Marisol, you get the corkscrew and some glasses. Maybe we should all sit down and have a drink. You've got the gin." Eric nodded at Albie, then he turned to

Franny. "The Hollingers are here. They came while you were in town. Just come out and say hello."

Eric was trying to turn the evening back into a dinner party. It occurred to Franny then that of course he wouldn't know who Albie was, he wouldn't know who she was either, other than Leo's girlfriend. Because when Leo called her his inspiration, and he always did, no one thought he meant it literally. The story of two couples moving in next door to each other, their awful children, that was nothing more than the plot of a novel as far as Eric was concerned. Franny wanted to go to Leo, to reassure him, but Marisol had opened the door from the kitchen. Everyone could hear the voices coming in from the front hallway, so many voices! *Hello! Hello!* the sound of car doors, of laughter, the sound of Ariel's voice calling out for her father.

* * *

If **Beverly or** Bert were to tell the story now, they would say they divorced after Cal died. And of course that was true, they had, but in this instance the word "after" would be misleading. It linked together the death and the divorce as if they were cause and effect, as if Beverly and Bert were one of those couples who, upon a child's death, are led down such separate paths of grief that they can no longer find their way back to one another. This was not the case.

Bert blamed Beverly for leaving the six children alone on the farm with Ernestine and his parents, for not telling anyone she was taking his mother's car into Charlottesville to sit through two back-to-back showings of *Harry & Tonto*. (She hadn't planned to see it twice, but the theater was so empty and quiet and cool. She had cried at the end of the picture and all through the credits, and rather than walk into the lobby with her mascara running she just decided to stay where she was.) Did he really think she supervised the children every minute? Did he think that had she stayed home that afternoon, after reading another book up in their room, another magazine, taking one more nap, after she had officially died of boredom she might have gone with them to the barn and curried the horses? The truth was she left the children alone in Arlington too, she left them in order to preserve her sanity. At least at the farm there was adult supervision. Did his parents bear no responsibility for what happened on their property? And what about Ernestine? Beverly had left the children in Ernestine's care even if she hadn't told Ernestine that's what she was doing. Ernestine had more parental sense than Beverly and Bert and Bert's parents all combined, and Ernestine thought it was fine for them to walk the half a mile to the barn.

Bert should not have insisted that Beverly and the children stay at his parents' house in the country for the week while he took the station wagon back to Arlington for work. If he thought that the children needed an escort to the barn then he should have stuck around and escorted them himself. Beverly didn't want to be a guest in his parents' house. They were forever asking the children about their wonderful mother—*How's Teresa? What's Teresa doing now? I hope your mother knows she's always welcome to come and stay with us.*

The children didn't want to stay with Bert's parents either. They had been much happier at the Pinecone, where they had stayed in summers past. At Bert's parents' house they had to take their shoes off at the back door and wipe their feet with a towel. Because they weren't allowed in the living room under any circumstances, they had inevitably made a game out of dashing through at top speed on dares whenever they heard someone coming down the hall. A porcelain figurine of an English gentleman and his wolfhound was knocked from an end table and smashed.

Bert's parents didn't want them there. They had made the offer of this extended and highly unusual visit in hopes of seeing their son, not his children or his second wife or her children. But then Bert left.

Ernestine didn't want them there. She couldn't have. It meant eight extra mouths to feed (seven after Bert decamped), piles of laundry, games to invent, fights to break up, employers to soothe. The load fell heaviest on Ernestine's shoulders and yet she alone carried her burden without complaint.

Bert went back to Arlington because under the circumstances of a normal work week it was expensive, impractical, and stimulatingly dangerous to find a place to continue his affair with his paralegal. Linda Dale (two first names; she did not answer to Linda) said for once she would like to have dinner together in a restaurant like regular people, go to bed in a real bed, wake up in the middle of the night and make love while they were still half asleep, and then do it again in the shower the next morning. Bert was not crazy about Linda Dale, she was petulant and demanding and very young, but she talked like this on the phone when he called the office, so what was he supposed to do? Stay at the farm?

He was in the office when his mother called to tell him about Cal. He jumped in his car and broke every speed limit, making the two-hour drive to the hospital in Charlottesville in just under one and a half like any parent would do. There wasn't time to go home and straighten up the house. He never thought of it.

Sometimes it was hard for Beverly and Bert to remember what had destroyed them. When Beverly wept over the affair, the unfamiliar red panties surfacing in her unmade bed, Bert was aghast. The death of a child trumped infidelity. The death of a child trumped everything. It was a logic Beverly could nearly embrace. If pain and loss could be ranked then surely Bert had won and this was the time for them to pull together, for the sake of their marriage, or their remaining children. But accepting the circumstances didn't turn out to be the same as forgiveness. They bound themselves together with a little tape and soldiered on, and even though their marriage held for nearly six years after Cal's death, neither of them would remember it that way. They would say that their separate griefs had broken them apart much earlier.

If the end of Beverly and Bert's marriage could not rightfully be attributed to Cal, neither could it be pinned on Albie, though the couple's emotional resources were so depleted by the time Albie arrived from California that he didn't have to do much of anything but watch them go over the cliff. The mere fact that he had come turned out to be enough. Five years, two months, and twenty-seven days after Cal died, Albie had dropped a lit book of matches in the trash can of the art room of Shery High, in Torrance. Teresa called Bert and told him about the fire, told him through her exhausted tears that Albie was being held in Juvenile. Bert hung up and had Beverly call her ex-husband to get the kid out. With that behind them, Bert called Teresa back to tell her what an incompetent parent she was. Saturday morning and she didn't even know where their only son had gone to on his bike? He told her the home she provided was unfit, unsafe, and she had no choice but to send Albie to him. Bert had this conversation on the phone in the kitchen where Beverly was sautéeing onions to start a Stroganoff for dinner. She turned off the fire beneath the pan and walked slowly up the stairs to Caroline's bedroom. She often hid in Caroline's room now that her older daughter had gone to college. Bert never thought to look for her there.

Of course there were many things Teresa could have volleyed back, but at the heart of her ex-husband's bombastic cruelty was one simple truth: she couldn't keep Albie safe. She didn't necessarily think Bert could do it either, but different friends, a different school, the other side of the country, might afford Albie a better chance. On Monday morning the principal called to say that Albie and the other boys were suspended pending investigation, and if the investigation found them guilty (which was likely considering they had been seen running out of the burning building on a Saturday morning and had confessed to starting the fire) they would be expelled. On Tuesday she called Bert back. She was putting Albie on a plane.

Albie, nearly fifteen, walked as far as the back patio, dropped his suitcase, sat down in a white wrought-iron chair, and lit a cigarette. His father was still trying to wrestle the giant sheets of cardboard that had been taped together to form a sort of box around the bicycle from the back of the station wagon. Bert had already told him on the ride in from Dulles that Beverly wouldn't be home for dinner tonight. On Thursday nights Beverly took a French class at the community college and after that went to dinner with her school friends where they practiced conversational French. "She's trying to find herself," his father said, and Albie looked out the window.

"How is he getting home from the airport then?" Bert had asked her when Beverly announced she wasn't going to be there. He walked right into that one.

When he got the bike unwrapped, Bert wheeled it out of the garage like it was Christmas morning. He had meant to say, *Look at this! Good as new!* but instead he saw the pack of cigarettes and, more distressingly, the red Bic lighter sitting on the table in front of his son. The bike didn't seem to have a kickstand so he leaned it against one of the patio chairs.

"You aren't allowed to have a lighter," Bert said, though it came out as more of a question than he'd meant it to.

Albie looked at him, puzzled. "Why not?"

"Because you burned down your goddamn school. Are you telling me your mother didn't ground you from fire?"

Albie smiled at the sheer expansiveness of his father's stupidity. "I didn't burn down the school. I set a fire in the art room. It was an accident, and they needed a new art room. The school is already open again."

"I'll say it then: You're grounded from fire. That means no arson and no cigarettes."

Albie took a long draw on his cigarette. He turned his head respectfully and blew the smoke to the side. He was respectfully smoking the cigarette outside the house in the first place. "Fire is an element. It's like water or air."

"So you're grounded from an element."

"Can I use the gas stove?"

They were both looking at the lighter on the table. When Bert reached down to take it Albie swept it into his hand, looking right at him. That was the moment: either Bert would hit his son or he would not. Albie held his cigarette down and lifted his face, eyes wide open. Bert straightened up, stepped back. He had never hit his children. He would not hit them now. The few times he'd ever smacked Cal played in his daydreams on a continuous loop.

"Don't smoke in the house," Bert said, and went inside.

Albie stared up at the house. It was not the one he'd come to as a child. It wasn't any house he'd ever seen before. At some point between the last time he was in Virginia and now, Bert and Beverly had moved and failed to mention that fact to Holly or Albie or Jeanette. And why should they, when no one thought that Holly or Albie or Jeanette would ever visit again? But his father hadn't mentioned the new house at the airport either. Did he forget? Did he think Albie wouldn't notice? This place was bloodred brick with fluted white columns in the front, a junior relation of the house his grandparents lived in outside Charlottesville. It was heavily landscaped with plants and trees he didn't recognize, everything orderly and neat. He could see the edge of a swimming pool already covered in tarp for the winter. He could look in the window from the patio and see the kitchen, see the fancy copper pots that hung from a rack on the ceiling, but if he got up and opened the door and walked through the kitchen, he wouldn't know which way he was supposed to turn. He wouldn't know what bedroom he was supposed to sleep in.

Caroline would be off in college by now, and if Albie were to guess he would guess that she had plenty of friends who invited her to their houses for the holidays. She probably had some all-encompassing summer job as a camp counselor or government intern that prevented her from ever coming home or even using a pay phone. Caroline had always made it clear that once she got out of there she wasn't coming back. Caroline was a bitch by any standard, but she was also the one who had organized all the subversive acts of their childhood summers. She hated them all, especially her own sister, but Caroline got things done. When he thought of her cracking open the station wagon with a coat hanger and getting the gun out of the glove compartment, he shook his head. He had never in his life adored anyone the way he adored Caroline.

That meant it would just be Franny. He hadn't seen either of the girls since summer visits to Virginia had stopped five years ago, but Franny was harder for him to fix in his mind. It was weird since she was the person in the family closest to him in age. He remembered that she was always carrying the cat around, and in his memory the girl and the cat had merged: sweet and small, eager to please, quick to nap, always crawling into somebody's lap.

Albie stayed on the back patio and smoked while the light turned gold across the suburbs and the cold air pricked his arms. He didn't want to go in the house and ask his father where he'd be sleeping. He thought about rummaging through his suitcase and finding the generous bag of weed his

friends had put together as a going-away present but he figured he'd already pushed the limits of brazenness for one day.
It would have been one thing if his lighter were confiscated
in a world full of free matchbooks but he didn't want anyone
taking his pot away. He could ride his bike around the new
neighborhood, acquaint himself with what was there, but he
stayed seated. Thinking about moving was as far as he'd gotten when Franny pulled into the driveway and parked.

She was wearing a white blouse with the sleeves rolled up
and a blue plaid skirt, knee socks, saddle shoes, the universal
attire of Catholic school girls. She was skinny and pale with
her hair pulled back, and when he stood up and dropped his
cigarette he had a split second of uncertainty as to whether or
not there was good will between them. Franny dropped her
backpack on the ground and came straight to him, arms out.
Franny, not understanding that he lived on the other side of a
thick wall and so no one could take him into their arms, took
him into her arms and squeezed him hard. She was warm
and strong and smelled slightly, pleasantly, of girl sweat.

"Welcome home," she said. Two words.

He looked at her.

"Are they making you stay outside?" she asked, looking
down at his suitcase. "Can you at least go in the garage?"

"I like it out here."

Franny looked at the house. The light in Bert's study was
on. "Then we'll stay out here. What can I get for you? You
must be hungry."

Albie looked hungry, not only in the unnerving thinness
that all the Cousins children possessed, but in his hollow
eyes. Albie looked like he could eat an entire pig, python-

style, and it wouldn't begin to address the deficit. "To tell you the truth I could use a drink."

"Name it," Franny said. She was half-turned towards the house, her mind already considering the secret stash of 7-Up her mother disapproved of.

"Gin."

She looked back at Albie and smiled. Gin on a Thursday night. "Did I tell you I'm glad you're here? Probably not yet. I'm glad you're here. Are you going to come with me?"

"I will in a minute," he said.

While she was gone Albie looked at the sky. There were animals zipping around up there—sparrows? bats?—along with the near-deafening roar of something cricket-ish. He wasn't in Torrance anymore.

In a minute Franny came back with two glasses half-full of ice and gin, a bottle of 7-Up under her arm. She topped off her glass with the soda, used her finger to stir it around, and then looked at him, wagging the 7-Up back and forth.

"Pass," he said.

"Very manly." They tapped their glasses together the way people did in movies, the way her girlfriends did at slumber parties after siphoning off what could be taken discreetly from the family supply. Franny had had some drinks before, just not at home, not on a school night, not with Albie, but if ever there was a day to break the rules it was today. "Cheers."

She made a little face at the taste while Albie just sipped and smiled. He lit another cigarette because it went so nicely with the gin. It felt like they were catching up just sitting there not talking. Too much had happened, too much time had passed, to try putting it into words now.

After a while Bert came back out. He seemed so happy to see Franny there. He kissed the side of her head, the cloud of cigarette smoke eradicating the smell of gin. "I didn't know you were home."

"Both of us," Franny said, smiling.

Bert jingled his car keys. "I'm going to get a pizza."

Franny shook her head. "Mom made dinner. It's all in the fridge. I'll heat it up."

Bert looked surprised, though it would be hard to say why. Beverly always made dinner. He picked up Albie's suitcase. "You kids come inside now. It's getting cold out here."

The three of them went inside just as the deep darkness of night was setting in. Franny and Albie picked up their glasses, the cigarettes and the lighter, and followed Albie's father through the door.

7

"So Bert Cousins's kid was the one who broke you and the old Jew up?" Fix said. They were on their way to Santa Monica, the car windows down. They were going to the movies. Caroline was driving. Franny was in the back, leaning forward between the two seats.

"How have I never heard that part of the story?" Caroline asked.

"Would you please not call him 'the old Jew'?" Franny said to her father.

"Sorry." Fix covered his heart with his hand. "The old drunk. May God rest his soul in Zion. Hats off to the kid is my point. He's finally earned my respect."

Franny imagined calling Albie with that bit of news. "It wasn't like I left the house that night and never went back. We stayed in Amagansett all summer." There was still Ariel and her intolerable Dutch boyfriend and sad little Button to deal with, the entire long, horrible summer of houseguests to endure. The end of Leo and Franny's relationship played to a full house. It was more than twenty years ago and still the complete misery of that time was fully accessible to her.

"But essentially that was that, right?" Fix said. "The kid put the nail in the tire."

Caroline shook her head. "Albie identified the fact that the tire had a nail in it," she said, and Franny, surprised by the accuracy of her sister's assessment, laughed.

"I should have stayed in law school," Franny said. "Then I'd have been as smart as you."

Caroline shook her head. "Not possible."

"Get over a lane," Fix said, pointing. "You're taking a left at the light." Fix had his Thomas Brothers street guide in his lap. He refused to let Franny put the theater's address into her phone.

"Do you have any idea how it could have taken this long to make the movie?" Caroline glanced in the rearview mirror then accelerated deftly to get the better of an oncoming Porsche. As with so many other things in life, Caroline was the superior driver.

"It happens. Leo wouldn't sell the film rights so nothing could have started until after he died. I can't imagine his wife was easy to work with." Natalie Posen. They were, miraculously, still married when Leo died fifteen years ago, still battling it out. All those years his wife and now his widow. Franny saw her just that one time at the funeral, so much smaller than she would have imagined, sitting in the front row of the synagogue flanked by two sons who looked like Leo—one from the nose up and the other from the nose down—as if each had inherited half his father's head. Ariel was on the other side of the synagogue with a very grown-up Button and her own mother, the first Mrs. Leon Posen. Eric was listed in the program as an honorary pall bearer, too old himself to lift one sixth of the casket's weight by that point. He'd been the one to call Franny with the news of Leo's death, thoughtful considering all the time that had passed. She asked about the next book, the one of the long-ago advance that he was always supposed to be writing. Eric said no, sadly, it wasn't there.

They were all there, time having run them down: Eric and Marisol, Astrid, the Hollingers, a dozen more—all the summer guests come to claim him along with the rest of the world. Franny stayed at the back, standing against the wall in the peanut gallery of former students and devoted fans and old girlfriends. Natalie Posen had chosen to bury her husband in Los Angeles, giving her spite the air of the eternal.

"The wife," Fix said. "As long as we're thinking of things to feel good about, let's thank the wife."

"Leo's wife?"

Fix nodded. "She's the unsung hero in all this."

"How do you figure?" It was Fix's birthday, eighty-three, with metastases to the brain. Franny was making her best effort.

"If she hadn't hung in there like a pit bull to get more money, Leo Posen would have been a free man."

"Ah." Caroline nodded. She colored her hair the warm reddish shade of brown it had been when they were children, she went to Pilates three times a week. She had followed their mother's example, kept herself up. Caroline had become the younger sister.

"I'm not seeing your point," Franny said.

Fix smiled. Caroline, as far as he was concerned, had never missed a trick.

"If Leo had ever gotten a divorce," her sister explained, "he would have married you."

"Franny girl," their father said, turning with difficulty to look at her, "that may have been the only bullet you ever dodged."

Franny and Caroline had long agreed it was a waste of resources for them to visit either parent at the same time. With divorced parents on opposite sides of the country, and husbands whose parents also required a certain number of family holidays, Franny and Caroline divided their burden in order to conquer it. There were only so many vacation days, personal leave days, plane tickets, missed school plays, and unexcused absences between them. Whatever affection the two sisters had found for each other later in life would not be manifesting itself in visits. Los Angeles was as close as Franny ever got to the Bay Area, though she meant to go. Albie lived there now, two hours away from Caroline. Caroline's oldest child, Nick, was a senior at Northwestern, so at least when Caroline and Wharton came out for parents' weekend Franny could drive up to Evanston to see the three of them. Caroline's other two children, the girls, Franny had missed out on entirely, much the same way Caroline had missed out on Franny's two boys. But Ravi and Amit, no matter how long she'd had them, were not actually Franny's. They had come with the marriage, and Caroline, try as she might to feel otherwise, could never grant full citizenship to stepchildren.

All of which was to say that under normal circumstances neither Franny nor Caroline would necessarily have traveled to Los Angeles to celebrate Fix's birthday, but since Fix had already exceeded the outer limits of his oncologist's predictions, they both stepped up their game. This birthday was going to be his last, a quick glance over to the passenger seat confirmed this, and in honor of the occasion the two sisters broke their own arrangement and met in California.

"So what are we going to do for the big day?" Caroline had asked the night before. "Sky's the limit."

They were sitting in the den, the four of them, in the house in Santa Monica that Fix and Marjorie had moved to when they finally left Downey after retirement. It was something of a miracle, that house, in no way splendid except that it was two blocks from the beach. It was forty years ago that Fix had known a cop who played poker with a bankruptcy judge. He had a tip the place was coming up at auction. That was when Fix finally told Marjorie he'd marry her. They would use her recent inheritance from her aunt in Ohio as the down payment. They would buy it, rent it out for twenty years or so, and by the time they were ready to retire they'd practically own it.

"That's your proposal?" Marjorie had said, but she took the offer.

"But what was Dad's part in all of it?" Franny had asked her years later when she finally heard the full story. Fix and Marjorie had driven the girls by the Santa Monica house every time they came to visit. They would point it out from the car, saying they owned it, saying one day they were going to live there. "If you were the one with the money then why did you have to marry him? You could have just bought the place yourself and rented it."

"Your father wanted a house at the beach, and I wanted to marry your father." Marjorie laughed when she heard how that sounded. She tried again. "He wanted to marry me. He was just slower to figure it out. I like to think that in the end everybody won."

Marjorie had just finished pushing the nutritional supplement into Fix's PEG tube. She was a young seventy-five to his old eighty-three, but it seemed that Marjorie had stopped eating about the same time her husband did. Her shoulder blades pushed out like a wire rack beneath her sweater.

"Let's go to the show," Fix said. "We'll see a matinee of Franny's movie."

"Fix," Marjorie said, her voice tired. "We talked about this."

"My movie?" Franny asked, but of course she knew what he was talking about. He'd called it her book.

"The one your boyfriend wrote about us. I figure I've got one chance to see a movie about my life." Fix appeared wonderfully satisfied by the thought. "I never read the book, you know. I wasn't going to give the son of a bitch my money. But now that he's dead and the money will go to his wife, it's fine by me. Plus I read the review in the paper that said the woman who plays your mother wasn't any good. I'm thinking that must really burn her up."

Marjorie raised a slender hand. "I'm out. You and the girls make a day of it. I'll be here with cupcakes when you get back. " A few free hours were worth a month of pension checks.

"Oh, Dad," Caroline said. "Wouldn't it be more fun to stay home and pull our toenails out with pliers?"

Franny had her share of guilt and dread when *Commonwealth* was published, but still, she would never deny that those were glorious days: the publisher's luncheon at La Grenouille, the award ceremony in which Leo was called to the stage, the never-ending book tour where night after night he read to the spellbound crowds and then waited while the crowds formed a line at a table, supplicants come to tell him how his work had changed their lives. He was famous again, back in the light of the world, and every night in a different hotel room he gave her full credit, cradling her head in his hands while they made love. He could not look away from her. He loved her and thanked her and needed her, Leo Posen did. So for all the many costs she had been rewarded.

But seeing the movie now would bring back more than just her betrayal of her family. The movie also spoke to the failure of her long-ago relationship and the lonely death of the man she had loved, as sold by his second wife.

Franny hadn't understood what it would be like to live with *Commonwealth* when Leo was writing the book, and once she'd read the book it was too late to do anything about it. The movie, however, was another matter. The movie had yet to be made. Franny begged Leo to keep the rights. She understood that such a promise would constitute a significant financial loss, and still, with the manuscript in her hands, she begged him.

Leo gave them to her on a three-by-five card, because Franny was the sun, the moon, and every last glittering star.

> *To Frances Xavier Keating,*
> *on the occasion of her twenty-seventh birthday,*
> *I give you the film rights to Commonwealth,*

> *for now and forever,*
> *as a token of my enduring love and gratitude.*
>
> LEON ARIEL POSEN

He honored it, even later when they rarely spoke and she suspected he needed the money. She didn't mention his promise to anyone after he died. Who would she have told? His wife? She knew an index card didn't stand a chance against the flotilla of lawyers. Irrationally, she had gotten it in her head that they might try and take the card away from her.

"No," Franny said. No, it wasn't a movie she wanted to see, especially not with her father and sister and a hundred strangers packed into the Santa Monica AMC 3, eating popcorn.

Fix laughed and smacked his hands flat against the arms of his recliner. "Boy, did you two turn out to be a couple of little girls. There's nothing in that movie that's going to hurt you. You should be able to see how a dying man stuck in this rattrap frame might want to see himself portrayed by a handsome movie star. And anyway, this story is ancient history. You've got until tomorrow to pull yourselves together. It's my birthday and we're going to the show."

Caroline parked and Franny got the wheelchair out of the trunk. Fix had long since stopped driving but he wouldn't sell the car. There was always the chance that fate could reverse itself, that a cure could be found in the latter part of the eleventh hour and the parts of himself that had been devoured by cancer could be restored. Hope, Fix said, was the blood of life, and the car could never be replaced. It was a

Crown Victoria, a former unmarked police car he'd bought from the department. Franny called it the Batmobile for its ability to go a hundred and forty miles per hour if need be. Not that he'd ever driven it at a hundred and forty, but he liked to say he felt better just knowing what was possible.

Franny opened the car door and picked up her father's feet from the floorboard, swinging them gently out and then taking his arm. "Count of three," she said, and together they counted while he rocked back and forth to gain momentum. The car that could catch a stolen Ferrari could not help him up. Franny pulled him out and Caroline caught him in the chair the moment he stood. Even a month ago Fix had fought this. A month ago he wouldn't use the walker, insisting instead on holding on to Marjorie, even after the falls. But that was behind them now. Now he let Franny put his feet on the paddles. He said thank you.

The actress who owned the house in Amagansett had wanted to play Julia in the movie, which was to say she wanted to play Franny's mother. She didn't know, of course, that Franny was a real person who would be sleeping in her bed on her Egyptian cotton sheets. Leo had blamed Albie for the end of their affair. He believed that had Albie never found them they would have gone on happily together. But Caroline was right: Albie didn't put the nail in the tire, the nail was already there. Still, as long as Leo got to blame their personal problems on an innocent party, Franny would like the chance to blame the actress and her ridiculous goddamn house. No one should have so much money that they could own a house like that and then not even bother to live in it. The swimming pool was long and deep and looked nothing like a swimming pool at all. It looked like the foundation of a shotgun house that had been built in the 1800s and then blown away in a storm. The swimming pool was fed by a spring. No one knew exactly where it came from, not the spring, not the pool, both having been there longer than the actress's house. And that was just the beginning: there were climbing roses that covered the east wall and then sprawled in a giant tangle over the sloping roof, a miraculous profusion of blooms. It was a storm of roses, white and red, a half a dozen shades of pink, that piled over themselves all summer long, one breed dying out just as another was peaking. A carpet of blown petals covered the lawn throughout the summer. And there was a Klimt in her bedroom, small but unarguably real, a painting of a woman who bore an almost ancestral resemblance to the actress. Who kept the Klimt in their summer house? It was the house, Franny believed, that had done them in. No one could stay away from it except the actress herself. Leo had called Franny one night long after their relationship was over to tell her the actress had invited him back to Amagansett for dinner. She said she wanted to talk about the movie, even though he told her there wasn't any movie.

"Come anyway," she'd said.

"You remember all that champagne in the refrigerator?" Leo said to Franny on the phone.

Franny remembered the champagne.

"Well, we drank it." From his apartment in Cambridge, Leo sighed. "Nothing happened. That's what I wanted to tell you. In the end I couldn't go upstairs with her. It was still our bedroom, Franny. I wasn't going to do it."

By the standards of the film industry, both the actress

and her attempts to land a part by any means possible were now ancient history. She had long ago ceased to be the romantic interest in films. She had stopped playing the mother roles. At sixty, she was even too old to play fairytale witches. She was left with a handful of dowager parts, the occasional senior senator, a ruthless CEO in a well-reviewed cable series. That was what Franny had to content herself with as the lights in the movie theater in Santa Monica went down: somewhere the beautiful actress was going to see the movie of *Commonwealth* and remember how hard she'd tried to be Julia.

But that turned out to be no comfort whatsoever.

Franny and Caroline, sitting with their father, were joined in the darkness by a single improbable thought: Would it have been worse to see a film of their actual childhood? There was the summer that Bert had the Super 8 and stalked them like Antonioni as they ran through the sprinklers and weaved their bikes in and out of the frame. Holly swirled a hula hoop around the straight pole of her hips. Albie jumped in front of her, pulling off his shirt. The sound of Bert's voice came from the other side of the camera, barking at them to do something interesting, but they were being children, and so, in retrospect, they were fascinating. Maybe that film still existed in a box in her mother's attic or somewhere in the bottom of a file cabinet in Bert's garage. Franny could try to find it the next time she was in Virginia and thread the tape into a projector. That way they could see the real Cal running again and erase the memory of this sullen boy who played him. A film of life would definitely be better than this, even if there had been a camera behind them every minute recording the entire disaster of childhood, all the worst moments preserved, it would still have been better than having to watch these strangers making some half-assed attempt to replicate their lives. Holly and Jeanette had been collapsed into a single girl who was neither Holly nor Jeanette but some horrible changeling who stamped her foot and slammed the door when she argued. When had Holly or Jeanette ever done anything like that? But of course the child actors weren't trying to play real children. They wouldn't have known that the book had anything to do with real people, and anyway, they wouldn't have read the book. So was the movie excruciating to watch because nothing was right, or was it excruciating to watch because, impossibly, some things were? Every now and then there was a flash of familiarity in the minute cruelties the two families exchanged.

"It isn't you," Leo had said when she finished reading the book. "It isn't any of you." He was sitting in the second bedroom he used as an office in their apartment in Chicago, the little apartment they had before there was money. He held her in his lap and stroked her hair while she cried. She had made a terrible error in judgement and he had turned it into something permanent and beautiful. That was the nail in the tire. Or not even that. Not her reading it, not his writing it, but a day all the way back in Iowa when Leo, brushing his teeth while Franny was in the shower, had spit out his toothpaste, pulled back the curtain just a bit, and said, "I've been thinking about that story you told me about your stepbrother."

What she had thought at that moment, naked in the water, the shampoo running down her neck, was that Leo Posen had listened to her, that he had found Cal's death worthy of his further reflection. He reached into the water, ran his finger in a circle around her small soapy breast.

What she hadn't thought of in the shower was that one day she would be fifty-two and have to watch the outcome of her smiling acquiescence play out on a screen. Cal's character wasn't dead yet, that was waiting up ahead. Albie's character had been drugged a couple of times by the other children, the character who was Caroline had slapped and pinched the character who was Franny every time the camera panned in their direction, and the movie wasn't even about the children. It was about the mother of one family and the father of the other and how they looked at each other at night from across the driveway. The character who was Franny's mother pushed her hand repeatedly through her long blond hair while staring off into the distance, proof that she struggled with the weight of her infidelity. She wore blue surgical scrubs that seemed to have been tailored to her pretty figure. The mother in the movie was pulled in so many directions: the hospital, her children, her neighbor who was her lover, his wife who was her friend. Only her hapless husband seemed to ask nothing of her. He moved along the edges of the screen, picking up the children's dishes as she cut a line through the center of the kitchen. She was being called away again.

"Enough," Fix howled. He pushed himself halfway up to standing, as if he meant to walk out of the theater on his own, but his feet were still on the paddles. Caroline shot from her seat, catching him just as he pitched forward into the wide open space in front of handicapped seating, breaking his fall with her body. They were clambering around in the darkness, each with a knee and both hands on the sticky floor.

Franny had her arms around her father's chest but he was thrashing, fighting her off.

"I can get up!" he said.

The collective eyes of the movie theater fell upon them. No one hushed them. Up on the screen the scene had changed. Now Cal's character was running down the street past the neighbors' houses in the middle of the day, his brother running behind him, trying to catch up. There was for that moment enough light that the patrons could see the noise was coming from an old man in a wheelchair. There were two women trying to help him up. No one knew that they were the movie.

"Get out of here," Fix said, his voice keening. "Get out!" They had him back in his seat but his legs were still twisted. He kicked at Franny but she got his feet back on the paddles. Caroline got behind the chair and Franny grabbed their purses. They were not exactly running with their father but they were going as fast as they could. Franny raced ahead and held open the door to the long, carpeted hallway, and then they were through the lobby, past the crazy neon rainbow pulsing above the popcorn stand, past the teenaged ticket-takers in their brown polyester vests. Bang! They burst through the glass double doors and out into the unbearable flood of sunlight.

"Fuck that!" Fix screamed at the parking lot. A mother with two children was crossing towards them but then stopped, reconsidered, and went the other way. Franny laughed and then buried her face in her hands. Caroline bent from the waist, putting her head on the curve of her father's shoulder.

"Happy birthday, Dad," she said. She gave him a small kiss on the neck.

"Fuck that," Fix said again, this time discouraged.

"Yeah," Franny said, and rubbed his other shoulder. "Fuck that."

After the movie they went to the beach. Franny and Fix were against it. They said they were tired and wanted to go home, but Caroline was the one who was driving the car.

"I will not allow that to be my memory of Dad's birthday," she said, tapping at the accelerator to remind them what the car was capable of, what she was capable of. "I want to wipe that movie off my eyeballs. We're going to go look at the ocean."

"Turn on Altamont," he said. His voice half-vanished, as if the roar of his invective to the movie theater parking lot was all he had left.

"Do you think we might kill him, going to the beach now?" Franny said to Caroline.

Fix smiled. "That's how I want to go. I want to die at the beach with my girls. We could call Joe Mike to come out and give me last rites."

"Joe Mike's not a priest anymore," Caroline said.

"He'd do it for me."

It was harder getting their father out of the car the second time. He wasn't as able to help them, but Franny and Caroline managed. Caroline had, of course, been right about the beach. Almost all of the days in Santa Monica were beautiful, and this one, by virtue of the fact that it was no longer playing out in a movie theater, was more beautiful than most. Fix had a permanent handicapped placard for the Crown Victoria and they got a magnificent parking space when no parking spaces were available.

"Writing out a two-hundred-dollar ticket to some able-bodied asshole in a handicapped spot." Fix shook his head. "That is a pleasure you'll never know."

Franny pushed the chair down the sidewalk blown over with sand. They took it all in: the gulls and the waves, the bikini-clad girls, the boys in board shorts, the lifeguard in his wooden tower watching over them like a god. Young people so beautiful they should have been making commercials for tanning lotion or everlasting youth played volleyball with no one watching. People ran with their dogs or ate sno-cones or stretched out on brightly patterned towels the size of bed sheets and baked.

"Don't you wonder who all these people are?" Caroline marveled. "It's Thursday. Doesn't anyone have a job?"

"They're celebrating my birthday," Fix said. "I gave them all the day off."

"Why aren't those kids in school?" Caroline looked at a half dozen children with buckets beavering away on the rear-rangement of sand.

"Do you remember when I used to bring you girls to the beach?" Fix said.

"Every year," Franny said.

Fix looked out at the waves, at the tiny figures of men skating the water on bright-yellow boards. "I don't see any girls out there," Fix said.

"The girls are lying on their towels," Franny said.

Fix shook his head. "That isn't right. I would have taught

you to surf. If you had lived out here with me I would have taught you to surf."

Caroline reached out and combed back her father's hair with her fingers. All she had ever wanted when she was young was to live with her father and no one would let her. "You didn't know how to surf."

Fix nodded slowly to the waves, taking it all into account. "I wasn't a good swimmer," he said.

They watched a boy with a pink-and-red dragon kite that raced straight up, spun in wild circles, and then plummeted down. They watched two girls in bikinis roller-blade past them, their long legs nearly brushing Fix's knees.

"Your mother wasn't like that," Fix said, his eyes still on the surfers.

Franny didn't know what he was talking about, the roller-blading girls? but Caroline picked it up. "Mom wasn't an orthopedic surgeon?"

"Your mother was better than that, that's all. I'm not one to go sticking up for your mother but I want you to know, she wasn't the way that woman played her in the movie."

The two sisters looked at each other over the wheelchair. Caroline gave her head a sideways tilt.

"Dad," Franny said. "None of those people were us."

"That's right," Fix said and patted her hand as if to say he was glad she'd understood.

When they got back in the car Caroline and Franny both checked their phones. They'd turned them off for the movie and in the aftermath had forgotten to turn them on again.

"I wish I had a phone," Fix said. "I could be a part of the club."

"Check your Thomas Brothers guide," Caroline said, her thumb rolling down an endless stream of texts from work.

Franny had two texts, one from Kumar wanting to know where the checkbook was, and one from Albie that said "CALL ME!!"

"One second," Franny said, and got back out of the car.

He picked up on the first ring. "Are you still in L.A.?"

They had e-mailed a week or two ago. She had told him she was coming out for her father's birthday. "I'm standing in front of the ocean right now."

"I need a huge favor, which you owe me for not telling me that fucking movie was coming out this week."

"Don't see it," Franny said. The kid still had the dragon kite up. There was just enough wind.

"My mother's sick. She's been really sick for three days and she won't go to the hospital. She tells me she's fine and she tells me she's sick all at the same time, and I don't think she's fine. I can get down there by tonight but I'm worried she needs to go to the hospital now. I can't get her neighbors on the phone, her best friend's out of town. Mom was never exactly what you'd call social, or if she was social she didn't tell me about it, so I don't have a lot to work with. I don't want to send an ambulance and scare her to death when maybe there really isn't anything wrong with her." Albie stopped for a minute, breathed in. "What I want to know is if you'd go over there and check on her. Jeanette's in New York, Holly's in fucking *Switzer*land. I can call Mom and tell her you're coming. She'll be mad but at least that way she'll open the door."

Franny looked back at the Crown Victoria, knowing the car could fly there. She looked at her father and sister in the front seat, staring at her through the window like two people who were late for an appointment. "Sure," she said. "Give me the address. Then I'll call you and tell you whether or not you should come."

There was a pause on the line and Franny wondered if her phone had gone dead. She wasn't great about remembering to plug it in. Then Albie's voice came back. "Oh, Franny," he said.

"Your mom doesn't know about the movie, does she?"

"My mom doesn't know about the book," he said. "It turns out a novel isn't the worst place to hide things."

It was more than twenty years since Albie had taken the train to Amagansett. He had finished reading the book before he left and had given it to Jeanette. He had walked the three miles to the actress's house from the station and knocked on the door to find out how his life had fallen into someone else's hands.

Later, after the argument with Leo, she and Albie had gone out the back door without ever seeing Ariel or Button. They were only going as far as the cabin at the back of the property, and they passed John Hollinger in the backyard on their way. He was wearing a perfectly crumpled summer suit and was smoking a cigarette. He was taking in the beauty of the night. "Isn't this place something," he said to them in wonder.

Franny and Albie kept the lights in the cabin off and drank the gin, passing the bottle back and forth between them. No one thought to look for them there, but then there was a good chance that no one had thought to look for them at all. Instead, Leo and his guests would be sitting on the screened-in porch on the other side of the lawn, smoking and drinking the gin the Hollingers had brought. Leo would be railing about Franny's crazy ex-stepbrother who had shown up out of nowhere in a rage, but he wouldn't mention what the stepbrother might have been mad about.

"Did you tell Jeanette you were coming?" Franny asked him.

"No, no." Albie shook his head in the dark. "Jeanette would have wanted to come with me, and Jeanette really would have killed him."

"Not him," Franny said. The burn of the gin was pleasant and familiar. She realized now she'd been saving this drink for the necessary occasion. "It was my fault."

"Yeah," Albie said. "But I wouldn't let Jeanette kill you."

"Quick errand of mercy," Franny said when she got back in the car. She explained the situation to Caroline and their father. "Let me drop the two of you off at the house and I'll go check on her. It shouldn't take long."

"That was Albie on the phone just now?" Fix said.

"That was him."

"That's crazy!" Caroline said. "What are the chances?" Even Caroline was impressed.

The chances were unremarkable. Franny and Albie were friends. She and Kumar had gone to his wedding. She had a picture of his daughter Charlotte on her refrigerator. Most years they remembered each other's birthdays.

"Well, I can't speak for your sister but you aren't dropping *me* off at the house," Fix said. "I haven't seen Teresa Cousins in a dog's age."

"Since when do you know Teresa Cousins?" Caroline asked. The four girls used to talk about it in their bunk beds at night when they were all together for the summer, how perfect it would be if Caroline and Franny's father could marry Holly and Jeanette's mother. Then everything would be settled.

"When Albie burned down the school. Haven't I ever told you that story? Your mother called and asked me to get him out of Juvenile as a favor to her, like I was in the business of doing your mother favors."

"We know this part," Caroline said. "Get to the Teresa part."

Fix shook his head. "It's amazing when you think about it, those guys in Juvenile releasing him to me. They didn't know me from Adam. I just showed them my badge and said I was there to pick up Albert Cousins. Two minutes later I'm signing for the kid and they're handing him over. I would bet they don't do it like that now, at least not with a juvenile. There were two or three other boys in his gang if I remember, a couple of blacks and a Mexican. The desk sergeant asked me if I wanted them too."

"What did you do with them?" Franny said. How could she have heard a story so many times and just now realize that all of the interesting parts had been left out?

"I left them there. I didn't want the one kid, I sure as hell wasn't going to take all four of them. I remember he'd gone to the hospital first. He had a burn on his back from where his T-shirt caught fire. They gave him a scrub top to wear but he still stank of smoke. I made him keep the windows down in the car."

"You've got a cold heart, Pops," Caroline said.

"Cold heart my ass. I saved that kid. I was the one who got him out. I took him over to the fire station to see your uncle Tom. He was working Westchester then, all the way out by LAX. I was stuck in that airport traffic with Bert Cousins's kid who smelled like a charcoal pit. He and Uncle Tom had their heart-to-heart about arson. You know your uncle was a childhood arsonist, used to burn things up all the time. Not schools, mind you, just empty lots and little things no one cared about. Lots of firemen got their start setting fires. They learn to set them, then they learn to put them out. Tom explained all that to Albie and then I drove him back to Torrance. It was a whole goddamn day in the car."

"And that's when you met Teresa Cousins," Caroline said.

"And that's when I met Teresa Cousins. Nice woman, I remember that. She'd really been through it but she kept her head up. That kid of hers, though, he was a wolf."

"He improved," Franny said.

"I'll say he's improved. First I find out he broke up your engagement to the Jew—" Fix held up his hand. "Wait, I did it again, sorry, the drunk, and now he's worried about his mother."

"We weren't engaged," Franny said.

"Franny," Caroline said. "Let Albie have his due."

"Same house out in Torrance?" Fix asked.

Franny read him the address.

He nodded. "Same house. I'll tell you how to get there. We can do the whole thing on surface streets."

All the stories go with you, Franny thought, closing her eyes. All the things I didn't listen to, won't remember, never got right, wasn't around for. All the ways to get to Torrance.

In Virginia, the six children had shared two bedrooms and a single cat, picked food from one another's plates and indiscriminately used the same bath towels, but in California everything was separate. Holly and Cal and Albie and Jeanette had never been invited to Fix Keating's house, just as Caroline and Franny had never seen where Teresa Cousins lived. Bert and Teresa bought the house in Torrance in the sixties when Bert took the job in the Los Angeles D.A.'s office: it wasn't too far from downtown or too far from the beach. There were three bedrooms, one for Bert and Teresa, one for Cal, and one for Holly. When Jeanette and Albie came along everybody shared. It was the starter house, the port from which they planned to embark on their grand life. In the end, everyone left but Teresa, first Bert then Cal then Albie then Holly and finally Jeanette. Jeanette started talking that last year before college when she and Teresa lived alone together. They had a good time, made each other laugh, which surprised them both.

In truth, the story didn't turn out to be such a bad one. While Teresa went to work day after day and year after year at the D.A.'s office, Torrance improved. The neighborhood, which had once been a place to leave as soon as there was money, became up-and-coming, and then fully arrived. Teresa planted a succulent garden in a rock bed with plans she took from a magazine. She added a deck. She turned the boys' room into a den. Real estate agents left handwritten notes in her mailbox asking her if she was interested in selling and she put the notes in the recycle bin. Teresa liked her job as a paralegal and she was good at it. The lawyers were always telling her to go to law school—she was smarter than most of them—but she wanted none of it. She stayed with the county until she was seventy-two, leaving with one of those plush California pensions that would eventually drive the state into bankruptcy. Lawyers who had long since moved on to other jobs came back to raise a glass to Teresa at her retirement party. They chipped in together and bought her a watch.

Once a year she went to New York to see Jeanette and Fodé and the children. She loved them but New York overwhelmed her. Californians were used to their own houses and cars and lawns. She missed the sprawl. She saved up her money and bought a ticket to Switzerland to see Holly at the Zen center. For ten days she sat beside her oldest living child on a cushion and did nothing but breathe. Teresa liked the breathing up to a point but then the silence overwhelmed her. She considered the life of her daughters in terms of Goldilocks coming into the cottage of the three bears: too hot and too cold, too hard and too soft. She kept her opinions to herself, wanting most of all to not be seen as critical. Albie came back to Torrance two or three times a year. She would make up a list of the things that needed taking care of and he would tick them off, putting a new motor in the garage door and flushing out the hot water heater. After a life of scraping by in odd jobs, Albie had, by necessity, become a person who could do absolutely anything. These days he worked for a company up in Walnut Creek that made bicycles. He liked that. At Christmas he sent his mother a plane ticket so that she could come and sit around a tree with him and his daughter and his wife. Sometimes the popcorn and the fireplace and the endless hands of Go Fish would overwhelm her and she would have to excuse herself and go to the bathroom just to stand beside the sink for a minute and cry. Afterwards she'd rinse her face and dry it off again, coming back to the living room good as new. It was what she had hoped for but never for a minute what she'd expected.

Teresa dated a few lawyers after Bert left, a couple of cops, none of them married. That was her rule and she never broke it, not even for a drink after work, which, as they were quick to remind her, was all they were asking for. Around the time Jeanette left for college Teresa fell in love with Jim Chen, a public defender of all things, and they had ten good years before he had a heart attack in the parking lot outside the county courthouse. There were people all over the place, people who saw him fall and called 911. A secretary who had taken a life-saving course when her children were small did CPR until the ambulance came, but sometimes all the right things are as useless as nothing at all. Life, Teresa knew by now, was a series of losses. It was other things too, better things, but the losses were as solid and dependable as the earth itself.

Now there was this thing in her stomach that was doubling her over, enough pain to make her shake, and then it would pull back and let her breathe. If she'd had the sense to go to her doctor three days ago when it started she could have driven herself over, but after three days of not eating she was too weak to drive anywhere. She could call Fodé and ask him what to do, Fodé was a doctor, but she was perfectly capable of having that conversation in her head without bothering him on the other side of the country: he would tell her she should call a friend and go to the hospital, or, short of that, call an ambulance. She didn't want to do either of those things. She was so tired she felt lucky to make it to the bathroom, to the kitchen for a glass of water, and then back to bed again. She was eighty-two years old. She imagined her children might use this particular stomach pain to answer their questions about whether or not she could continue to live alone in her house or whether she'd have to move to a facility up north someplace near Albie. She couldn't go to Jeanette, people moved to Brooklyn to fall in love and write novels and have children, not to get old, and she couldn't go to Holly, though she imagined dying in the Zen center might come with spiritual advantages.

Then on the second day it occurred to her that maybe this pain, whatever it was, could answer the question of her future in a larger way: maybe this pain that felt like it was killing her would actually kill her. Her appendix was still in there somewhere, and while appendicitis seemed like the kind of thing schoolchildren died of on camping trips, it was possible that hers had hung around all these years in order to detonate late in the game. That wouldn't be the worst thing, would it? Peritonitis? Not as quick as dear Jim Chen going out in a parking lot, but still. When she was having a better moment she found the key to the lockbox, the title to her car, her will. Only a person in deep denial about the future would work her entire life in the legal profession without having a good will. Everything she had was divided three ways. The house, long since paid for, had ticked steadily up in value, and there were savings. Once the kids were out of school she never spent what came in. She laid everything out on the kitchen table and sat down to write a note. She didn't want it to seem like a suicide note because she was most definitely not committing suicide, but she thought whoever came to the house eventually should find more than the car keys and her body. She looked at the pad of paper she used to make grocery lists. The top was lined with cheerful daisies dancing in their pots above a series of chaotic pink letters that spelled out *Things To Do*. She had never stopped to think about how stupid it was to buy a pad of paper that said *Things To Do* but she didn't have the energy to go look for a plain white sheet. The pain was ramping up again and she wanted to go back to bed.

Not feeling great.
Just in case.
     Love, Mom

That was good enough.

Albie was the single distraction from what, on the third day, she had rather hazily decided was a very intelligent plan. He had called too many times to check on her, and how she explained the situation to him had everything to do with where the phone call fell in the cycle of pain. A few times she simply hadn't answered. The idea of picking up the phone had overwhelmed her. But then she did answer, and he told her to get up and open the front door. He said that Franny Keating was coming over to see her.

"Franny Keating?"

"She's in town visiting her father. I asked her to come over and check on you."

"I know people who can check on me," Teresa said, sounding pathetic even to herself. She *did* have friends, she had just made a decision to stay home and experiment with dying.

"I'm sure you do but I was tired of waiting for you to call them. Go open your door. She's going to be there in a minute."

Teresa hung up the phone and looked down at herself in her zip-front cotton robe, what her mother had called a model's coat back in Virginia. She'd been wearing it for three days and it had been crushed by restless sleep and perspiration. She hadn't taken a bath or brushed her teeth or looked in a mirror since this all began. Franny Keating coming to the house was not the same as Beverly Keating coming to the house, but at this moment Teresa was having a hard time distinguishing the two of them in her mind. Beverly Keating, who was Beverly Cousins, who was now Beverly-something-else, Teresa couldn't remember what Jeanette had told her other than she'd married again after Bert. Beverly-Something-Else was so bone-crushingly beautiful that even now, fifty years later, it hurt to think of it. Beverly was always in the pictures the children brought back from summer, as if Catherine Deneuve happened to wander by while they were playing in the pool or swinging in swings and stepped accidentally into the frame as the shutter snapped. She did not want to die thinking of Beverly Keating's beauty. Beverly was younger than Teresa too, not by a lot but it mattered. Beverly wouldn't even be eighty yet.

A wave of pain broke over her and she had to cling to the back of the recliner to remain upright. It was deep in her pelvis, top to bottom, hip to hip. Uterine cancer? Bone cancer? Could it come on this fast? If she didn't answer the door the Keating girl would call her father. Albie said she was visiting her father. He would be old himself by now but he would call some cop friend over to break down her door. That's the way cops work: straight from thought to battering ram. She could feel the sweat breaking out over her scalp. Her short gray hair would be soaked through in a minute. She let go of the recliner and made it over to the front door. Every step made her swear in her head, sonofabitch, sonofabitch. She used it as a mantra, a focal point to calm her breathing, the way Holly had taught her. She opened the front door wide and unlatched the screen, then, having no speed to work with, shuffled back to change her clothes and splash some water on her face. She was hoping there was mouthwash. She didn't think she had the energy to brush her teeth.

It wasn't five minutes before she heard a voice, "Mrs. Cousins?" and then five seconds later, the voice was more familiar, "Teresa?" She heard the screen door open.

"One minute." She pulled up her track pants and pushed her feet into sneakers, ran a towel over her head. It hurt. Her hair was so short but who did she have to impress? Jeanette said she looked like she was coming back from chemo. Holly said she looked like a Buddhist nun. Albie never mentioned her hair.

"It's Franny," the voice said.

"I know, Franny. He told me." Teresa closed her eyes, waited, inhaled sonofabitch, exhaled sonofabitch. It helped a little.

When she came into the living room there were two of them there, a blonde and a brunette. The blonde was aggressively natural, gray in her ponytail, no makeup, a cotton top that tied at the neck with a string. The brunette had more polish but the truth was you wouldn't look at either one of them twice. Neither was as pretty as Holly or Jeanette. Teresa pushed her mouth into a smile by the sheer force of will.

"This is my sister, Caroline," the blonde said. "I hope you don't mind us coming over. Albie was worried about you."

"He turned out to be a worrier," Teresa said. She was trying not to pant. "It's strange, when you think about all the worry he caused us, that he would turn around and worry."

"I guess it happens," Caroline said.

Teresa looked at them for a long time. She had seen so many pictures, heard so many stories. Caroline was the aggressive one, Franny placating. They both made good grades in Catholic school but Caroline was smarter. Franny was kinder. "I know this sounds crazy but have I ever met you girls before?" One of them finished law school and one of them dropped out. She couldn't say she remembered which was which but she could sure tell by looking at them.

"Cal's funeral," Franny said. "I think that was the only time."

Teresa nodded. "I wouldn't remember it then."

"How are you feeling?" Caroline asked. Straight down to business. She had authority. Teresa had the feeling that if she lied about anything Caroline would walk over and poke her in the stomach.

"I've been sick," she said, putting her hand on the chair. "But I'm getting better. I'm up now. It's hard when you get to be my age. Little things knock you out."

"Wouldn't you like to see a doctor?" Franny asked.

Had I liked to see a doctor, Teresa thought, I would have seen one. But she wouldn't be nasty. There was nothing wrong with these girls. Albie had asked them to come. It wasn't their fault. "No," she said.

The smarter one squinted slightly. "We're here. We can drive you over to the hospital. If you have to call an ambulance at eleven o'clock at night it's going to be a lot harder. I'm sorry to say this but you don't look great." Miss Rational Argument. She'd probably already made partner.

"I'm eighty-two," Teresa said. She could feel the sweat on her face. "I haven't looked great in a long time."

"So you're not going?" Caroline asked. Let the record state the defendant declined the offer for transportation to the hospital despite the advice of counsel.

"I'm sorry my son made you come all the way over here for nothing. If he'd asked me first I would have told him not to call." They would leave in just a minute and she could sit down. She could fall down. She wouldn't make it back to bed but the living room couch was all she could ever want.

"Okay," Franny said, "but my father's in the car and he wants to say hello to you. Come say hello to my father and we'll leave you alone."

"Fix is in the car?"

Franny nodded. "Today's his birthday. He's eighty-three. That's why we're out here." Franny waited for a minute but Teresa didn't make any offers. She decided to up the pot. "Dad has esophageal cancer. He's very sick."

"I'm sorry to hear that." Teresa liked Fix Keating. She'd only met him that one time on the terrible day of the fire, but she remembered him as being a very nice man. Albie, radiant in his silent fourteen-year-old rage, had gone to his bedroom and slammed the door while she and Fix sat in the kitchen and had a drink together. There was fresh orange juice in the refrigerator and she made them each a screwdriver. When he tapped his glass to hers he looked her straight in the eye and said, *Solidarity*. She thought that was just the classiest thing in the world.

"Ask him to come in," Teresa said, wondering how much time this was going to take and if she'd have to offer anyone a drink. That would not be possible.

Caroline shook her head. "We've been out all afternoon. We could never get him up the stairs."

There were three short steps to the front door, a decorative wrought-iron handrail on either side that Albie had put in for her last year. If Teresa made it down the stairs she wouldn't make it back up. "Tell him I said hello," she said.

"Dad's dying," Franny said.

So am I, Teresa wanted to say. She looked from one girl to the other. Suddenly she could see they were tag-teaming her: good-cop daughter, bad-cop daughter. They weren't going anywhere. Another wave of pain crested up from below her navel. She'd been standing there too long being nice. She closed her eyes and tried breathing through her mouth, her fingers digging deep into the back of the chair.

"I'll get your purse and lock up," Franny said. "Is your purse in the kitchen? Are all your insurance cards in your purse?"

Teresa moved her head a quarter inch in confirmation while the other one came and put her arms around her. She was gentle but she was undeniably holding her up.

"Are you ready to walk?" Caroline asked.

She had been up and down those steps countless thousands of times, and now she felt like Eva Marie Saint looking over the edge of Mount Rushmore in *North by Northwest*. A

Keating girl stood on either side and lifted her up. She had never been a big woman, never tall like her children, even before she'd started shrinking. She didn't feel like a burden to them. They were strong girls, obviously. They were her kidnappers, sailing her across the lawn and into the backseat of the car, lifting up her feet while pivoting her around in a way that was disturbingly professional, as if stealing old people was what they did. They clicked the seat belt to lock her into place and when she cried out briefly in pain because nothing should touch her stomach, they took it off again.

"Teresa Cousins," Fix said from the front. "We meet again."

"Dad," Caroline said. "Tell me where I'm going."

Teresa heard the urgency in Caroline's voice. It wasn't enough just to take her to the hospital, they had to get there immediately.

Fix gave her directions to Torrance Memorial Medical Center. He didn't even pick up the Thomas Brothers guide. Every page was muscle memory.

The pain subsided a bit and Teresa took in the view. She sighed to be in the backseat of the car, to be moving away from her plan. Maybe dying hadn't been her best idea. Look at this day, another beautiful Southern California day. "Happy birthday," she said to Fix. "I'm sorry to hear about your health."

"Cancer," he said. "What about you?"

Franny was on her cell phone. "We've got your mother in the car. We're going to the hospital now."

"No idea," Teresa said. "Ruptured appendix maybe?"

Caroline pressed the accelerator and the Crown Victoria sprung forward like a racehorse.

"Is that Albie on the phone?" Fix said. "Let me talk to him."

"Dad," Franny said. Her father was holding out his hand to the backseat. Teresa put her hand in Fix's hand and squeezed very lightly.

"Albie, Dad wants to talk to you."

"Your dad?" he asked.

Franny handed her father the phone.

"Son?" Fix said, somewhere he'd found some boom to add to his voice. "We've got your mother here with us. We're going to get her taken care of so don't worry."

"Thank you," Albie said. "You've saved me twice now."

"We'll stay with her until they get to the bottom of this thing. I don't want you to think we'd just drop her off at the door."

"That's nice," Teresa said, looking out the window as her neighbors' houses flew by.

"Should I come down now?" Albie asked.

Fix looked at Teresa there in the backseat, like one of those little featherless birds that's dropped out of the nest and onto the sidewalk, still breathing but completely translucent, everything at the wrong angle. "Why don't we say we'll see you in the morning, how's that? We'll call you again. How do I hang this thing up?" He said this last bit to all of them and then hit the red button.

"We have good children," Teresa said to Fix. "After all the trouble they gave us they turned out okay." She was shocked by how bad he looked. Cancer really was the devil's hand-shake.

Caroline pulled the car into the emergency entrance. Franny went inside to get a wheelchair for Teresa while Caroline got the wheelchair out of the trunk for their father. Caroline and Franny worked together to get the two of them out of the car. Teresa was easier. She squinched up her eyes and pressed her lips together but she didn't say anything. She was very light. Fix was in a good bit of pain now, his limbs so stiff it was hard to wedge him out. It had been a longer day than anyone had anticipated, and they hadn't brought the Lortab. He was resting a hand on either rib the way he did when he was tired, like he was trying to hold himself together. Franny wondered if it would be possible to score a single pill from the emergency room so they could get him back to Santa Monica. Probably not. Caroline and Franny rolled Teresa and Fix up to the registration desk where a young Latin girl with heavy eyeliner and a low-cut T-shirt looked from one wheelchair to the other and then back again. The bottom of a gold crucifix dipped into the top of her extravagant cleavage.

"Both?" she asked.

"Her," Franny said.

Caroline went out to park the car. "I'll call Marjorie and tell her to put the cupcakes in the refrigerator."

"Your birthday," Teresa cried, remembering his wife. "I've ruined it."

Fix laughed, a real laugh that none of them had heard in a while. "You've ruined my eighty-third birthday? Seriously, you can have it."

"Insurance cards?"

Franny had Teresa's purse, and she asked if it would be okay to go through her wallet. She dug past the balled-up Kleenex, the house keys, a roll of mints. In her wallet she found the Medicare card, supplemental Blue Cross Blue Shield, and her driver's license. Did she still drive?

"Name?" the girl began, reading from the questions on her computer screen, having committed none of them to memory.

"I used to come here all the time when the kids were growing up," Teresa said, looking around as if she was just that minute waking up from a dream. "Stitches, tonsils, earaches. But after the kids were gone I never came here anymore. No kids, no emergencies. I'd come to the hospital to have a mammogram or see a sick friend but I don't think I've been to the emergency room even once."

"It's all on the cards," Franny said to the girl.

"I brought Cal here when he was stung by a bee," Teresa said.

"He was stung by a bee in Virginia," Fix said, trying to be helpful.

"We're supposed to ask the patient," the girl said. "It helps us assess."

Franny looked at her, then looked pointedly over to Teresa. The girl sighed and started typing.

"The first time he was stung we came here."

"I guess I didn't know he'd been stung another time," Franny said. Bert had brought all of the children together in the living room in the house in Virginia on the morning of Cal's funeral. He told them a bee sting was something Cal could not have survived. He'd said it to be comforting, so they wouldn't think there was something they could have done to save him. Although, of course, they could have saved him. They could have stopped insisting that Cal feed all his Benadryl tablets to Albie whenever they wanted Albie to shut up, and they could have encouraged Cal to stop giving Albie the pills himself when none of them were around, just so he would have had a few left when he needed them. They could have gone to him when he fell instead of ignoring him for half an hour, thinking he was doing it for show.

"That's how we knew he was allergic," Teresa said. "It was that first time."

"How old was he then?" Caroline said. Caroline was standing behind them. They didn't know she'd come back. Caroline was thinking of her own children. Had they all been stung by bees? She tried to remember.

Teresa closed her eyes. She was counting her children up, arranging them in her memory according to size. "He must have been seven. Albie was just trying to walk, so the girls would have been three and five. I think that's right. Cal and Holly were playing in the backyard and I had the little ones inside. Four children on my own, it was really something. Do you girls have children?"

"Three," Caroline said. "A boy and two girls."

"Two boys," Franny said.

"But they aren't hers," Fix said.

"Cal was stung by a bee," Caroline said, trying to steer the ship.

"Medications?" the Latin girl asked.

Franny dug back into Teresa's purse and pulled the two

bottles she'd found on the sink in the bathroom, Lisinopril and Restoril.

Teresa looked at the orange plastic bottles on the desk and then looked at Franny.

"I thought they might ask," Franny said, though maybe collecting medication had been overstepping. She wouldn't want anyone going through her medicine cabinet.

"I always taught the girls to be thorough," Fix said.

"Next of kin?"

They looked at each other. "Albie, I guess," Franny said.

"Local?" the girl asked, her fingers hovering over her keyboard.

"Oh, me then. Frances Mehta." She gave the girl her phone number.

"Relationship?"

"Stepdaughter," Franny said.

"Wait," Fix said. He was doing the math in his head, trying to figure out the right word for what Teresa and his daughter actually were to one another.

"That's right," Caroline said to the girl.

When she was finished with the forms, the girl at reception told them where to wait. "The nurse will come get you."

"It needs to be soon," Caroline said to her in that very direct way she was capable of. "She's very sick."

"I understand that, missus," the girl said. The weight of her eyelashes was a burden to her. She looked like she was just about to fall asleep.

Franny wheeled Teresa and Caroline wheeled their father as far away from the television set as was possible. It was still light outside.

"You should go home now," Teresa said when they were settled in their corner. "I'm here, they'll come and get me. You don't have to worry about me running out."

"I'll take Dad home," Caroline said. "Then I'll come back for Franny."

"Too much traffic," Fix said. "It's better that we stay together, see this through. If I get sick they can always admit me. I like Torrance. Lots of cops used to live out here."

"Finish your story," Franny said to Teresa.

Fix answered instead. "I worked an accident once, a guy was stopped at a traffic light with his windows down and a bee flew in and stung him. That was that. His foot fell off the brake and the car went out into the intersection where it was T-boned by another car. He was probably already dead at that point. Nobody knew what had happened until the autopsy. I went back to the site a couple of days later, not that I was looking for a bee exactly, but I wanted to take a look around. There was a bottlebrush tree just before that traffic light and it was swarming. I mean half of it was bees."

Teresa nodded, as if the story were perfectly relevant. "When Cal came in from the backyard he was dead white. I remember his little face, how terrified he was, and really, I thought it was Holly. They were always going after each other with rakes and brooms and I thought something had happened to her. I said, 'Cal, where's Holly?' And when I started to turn away from him to go out to the yard to find her, he made this horrible high-pitched noise, like he was trying to suck air through a pinhole. He held his arm up to stop me and then he fell straight back. His lips were swelling, his hands. I went to pick him up and there

was a bee on his shirt. The bee was right there on him, like someone who commits a murder and then sticks around."

"It happens," Fix said.

Caroline reached over and took her sister's hand. No one
would have thought a thing about it. They were listening
to a terrible story, that was all. Franny wrapped her fingers
around Caroline's fingers.

"If it hadn't been for that bee I feel sure he would have
died when he was seven, but somehow I understood exactly
what had happened. I was up and out the door like lightning.
I had him in the car in two seconds. It isn't far to the hospital,
you know that, and in those days there wasn't half the traffic.
I just kept telling him to slow down, slow down and concentrate on breathing."

"What did you do with the rest of them?" Caroline said.

"I left them there. I don't think I even closed the door. Bert
was so mad at me when I told him what had happened. I was
scared to death at the time, but really I was proud of myself too.
I'd saved Cal's life! Bert said, you can't leave children alone like
that. You should have put them in the car. But Bert wasn't there,
and he thought I was a terrible mother anyway. If I'd rounded
up all those kids and thrown them in the car Cal would have
died. The doctor told me so. He told me how serious a bee sting
was for Cal, and how the next time it would be even worse. But
you can't keep a boy inside for the rest of his life, at least not
a boy like Cal. I was always on him about carrying his pills,
and I had a vial of epinephrine and a syringe in the house, but
Bert hadn't brought the epinephrine to his parents' house, and
I doubt they would have known how to give the shot anyway.

No one ever checked to make sure Cal had his pills." Teresa shook her head. "I don't blame Bert though. I used to but I don't anymore. The things you really need are never there when you need them. I know that. It could have happened when he was home with me."

"There's no protecting anyone," Fix said, and reached over from his wheelchair to put his hand on hers. "Keeping people safe is a story we tell ourselves."

"Bert swore he was going to cut down the orange trees in the back. They're always covered in bees when they're in bloom. He was in a rage about those trees, like they had done this to his son, but after a couple of days he forgot all about them. We all did."

She stopped and looked around the place they were now. "The emergency room was in the back of the hospital in those days. It's a lot nicer now. All of this is new."

After the CAT scan and an examination, the doctor came out to talk to them. "Mr. Cousins?" he said to Fix.

"Nope," Fix said.

This didn't seem to trouble the doctor a bit. He was there to relay the news and so he went ahead. "It looks like Mrs. Cousins has a diverticular abscess in her sigmoid colon. We're going to cool things down with antibiotics, give her something to keep her comfortable. We'll watch her white blood count and fever through the night. Keep her NPO, then we'll reexamine her in the morning and see how she's doing. Has she been sick very long?"

Caroline looked at Franny. "Maybe three days?" Franny said.

The doctor nodded. He made a note in the file he carried, told them she had been transferred to a room, and then excused himself. They imagined him imagining their neglect. Why hadn't they brought such a sick old woman to him sooner? There was no point in explaining themselves.

"Not cancer," Teresa said to the Keatings when they came to tell her goodbye. "But it still looks like I'm going to have to spend the night." She had a heart monitor now, an IV dripping into the back of her hand.

"Lucky you," Fix said. He was happy for her.

"Oh," Teresa said, touching her untethered hand to her forehead. "Cancer. I'm sorry. I shouldn't have said that. They're giving me morphine now. I'm loopy."

Fix gave a little wave to say it meant nothing.

"I'll come back later tonight and check on you," Franny said.

Teresa told her not to. "I talked to Albie. He'll be here first thing in the morning. I'm going to sleep straight through until then. To tell you the truth I'm very tired. And anyway, you've come out here to be with your father, not me. I've eaten up half your day."

"I just wish you could have had all of it," Caroline said. "The second half was definitely better than the first."

"We can wait here until you go to sleep," Fix said, feeling both chivalrous and uncertain. He'd been in the wheelchair too long. He needed to get home and into his recliner. It had felt good to take someone else to the hospital for a change, to think of Teresa's condition rather than his own. But pain was only going to be ignored for so long. It had come back on him with a baseball bat.

"I'm closing my eyes now. By the time you get to the door I'll be asleep." She smiled at Fix in his wheelchair and then, true to her word, closed her eyes. She should have married Fix Keating, that's what she was thinking when sleep wrapped her up in its soft arms. Fix Keating was a good man. But he was sick now, and she was sick. How was she going to be able to take care of him?

Caroline and Franny wheeled Fix down to the elevator. They were in a different part of the hospital now, having come in through the emergency room and then traveled to the other side of the world to get to the patient rooms. When they came outside they were someplace they'd never seen before and it took Caroline a while to find the car. By the time they got the wheelchair in the trunk and found the exit to the parking lot, Fix was asleep in the front seat, leaving Franny to put the address to the Santa Monica house into her phone.

Neither Caroline nor Franny said anything for a long time. Maybe they were each waiting to be sure their father wasn't going to hear them, but why? What had they done? Fix's head fell back against the headrest. His mouth was open. If he hadn't been snoring very lightly they might have wondered if he was dead.

"When she said that about Cal turning white, and then making a noise," Caroline said.

Franny nodded. Kumar's oldest son, Ravi, had asthma. There had been the summer at the lake in Wisconsin when she was clawing through his backpack trying to find the inhaler. The sound he was making was the sound Cal had made right before he died, that same high-pitched whistling that was, if not the opposite of breathing, at least the very end of breathing.

"It's so hard to remember what I was thinking," Caroline said. "Cal was already dead but I still felt like I could do something about it. I could make sure no one knew we'd given Albie the Benadryl. I could get the gun back to the car. Why did Cal have that goddamn gun?" Caroline said, turning to look at her. "Who leaves a gun in the car and never knows their teenaged son has it tied to his leg? And why did I care? Cal was dead and the gun didn't have anything to do with it. It's like this enormous tree had just crashed through the house and I was picking up leaves so no one would notice what had happened."

"We were kids. We had no idea what we were doing."

"I made it worse," Caroline said.

Franny shook her head. "You couldn't have made it worse. There isn't anything worse." She laid her forehead on the seat in front of her.

"Maybe I should have told her."

"Told her what?"

"I don't know, that Cal wasn't alone, that we were all there with him when he died."

"Holly and Jeanette were there too and they never told her. Or who knows, maybe they did. We have no idea what Teresa knows about what happened in Virginia."

"Unless she goes to the movies this weekend."

"Your guilt's got nothing on my guilt," Franny said. "Your guilt isn't even in the ballpark."

Caroline and Franny lost their father's eighty-third birthday. The traffic, which had been manageable driving over to Teresa's, was at a standstill going out to the beach from Torrance, and so they got home well after dark. The consequence of their kindness was that Fix had been too long in his wheelchair and too long in the car. His pain radiated out to his feet and hands and into the bones of his face, though it was nothing like the pain that concentrated into the white-hot center of himself.

"Just let me go to sleep," he said to Marjorie when they got him in the house. She had to bend over to hear him he had so little voice left. "I can't stand this," he said. He was tugging at his shirt, trying to get it off.

Marjorie helped him with the buttons. During the course of his illness, Fix had lost his reserves. He had no buffer to carry him through the unexpected. They had stayed out too long and now he was bone on bone.

"You were with Teresa Cousins?" Marjorie said to Franny, in the same way she might have said, *You took him to South Central to smoke crack?*

"Her son called right after we got out of the movie. She had to go to the hospital," Franny said.

All she had to do was bring him home first. They were practically at the house when Albie called, but it hadn't occurred to her that she was the one to make that decision, not Fix. "We didn't know it was going to take this long."

Caroline put a Lortab in a tiny spoonful of applesauce and gave it to her father. The pills were easier to swallow that way.

"Doesn't she have her own family?" Marjorie had always been so patient with the girls, right from the beginning when Fix used to bring them over to her mother's house to take them swimming. But dragging their dying father along on

an errand of mercy for someone they didn't know was tantamount to trying to kill him.

"She does," Franny said. "But none of them live in town.
Dad said he wanted to see her."

"He didn't know her. Why would he want to see her?"
Marjorie ran her hands across the shoulders of his rumpled
undershirt. "I'll get you to bed," she told him.

Franny looked at her sister, the two of them still standing in the den once Marjorie had rolled Fix away. "If there's
anything else I can fuck up today you let me know."

"It wasn't your fault," Caroline said, and rubbed her face.
Neither of them had eaten and neither of them would. "You
didn't know. And anyway, we had to go, all three of us. We
owed her that. I understand that it makes no sense to Marjorie, but even if it was a mistake, we owed it to Teresa."

Franny gave her sister a tired smile. "Oh, my love," she
said. "What do the only children do?"

"We'll never have to know," Caroline said.

Caroline went up to the bedroom they shared to call
Wharton and say goodnight. Franny went into the backyard
to call Kumar.

"Did you find the checkbook?" Franny asked.

"I did, but you could have texted me back six hours ago
when I asked you."

"Really, I couldn't have." She yawned. "If you'd been here
today you'd be overwhelmed with sympathy for me right
now. Did the boys make it home from soccer practice okay?"

"I haven't seen them," Kumar said.

"Don't give me a hard time. I'm not up for it."

"Ravi's in the shower. Amit is pretending to do his homework on the computer but he switches over to some horrible video game whenever I stop watching him."

"Are you watching him now?" Franny asked.

"I am," her husband said.

Marjorie tapped on the kitchen window and waved her inside.

"I have to go now," Franny said.

"You're still coming back?"

"That's one thing you don't have to worry about," she said, and hung up the phone.

"Your father wants you to come in and say goodnight," Marjorie said, looking tired. "I can't believe he's still awake."

"Is Caroline in there?"

Marjorie shook her head. "He said he wanted to talk to you."

Franny promised not to keep him up.

Marjorie had pushed their two single beds together and covered them with a king-sized blanket and bedspread to make it look like it was still one bed, even though Fix's side was a hospital bed. Sitting halfway up helped with the pain in his chest and made it easier for him to swallow his own saliva so he slept that way. That was how Franny found him, in his light-blue pajamas, staring at the ceiling.

"Close the door," Fix said, and patted the space in the bed beside him. "This is private."

She went and sat down next to her father. "I'm sorry I dragged you out to Torrance," Franny said. "I was thinking about Albie and Teresa when I should have been thinking about you."

"Don't listen to Marjorie," Fix said.

"Marjorie's looking out for you. That's why we had to go to Teresa's in the first place, because she doesn't have someone like Marjorie to take care of her."

"Forget about all of that for two minutes. We need to have a serious talk. Can you listen to me?" Fix in his bed seemed particularly hollow and small, her father's husk.

"Bring the bed up a little more," he said, and when Franny did he said, "Good. There. Now open the bedside table drawer."

It was a big drawer, deep and long and full of crossword puzzle books and envelopes, a paperback guide to the great hiking trails of California, a book of Kipling's poems, a pair of exercise grips to strengthen the hands, loose change, Vicks VapoRub, a rosary. The rosary surprised her. "What am I looking for?"

"It's in the back."

Franny pulled the drawer out farther and shifted the papers around. There she found the gun. She didn't have to ask. She took it out and held it in her lap. "Okay," she said.

Fix reached over and touched her hand, then he put his hand on the gun and smiled. "Marjorie made me promise that I'd turn everything in when I retired. She said no more guns once we move to the beach, so I didn't tell her."

"Okay." Franny put her hand on top of her father's hand. She felt the delicate structure of his skeleton beneath his paper skin. She imagined it was like touching a bat's wing.

"Thirty-eight Smith and Wesson. This was my gun for a long, long time."

"I remember," she said.

"I never left the house without that gun."

"Do you want me to take care of it for you?" Franny wasn't exactly sure how she would do that. She couldn't put it in her luggage. She couldn't take it on the plane or bring it into her house in Chicago with Kumar and the boys. She didn't want the gun but was sure she could figure something out.

"I can't pick it up anymore," he said. "It's too heavy. I can't get it out of the drawer. All the different things you think about, but I never thought about that."

They would go down to the firing range at the police academy in the summer and shoot paper targets when she and Caroline were girls. It was in all the world the one thing Franny was better at than Caroline. She could shoot a gun. Fix's friends would come by and marvel at Franny's target paper when they pulled them in. "Sign that girl up!" the cops would say, and Franny, clear of eye and steady of hand, would beam.

"Don't worry about that," Franny said.

"Could you shoot me, do you think?" her father asked.

"Your Lortab is kicking in, Dad. Go to sleep." She took her father's hand off the gun, then leaned over and kissed his forehead.

"It is kicking in so you have to listen to me. There's no time for us to talk anymore, just the two of us. I can't pick up the gun but no one knows that but you. No one would think of that. Lots of cops shoot themselves in the end, when the end comes to this. There's nothing wrong with it."

The gun lay heavy in her lap. "I'm not going to shoot you, Dad."

He looked at her then, his mouth open, and without his glasses she could see his eyes were fogged with cataracts. Was this the way Cal had looked at Teresa the summer he was seven, the bee crawling over his shirt? Was it the way Cal had looked at her when he died? She couldn't remember.

"I need your help. *Your* help, Franny. Marjorie puts the pills away. I don't know where they are, and if I did know I couldn't get up to get them. I wouldn't know which ones to take. She fills up this feeding tube like I'm a car. If I shot myself, no one would mind."

"Trust me, they would mind. I would mind."

"Marjorie and Caroline will go to the grocery store tomorrow and you'll stay here with me. Put on two pairs of those gloves, the disposable ones, one on top of the other. You put my hands on the gun and then hold your hands over my hands."

Franny put her hands over her father's hands. She couldn't write it off to the Lortab or the pain. "Dad."

"Face the grip out, not to the throat but away from the throat. Do you understand me? I'll be right here with you. We can go over it step by step. You hold it right under my chin, then tilt it back just a little, maybe twenty degrees. Once you get it set up I want you to lean back. You won't get hurt."

Why wasn't he asking Caroline? That's what she wanted to know. Caroline was his favorite. She was the one he trusted. But Caroline wouldn't have listened to him.

"I can't," she said.

"When the gun fires you'll drop it. Leave it however it falls. You pull off the gloves and stick them in your pocket. Go look in the mirror, make sure there's nothing on your face, then call 911. That's all you've got to do. No one is ever going to think it was you. And it won't be you, it's me. It's you helping me. I wouldn't put you in a bad spot." His eyes were closing, down and up then down.

"It would be a bad spot," she said. There had always been the sensation of letting her father down, living with her mother, living on the other side of the country, living with Bert. How strange it was that even now all of that stayed with her, that she would think, even for an instant, of not shooting her father as failing him again.

"People are scared of the wrong things," Fix said, his eyes closed. "Cops are scared of the wrong things. We go around thinking that what's going to get us is waiting on the other side of the door: it's outside, it's in the closet, but it isn't like that. What happened to Lomer, that's the anomaly. For the vast majority of the people on this planet, the thing that's going to kill them is already on the inside. You understand that, don't you, Franny?'"

"I understand," she said.

He reached out and patted her hand again, her hand and the gun. "I depend on you so much," he said. His mouth opened as if for one last thought, and then he fell asleep.

Sitting on the edge of her father's bed, Franny unloaded the revolver. Unloading, cleaning, reloading, that was all part of their childhood education. There were six bullets in the chamber and she put them in the front pocket of her jeans and stuck the gun in the back of the waistband beneath her shirt. Her pants were snug around the waist these days and for once she was glad about it.

When she came back to the den Caroline and Marjorie were watching *The Man Who Came to Dinner.* Caroline pushed the mute button while Monty Woolley tyrannized the secondary characters from his wheelchair.

"How's your father?" Marjorie asked.

"Asleep." Franny could feel the cold of the metal pressing into the small of her back. It was ridiculous, walking through the room with a gun and not mentioning it, but she didn't think the gun was anything Marjorie needed to know about, nor did she need to know about his request. She would tell Caroline in the morning, but there was nothing more that needed to be said tonight, not one more conversation. Franny said she was going to get into bed and read.

That night, after putting the gun in her suitcase and the bullets in a sock, Franny dreamt of Holly. It had been so many years since they had seen each other but there she was, still fourteen, her straight dark hair divided into pigtails, her cropped yellow top knotted halfway up her skinny white torso. She was still a girl, freckles unfaded, braces on her teeth. They were back in Virginia, back at Bert's parents' house, and they were walking through the long field that lay between the house and the barn. Holly was talking, talking, the way Holly was always talking, explaining the history of the commonwealth and the Mattaponi Indians who had once lived along the banks of the river. The Mattaponi, she said, had fought the English in the second and third Anglo-Powhatan Wars.

"Right here," she said, holding out her hands. "There weren't many of them to begin with, and between the two wars and all the diseases the English brought with them most of the Mattaponi died. Do you remember how Cal would look for arrowheads? Our grandfather had a dish of them on his desk but he'd never give us any. He said he was saving them. What was he saving them for do you think? An uprising?"

Franny looked out over the green slope of grass. There was a shallow pond beyond the barn where the horses liked to wade on hot days, where they themselves had ventured in on some occasions despite the thick, sucking muck at the bottom. She looked at the distant line of trees that rimmed the field to the left and the stand of hay to the far right that the Cousinses leased out. She was trying to take in how beautiful it all was—the grass and the light and the trees, the entire valley. This was where Cal had died, where Holly and Caroline and Jeanette had run through the field once they realized what had happened, back to the house to get Ernestine, Caroline telling her to stay with Cal in case he needed help. Why had Caroline told her to stay?

"You took the gun then, remember?" Holly said. "You brought it back to Caroline later that night."

Cal's eyes were shut but his mouth was open like he was still trying to pull in air. His lips were thick and swollen and his tongue was coming out of his mouth. Franny stood over him, looking back in the direction of the house and then looking down. When she remembered the gun she pulled back his pants leg. There it was, stuffed in his sock and tied to his calf with a red bandanna. Franny got it in her head that Ernestine or the Cousinses or whoever was coming out to save her shouldn't find the gun. They would all get in trouble for that. "I don't know why I took it," she said. She really didn't.

Holly shook her head. "You couldn't have left it there. We were all so obsessed with the gun. It was all we ever thought about."

Franny had untied the bandanna and, carefully, pointing the gun away from herself and away from Cal, unloaded it the way her father taught her. She put the bullets in the front pocket of her shorts, holding the open revolver up to the light, spinning the cylinder and looking down the barrel to the sun to make sure it was empty. She tied it up in the red cloth but there was really no place to put it. She tried to put it in her waistband but of course it showed. Finally she decided to hide it behind a tree nearby. When everyone was gone she would go back and get it and take it to the house. She would get Jeanette to come with her and they would put the gun in Jeanette's purse. No one would think that was strange because Jeanette always carried her purse. She remembered being glad to have something else to worry about, something other than Cal.

Franny looked over at the barn. "I always thought I did the wrong thing."

"What would the right thing have been?" Holly put her arm around Franny's waist. "We had no idea what was going on. We didn't even know he'd been stung by a bee."

"We didn't?"

"Not until later. We did that night when Dad came back from the hospital, but before that we didn't have a clue."

"I loved it here," Franny said, though she had never known it before.

Holly looked surprised. "Did you? I hated this place."

Franny looked at her. Holly had been such a pretty girl. Why had she never noticed that? She thought of her as a sister now. "Why did you come back then?"

"To make sure you were going to be okay," Holly said. "We always stuck together. Don't you remember that? We were such a fierce little tribe."

"Listen," Franny said, looking up. "Do you hear the birds?"

Holly shook her head. "It's your phone. That's what I came to tell you. You shouldn't worry."

"About the birds?" Franny asked, but then Holly was gone and the room was dark again. She could still hear them.

"Answer your phone," Caroline said from the other bed.

The room was dark except for the light of her phone. She picked it up, even though nothing good ever came from answering the phone in the middle of the night. "Hello?" Franny said.

"Mrs. Mehta?" a voice said, a woman's voice.

"Yes?"

"This is Dr. Wilkinson. I'm calling from Torrance Memorial Medical Center. Mrs. Mehta, I'm sorry to tell you that your stepmother has passed away."

"Marjorie's dead?" Franny sat straight up, the news pulling her awake. How was that possible? When had she gone to the hospital? Caroline got out of her bed and turned on the light on the table between them. There was only one person who was going to die and that was their father.

"What?" Caroline said.

"Mrs. Cousins," the doctor said. "Her heart monitor alerted the nurse a little after four o'clock this morning. We attempted resuscitation but it was unsuccessful."

"Mrs. Cousins?"

"Teresa died?" Caroline said.

"I'm sorry," the doctor said again. "She was very sick."

"Wait a minute," Franny said. "I don't think I'm understanding what you're saying. Could you say this to my sister?"

Franny gave the phone to Caroline. Caroline would know what questions to ask. The digital clock on the bedside table said it was 4:47 in the morning. She wondered if Albie would be awake by now, if he had set his alarm. He was taking an early flight to Los Angeles to see his mother.

8

Six months in advance of her retirement, Teresa bought herself a ticket to Switzerland to visit Holly at the Zen center. She did it so she'd have something to look forward to. She wasn't sure about retiring so much as she feared becoming a doddering presence in the job she had loved for so long. Over time she'd seen everyone come and go, rise and fall and pack the contents of his or her desk into a box. Sooner or later she'd have to do the same, and wouldn't it be better to do it before they started nudging her towards the door? At seventy-two she might well have the time to figure out another life, not that she was sure what that meant exactly. She thought she might take a bridge class or do a better job with her yard. She'd thought that she could go to Switzerland.

Two weeks after her retirement party, a pretty gold watch on her wrist and a ticket in her purse, she called a taxi for the airport.

Holly didn't come home anymore. When she first went to Switzerland twenty-five years ago, she had planned to be gone for a month. She came back after six months, and then it was only to apply for a permanent visa. She officially quit her job at Sumitomo Bank, which they had held for her. Holly had been an economics major at Berkeley and even though she was young she'd been valued at her job. She gave up the lease on her apartment which had been sitting empty all this time. She sold her furniture.

"Are you in love?" her mother asked. She didn't actually think that Holly was in love, even though she exhibited all the classic signs: distraction and dewiness, a loss of appetite. Holly had cut her dark hair close to her head. Her face was scrubbed, and for the first time in years Teresa could see that a smattering of freckles still remained. Teresa was afraid her oldest daughter had been kidnapped even though they were sitting together at the kitchen table drinking coffee, that her brain had been taken over by a cult that had allowed her body to come home long enough to sort out her possessions, throwing everyone off the trail. But asking Holly if she'd been taken over by a cult was a harder question.

"Not in love," Holly said, picking up her mother's hand and squeezing it. "Not exactly."

It used to be that Holly came home from time to time, first once a year, then every two or three. Teresa suspected that Bert bought the tickets but she never asked. After a while the small trickle of occasional visits dried up. Holly said she didn't want to come back to the States anymore, making it sound like it was her country she was letting go of rather than her family. She said she was happier in Switzerland.

While Teresa ardently wished for her children's happiness, she didn't understand why they couldn't have found it closer to Torrance. With one of them gone, the other three might have chosen to circle the wagons, but it seemed just the opposite had happened, that Cal's death had flung each of them to their own far corner. She missed them all but mostly she missed Holly. Holly was the least mysterious of her children, the only one who on occasion would crawl into her bed at night, saying she wanted to talk.

You could always come see me, Holly would write whenever her mother complained, first in slow Aérogramme letters and then, blessedly, in e-mails once the Zen center, called Zen-Dojo Tozan, got its own computer. Teresa never could remember the actual name of the place so it helped to see it printed out.

What would I do in Switzerland? her mother wrote back.

Sit with me, Holly wrote.

It wasn't so much to ask. Certainly she'd sat with Jeanette and Fodé and the boys in Brooklyn. She'd sat with Albie in any number of places including her own living room. Over the long years, Teresa had gotten past her suspicion of Buddhism and meditation. Holly, the times she'd seen her, had still been Holly. And while there had been plenty of good reasons not to go when she was working, without work all she could tell herself was that she was too old, the trip too long, the tickets too expensive, and the connections too intimidating. None of those were reason enough to miss seeing her own daughter.

The flight from Los Angeles to Paris was twelve hours. Teresa accepted the free wine whenever the cart rolled down the narrow aisle, slept fitfully against the window, and tried to read *The English Patient*. By the time the plane landed in France she had aged twenty years. Prosecutors should insist the trials of murderers and drug lords be held in economy class on crowded transatlantic flights, where any suspect would confess to any crime in exchange for the promise of a soft bed in a dark, quiet room. Off the plane, stiff and slow, she shuffled into the river of life: the roll-aboard suitcases trailing behind the cell-phone-talkers like obedient dogs, everyone walking with such assurance that it never occurred to her not to follow them. She was too muddled to think for herself, yet when she finally did, snapped back to reality by the sight of an information desk, she was told that her departure gate was in another terminal that could be accessed by shuttle bus, and that the flight to Switzerland was three hours delayed.

Teresa accepted a highlighted map of the airport from the startlingly handsome informational Frenchman and started making her way back in the direction from whence she came. Her feet had swollen on the flight and were now a full size larger than the shoes she was wearing. It wasn't that she expected someone was going to show up and escort her to her gate, but she couldn't help but remember the way things had gone the last time she was in this airport fifty years ago: she was a different person under considerably different circumstances.

Bert had taken Teresa to Paris for their honeymoon. It was all a surprise. He made the hotel reservations, ordered francs from the bank, asked Teresa's mother to pack her daughter's suitcase. His parents drove them to Dulles the morning after the wedding to catch their flight and she still didn't know where they were going. She had majored in French literature at the University of Virginia and had never left the country. She had never spoken French outside of class.

She stopped at a little café on the concourse, collapsed

into the white molded-plastic chair, and ordered a café au lait and a croissant, that was easy enough. She had nothing but time. She eased her heels out of the backs of her shoes even though she knew it was a mistake. Her feet would expand like bread dough and she would never be able to cram them back in. For the first time since she was in her twenties she thought about what a beautiful boy Bert Cousins had been, tall and sandy blond, with such dark blue eyes they startled her every morning when he opened them. His family was rich as Croesus, her grandmother liked to say. His parents had given him a little green Fiat when he graduated from college.

When they met he was in his second year of law school at UVA, the top of his class, and she was in her senior year of college. She slipped on a patch of ice one snowy January morning hurrying to class and had gone down hard, books and papers fanning out around her, the icy air knocked from her lungs. She was lying on her back, too stunned for the moment to do anything but watch the flakes of snow wafting towards her, when Bert Cousins leaned into her view and asked if she would allow him to help her. Yes, she would. He picked her up, a stranger, picked her up in his arms and carried her all the way to the infirmary, missing his next class to wait while they wrapped her ankle. A year later, when he asked her to marry him, he told her that he wanted them to move to California after he finished law school. He would take the California bar and they would start a whole new life together where nobody knew them. He wasn't going to spend his days drawing up contracts for real estate sales, he was going to practice real law. And he wanted children, he said, lots and lots of children. As an only child he had wished for nothing but brothers and sisters. Teresa looked back and forth between Bert and the pretty ring on her hand and thought she must be emitting light from her entire body she loved him so much. It was unnerving to remember that now, at seventy-two, spreading strawberry jam on the tip of her croissant, how much she had loved him. She could barely hold the thought in her mind. She had loved Bert Cousins, and then grown used to him, then was disappointed in him, and then later, after he left her with four small children, she had hated him with the full force of her life. But in the airport when she was twenty-two, her love for him had precluded all thoughts of ever not loving him. They held hands on the way to baggage claim, and while they waited beside the shining silver luggage chute he kissed her, full and deep, not giving a thought to who might be watching, because they were married, they were in Paris.

Teresa looked at all the people walking past her table at the airport coffee shop and wondered how many of them were starting their honeymoons and how many of them were in love and how many of them would not be in love later on. The truth was she had more or less forgotten about Bert. It took a long time but it was a fact that now entire years would pass when she failed to ask the children how their father was because she simply didn't think of him. She had lived long enough that Bert and all the love and rage he had engendered were gone. Cal was still with her, Jim Chen was there, but Bert, alive and well in Virginia, was gone.

Revived by the coffee and the rest, Teresa stuffed her feet painfully back in her shoes and beat a slow path to her gate. Maybe she would stay in Switzerland forever, maybe she would become a Buddhist. She couldn't imagine doing this again.

Holly had neglected to go into the tiny room that had once been a broom closet beneath the kitchen stairs to check the computer for the status of her mother's flight from Paris. It was only now that she was at the airport in Zurich standing in front of the arrival board that she could see the plane was three hours late. True, she didn't have occasion to go to the airport very often, but what kind of an idiot forgets to check the time before making an hours-long drive? Because it was a rule that whoever took the car also had to take the phone, she was able to send a text to Mikhail and explain the situation. She knew he wouldn't care. He told her they didn't need the car but still, she felt like she was inconveniencing the community by keeping it for so long. Assuming that the time now listed was in fact correct, they would not be returning until after two o'clock. She had told her mother to take the train from Paris. No one flew from Paris to get to Lucerne. The train was a snap. But her mother had despaired at the thought of taking a train from the airport to the Gare de Lyon and then finding the train to Lucerne. And maybe it would have been impossible, with the jet lag and the luggage. Holly could have taken the train up and met her in Paris but she never suggested that. She didn't want to be away that long.

Holly had completed her morning kitchen work early, washing and peeling ten pounds of potatoes, cutting them into chunks, and leaving them covered in cold salted water while at every moment striving to remain present in her task. She had gone to the guestroom where her mother would be

sleeping to make sure there were towels and a washcloth beside the basin and a bottle of water and a glass beside the bed.
She excused herself from morning meditation early, stepping
around the cushions of others as quietly as possible to leave
for the airport, though of course now she realized she hadn't
had to do that at all. She could have stayed. Her sense of irrita-
tion with herself was so ridiculously disproportionate to the
event that she had to wonder if the problem wasn't really that
she didn't want her mother to visit. While she understood the
importance of letting all thoughts rise without judgment, to
see them and to let them go, she decided it would probably be
best just to squelch this one.

Holly bought a Toblerone bar at the news kiosk and then
looked around the waiting area for discarded newspapers,
as chocolate and news were the two things her life was lacking. And sex. Sex was lacking but she had enough sense not
to look for that in the airport. She found copies of *Le Matin*,
Blick (but she didn't do so well reading German) and, wonder of wonders, a complete Tuesday edition of the *New York
Times*. Suddenly she was soothed. The idea of spending three
hours in the airport with three newspapers and Toblerone
was nothing short of a miracle. She peeled back the tinfoil
and broke off a piece of candy, resting it on her tongue to melt
before she read the science section of the *Times*: Tasmanian
devils were dying of oral cancer; there was reason to think it
might be better to run without running shoes; and children
living in poverty in the inner cities were as likely to suffer
from asthma as children in war zones. She tried to figure
out what she was supposed to do with the information. How
could she save the devils, get them to stop biting one another,

which appeared to be how the cancer was spread, and why was she worrying about a small, vicious marsupial in Tasmania and feeling next to nothing about the asthmatic children? Why had she read the entire article about running when she wasn't a runner but skipped the piece about geothermal energy? Exactly how shallow had she become? She folded the paper in her lap and sat with the information for a moment. She thought that she should leave Zen-Dojo Tozan more often, or maybe leave it altogether, and she thought that she should never leave it under any circumstances, like Siobhán, whom Holly had never seen go farther than the mailbox at the end of the driveway.

When Holly remembered her life in California, she remembered seeing everything in terms of who had less than she did and who had more, who was prettier, smarter, who had a better relationship (everyone, usually), who was getting promoted faster, because as much as they had praised her at the bank there seemed to be people they preferred. She was constantly trying to figure out how to do it better, how to get it right, and in doing so she had started to grind her teeth at night. She had chewed a soft crater on the inside of her left cheek, and was picking at the cuticles of her thumbs until they bled. She made an appointment with an internist, told him her problems, and then showed him the inside of her mouth. He peered around her tongue and teeth with a penlight, looked at her hands, and then suggested meditation. Or that's what she thought he had said, "You're going to need meditation."

The instant she heard the word she felt her heart surge, as if her heart had been waiting for this exact moment. *Finally!*

her heart said to her. *At last!* "Where can I learn to meditate?" she asked. Just the word in her mouth brought forth joy.

The doctor looked at her as if wondering how crazy she might actually be. "Med-i-*ca*-tion," he said again, slower and louder this time. "You'll need medication for your anxiety. I'm going to write you a prescription for Ativan. We'll work with the dosage. We'll have to figure out what's right for you."

But Holly dropped the white slip of paper in the trash can after giving the receptionist a twenty for her co-pay. However unwittingly, the doctor had told her how she would be cured. She didn't even understand exactly what meditation entailed at that point but she knew she was going to find out. She read a couple of books, listened to some dharma talks on cassette tapes in her car, and then found a group that sat on Wednesday nights and Saturday mornings. She started a sitting practice at home, getting up early before she went to the bank in the morning. Six months later some people from the Wednesday group invited her along for a weekend retreat. Later, she sat in silence for a week at a spirituality center just north of Berkeley. It was there she saw a notice on the corkboard about Zen-Dojo Tozan. She felt the same acceleration in her heart that she had felt when she first misunderstood her doctor. *There I am*, she thought, looking at the picture of the chalet balanced on a soft sweep of mountain flowers. She pulled the push-pin from the brochure and let it drop into her hand.

Things like this happened to Holly. At times she had a sense of being guided, and when she did she attributed it to Cal.

For years after Cal died, Holly was rocked with regret that they hadn't been closer (and there was regret about other things as well). But since coming to Switzerland, she'd started to see that for a fifteen-year-old boy and a thirteen-year-old girl in a stressful living situation they'd done pretty well. They yelled at one another but carried no grudges. They shoved but never slapped or pinched. They threw couch pillows at one another, not dishes. Holly corrected Cal's homework without condescension, and Cal, in the shining memory of her childhood, had once yanked two girls off of her in the hallway at school, one by her ponytail and the other by her shirt collar, as they were attempting to stuff Holly into her locker. "You bitches get off my sister," he had said as the bitches stumbled backwards and then ran down the hall in tears. He had hurt them, scared them senseless. Holly, who made it her business to look after everyone else, was for that one golden moment protected. By her brother.

As the two oldest children, Holly and Cal worked together to look after Albie and Jeanette, keeping them away from the stove and the knives when they were younger. And they looked after their mother too, maybe not in tandem, but they made an effort to lighten her load, to keep things from her whenever possible. The more Holly felt Cal's presence in her life now, the more she knew he cared for her, that he forgave her. The better job she did at keeping her life quiet, her eyes open to the simple beauty that surrounded her, the better she was able to hear him. She didn't hear him in any nutty way, they didn't sit around and talk politics, it was more a pleasant feeling, easy enough to achieve at Zen-Dojo Tozan but she could even do it here, in the waiting area of the Zurich airport. She believed that most of the human population didn't avail themselves to their full psychic potential. They lived in a state of mental clutter, the bombardment of goods and services, information and striving. They wouldn't be able to recognize true happiness if it were standing on their foot. It had been almost impossible to hear her brother when she was at Berkeley, at the Sumitomo Bank, or anywhere in Los Angeles, but in Switzerland, this place where he had never been, well, it was better.

Holly went back to her newspapers. She read about Broadway plays. She read a book review and an op-ed about flooding in Iowa. She read about the plight of women in Afghanistan. She finished half of her chocolate and put the other half in her purse for later. Seeing the time, she got up and went to stand with the families and the drivers holding hand-lettered signs. When she saw Teresa walking towards her—so tiny! so much older! how long had it been now? ten years? more than that?—she was flooded with love, such a huge wave, both her love and her brother's. She held out her arms. "Oh, Mom," Holly said.

Where to begin with the marvels? First of course was Holly, who, with her cropped black hair touched in gray and her Birkenstocks and wooly socks, was radiant. All those people packed together on the other side of security, all those people making a single, indistinguishable mass, and then, *bam!* Holly. She was something else entirely, no one could have missed her. When Teresa fell into her embrace it was as if they had never been parted. She had such an overwhelming memory of the nurse coming into her room the morning Holly was born, laying that perfect baby in her arms, the baby who was now this beautiful woman. Teresa kissed her neck, pressed her cheek to her daughter's sternum. "I'm sorry you had to wait so long," she said, not knowing if she meant the three-hour delay or all the years it had taken her to get there.

"I had a nice time," Holly said, running her hand across her mother's head. She took the carry-on and her purse, slung them over her shoulder like they were nothing, like she could have just as easily slung Teresa over her shoulder too. She walked her straight to the restroom without asking if she had to go, and she did. This was the person Holly had always been: in charge, making decisions, being helpful without being asked. When Teresa pointed out her luggage at the baggage claim, Holly scooped it up and laughed.

"You pack like a Californian!" she said, thrilled by such a small thing. "I do, too."

"How do Californians pack?" Teresa was laughing without getting the joke, her smile so wide she felt certain she was showing teeth that had not been seen in years.

Holly held up her mother's black wheelie-bag. It was small and discreet, a footnote to all the giant bright-pink hard-sides reinforced with bungee-cords that circled before them. "Europeans pack like they're never coming home. I think it has to do with the war."

Outside the air was bright and cold despite it being the first of September. It had been ninety-six degrees when she left Los Angeles. Holly helped her on with her coat. Teresa was proud of herself for having brought the coat in the first place. At home in her living room she had put it on and then taken it off, locked the front door, gone to the taxi, gone back inside and put the coat on again. She could see the Alps in the distance from the parking lot now. She had seen them from the plane, the snow-covered peaks. Alps. She pulled the coat tighter. Who would have thought Teresa Cousins would ever see Alps?

The Zen-Dojo Tozan's Citroën that Holly drove was more like a soup can than a car. The flimsy metal shuddered as she downshifted around the curves, the gearshift a long stick coming up from the floorboard. Back home on the 405, such a car would be crushed by the blowback from a passing SUV, but on this perilous mountain road it felt like all the other tin cans. They could bump into one another without significant harm, like people brushing past on a crowded street. No one had upped the ante in order to save themselves, built a daily tank that would obliterate the competition. They were all in this together. The guard rail that separated them from the vertiginous drop off the side of the mountain seemed similarly unprepared to save a life, but what difference did it make? They were all going to die anyway, all of them. They weren't even at the Zen center—whatever it was called—and already Teresa felt she was getting the point. Who needed air bags? The reinforced steel-cage construction that created a barrier to the world? Teresa rolled down her window—rolled it down with a hand crank!—and breathed in the bright Swiss air.

"So beautiful," she said. They shot into a stone tunnel cut through the side of a mountain: light then darkness then pine trees.

"Just you wait," her daughter said.

"I have to tell you, Holly, I didn't understand until now.

I mean, I've been happy for you, but in the back of my mind I was always thinking, *What's wrong with Torrance?*" They drove past two shaggy mountain goats on the side of the road, their curled horns looking like crowns. No doubt they were waiting for Heidi and Grandfather to herd them back into the mountains. Teresa looked over at Holly. "Why would anyone live in Torrance?"

"There's nothing wrong with home," Holly said, feeling so pleased to receive her mother's affirmation. "But it's quieter here. It's better for me."

"I think about Jeanette in Brooklyn with Fodé and the boys. I think she likes all the noise, her tight little space. I think that's what holds her together. And Albie, always picking up and going someplace else, always looking for something new. That probably works for him. He's in New Orleans now."

"He e-mails me sometimes," Holly said, feeling such a sudden longing for her brother and sister, wanting them all to sit together in the same room with their mother.

"That's good."

"What about you?"

"What about me?" Teresa said, craning around to catch another glimpse of the view that receded behind them.

"Has staying in Torrance been good for you? Was it the right choice?"

They were driving through a forest now. The trees, their lower trunks furred with moss, got thicker and taller and started to cut into the light while ferns stretched across the forest floor. There were enormous rocks, boulders really, that looked like they'd been placed by set designers around a fast-running stream. *Show me an enchanted forest!* the producer must have said.

"Your father wanted me to move all of us to Virginia when he left with Beverly, so we'd be close by. I didn't even consider it, to tell you the truth. Maybe I should have. It would have made things easier on you kids. I just couldn't find it in myself to be that accommodating."

"That's the stupidest thing I ever heard," Holly said, foolishly taking her eyes off the road for a second to stare at her mother. "I never knew he said that."

"Then after Cal died." Teresa shrugged. "Well, you remember that. We sure weren't moving to Virginia after Cal died, though I'll tell you, it bothered me to have him buried there. It was just about going forward in those days, one step, one step, not falling all the way down into myself. I didn't think about changing my life. My life had already been changed. I just had to get through it."

"You got through it." Holly took the car down to second. They were behind a truck, climbing and climbing.

"We all did, I guess, in our own ways. You don't think you're going to but then you do. You're still alive. That was the thing that caught me in the end: I was still alive. You and Albie and Jeanette, still alive. And we wouldn't be forever, so I had to do something with that."

Teresa put her hand over Holly's hand, felt the deep rattle of the gearshift. "Listen to me talking. I never talk like this."

"It's Switzerland. That's what it does to people." Holly stopped to reconsider. "I should say that's what it's done to me. Actually, most of the people I've met here are pretty quiet."

Teresa smiled and nodded. "Well, it's good. I like it."

Zen-Dojo Tozan was not in Sarnen or Thun but somewhere between the two, not in a village but in the tall grass and blue flowers. It occupied a large chalet that was built high into the slope of a mountain. The chalet had been the country home of a banker from Zurich. In the summer he and his wife swam with their five children in the lake and in the winter they skied, and in between, unbeknownst to anyone in Sarnen or Thun or Zurich, they sat together on zafu cushions, all seven of them, and closed their eyes and cleared their minds as surely as the bracing mountain air had cleared their lungs. The house was left with a trust to form Zen-Dojo Tozan, with the understanding that the family's children and their children and all of the children to come would be welcome. Katrina, the fourth daughter, now in her seventies, lived there full time in the small back bedroom she had slept in as a child. Along with Katrina there were fourteen other full-time residents. Twice a year they hosted retreats, running a rented shuttle bus back and forth from the inn in Thun, but most of their income came from walking sticks.

All of the residents participated in some way in the carving or distribution of the sticks, either the art or the business, they liked to say. The sticks were highly sought after, especially by American and Australian meditators who knew that they would never make it to Switzerland. Holly, who displayed no talent with wood or knives, did the accounting. She had found there was virtually no ceiling on what could be charged for a long pole of Swiss stone pine with a carved fish for a handle. Drop a five-euro compass into the fish's back and double the price, even though no one seemed to understand the basic tenets of orienteering anymore. They bought the wood from a mill in Lausanne, and while they could have had a cheaper and more compelling stock from Germany, they had made the decision to keep the sticks Swiss. That's what it said on their website: Swiss walking sticks carved from Swiss stone pine by meditators in Switzerland. Every day after meditation and community chores, a few hours were devoted to the sticks: Paul whittled the wood into sticks, Lelia blocked out the crude bodies of the fish with a carving knife, and then Hyla began the delicate work of scales. These sticks, along with their modest endowment, kept up the roof and paid the taxes and put cheese and bread on the table. They had a wait list of eight months for walking sticks. The wait list for residences had gotten too long to be useful and was stuck in a desk drawer and forgotten.

"We're lucky there's a guest room open," Holly said, taking her mother's hand as she walked her up the steep wooden steps. Her mother, steady enough, would benefit from a stick. The wind could knock a person over some days. "People come as a guest for a month and then they refuse to leave. There are three guest rooms and the schedule is always messed up. People just stay and stay. They think one of us is going to leave and make a space for them."

The chalet was ringed by a wide wooden porch that jutted out over the crystalline world. Heavy wooden chairs hewn by a careless axe were spread around so that a disciple might rest while taking in the view. The Alps looked like a drawing of the Alps on a candy wrapper, an idealized version meant to draw strangers in. Teresa had to stop and catch her breath, from the view, the thinner air, from the fact that she had actually done it and was there.

"It worked for you," she said, huffing slightly.

Holly stood there, seeing it all again through her mother's eyes. "Well, someone actually died while I was waiting them out. That's when I came back to California and quit my job. He was a Frenchman named Philippe. The walking sticks had been Philippe's idea years before when they were running out of money and worried they'd have to give the place up. He was a sweet old bird. I still have his room."

"Do other people's mothers come?" Teresa asked, trying not to sound competitive but feeling exactly that. She was so proud of herself.

"Sometimes. Less than you'd think."

As soon as she saw the bed in her room Teresa took a nap. Then before dinner and the dharma talk and the last sitting of the day, Holly did her best to give her mother a crash course in meditation. Breathing in and out, following the breath, letting thoughts come up and pass away without judgment. "You just have to do it," she said finally, fearing her explanation was doing more harm than good. "It's pretty straightforward."

So Teresa, wearing the track suit she wore in the mornings when she did her power walk with her neighbor, sat down on a cushion beside her daughter and closed her eyes.

Nothing much happened at first. She thought about the ache in her left knee. Then there was the thought that the other people seemed nice. She liked Mikhail, the Russian who she had called Michael. Did he run the place? Very welcoming. All of them with their hair cut short like Holly's. And why not? What difference did it make? There was no one to impress. She could see that Holly was happy here, but was it a real life? And what would she do when she was Teresa's age? Would they take care of her? She could ask the older woman, the one who'd grown up in this house. Imagine this place as a *house*, a home for a single family. How many servants must they have had to keep this up? Both of her feet were asleep.

She caught herself then. Such babble! Teresa was shocked by the roaming idleness of her mind, as if she were sifting through trash on the side of the freeway and was stopped, enchanted, by every foil gum wrapper. She came back for a single breath but found herself reflecting on the bean salad they'd had for dinner, some kind of pink beans in there she hadn't seen since childhood. She couldn't remember what they were called. Her mother would ask her to pick through the beans before she soaked them, to look for little rocks, and she would be so meticulous until she lost interest, dumping the unchecked beans on top of the ones she had vetted, ruining everything. Did anyone in her family ever bite down on a rock?

One breath? She couldn't manage that? Maybe a single inhalation that wasn't burdened by thought? She tried. There. Okay. Her back hurt. Without warning her head dropped forward and for an instant she was sound asleep. She made a small, startled sound like a dog or a pig having a dream. She sat up straight again, opened her eyes slightly to see if anyone had caught her. She looked around at the peaceful faces of her neighbors, her daughter, as if she could see the clarity of their untroubled minds. She was ashamed of herself.

At the end of the session Holly helped her stand. Everyone came to shake her hand, give her a small embrace. They were so fond of Holly. They were so glad Teresa had come to visit.

"Don't worry about the meditation," a woman named Carol said, her eyes as placid as a glacial lake. "It doesn't make a lot of sense at first."

"I meditated on my own every day for years before I came to this place," Paul the stick-maker said. "But to meditate here for the very first time in your life? That would be like taking your first run at the Olympics." He patted her shoulder. "You should be very proud of yourself."

In the single bed of the guest room, Teresa, wide awake, looked at the ceiling, the regular notches around the crown molding like evenly spaced teeth. She'd flown halfway around the world for this? To sit? She had sat at her desk half her life. She sat in her car, on the plane. What could she have been thinking? She had wanted to see her daughter. Had Bert ever been to visit Holly here? Did Bert sit? Why hadn't she thought to ask? Light from the enormous moon flooded her little room, painting the walls and covering her bed. She thought of all the women and men, mostly men, she had in her own small way helped the Los Angeles District Attorney's Office send to prison. All of the cases she had worked to prepare so that they would be prosecuted and spend their nights in narrow beds and spend their days in silence. How was it that she'd never really wondered what became of them before? There were hundreds of cases that had come across her desk over the years. There were thousands. Were those men staring up at their ceilings now in the cells where they lived, trying to empty their minds?

It went on like this for Teresa day after day, three times a day. She filed into the meditation room with the others and someone would stoke the blue ceramic stove with coal and then everyone would sit together in a circle on the dark green cushions and wait for Mikhail to tap the little gong that signaled the beginning. It was madness. She would have quit—taken her copy of *The English Patient* to the second-floor balcony or walked alone through the tall grass while the others looked for inner peace—had it not been for the fact that Holly was so proud of her. Her daughter kept an arm looped through her arm, dragged her cushion closer to be near her. The other residents gazed upon the two of them in deep appreciation—in the kitchen, at meals, while meditating (Teresa would sometimes cheat and briefly open her eyes, causing the others to immediately shut theirs)—other mothers did not visit, and if they did visit, they most certainly did not sit.

Teresa kept sitting.

Lelia gave a dharma talk about letting go of self-definition: I can't do this because of what happened to me in my childhood; I can't do that because I am very shy; I could never go there because I'm afraid of clowns or mushrooms or polar bears. The group gave a gentle, collective laugh of self-recognition. Teresa found the talk helpful, as she had been having an extended interior dialogue during meditation about how septuagenarians from Torrance were fundamentally unsuited for Buddhism. Pretty Hyla, whose fine bones were beautifully featured by her lack of hair, took her for a walk and told her the name of every plant and every tree they passed. They saw an ibex in the distance. She rolled a piece of juniper between her palms and let Teresa sniff her open hands, the hands that found the fish inside the handles of the sticks. Hyla told Teresa her mother had died five years ago and that she was very lonely. After that she held Teresa's hand as they walked back to the chalet. Okay, Teresa thought, I can be your mother today. They went back to the kitchen and sliced apples for a pie.

"I want you to cut off my hair," she said to Holly before dinner.

"Really?" Holly leaned over and touched her mother's hair. It was thick and gray and she wore it in a bob with the sides pulled back in barrettes for lack of a better idea.

"I've gotten used to the look, and anyway, I think it will help me fit in." Teresa wouldn't have done it had she been going back to work. At work her hair would have been a point of conversation, but when she got home it would be a signal of her new life. Her neighbors would see her, the checkers in the grocery store, and they would know she was different now.

Holly went and got the electric clippers out of the small plastic tub where they were kept in the downstairs bath. She took her mother outside on the deck and pinned a towel around her neck. They all cut one another's hair. They could have done it themselves but it was nice, having someone else's hands on your head every month or so.

"You're sure?" Holly asked before she turned the clippers on.

Teresa gave a single nod of assurance. "When in Switzerland."

And there went her hair, the thick gray tufts settling down around their feet like storm clouds dispersed. When she was finished Holly came around to assess her work.

"What do I look like?" Teresa asked smiling, running her hand over the velvet.

"Like me," Holly said, and it was true.

Sometimes Holly came into the guest room at night, the same room she had slept in when she first arrived twenty years before. She liked it in there. Teresa scooted over as far as she could in the little bed to make a place for her. The two lay together on their sides, the only way there was room, and talked, two women who hadn't talked in bed with anyone for years.

"Do you think you'll stay here?" Teresa asked, pulling up the blankets over their shoulders. It was freezing at night. Holly was forty-five, and while this life was all very beautiful, if she was ever going to want something else, a husband or a job, she had to think about that.

"I won't stay forever," Holly said. "I don't think I will. But I've never come close to figuring out how I'd leave. It's like I expect destiny to throw open the door of the Dojo one day and say, 'Holly! It's time!'"

"Call me when that happens," her mother said.

"You should see how pretty it is here in the snow."

They were quiet for a while, maybe both of them nearly asleep, and then Holly said, "Do you ever think about staying? You could be one of those people in the guest room who we think is going to leave and never does."

Teresa smiled in the dark, though she realized then she couldn't exactly imagine leaving either. She put her arm around Holly's waist and thought of her body as something she'd made, something that was so completely separate from her now. "I don't think so," she said, and then they did both fall asleep.

On the eighth day of her eleven-day visit to the Zen center, Teresa went to morning meditation, sat down on her cushion next to Holly, closed her eyes, and saw her oldest son. He was so clear it was as if he had been in the room with her all this time, as if he had been with her in every room she'd ever been in in her life and she had simply failed to turn her gaze in the right direction until now. She wasn't having a dream or an out-of-body experience. She understood that she was still in the chalet, still sitting, but at the same time she was with Cal and his sisters. She was with the Keating girls, Caroline and Franny. She saw the five of them going out the kitchen door of Bert's parents' house, the door that she had gone through countless times when she and Bert were dating, when they were planning their wedding.

Ernestine, the cook, is telling them not to be a bother to Ned down at the barn and to do what he tells them, and the girls say yes ma'am. She gives a half bag of withered carrots dug out from the bottom of the refrigerator and two small apples to Jeanette, who in return gives her a grateful smile. No one ever gave things to Jeanette. Cal is already across the porch. He doesn't say anything to Ernestine. He doesn't wait for the girls.

"Cal!" Ernestine calls out through the screen. "Where's your brother at?"

He doesn't stop. He doesn't turn around. He shrugs his shoulders and lifts up his hands, keeping his back to her. *Cal*, Teresa wants to say, *speak to her!* But she says nothing. She is watching a day that happened thirty-five years ago, a half a world away. She cannot correct his behavior. She cannot change the outcome. She is only allowed to sit and watch, and that is miraculous.

The five of them walk down the blacktop drive out the back, then turn onto a dirt road that eventually becomes not a road but two rutted tracks, the grass growing up in between the two halves to form a median. Holly and Caroline are chattering while Jeanette and Franny listen. Cal is off in front, walking fast enough that from time to time the girls have to break into a trot to keep up. They want to stay together without staying with him, and all five of them have a sense of what is close enough. Cal is tall and blond like his father, his eyes the same blue, his skin brown from the summer spent outside. His expression is one of simmering fury, but then it always is. He doesn't want to be in Virginia, doesn't want to be with his sisters, with the Keating girls, with his stepmother, with his grandparents. He doesn't want to curry the horses, to be bitten by the flies and mosquitoes, to stand in the stink of shit and hay, but there is nothing better to do. That's the trouble with being fifteen—all he can think of is what he doesn't want. He's wearing a UCLA T-shirt and Levi's though the day is hot. If Cal's wearing long pants it means he's taken the gun again. All the children know that.

Jeanette had told Teresa that Cal kept the handgun tied to his leg with bandannas. Jeanette had told her mother everything a long time ago, in that year they lived alone together in the house in Torrance. Without Holly and Albie around she was free to talk about the day Cal died, how they'd wasted the Benadryl to put Albie to sleep, the route they took to the barn, how they had ignored Cal while he was dying, thinking that he was playing a game so that they would come close enough that he could hit them. They had waited a long, long time, sitting in the grass making daisy chains to show him they weren't falling for it. Jeanette had told her all of this but Teresa didn't see it then. She had never seen anything before.

Holly, who has the nicest voice of all the girls, the nicest voice in her school, starts to sing, her arms swinging back and forth, "Goin' to the chapel, and we're—"

"*Gonna get married.*" Caroline and Franny join her.

"Goin' to the chapel and we're—"

"*Gonna get married.*" Caroline and Franny. Jeanette doesn't sing at first but she's moving her lips.

"Gee, I really love you and we're—"

"Could you shut up for two minutes?" Cal asks, turning around while he's walking. He is far out ahead of them now, in the tall grass, far enough away that it doesn't seem like the singing should bother him so much, but it does. "Would that be too fucking much to ask?"

Those are her son's last words.

"*Gonna get married.*" It's all four of them now, even Jeanette is belting it out, and suddenly Cal charges them. It's impossible to say if he's really angry or making a joke, but the girls scatter and scream, running in four different directions. Cal could have caught any one of them but now he has to choose and he stops. Something happened, he feels a sharp pain in his neck while the sisters and the not-sisters run a circle around him. He stops and puts his hand high up on his chest near the base of his throat. Teresa, on her cushion in Switzerland, can feel the constriction, her own breath closing off, because she is watching him and she is him. The girls are singing and running and she wants them to stop. He wants them to stop but he can't say it. The bee is still on the back of his neck, crawling there. He feels it but he can't knock it away. He is falling, not just into the grass but someplace farther, the sound of the girls' voices washed away by the tide of blood, his thrumming heart, the color stripped from their T-shirts, the sun and sky and grass, stripped. His tongue is filling up his mouth. He tries to put his hand in his pocket to search out the last of the Benadryl if there's any left but he can't find his hand. He spins straight back with the full force of gravity and the earth thumps up against him hard, driving the bee in, and takes with it the last of the air, the last of the light. He is fifteen and ten and five. He is an instant. He is flying back to her. He is hers again. She feels the weight of him in her chest as he comes into her arms. He is her son, her beloved child, and she takes him back.

9

Fix was still alive the Christmas after Teresa Cousins died. Impossible but true. It would be his last Christmas, but then the last two Christmases had been his last Christmas, as this past Thanksgiving was his last Thanksgiving. Franny didn't want to leave Kumar and the boys again for the holidays, nor did she want to bring them with her to Santa Monica. It was too depressing. Franny and Caroline also considered the question of their mother who had been increasingly neglected in every year it was taking their father to die.

"Dad's not the only one to worry about," Caroline said, thinking of their mother's husband. Their mother confided in Caroline now, maybe more than she did in Franny. This was the pleasure of a long life: the way some things worked themselves out. Caroline and her mother had become very close.

"I'm flipping a coin," Caroline said over the phone. "You're just going to have to trust me."

"I trust you," Franny said. There was no one she trusted more than Caroline.

"Heads you go to Dad's for Christmas, tails I go to Dad's." This was what they'd come to, an instant of anticipatory silence and then the clatter of a quarter coming to rest on Caroline's kitchen table in San Jose.

The plane had circled in a holding pattern for forty-five minutes before delivering Franny, Kumar, and the boys to Dulles in harrowing weather—snow and pitch-black dark. Ravi, fourteen, and Amit, twelve, sat in the back of the rental car, earbuds stuffed deep into their ears, their heads bobbing gently in discordant time. The boys had been untroubled by the icy skid of the landing gear against the runway, just as they were untroubled by the interstate to Arlington, which was a soup of accidents and ice, cars crawling back to the suburbs like beaten dogs, holiday travelers anxious to arrive on time, holiday travelers desperate to flee. Franny called her mother to tell her not to hold dinner. There was no saying how late they'd be.

"Be as late as you need to be," her mother said. "If things get bad we'll eat the onion dip." She always made onion dip for Ravi, who liked things salted, and a caramel cake for Amit, who liked things sweet.

"As if my mother has ever eaten onion dip," Franny said to Kumar after hanging up her phone. She was inching the car forward while Kumar attended to the last of his work e-mails. Kumar worked in the mergers and acquisitions department in the behemoth Martin and Fox. He was making plans to defend his client from a hostile takeover even as his wife drove through the blinding snow. It was only fair. Had they been going to see his mother in Bombay she would not have been driving.

"I've never seen your mother eat anything," Kumar said, his thumbs burning up the screen on his phone. "Which is my best proof that she is a goddess."

Beverly and Jack Dine were both in their sixties when they married: hers early, his late. Kumar had only known Franny's mother as Jack Dine's wife, the empress of the Arlington car dealerships, and so he regarded her as happy and powerful, a source of bejeweled splendor. Kumar believed his mother-in-law to be the person she was in this present moment, free from history, and in return for that gift Beverly loved him like a son.

Jack Dine's house had once been owned by a four-term senator from Pennsylvania. It had a wall and a gate, but they kept the gate open and for Christmas draped the wall in swags of pine punctuated by oversized wreaths. The great circular driveway was parked up with cars. Every light in every window was on, the lights pinned to the high branches of the trees were on, and the snow threw back the light and illuminated the world. From the car they could see all the people through the long front windows packed together like dolls in an enormous dollhouse.

"Is she having a party for us?" Amit asked from the backseat. At their grandmother's house anything was possible. There were only a few parking spots left down at the end of the driveway, and so they wrestled their bags from the back and made their way through the snow.

"Merry Christmas!" Beverly said when she threw the door open. She hugged Amit first, then Ravi, then hugged them both together, each in one arm. Beverly's seventy-eight could rival anyone else's sixty-five. She had stayed slim and blond while having the sense to never push things too far. A life spent as a great beauty was still clearly in evidence. Behind her the house was full and overflowing, lights and pine and glasses of champagne. The Christmas tree in the living room brushed the ceiling with its highest branches and seemed to have been encrusted with diamonds and pink sapphires. Somewhere on the other side of the house someone was playing the piano. Women were laughing.

"You didn't tell us you were having a party," Franny said.

"We always have a Christmas Eve party," Beverly said. She was wearing a smart red dress, three ropes of pearls. "Now would you please come in the house and not stand on the porch like a bunch of Jehovah's Witnesses?"

Kumar and Franny pulled in their luggage and brushed the snow off their shoulders and hair. At least Kumar was wearing a suit. They had picked him up from the office on the way to the airport. But Franny and the boys looked like nothing but the disheveled travelers they were. The boys had seen guests walking around with plates heaped with food and so they dropped their bags and headed for the dining room to find the buffet. The boys were always starving.

"It isn't Christmas Eve," Franny said.

"Matthew's family is going skiing in Vail for Christmas so I moved the party up. It was easier for everyone this way. Really, I think I'll always have it on the twenty-second."

"But you didn't tell us."

Kumar leaned in and kissed Beverly on the cheek. "You look beautiful," he said, changing the subject.

"Franny!" A heavyset man past middle age wearing a red houndstooth button-up vest came and swept her up in too zealous a hug, shaking her back and forth while making growling sounds. "How's my favorite sister?"

"That's only because Caroline isn't here," Beverly said. "You should see the way he makes over Caroline."

"Caroline gives me free legal advice," Pete said.

"If you get sued over the holidays I'd be happy to help," Kumar said.

Pete turned and looked at Kumar, trying to place him. His face lit up with pleasure when finally he was able to put it all together. "That's right," he said to Franny. "I forgot he was a lawyer too."

"Merry Christmas, Pete," Franny said. Surely she would burst into tears at some point in the evening. It was only a question of how long she could hold off.

"Pete and his family are going to New York to see Katie and the new baby," Beverly said. "Did I tell you Katie had her baby?"

"Christmas in New York." Pete smiled and his teeth made Franny think of ivory, like elephant's tusks carved down to the size of human teeth. He was drinking eggnog from a small crystal cup. "Can you imagine that? Sure you can. You're a city girl. Are you still in Chicago?"

"Let them go upstairs and settle in," Beverly said to Pete. "They'll be back in a minute. They just got off the plane."

But then Jack Dine was there, wearing a needlepoint vest, a leaping stag rendered convincingly in small stitches. Jack had always been such a big man, tall and broad, though now he seemed no larger than his wife. "Who's the pretty girl?" he asked, pointing to Franny.

Beverly put her arm around her husband. "Jack, this is Franny, my Franny. You remember."

"She looks like you," Jack said.

"And Kumar. Do you remember him?"

"He can get the bags," Jack said, waving him away. "Go on now. Take them upstairs."

Kumar smiled, though it would be hard to say how. He was a generous man, and the boys weren't there to bear witness.

"Jack," Franny said, putting her hand on her stepfather's trembling forearm. "Kumar's my husband."

But Kumar was not about to miss his exit. He would take what was available. "Sir," he said and nodded his head. Somehow, in an impossible feat of balance and strength, he managed to scoop all of it up. He looped the boys' duffels across his chest.

"Go through the kitchen," Jack said when Kumar had taken a single step in the direction of the sweeping staircase. The luggage was just about to overtake him, and still he turned and took the bags to the kitchen. There was a narrow back staircase that the servants had used when there were servants.

"They think they can go right through the middle of your party," Jack said to Franny, his eyes tracking Kumar's back. "You've got to watch all the time."

"That was my husband," Franny said. Was she choking? She had the strangest feeling in her throat.

Jack patted her hand. "Tell me what I can get the pretty lady to drink."

"I'm fine, Jack." Franny had thought that she had won the toss. When she heard the quarter come down on Caroline's table, when Caroline told her to go and spend Christmas in Virginia, she thought she had gotten the better deal. Now Franny found that she was longing for her dying father, her father who was nearly dead.

"I'll get you some eggnog," Jack Dine said and then turned and walked back into the crowd.

"Worse." Pete followed his father with his eyes. "In case you didn't catch that. He's a lot worse. Has he started any fires yet?"

"Why would you say that?" Beverly asked, her voice gone flat. She loved Jack Dine, or she had loved him when he was still someone she knew. His sons, on the other hand, often required more consideration than she cared to give.

"Because sooner or later he will," Pete said. He was scanning the crowd, looking for someone better to talk to. "Matthew!" He raised a hand and waved to his brother. "Look! Franny's home."

Matthew Dine's vest was black, but he wore a gold watch chain with a small red Christmas ornament hanging from it, a single glass ball that made him look more festive than all the rest of them. Franny had forgotten that Jack Dine's Christmas parties required vests for men. Glancing across the room the theme emerged: women in red, men in vests. Matthew took both of Franny's hands in his hands, kissed her on the cheek. "You haven't made it three steps past the door," he said in a solemn voice.

Franny liked Matthew the best. Everyone did. "Where's Rick?" she said, thinking she might as well get all three of the brothers out of the way before she tried to fight a path to the staircase.

"Rick has his nose out of joint about something," Beverly said. "He said he wasn't coming."

"He'll come," Matthew said. "Laura Lee and the girls are already here."

As I was going to St. Ives, I met a man with seven wives. Each wife had seven sacks, each sack had seven cats. Franny couldn't keep them straight. She knew the Dine boys, that's what they were called late into their fifties, but their wives and second wives confused her, their children, in some cases two sets, some grown and married, others still small. *Kits, cats, sacks, and wives.* There were members of the Dine family who considered her in some vague sense to be a sister, a cousin, a daughter, an aunt. Katie Dine in New York had a baby. She couldn't follow all the lines out in every direction: all the people to whom she was by marriage mysteriously related. Jack Dine's first wife, Peggy, had died more than twenty years ago but Peggy Dine's sisters, along with their husbands and children and children's spouses and their children, were still invited to the party every year—cherished guests! Every year they came and stood in the house that had once been their sister's and catalogued the changes while eating the canapés that Beverly had made herself—the new sofa and a different color of living room paint and the painting of birds above the fireplace—it was a desecration of Peggy's memory. The rearrangement of objects was more than they could bear.

The guests were catching on to the fact that Beverly's

daughter had arrived, and the ones who knew her were anxious to see her, and the ones who didn't know her had heard so much about her. Matthew leaned towards her, whispered in her ear, "Run."

Franny gave her mother a kiss. "I'll be right back," she said.

She went through the kitchen, where two black men in black pants with white shirts and vests and ties piled ham biscuits onto silver trays, while a third man arranged boiled shrimp around a cut-glass bowl of cocktail sauce on a massive silver platter. They didn't lift their heads from their work when she came through the room. If they saw her at all they said nothing about it. She went up the back stairs to the room where she and Kumar always slept. All of the Dine boys lived in town, all in beautiful houses of their own, so even at Christmas there was never a worry about space. In his retirement Jack Dine's empire had been divided three ways, giving Matthew the Toyotas, Pete the Subarus, and Rick the Volkswagens. Rick, who was lazy, was also bitter, and often said it wasn't fair that Matthew got Toyota. No one could compete with Toyota. He particularly envied his brother the Prius.

Franny opened the door quietly and found her husband lying on top of the bedspread in the dark. His jacket and tie were hanging in the closet, his shoes tucked beneath the bed. Kumar had always been neat, even when they were in law school. She dropped her coat and scarf on the floor, pushed out of her snow boots.

"I would feel very sorry for myself," he said quietly, his hands folded over his stomach, his eyes closed, "except that I'm feeling sorry for you."

"Thank you," she said and crawled the length of the vast mattress to lie beside him.

He put his arm around her, kissed her hair. "A different couple would make love now."

Franny laughed, pushing her face into his shoulder. "A couple whose children wouldn't be walking in the room any minute."

"A couple whose host wouldn't shoot the son-in-law for miscegenation."

"I'm sorry about that," Franny said.

"Your poor mother. I have to feel sorry for your mother, too."

Franny sighed. "I know."

"You have to go to the party," he said. "I'm not brave enough to go back down there with you, but you have to go."

"I know," she said.

"Ask the boys to bring me up a plate, will you?"

Franny closed her eyes and nodded against his chest.

If Kumar had his way they would leave for Fiji every year just before Thanksgiving and not return until the New Year rang in and the decorations came down. They would swim with the fishes and lie on the beach eating papaya. On the years they were tired of Fiji they would go to Bali or Sydney or any sunny, sandy place whose name contained an equal number of consonants and vowels.

"What about school?" Franny would ask.

"Aren't we capable of home-schooling for six weeks out of the year? It wouldn't even be a full six weeks. We would subtract the weekends and vacation days."

"What about work?"

Kumar would look at her sharply then, his dark eyebrows pushing down. "Just participate in the fantasy," he said.

Kumar's first wife, Sapna, had died on Pearl Harbor Day in the full tilt of the holiday season, four days after Amit was born. It was easy enough to remember how long ago that was as Amit was twelve. Sapna had been ten years younger than Kumar.

"Ten years kinder," he would say to her on her birthday. "Ten years more forgiving." It was true, Sapna's joy in life could make her seem uncomplicated, when in fact she was probably as complicated as anyone else. "No stupidity in happiness," she liked to say. She loved her husband, she loved her sons. She loved that she had managed to escape northern Michigan for Chicago. Their lives, however busy and freezing cold, were good lives. She had come through childbirth for a second time without a hitch. They were all home together. Ravi, who was two and a half, was taking a nap. Sapna was sitting on the couch, the baby in her arms. She looked right at Kumar and said, "It's the strangest thing." Then she closed her eyes.

The autopsy showed a genetic abnormality of the heart—long QT. Considering the severity of her condition, the real surprise was that she hadn't died after Ravi was born. But sometimes people didn't. Sometimes they lived their entire lives never knowing the fate they missed. When tested, they found out Sapna's mother had the gene as well. Her sister had it.

"For the vast majority of the people on this planet," Fix had said, "the thing that's going to kill them is already on the inside."

It was less than a year after the death of his wife that Franny came to Kumar's table at the Palmer House and asked him what he wanted to drink.

"Jesus," he said, staring up at her in disbelief. "Tell me that you're not still working here."

Kumar, she thought. How had she forgotten Kumar? "Every now and then, only on the weekends," Franny said, leaning over to kiss his cheek. "I have a real job in the law library back at the University of Chicago but the pay is appalling. Plus I like it here."

Kumar was waiting to pick up a client and take him to dinner. "I'm offering you a job," he said. "You can start Monday. A single job that will pay you more than your two jobs combined."

Franny laughed. Kumar hadn't changed. "Doing what?"

"Due diligence." He was making it up. "I need you to compile financial records for a merger."

"I never finished law school."

"I know how far you got in law school. We need someone we can count on. This is your interview. There, I've hired you."

A tall black man in a charcoal suit came to the table and Kumar stood to greet him. "Our new associate," Kumar said to the man, holding out his hand towards Franny. "Franny Keating. Is it still Keating?"

"Franny Keating," she said, and shook the man's hand.

Later, Kumar would say he worked it out on the spot: he would marry Franny, and in doing so solve everything except the unsolvable. He had loved her when they were young—if not in the year she had shared his apartment then at least after she had left with Leo Posen. If she were free he saw no reason he wouldn't be able to love her again. The problem was time. Sapna's parents had come from Michigan to take care of Ravi when Amit was born and almost a year later they were still living in his house. Between work and his children, between his life and the enormous burden of grief, there wasn't a minute in any day that wasn't devoured. His genius would be to hire Franny rather than date her. He didn't want to date her anyway. He wanted to marry her. If she came to work in his law firm they would see each other every day. They would come upon each other's stories naturally, in the elevator or exchanging files. He could make sure that his idea was as good as he thought it was before entrusting her with his children and his life.

Settled, he thought when he handed her his business card and said goodnight, everything's settled.

The bar was still playing the same tape all these years later, or a tape that was remarkably similar to that other tape. Franny would have laughed to think how much it used to bother her. She never heard it anymore. But when Kumar and his client left the bar and she put his business card into her apron pocket, she could half-hear Ella Fitzgerald singing as if in the back of her mind,

There's someone I'm trying so hard to forget
Don't you want to forget someone too?

Lying in the darkness of her mother's house, Franny tried to imagine a world in which Sapna had lived. Maybe Franny and Kumar would have met again, bumped into each other in a bookstore one day, laughed and said hello and gone on, but she never would have married him, and his sons would never have been her sons. If Sapna could have lived then certainly Beverly could have stayed married to Fix, which would mean no Jack Dine, no Dine stepbrothers, no Christmas party in Virginia. It would also mean no Marjorie though, and that would be a terrible loss when Marjorie had given Fix the benefit of great love. But maybe Bert would have stayed with Teresa then, and fifty years later he might have saved her life by insisting she go to the doctor in time. Cal would have missed the bee that was waiting for him in the tall grass near the barn at Bert's parents' house. He could have lived for years, though who's to say another bee wouldn't have found him somewhere else? With Cal alive, Albie would never have set the fire that brought him to Virginia, though he wouldn't have come to Virginia anyway because Bert would have stayed in California. Franny, half asleep on top of the bedspread beside her husband, was unable to map out all the ways the future would unravel without the moorings of the past. Without Bert, Franny would never have gone to law school. She would have gotten a masters in English and so she never would have met Kumar at all. She never would have been in Chicago working at the Palmer House and so she never would have met Leo Posen, who sat at the bar so many lifetimes ago and talked about her shoes. That was the place where Franny's life began, leaning over to light his cigarette. Somehow, out of all that could have been gained or lost, the thought of having never met Leo was the one thing she couldn't bear.

The sound of Kumar's breathing had deepened and slowed, and she got up carefully, felt for her dress and shoes in her suitcase, and changed clothes in the dark.

When she came down the back stairs to the kitchen, Franny found her mother at the breakfast table by herself, arranging petits fours on a tray.

"You know there are people here who will do that for you," Franny said.

Her mother looked up and gave her an exhausted smile. "I'm hiding for just a minute."

Franny nodded and sat down beside her.

"This party always seems like such a good idea in the abstract," Beverly said. "But every time I have it I can't imagine why."

They could hear the guests in the other room, the hilarity in their voices raised by the eggnog and champagne. The piano player was playing something faster now, maybe a jazzed-up version of "The Twelve Days of Christmas" but Franny wasn't sure. Twelve days, she thought, she would have killed herself before she ever got to the five golden rings.

Beverly put out the last of the tiny square cakes from the box, pink and yellow and white, each one crowned with a sugared rosette. "Rick came after all," she said, turning the squares to diamonds. "Now he's drinking."

"Matthew said he'd come."

"I can't take them all together," Beverly said. "One on one the boys are fine, or mostly fine, but when they're together they always have an agenda. They have so many ideas about the future: what I'm supposed to do with Jack, what I'm supposed to do with the house. They don't seem to have any sense of what conversation is appropriate for a Christmas party. I don't know what's going to happen in the future. I don't know why they keep asking me. Do you have any ideas about the future?"

Franny picked up a pale-yellow petit four, the color of a newly hatched chick, and ate it in a single bite. It wasn't very good, but it was so pretty that it didn't matter. "None," she said. "Zero."

Beverly looked at her daughter and the look on her face was a pure expression of love. "I wanted two girls," she said. "You and your sister. I wanted exactly what I had. Other people's children are too hard."

If her mother hadn't been so pretty none of it would have happened, but being pretty was nothing to blame her for. "I'm going out there," Franny said, and got up.

Her mother looked down at the plate of tiny cakes. "I'm going to divide them by color," she said, pushing them all onto the table with the side of her hand. "I think I'd like them better that way."

Franny found Ravi and Amit in the basement watching *The Matrix* on a television set the size of a single mattress.

"That's rated R," she said.

The boys looked at her. "For the violence," Ravi said. "Not sex."

"And it's Christmas," Amit said, operating on the logic of wishes.

Franny stood behind them and watched as the black-coated men dipped backwards to avoid being split in half by bullets and then popped up again. If it was going to give them nightmares the damage was already done.

"Mama, have you seen it before?" Amit asked.

Franny shook her head. "It's too scary for me."

"I'll sleep in your room with you," her younger boy said, "if you're scared."

"If you make us stop now," Ravi said, "we'll never know what happens."

Franny watched for another minute. She was probably right, it probably was too scary for her. "Your father fell asleep," she said. "Wait a little while and then go take him a plate for dinner, okay?"

Pleased by their small victory, they nodded their heads.

"And don't tell him about the movie."

Franny went back upstairs and did one full loop around the room but there were so few people she remembered. She hadn't lived in Arlington since she'd left for college. The wives of Jack Dine's three sons all wanted to talk to her but none of them particularly wanted to talk to one another. The wife of the son she liked the most was the wife she liked the least, and the wife of the son she liked the least was the wife she greatly preferred. What was interesting though, not that any of it was interesting at all, was that the wife of the son she had the hardest time remembering was also the wife she had the hardest time remembering.

At some point in the evening before even a single guest had departed, Franny found herself back in the foyer, and there, without looking for it, she saw her own handbag on the floor, slightly behind the umbrella stand. She must have dropped it there when she came in, putting the luggage down, and without a thought she picked it up and went out the door.

The dress she'd brought for the party, the party she'd thought was still two days away, was not red. It was a dark blue velvet with long sleeves but still it was no match for the cold, as her shoes were no match for the snow. It didn't make any difference. She had left the party, slipped away after everyone had seen her. "Where's Franny?" they would say, and the answer would be, "I think she's in the kitchen. I just saw her in the other room."

The cars were all covered in snow, and hers was a rental, rented in the dark no less. She didn't know what color it was because she'd never actually seen it. It was an SUV, she remembered that, but all the cars were SUVs, as if SUVs, like vests for men, had been a requirement of the invitation. She went down the hill at the end of the drive and when she was in what she thought might have been the general vicinity, she hit the automatic key. A horn beeped just to the left of her and the lights came on. She brushed off the windows with her wrist and got inside. Once she got the heater running she called Bert.

"I thought I'd come by and say hello if it isn't too late." She worked to keep her voice casual because she felt frantic.

Bert was always up late. She had to discourage him from calling the house after ten o'clock at night. "Wonderful!" he said, as if he'd been waiting for exactly this call. "Just be careful in the snow."

Bert still lived in the last house he and Beverly had lived in together, the same house she and Caroline had lived in during high school, the house that Albie had come to for a year after Caroline was gone. It wasn't that far from where Beverly lived with Jack Dine, maybe five miles, but in Arlington it was possible to live five miles from someone and never see them again.

He was waiting for her on the front porch when she pulled up, the front door of the house open behind him. He had put on his coat to come outside. Bert was as old as the rest of them but age arrived at different rates of speed, in different ways. Coming up the walk in the dark, the porch light bright above his head, Franny thought that Bert Cousins still looked like himself.

"The ghost of Christmas past," he said when she stepped into his arms.

"I should have called you sooner," Franny said. "It's all been sort of last-minute."

Bert did not invite her in, nor did he let her go. He only stood there holding Franny to his chest. Always she was the baby he had carried around Fix Keating's party, the most beautiful baby he had ever seen. "Last-minute works for me," he said.

"Come on," she said. "I'm freezing."

Inside the door she took off her shoes.

"I made a fire in the den when you called. It hasn't really caught yet but it's starting."

Franny remembered the first time she'd ever been inside this house. She must have been thirteen. The den was why they'd bought the place, the big stone hearth, the fireplace big enough for a witch's pot, the way the room looked out over the pool. She thought it was a palace then. Bert had no business keeping this house, it was entirely too big for one person. But on this night Franny was grateful he'd held on to it, if only so she could come home.

"Let me get you a drink," he said.

"Maybe just some tea," she said. "I'm driving." She stood up on the hearth and flexed her stocking feet on the warm stones. She and Albie would come downstairs in the winter late at night when they were in high school and open up the flue when it was too cold to go outside and smoke. They would lean back into the fireplace with their cigarettes and blow the smoke up the chimney. They would drink Bert's gin and throw away the empty bottles in the kitchen trash with impunity. If either parent noticed the dwindling stock in the liquor cabinet or the way the empties were piling up, neither one of them ever mentioned it.

"Have a drink, Franny. It's Christmas."

"It's December twenty-second. Why does everyone keep telling me it's Christmas?"

"Barmaid's gin and tonic."

Franny looked at him. "Barmaid's," she said sternly. Bert had shown her that trick when she was a girl and would play bartender for their parties. If a guest was already drunk she should pour a glass of tonic and ice and then float a little gin on the top without mixing it up. The first sip would be too strong, Bert told her, and that's all that mattered. After the first sip drunks didn't pay attention.

"If you get sloppy you can sleep in your old room."

"My mother would love that." It was always a trick getting out to see Bert. For all the times that Beverly had forgiven him, she couldn't understand that Franny and Caroline might forgive him as well.

"How is your mother?" Bert asked. He handed Franny her drink, and the first sip—straight gin—was right on the money.

"My mother is exactly herself," Franny said.

Bert pressed his lips together and nodded. "I would expect nothing less. I hear old Jack Dine is slipping though, that she's having a hard time taking care of him. I hate to think of her having to deal with that."

"It's what we'll all have to deal with sooner or later."

"Maybe I'll give her a call, just to see how she's doing."

Oh, Bert, Franny thought. Let it go. "What about you?" she said. "How are you doing?"

Bert had made his own drink, a gin with a splash of tonic floating on the top to balance her out, and came to sit on the sofa. "I'm not so bad for an old man," he said. "I still get around. If you'd called me tomorrow you would have missed me."

Franny stabbed at the logs with the fireplace poker to encourage the flame. "Where are you going tomorrow?"

"Brooklyn," he said. Franny turned around to look at him, poker in hand, and he smiled enormously. "Jeanette invited me for Christmas. There's a hotel two blocks from where they live. It's nice enough. I've been up there a couple of times to see them now."

"That's really something," Franny said, and she came to sit next to Bert on the couch. "I'm happy for you."

"We've been doing better these last couple of years. I e-mail with Holly too. She says that I can come to Switzerland and see her in that place she lives, the commune. I keep telling her I'll meet her in Paris. I think that Paris is a good compromise. Everybody likes Paris. I took Teresa there for our honeymoon. That would have been what? Fifty-five years ago? I think it's time to go back." He stopped himself then, remembering something. "You were out there, weren't you, when Teresa died? I think Jeanette told me that."

"Caroline and I took her to the hospital. We were with Dad."

"Well, that was nice of you."

Franny shrugged. "I wasn't going to leave her."

"How is your dad?"

Franny shook her head, thinking of her father. *How is old Bert?* Fix would always say. "I'd tell you he wasn't going to make it until New Year's but I'm sure I'd be wrong."

"Your father's a tough guy."

"My father's a tough guy," Franny said, thinking of the gun in his bedside table and how she had declined to help him when he asked. She'd done worse than that. She'd taken the gun to the police department in Santa Monica later, turned it in along with the bullets.

"I'm going to float a little more gin in there," Bert said.

"A tiny bit," Franny said, and handed back the glass. She wasn't drunk and so she was sadly aware that all the gin was gone now.

"We're not even up to half a jigger yet." Bert made his way to the bar at the side of the room.

"Just be careful."

"I remember seeing your father again after your christening party," Bert said. "I saw him at the courthouse. I don't know, maybe I saw him all the time and never knew it before, but that Monday he came up to me and shook my hand, said he was glad I'd come. 'Glad you could come to Franny's party,' is what he said." He handed Franny her drink.

"It was a long time ago, Bert."

"Still," Bert said. "It bothers me to think of him now, so sick. I never had anything against your father."

"Do you hear from Albie?" she said, wanting to change the subject. It was a question she could have asked Albie but for some reason she never did. They didn't talk about Bert. Even all those years ago when they'd lived together under this roof they didn't talk about him.

"Not so much. Every now and then one of us gives it a try but we haven't had a lot of success. Albie was very attached to his mother, you know. That's the way it happens—girls to their fathers and boys to their mothers. I don't think he ever got over my leaving his mother." For Bert the past was always right there with him, and so he assumed that everyone else felt the same way.

"You should give him a call. It's a tough time of year now, with Teresa gone." Franny thought of her own father, of this time next year.

"I'll call him on Christmas," he said. "I'll call from Jeanette's."

Franny wanted to tell him it was three hours earlier in California and that he could call his son tonight, could call him right now, but Bert wasn't going to call Albie and there was no sense trying to make him feel bad about it. She tilted back her glass and went past the gin for a second time. She pressed through the fizzy sweetness of the tonic and drained the glass down to the ice and the lime. "I wish I could stay," Franny said, and part of her meant it. She would have liked to go upstairs to her room and lie down on her bed, though what were the chances that the bed was still there?

Bert nodded. "I know. I'm just glad you came by at all. I really appreciate that."

"What time are you flying out?"

"Early," he said. "That way I'll beat the traffic."

Franny got up and gave her stepfather a hug. "Merry Christmas," she said.

"Merry Christmas," Bert said, and when he stepped back to look at her his eyes were damp. "Be careful now. If anything happened to you your mother would kill me."

Franny smiled and gave him a kiss, thinking that Bert still saw the world in terms of what Beverly would and would not forgive him for. She stepped into her shoes beside the front door and let herself out into the snow. Inside the house Bert was turning off the lights, and she stood there on the front porch for a minute and watched the snow come to rest on the sleeves of her velvet dress. She was thinking about the night she couldn't find Albie. Bert was in his study downstairs working and her mother was in the kitchen going over her French homework. It was long past dinner. It was snowing just like this and the house was perfectly quiet. Franny was wondering where Albie was. Usually by this time he had come into her room to do his homework or talk to her instead of doing his homework. She was lying across her bed reading *The Return of the Native* for AP English. It wasn't that he came in every night, but if he wasn't in her room then she could usually hear him, watching television, walking around. She kept listening until finally she put the book down and went to look for him. He wasn't in his bedroom or the bathroom or the den or in the living room where he never went anyway. When she had looked everywhere in the house she could think of she went into the kitchen.

"Where's Albie?" Franny asked her mother.

Her mother shook her head and made a little sound that stood in for the words *no idea*. Her mother never did learn to speak French.

"If you see him would you let me know?"

Her beautiful mother, maybe embarrassed now, looked up from her book for just a second and nodded. "Sure," she said.

Franny didn't think of knocking on the door to Bert's study and asking him if he'd seen Albie, or checking to see if maybe Albie was in there with him. The thought never crossed her mind.

Instead, she went out the back door. She was still wearing her uniform from school: a plaid skirt and kneesocks, saddle oxfords, a sweatshirt from track over her white blouse. Her mother didn't tell her to put on a coat or ask her where she was going the way she would have had Franny walked out the back door on a snowy night a few years before. Her mother was lost in a sea of irregular verbs.

Franny looked in the garage but Albie wasn't in the garage. She walked a circle around the house and then went down the street, walking two houses down in one direction, three houses down in the other. She looked at the snow for bicycle tracks but there was nothing there, only her own footprints going in every direction. She was chilled now and her hair was getting wet. She was a little worried but only a little. She was thinking she could find him. She decided to go back to the house for her coat and as she was coming up the driveway she saw him, just a few inches of the side of his head behind the boxwoods beside the front door. He was wrapped in his red sleeping bag, staring up at the snow.

"Albie?" she said. "What are you doing?"

"Freezing," Albie said.

"Well don't. Come inside." She walked across the soft snow covering the lawn until she was standing right in front of him.

"I'm too high," he said.

Around every streetlight, every porch light, there was a soft halo of snow. Everything else was dark. "No one's going to notice."

"They will," he said. "I'm really high."

"You can't stay out here." Franny was starting to shiver. She was wondering what she had been thinking of, going out without her coat.

"I can," he said. His voice was so light, so airy, as if it were part of the snow.

Franny stepped between the boxwoods, thinking she would have to pull him up. Albie was taller than she was now but he was skinny, and anyway he wouldn't fight her. But as soon as she got back there with him she understood the appeal of this particular spot, the way you could see all things without being seen. The overhang of the roof kept them out of the snow for the most part. She could smell the pot on him now, sweet and strong. Franny and Albie drank together sometimes, and they smoked cigarettes, but they didn't smoke pot together. Later that would change.

"Let me in," she said.

And just like that Albie raised up his arm, never taking his eyes off the snow, and she sat down beside him. The sleeping bag was filled with down and when they were wrapped up together it was remarkably warm. They sat there like that, their backs up against the brick of the house, the coarse hedge just in front of them. They watched the snow fall and fall and fall until they thought that they were the ones who were falling.

"I miss my mother," Albie said. In the one year when they were very close it was the only time he said it, and he only said it that night because he was very high.

"I know," Franny said, because she did know. She knew it exactly, and she pulled the sleeping bag tighter around them and they stayed there together just like that until she lost the feeling in her feet and she told him they had to go inside.

"I lost the feeling in my feet a long time ago," he said.

They put their arms around one another in order to stand. The front door was locked so they went down the driveway, dragging the sleeping bag behind them. Franny's mother wasn't in the kitchen anymore but the light was still on beneath the door to Bert's study.

"I told you no one would know if you were high," Franny said, and for some reason this cracked Albie up. He sat down on the floor and pulled the sleeping bag over his head, laughing while Franny got out the cereal and the milk.

Franny brushed the snow off her shoulders and made her way to the rented SUV. She had never told that story to Leo. She had meant to but then for some reason she decided to hold it back. Now she understood that at some point far out in the future there would be a night just like tonight, and she would remember this story and know that no one else in the world knew it had happened except Albie. She had needed to keep something for herself.

About the Author

Ann Patchett is the author of eight novels, *The Patron Saint of Liars, Taft, The Magician's Assistant, Bel Canto, Run, State of Wonder, Commonwealth,* and *The Dutch House.* She was the editor of *Best American Short Stories 2006* and has written three books of nonfiction, *Truth & Beauty,* about her friendship with the writer Lucy Grealy, *What now?* an expansion of her graduation address at Sarah Lawrence College, and, most recently, *This Is the Story of a Happy Marriage,* a collection of essays.